The **GIRL** *with*
the **YELLOW**
STAR

BOOKS BY NATALIE MEG EVANS

The Dress Thief

The Milliner's Secret

A Gown of Thorns

The Wardrobe Mistress

The Secret Vow

The Paris Girl

Into the Burning Dawn

The Italian Girl's Secret

NATALIE MEG EVANS

The GIRL with the YELLOW STAR

bookouture

Published by Bookouture in 2022

An imprint of Storyfire Ltd.
Carmelite House
50 Victoria Embankment
London EC4Y 0DZ

www.bookouture.com

ISBN: 978-1-78681-059-5
eBook ISBN: 978-1-78681-058-8

This book is dedicated to my agent, Laura Longrigg, along with deepest thanks for discovering me, getting me published and being around for the last ten fabulous years

PROLOGUE

FRANCE, JULY 1942

Lotti traced the shape of the star on the front of her coat, feeling her pulse in the pads of her fingers. She didn't know why she had been woken up while it was still dark and told to pack a bag with things for a journey.

'You have to get dressed for outside,' her mother had told her. 'Warm clothes, but not your best ones.' Then Mutti had left her, going downstairs where Madame was waiting.

Obediently, Lotti brushed and plaited her own hair, and polished her shoes with a rag. Into her school satchel she put underwear and socks, handkerchiefs, a puzzle book, making sure to leave room for her most precious possession. Placing the satchel over her shoulder, she gave the attic bedroom a last glance. She knew she would not see it again.

'Mutti?' she called softly when she was on the ground floor. There was such a stillness in the house, the only sound the slow tick of a clock and the purring of a grey cat, curled on a cushion under the coat rack. As she passed, he gave a funny, corkscrew purr and lifted his head but Lotti did not stroke him. Mutti had said, 'Don't linger. Dawn comes early this time of year and we have to be ready.'

Ready for what, though? Madame and Mutti had been whispering all day yesterday, breaking off whenever Lotti came near. Grown-ups kept secrets sometimes.

She pulled open the front door with all her fingers because it was not made for a child's hands. Stepping into the courtyard, the air felt like a cool lemon drink. The roofs were shiny with dew, kissed with light the colour of pomegranate.

In the middle of the courtyard stood a tree and there he was, sitting on the only branch Lotti could reach, his arms poking sideways and his toes turned up. She plucked him free and kissed his damp fur. 'Hello, Rumtopf, did you mind being outside all night? I knew it wasn't going to rain because it doesn't in August. Not much. I heard Madame say so to Mutti.'

Mutti said Lotti was too old to still be carrying on conversations with a teddy and that Rumtopf was ugly with his single, orange eye, but that was what made him special. He had suffered much but never gave away secrets. So Papa had told her. Papa had said, 'Keep Rumtopf by you, don't let anybody separate you.'

That was why she'd left the bear outside. If Rumtopf had been sitting on her bed, Mutti would have been sure to say, 'Only bring the things you need.' Cradling the bear to warm him up, Lotti whispered, 'I don't know where we're going, but it's going to be windy.' Mutti had told her to fasten on her beret with lots of grips.

Lotti crossed the courtyard and went into a passage that ran beneath the house where one of Madame's daughters lived. When she and Mutti had arrived, so late one night only the moon had seen them, Lotti had marvelled at there being a whole secret house tucked behind another one. It had made her feel like a turtle who could pull in its head so nobody saw anything but its shell. Only now they were leaving their shell. The closing of the passage door behind her stole the dawn light.

A dark shape at the end of the passage split in two. It was Mutti and Madame, whispering by the street door. Madame flicked on a torch at her approach and took a breath.

'*Mon Dieu, ma petite*, what are you wearing?'

Mutti also gasped. 'Lotti – I said, put on a warm coat, not your red one!'

'No, you didn't say that.'

'I said *old* things, not your best. I meant the brown school coat.'

'I don't like my brown one. It makes me itch.'

'Red makes us noticeable. You have to change. Go back, quickly.'

Lotti regarded her mother sternly. 'You are wearing your gold hat, Mutti.'

'Call me "Maman", not "Mutti". How many times? Speak French, not German. Not ever. Anyway' – Mutti touched the beret that was pinned sideways to her head – 'it isn't gold, it's mustard-yellow.'

'If you can wear your best beret, why can't I wear my best coat?'

'Sometimes a lady likes to look beautiful.' Madame used a silly voice, as if Lotti were four years old and not nine going on ten. 'Tiptoe back inside, *ma petite*, and change. I'll take teddy.'

Lotti moved Rumtopf away from Madame's grasp.

'What is this?' Madame pointed the torch at Lotti's chest. She muttered urgently over her shoulder, 'Miryam, she still has her star stitched on.'

In her shock, Mutti forgot her own rules about not speaking German. '*Gott im Himmel*, get it off her!'

Lotti anchored Rumtopf to her chest and fancied she heard his heart thudding. Nobody would take her star. It was the rule, you had to wear one. Papa had said so.

'Let Madame take it off, Lotti. You can't go out—' The

sound of a vehicle in the street silenced Mutti and a moment later, there came a short knock. Madame slowly, slowly, opened the street door. Her voice wobbled as she said, 'Delivery for Cousin Jacques, as ordered?'

A gruff voice replied, 'Winter-weight suiting, best quality.' After a pause, the same gruff voice said, 'Two to collect in return. Ready?'

Madame glanced at Lotti. 'Almost. The child... never mind. Give us one minute.'

A second man took rolls of fabric from the rear of a dumpy green van. Lotti heard him say, 'Madame, get your little girl into the back. Quick, quick.'

Mutti dithered. 'There's no time to unpick that vile star. Lotti, you'll have to come without your coat.'

'Ah, no,' Madame objected, 'she'll be perished out on the water. It may be August, but at sea it's always November.'

Sea? They were going on a boat?

Before Lotti knew it, Madame had seized Rumtopf and, taking a tiny pair of scissors from her pocket, began cutting off the star on Lotti's breast.

Lotti writhed, but Mutti helped to hold her, hissing, 'It has to come off, now stay still.'

'But we have to wear a yellow star. It's the rules. Papa said so. I always do as Papa says.'

'Today is different,' Madame said. 'Do as your mother says, *petite*. If you wriggle, I might jab you. Nearly there.' The star was still attached by one of its points.

The men had run out of patience and one of them picked Lotti up in his arms. She smelled cigarettes on his jacket. In the blink of an eye, the rolls of cloth were thrown back in the van; Lotti and her mother were bundled in after them. Lotti screamed. She had seen her papa being put into a van, blood on his face. The man who had picked her up jumped in with them and shut the rear doors, plunging them into darkness.

'Sit down,' Mutti urged. 'He is a friend, risking his life to help us.'

The van's engine fired.

Lotti realised then that her arms were empty. 'Madame has Rumtopf!' She pounded against the rear doors, shrieking, 'Rumtopf!' Somehow, she got out and half fell into the road. Madame was still in her doorway, holding the bear by one ear.

Lotti seized Rumtopf and crushed him to her. The man who smelled of cigarettes had jumped out too. He picked her up again, like he had the pillars of cloth, and posted her headfirst into the van. As he slammed the doors once again, he flung words at Mutti, something about, 'Does she want to get us all killed? The Milice are like rats, scuttling in every gutter! You know who they are?'

As the van pulled away, Mutti said shakily, 'Of course we know. They're your police, who work with the Gestapo. I'm afraid Lotti only ever listened to her papa. She worshipped him.'

The man patted Lotti's shoulder, saying, 'For the next hour, pretend I am your papa.'

Mutti added more advice. 'If anything happens, this gentleman is your Oncle Gael, you understand?'

Lotti said he was not her uncle, and she said it in German.

'How many times – ouch!' The van lurched and Mutti's head cracked against the side. Lotti rolled, pedalling in the air like a beetle.

She heard the man say, 'If she gabbles in German at a police roadblock, we're finished. Tell her to keep her mouth shut.'

'Lotti' – Mutti's voice in the darkness was a nervous plea – 'if we're stopped, pretend you cannot speak. You don't know how. Is that clear?'

Lotti chose to obey at once, and so didn't answer. This man who wasn't her uncle was lighting another cigarette and its glowing end shook with every bump of the van's wheels. Lotti pulled out the last stitches holding her yellow star and squeezed it in her hand. Madame shouldn't have got her scissors out. You had to wear a star. Grown-ups told you to obey, and then they made you disobey. They were a muddle.

Except Papa. Papa had always explained why things had to be as they were, as if Lotti was as clever as he was. The last time she had seen him, he had been wet with blood. 'Get away,' his tears had told her. 'Run, go, now.'

LOTTI

LONDON, AUTUMN 1942

England was a muddle too.

Aunt Freda, whose house they lived in now, kept telling her that she and Mutti had found a safe haven, then spoiled it by saying, 'Only, never speak German outside this flat because not everyone understands what a refugee is.' They'd soon have her speaking the king's English, Aunt Freda promised. 'Chattering away, nineteen to the dozen.'

That sounded like a lot of words, nineteen and a dozen, but truthfully, Lotti was learning faster than Mutti, who still said 'vee' instead of 'we' and couldn't say 'the' without first stopping her tongue to think. Mutti would 'go in the shop' instead of 'to the shops' and if anything scared her, she melted into German and Lotti had to be the one to say, 'Shh!' She had heard Aunt Freda talking about them on the telephone, saying they were 'stateless'.

Whenever Lotti asked about her papa, the little trench would come between Mutti's eyebrows. 'Why must I keep saying it, Lotti? Papa is with us in our hearts, wherever he may be.'

Was he stateless, then, somewhere else?

Mutti would sigh, 'Enough, enough.' In bed at night, Lotti

whispered into the ear of the one person who never shushed her because his mouth was stitched with wool. Rumtopf didn't mind Lotti asking about Papa. She poured into his ragged ear the best thing Papa had ever told her:

'If ever you don't know what to say, *bubbeleh*, say nothing.'

1

TRURO, CORNWALL, SIX MONTHS LATER,
MARCH 1943

The Cornish Riviera Express rolled in, steam fogging its iron wheels. Gwenna Devoran positioned herself where the third-class carriages would stop. Those she was here to collect must not suffer a moment's anxiety. After what they'd been through, first in their home in Berlin, then France and then in London, they deserved an unflustered welcome to Cornwall.

Her friend Freda Fincham had written a couple of weeks back, asking if Gwenna would take in two guests, a mother and daughter. 'Miryam Gittelman is around your age, five foot six, slimly built with brown hair gathered up under a mustard-yellow beret. The child wears a red coat and since she never lets go of a tatty, one-eyed teddy bear, you can't possibly miss them.' They were coming to live with Gwenna in her remote farm-house because London had triggered a breakdown in the mother. Country air, peace and quiet, was what the doctor had ordered.

Doors were flung open, suitcases were lifted down from chocolate-and-cream carriages. Most of those disembarking had the look of early-season holidaymakers, with bulging luggage. Gwenna studied every face, but nobody matched the description she'd formed in her mind. She walked past the two front coaches, peering in at windows, ignoring the pinch of town shoes she hadn't worn in many months. Silly to dress up, really, but she'd wanted to put on her best show for Mrs Gittelman. Ought she to call her 'Frau Gittelman'? Probably not. She might prefer 'Miryam'.

Gwenna reached the third-class dining car. The Gittelmans were travelling third, there being no second class on the Riviera Express. They must still be on the train because they certainly hadn't got off. They'd better not be dozing, as this train only stopped a few minutes. Though they might be forgiven for nodding off, it being a five-and-a-half-hour slog from London to Truro. Apologising as she went, Gwenna picked her way through a knot of travellers. She was growing a little frantic. Any moment, the guard would blow his whistle and the train would steam off to Penzance where it terminated. Freda Fincham, Gwenna's old school friend and Mrs Gittelman's sponsor, had promised that this was the day, and the train. Freda's promises were as dependable as the chimes of Big Ben.

Mustard-yellow beret. Red coat. Mother and child.

Child. How would it feel, Gwenna wondered, for her lonely farmhouse to echo with a child's laughter?

The Riviera Express was a long snake and Gwenna was thoroughly out of patience with her high-heeled shoes as she reached the final carriage without seeing any sign of her guests. Back she went, having noticed a carriage in the middle with its window blinds down. At the time, it had struck her as odd. A railway journey into Cornwall offered views of rolling emerald countryside. Crossing the River Tamar by the Saltash Bridge was awe-inspiring, even if you'd done it dozens of times as Gwenna had. You'd have to be thoroughly jaded, or descended from bats, to want to travel the last miles in darkness. But clearly, somebody had chosen to. She was reaching for the carriage door handle when a guard stopped her.

'You can't get on that one, madam.'

She turned to him. 'This is a third-class carriage, yes?'

'It's a special carriage. Third class is up along, the two coaches behind the coal tender.' He jerked his head towards the front of the train, where Gwenna had begun her search.

'Thing is,' she said, 'I'm collecting people and I'm worried they're asleep and don't realise they've reached Truro. I've looked in every carriage but this one.'

'This one's out of bounds.'

'Why?'

'Never you mind.'

Oh, for goodness' sake! They were at war and secrecy had its place, but she had her duty too, which was to collect two vulnerable souls before they were borne off to Penzance and fined for exceeding their tickets. 'Is there royalty on board or—?' *Or...* Her mouth slowly opened. Had she heard correctly? She had. 'They're speaking German in there!'

'More than likely,' the guard answered grimly.

'Who *is* on board?'

'The War Office didn't see fit to inform me,' he answered. 'You'd best gather up those you're looking for, madam. We shan't move her for another five minutes.' By 'her', he meant the train. 'Did you look in the third-class dining car?'

'Yes, through the window.' Utterly distracted, Gwenna watched the doors at each end of the sealed carriage being flung open. The smoke of a hundred cigarettes rolled out, adding haze to the crisp spring air. A heavily armed British Tommy got out and adopted a guarding stance. A second armed soldier did the same. At the command of 'Step forward!' two very different-looking men emerged, blinking as they encountered daylight. One had a bloody gash to his chin. The other wore a leather cap, whose peak partly concealed a swelling black eye. The soldiers gestured them to one side with their gun barrels. More men then began to file out. Gwenna soon lost count.

They wore light-green overalls with splayed collars revealing grubby shirtfronts, some plain, some checked. All wore white or grey armbands. A formless rage simmered through her. They must be POWs, prisoners of war, and by definition, killers of British soldiers, sailors and airmen. A number of POW camps had sprung up in Cornwall, and a new one was being built a couple of miles away from Gwenna's farm. She'd assumed it would house Italians. If these men were headed there, she'd have Germans on her doorstep.

They kept coming, but the clothes were different now. This latest cohort wore dark-blue pea coats and heavy-duty trousers. Mariners, by the looks of them, captured off their ship. Hauled out of the Atlantic, maybe. If so, they were the lucky ones, she reflected bitterly. Some wore caps, some were bare headed, but one thing they had in common was several days' growth of beard and eyes dull with exhaustion.

The last man out was of a different stamp. Their captain, Gwenna reckoned, though his jacket of salt-slicked leather carried no badges of rank. Unlike his men, he looked neither angry nor beaten. Once he had both feet on the station platform, he took in the Victorian architecture with an air of resignation, staring up at the strip of sky between the platforms as though the intensity of the March sunshine was faintly disappointing.

'You men, get in line,' ordered one of the Tommies. Helpfully, he sketched a line in the air with his gun.

Nobody obeyed. The German captain seemed to shrug, almost in amusement. His gaze found Gwenna, and she felt his momentary surprise at the sight of her, an emotion expressed through eyes as clear as gin. He had dark-blond hair cropped very short, and the shadow of a beard a few shades darker. A silvery scar ran from the middle of his face to his ear, as though someone had swept a butcher's knife under his cheekbone.

The Tommy again ordered the prisoners to get in line. Still, nobody moved.

The captain gave the same order in German and the men arranged themselves as neatly as schoolchildren, two by two, and were marched away.

Well. Bless me. Gwenna had a strong idea that she would shake herself later and wonder if she'd experienced a hallucination. The Gittelmans! How could she have forgotten them? She dashed inside the vacated carriage and immediately began coughing. You'd think those POWs had been given the last cigarettes on earth, and ten minutes to smoke them. Pulling up window blinds, she saw the floor was littered with cigarette butts. Playing cards too, dropped in the dimness. 'Oh, honestly, sailors!' One card, the Queen of Hearts, showed a voluptuous woman in a state of undress.

A through train flashed past, giving a whistle, followed by a hollow bang. Brown carriages confirmed it as a mail train, probably on its way to Exeter and London.

Gwenna went through to the next carriage, whose only occupants were an elderly couple who peered at her curiously. She nodded politely and walked the length of the carriage, into a lobby where lavatories hid behind discreet woodgrain doors. It was much busier in the third-class dining car. Passengers, interrupted at their tea, were gawping out onto the platform from their banquette seats. The object of their fascination was the group of prisoners, which had been brought to a halt alongside this carriage. The train had been delayed to allow them off, but it wouldn't wait much longer.

Gwenna called out over the jabber of voices, 'Are any of you Mrs Gittelman and daughter?'

Nobody heard. Real-life Germans on the other side of the window glass were as thrilling as a troop of elephants, and the onlookers were loudly describing to each other what was right in front of them, with 'Gorblimey!' every other word. They sounded as though they came from the same two streets of London's East End.

Gwenna blew out her cheeks. Sometimes, you had to accept failure. She'd go to the post office and telegraph Freda. 'PRECIOUS CHARGES NOT ARRIVED. ADVISE WHEREABOUTS.' But as she walked back along the carriage, something caught her eye.

The last table in the dining car was laid for tea. Two cups and saucers, side plates with part-eaten scones on them. A butter knife. A smear of jam. Afternoon tea abandoned. In the corner of one seat sat a teddy bear in a sailor suit. Gwenna looked into a threadbare face from which stared a single amber glass eye.

She called urgently up the dining car, 'Excuse me, who was sitting here?'

Her voice made no inroad on the chatter. Doors were now being slammed up and down the train and Gwenna knew she was in danger of being carried onwards with only a platform ticket in her pocket. But something held her still.

Gut instinct said her guests had sat here and had left in a tearing hurry.

So why hadn't Gwenna seen them? A very human possibility struck her. In the lobby between the carriages, she rapped anxiously on one of the lavatory doors.

'Um, Mrs Gittelman, are you in there? This is Mrs Devoran. It's our stop. You have to—'

The toilet was empty. So was the one beside it. That's when Gwenna felt a breeze across her cheek. The trackside door swung open at her touch. She peered down at the rails. A mustard-yellow shape lay on the stony ballast between the sleepers. It was a hat. A single shoe was balanced inexplicably on one of the rails. A wink of bright crimson too. Blood? *Dear God, don't think it.*

Gwenna looked towards the passenger bridge some yards

up the track and her heart stopped. Under it, on the railway line, stood a girl in a red coat. Gwenna searched with her eyes for a railway guard, but the platform opposite was deserted. As she calculated how long it would take her to get off the train, run to the footbridge and reach the opposite platform, the empty rails began to whine and crackle. A train was coming. She didn't think twice. Hitching up her skirt, she jumped down onto the track.

Loose, dry stones swallowed the heels of her shoes. She stumbled onto her knees, sharp edges piercing her stockings, but she scrambled up. The rails were now singing. She was half aware that people had finally come onto the platform. They shouted warnings, but Gwenna ran onwards as best she could, driven by a primal need to save, to rescue. Her vision narrowed to admit only the outlines of a red coat. She seized the little body, lifted the child up like a dressmaker's dummy. Corn-coloured plaits swung, heels kicked, striking Gwenna's abdomen, her womb, but she didn't feel pain. The vibration of the oncoming train overwhelmed everything. The noise was like a landslide, racing to engulf her and this child. A whistle blasted four urgent notes.

'Lady!' A railway guard had leapt down and he plucked the struggling child from Gwenna's arms. In one move, he swung her into the arms of another man then heaved Gwenna up onto the platform.

A local passenger train pulled in in a skirl of brakes. Gwenna lay on her back, voices clamouring over her and hot steam washing her face.

She had saved the child, but where was the mother? Where was Miryam Gittelman?

The tracks. The blood.

2

'Still not a word out of her.' A policewoman addressed the whiskery sergeant seated at a creaky table opposite Gwenna who was writing out her statement. She paused to listen.

'I took her a glass of milk, Sergeant Couch,' the policewoman continued, 'but I might as well have saved my trouble. I've left her to bide alone awhile, see if that helps her find her tongue.'

Gwenna shook her head. The WPC's stiff collar and black tie would frighten any child into silence. She asked, 'May I see her, please?'

Sergeant Couch tapped the lined writing pad in front of Gwenna. 'When you've checked and signed your statement, Mrs Devoran.'

He pronounced her name 'Dev'ran' which was the Cornish way.

Gwenna had written everything she remembered of the minutes spent looking for Miryam Gittelman and her daughter. The German POWs, the abandoned tea table and the single shoe on the track. It had the clarity of a film, rolling frame by frame. Except that timings were hard to pin down. Had she searched the train for five minutes or ten? She asked, 'Shall I mention the teddy bear? I'm sure it's the little girl's. It was on a seat, left behind, I'm sure of it.'

'Likely so,' Sergeant Couch replied. 'Lost Property will hold it.'

'But she'll want it. Children get so attached—' She broke off, telling herself – *How on earth would you know how children feel? You have none.*

What she did know was that she was stuck here until she'd finished her statement, and so she read through what she'd written. Her handwriting was all over the place and when the pad had been put in front of her, she'd briefly forgotten her own address. She'd even misspelled the name of her own farm. She knew it was shock because she'd experienced this sensation before, a feeling like doors shutting in every direction and your mind slipping to one side of your brain.

She scrawled an approximation of her signature and said, 'May I see the little girl? I – I suppose I'm her guardian now, since her mother... they were coming to live with me.'

Sergeant Couch said, 'In due course,' and as the policewoman was still there, Gwenna tried appealing to her. 'It might help Lotti to see a different face.'

Not the most tactful remark. The WPC sized Gwenna up, taking in the scuffed suit and ruined hat, the chestnut-brown hair clumped against her neck, half in, half out of its net. In the police station toilet, Gwenna had done her best to wash dirt off her chin and cheeks with hard, green soap she could still smell. She must look unfit to be anybody's guardian. 'What I meant was, Lotti might respond to a new voice.'

The policewoman sucked her teeth. 'The little maid wouldn't touch a drop of her milk.'

'Yes, you said.'

'Like she's been turned to stone. Where's she from again, Mrs Devoran?'

'London. She and her mother were coming to Cornwall for...' Gwenna's voice broke. 'For peace and quiet.' She pulled a handkerchief from under her sleeve. It was damp from earlier tears.

Sergeant Couch let out a gusty sigh. 'It can't be wondered at, her not wanting her milk. Seeing your mother hit by a train in front of your eyes would turn any little maid to stone.'

'You do think her mother's dead, then?' Gwenna asked. 'There's no hope she could have survived?'

'We don't deal in hope, madam,' Sergeant Couch said heavily. 'We look at facts.'

Gwenna remembered the hollow thump she'd heard from inside the Riviera Express, which she'd put down to the mail train crossing a point. The possibility that she'd heard the moment of impact made her stomach clench. A very young constable came in and mumbled something.

'Speak up, lad,' Sergeant Couch ordered. 'The lady isn't the fainting kind, to my mind.'

'Body's been found, Sergeant.' The young policeman laid something on the table. 'And this was picked up beside the track.'

It was an adult's ration book. Gwenna was shown the name inside. Miryam Gittelman.

'Until the body is identified, the lady is still a missing person.' Sergeant Couch's eyebrows dipped sympathetically. 'But I wouldn't hang on to hope, were I you.'

'Does... does Charlotte know her mother is... I mean... was hit?' Gwenna couldn't say 'dead' and despised herself. Pretending was no charity. 'Do you think she saw?'

'From the look in her eyes, Mrs Devoran, I'd say she did.'

'That's her proper name?' the policewoman intervened. 'Charlotte. Earlier, you said "Lotti".'

'She's Lotti for short, so my friend told me. My friend who

arranged for them to stay.' Gwenna pointed to her statement. 'I've written her name as Charlotte Gittelman.'

'Sounds German to me.'

'They are German Jews, they came here to escape—' Gwenna couldn't say 'danger' because the irony was sickening. 'They got out of Berlin when life there became impossible and that was just the start.' A hat, bright as a sunflower, and a shoe that seemed to have been placed so neatly on the train line were the remnants of a woman she would never meet, whose story had stopped, pointlessly, mid-chapter. Gwenna put her hand to her mouth to keep in the dry sobs. 'I'm sorry.'

'That's all right.' The sergeant nodded. 'You've done your best, Mrs Devoran.'

'Who will identify the body?'

The exchange of glances between the sergeant and the young PC told Gwenna that the body was in no state to be identified. Cold. She felt ice cold. Freda had entrusted Miryam and Lotti to her and this had happened.

Rocking with pain, she found anger. 'The railway staff were busy ogling the German prisoners. If they'd been on duty, safeguarding their customers, they'd have stopped Miryam crossing the track. You need to summon the stationmaster, demand an explanation.'

'And we will,' the sergeant assured her. 'Your job is to pass on all you saw for the coroner.'

All she saw. Blood on the tracks. A hat, a shoe. 'It's there on paper, all I know.'

'Then we'll drive you home, madam. You and little Charlotte.'

'I can take her?' Gwenna felt a tentative joy, like a candle flame in a storm. Her fear had been that Lotti would be taken into the starched arms of an orphanage before being sent back to London. She had intended to fight that, but it seemed there was no fight to be had. 'I can take Lotti home to Colvennon Farm?'

'Best you do,' the sergeant replied, 'and let's see if anyone else claims her. Go with WPC Roper, and I'll get the keys to the police car.'

The WPC led her to a side room and stepped aside. 'In you go, then. She'll prefer your face to mine, no doubt.'

Walking in and seeing a diminutive figure sitting on a too-large chair, a red coat folded at her feet, turned a skewer in Gwenna's heart. 'Lotti... Lotti, dear?'

The child raised her gaze, eyes full of hope which died at the sight of Gwenna. *She thought I was her mother coming back.*

Uncertain how to break the silence, Gwenna picked up the coat. The room was cold and Lotti's cheeks were marble pale. 'Will you stand up, so we can put this on?' The red sleeves were covered in scuff marks. 'We'll give it a brush-down later, but best wear it for now, yes? Arms up!' How bright she sounded, like a tinny bell ringing on after everyone had stopped listening. She crouched beside Lotti's chair. 'I'm Mrs Devoran but you may call me Aunt Gwenna. I'm going to take care of you.'

The child's eyes were a deep shade of honey. The irises darted and switched focus as if the mind within was meeting a new threat. Perhaps it was. Gwenna persisted. 'Did your Aunt Freda tell you about me? We're old friends, because she used to live here and knows how lovely and quiet Cornwall is. You're going to stay with me, on my farm. I'm sure you talked about it with your mother and how it would be, moving to the country. Lotti? We're going home, soon as you have your coat on.'

There was no response. No movement. A footstep suggested that WPC Roper had given up waiting. Gwenna put her finger to her lips, desperate that Lotti should make her own choice to get up or not. But the policewoman leaned over them.

'There now, do as the lady tells you. You're to have a little ride in a car, won't that be nice? On your feet, then.' Two sharp claps underpinned the command.

Lotti stood at once and put her chill fingers into Gwenna's hand. The tiny act of trust shot unbearable pain into Gwenna's heart. *Let me deserve it.* They walked out of the police station but when they reached the black Wolseley car with Sergeant Couch behind the wheel, Lotti stopped dead.

'It's all right.' Gwenna recognised instinctive fear. 'We aren't in trouble, we're going home.' She climbed into the back and drew Lotti in after her. Perhaps the child hadn't been in a car before. Freda didn't drive, nor did Freda's husband. Nobody did any more, unless they had to.

'Ready?' The sergeant turned to them, nodded, then fired the engine. Night had fallen and with the blackout in force, the streets were inky-dark. The Wolseley's headlights were masked, just bright enough for the sergeant to cautiously navigate his way. They left Truro, heading towards the coast, swapping a wide road for lanes rimmed by banks and stone walls. The dampened headlights picked out the white striped face of a badger and flushed owls from the trees. Gwenna tried not to glance at Lotti's still profile, not wanting to shatter the child's fragile shell. What grief and shock it hid, Gwenna could only guess at. She was about to speak when she noticed lights in a valley some distance off. Of course! They were shining from Tregallon, the POW camp, and powered by generators. Local people were none too pleased at the glare, nor the noise they made through the night. She thought of the men, unshaven and sullen, penned behind the fence. Putting an arm out, she pulled Lotti closer and felt the narrow shoulders stiffen. 'Country-dark is different from town-dark,' she said comfortingly. 'You'll grow used to it.'

It was the sergeant who answered. 'I'd speculate you see more foxes than people out here.'

'Not really. Colvennon lies in the parish of St Wenna, so I

see others most days. I admit, it's no metropolis.' Gwenna had
lived in Truro after she married, and for two years before that in
London, so she had no illusions about how remote her home
was. 'It's where I grew up and I came back after my husband...'
She broke off, realising she'd almost said too much.

The sergeant concentrated on his driving as they rounded a
tight bend, then turned his head to say, 'It's just come to me –
you're the younger Mrs Devoran of Fendynick House.'

She let a moment go before answering. 'Yes, I was Edward
Devoran's wife.'

'Then I'm sorry for your loss, madam. I read about his death
in the *Cornishman*. A year or so back, wasn't it, when his ship
went down?'

Longer than that. Day, month, time were engraved on
Gwenna's mind. 'Eighteen months, actually: the 23rd of
November 1941.'

'Ah, it's cruel, how we lose track of time in this war.'

Gwenna disliked the drift of the conversation. To change
the subject, she said, 'When you're a farmer, the seasons flow
one into the next.'

'A farmer,' the sergeant echoed. 'Pardon me, Mrs Devoran,
but that's an odd thing for a lady to be doing.'

'What, feeding the nation?'

'Working the land... if you don't mind me saying it.'

'I don't mind, but I'm by no means the only one of my kind.'
Gwenna was used to the blink of surprise whenever she stated
her profession to strangers. They'd look at her hands, then take
in her modest height and slim build and more often than not,
seek to correct her. *You mean, 'farmer's wife'?* She leaned
forward. 'The turning to St Wenna is just up ahead, next on the
right. Yes – here!'

He'd almost driven past. The signpost had been removed at
the start of the war and the lane end was a black mouth
yawning between trees, invisible unless you knew what to look

for. As they passed through St Wenna, a village of stone houses with a church and a chapel, elms and oaks gave ground to wind-bent Monterey pines. Gwenna said to Lotti, 'If the windows were open, we'd smell the sea.' A layer of polished pewter between the horizon and the hills announced its nearness. A couple of miles outside the village, the headlights picked out the granite standing stone marking the boundary of Gwenna's farm, revealing it as a misty, elemental form. Gwenna suggested the sergeant pull up here. 'Your tyres won't like my sunken lane.'

Sergeant Couch accompanied them up to the farm with his torch. Gwenna, having come out in broad daylight for what she had assumed would be a two-hour round trip, had not brought her own. Its beam bounced off the mossy walls of the lane. A stream's merry gurgle accompanied them to an iron gate, beyond which stood a house, visible only as a rectangular shadow touched here and there by moonlight. 'This is home, Lotti. Can you smell the cows? I have pigs and chickens too, and two horses for ploughing. You'll meet the cows and horses in the morning.'

Lotti made no answer. She had yet to speak a single word.

'It's a strong perfume,' the sergeant observed. 'And not a proper light within miles. No electric up here, I suppose.'

'Not a jot,' agreed Gwenna. 'And we passed our running water as we walked up the lane.'

'The stream? I hope you've got a fire lit inside, Mrs Devoran. The little maid will be wanting something to eat.'

There was indeed a fire smouldering in the range, left by Hilda Hoskens, who came in each weekday to help with the chickens and do cleaning and cooking. A pan of soup on the hob was a welcome sight. There wasn't enough heat in the stove to boil a kettle, however, and Gwenna was desperate for tea. Having settled Lotti on a chair at the kitchen table, she lit oil lamps, then a Primus stove. The Primus was her lifeline, running on kerosene and methylated spirits. 'Tea, Sergeant?'

'I'd better be off. My good lady will be thinking—' He broke off, awkwardly. He'd been going to say, 'something dreadful has happened to me.' They were both aware of the absent fourth person: Lotti's mother.

Before he left, Gwenna said, 'If anything else of Mrs Gittelman's is found – I mean, if it's in a fit state... you will let me know? I need Lotti's ration book; she'll have to be signed up with the local shops.'

The sergeant promised to chase up the stationmaster for any items that had come to light.

Gwenna followed him to the door. 'And the teddy bear, don't forget that.'

'I'll do my best.' He bid her goodnight.

With his departure, an uncertain mood took over, which Gwenna attempted to lift with more bright suggestions. 'Let's take your coat and hat, shall we?' Lotti flinched as Gwenna touched the rim of a beret held in place by grips. Gwenna pulled them free, her movements slow and steady. She placed the beret on the kitchen dresser. 'It's there when you next need it and I've put the grips beside it.' Something told her that Lotti was a neat soul, not the messy, lose-everything child Gwenna had been. 'Do you drink tea, or would you prefer hot milk?' As she waited for a response, she felt the first shoots of panic. Lotti, being Jewish, might have all kinds of rules about what she might and might not eat. Gwenna was pretty sure milk was allowed. She had raised the question of the Gittelmans' meals with Freda, who had written back, 'Don't worry, they're not orthodox and they don't keep kosher. Pork is a definite "no" but most other things are on the menu. Miryam will discuss her specific needs when she arrives.'

Only, she never would arrive. Could a nine-year-old child be expected to provide the answers? When a streak of brown-and-white detached itself from the top of the dresser, crossing the floor to wind itself around Gwenna's ankles, her anxiety amplified.

'Here's Josephine come to say hello. Do you mind cats, Lotti? I can put her out if you like. She's supposed to catch mice around the farm but there are outdoor cats to deal with mere rodents, or so she tells me.' Before Gwenna could stop her, Josephine sprang onto the table and a nut-brown paw reached out to bat Lotti's arm. Gwenna held her breath. Lotti's expression shed some of its blankness and a small hand tentatively stroked Josephine's fur.

So that was all right, then.

Leaving the cat and the child to make each other's acquaintance, Gwenna brewed tea for herself and heated milk for Lotti, which she sweetened with honey from a neighbour's farm. Hilda's soup today was pearl barley and vegetable, mostly potato and carrot. Gwenna put it on the heat and stood stirring it, willing Josephine to keep working her magic. 'She's a calico cat, which is a smart way of saying three-coloured. White, brown and black, see? Her mother was a tabby and her father was pure white. She likes curling up on people's knees, so be prepared.'

Lotti continued to stroke Josephine, who arched in pleasure. When the soup was ready, Gwenna was sorry to have to lift Josephine off the table in order to set out the crockery. 'Sit down, my dear.' She lit a candle because oil lamps were too smelly to have under your nose as you ate, and served the soup.

'Blow on your spoon if it's too hot and say if you don't like it. Lotti? You don't have to eat, but I think you should.'

It was like speaking to a statue. The moment Josephine had been removed, Lotti had subsided, her arms pressed to her side. Gwenna picked up a spoon and held it out. 'Try a little.'

Lotti stared at her bowl.

Gwenna began to eat her soup, blowing theatrically on each

spoonful. 'Mm, this is a good one. Hilda, whom you'll meet tomorrow, is rather an expert on the soup front.'

Telling herself that she was expecting too much, too soon, Gwenna moved her chair to sit beside the child. She put an arm around her – ignoring the flinch – and lifted the spoon to Lotti's lips. 'Come on. Just one.'

The child's mouth opened. She delicately took in the soup. Another spoonful, and another. 'Good girl.'

They'd managed half the bowl when Lotti shook her head.

'That's all right. You've done really well. Would you like your milk? It's not all that hot now.' Gwenna handed the cup to Lotti, who wrapped her hands around it and drank, sip by sip. When Gwenna took the cup from her, candlelight reflected in tears on the girl's cheeks.

'Oh, you poor darling.' Sergeant Couch had been sure Lotti must know what had befallen her mother, but was that true? Her mother would have been there one moment, and the next the space would have been filled by a thundering train. Recalling her first sight of Lotti walking down the track made Gwenna wonder if the child had been searching for Miryam. 'I am so sorry,' Gwenna whispered. 'So very sorry. There now. It'll be all right.'

She so wanted to give comfort, but hugging the child might only make things worse. Gwenna repeated gentle assurances she didn't for a moment believe. It *wasn't* going to be all right, because Lotti had lost not only her mother, but to all intents and purposes, her father too.

Freda's letters had told Gwenna the sad fate of this little family. Having escaped Berlin weeks before the outbreak of war, the Gittelmans had found a tentative security in Paris that lasted for three years. Last summer came the round-up of Jews in France. 'Miryam and Lotti got away just in time, but Lotti's father, Leopold, was seized.' Freda was hoping that through her contacts in the Red Cross, she might learn what had befallen

Leopold Gittelman. She held out little hope for his survival, however. 'We hear of Jews being deported and then killed within hours of arrival at their destination, or set to work in appalling conditions,' Freda had warned Gwenna; 'Say nothing of this in front of Lotti as Miryam has not confided her fears to her daughter.'

I might be all Lotti's got, Gwenna thought. Tears inched over her cheekbones and she wiped them away with her sleeve. It wasn't her job to join in the grief. She had to be strong, to pull this poor child through a nightmare time.

The nightmares began that night. In the early hours, Gwenna was pulled from a dream by terrified screams. She was out of her bed even before her eyes had fully opened, shoving her feet into slippers. In the corridor she stumbled into Lotti, a ghost-child in a pool of moonlight shining through an uncurtained window. She was screaming in German. Gwenna recognised the words *'Bitte, nein!'*

Please, no!

'It's all right. Shh. It's all right.' Gwenna parcelled Lotti in her arms. The girl was not so much shaking as jerking, like a fish thrown on a bank. 'Hush. Hush.'

When the fit subsided, Gwenna took the trembling child back to her own bed. It was large, with a goose-down mattress that had been her parents' and was easily big enough for two slender bodies. Lotti fell immediately back to sleep. Gwenna lay wide awake, listening to owls calling to each other from the trees along the lane. She thought – *If the authorities realise I keep pigs as well as cows, will they let Lotti stay?*

Would they notice, or care? And who were 'the authorities' anyway, in a case like this?

An image shot into her head of German POWs filing from the train, looking as though they'd emerged from the hold of a ship. A trail of captive manhood... who had got in her way. Had she boarded the train five minutes earlier, she'd have found Miryam and Lotti at their tea table. She was filled with hate for every German. Warmongers. Killers. Cold as winter. By what miserable twist of fate had they arrived on the same train as the Gittelmans?

As the night bled away, Gwenna contemplated ways of reaching a fragile and traumatised child. Games, lessons, country walks? It would help if Lotti would speak. So far, Gwenna had got nothing from her beyond some terrified German. Freda had informed her that Lotti spoke good English, and had picked up French in Paris, but that they'd discouraged German while in England for obvious reasons. Gwenna had learned basic German at school but felt she ought to respect the veto on speaking it here.

She drifted off to sleep with another worry knocking at her brain. Freda didn't yet know about Miryam's death. She must inform her before the police did.

3

After what felt like ten minutes' sleep, Gwenna was woken by a din from the farmyard. She'd overslept! The cows were in for milking, lowing their displeasure at the disruption to their schedule.

She was out of bed in a flash, pulling clothes on over her nightdress. Her blouse smelled of the railway track and cigarette fumes from the German-filled carriage. Later, she'd heat water for washing and do her clothes and Lotti's too. The child slept on, curled like a shrimp under the blankets, one fair plait clutched in her hand. *Best not wake her,* Gwenna decided. *Let her rest.* From the sound of her breathing, she wouldn't wake for a while.

Downstairs, Gwenna stuffed her feet into wellingtons and pulled on a short coat before going outside. Her back ached. That railway guard had hauled her up onto the platform, straining her tendons as he did so. Mind you, he was a hero. He'd likely saved her life and Lotti's.

Despite her oversleeping, it was early still, and nippy. Dawn had laid mist across the bow-backed hills between the farm and the sea. A breeze brought the scent of salt spray. The cows were moving with undulating intent towards the milking parlour, dew sparkling on their caramel backs. They'd spent the night in the meadow, as they did from spring through summer, only coming inside in the colder months.

'Sorry, Ezra,' Gwenna called to the grizzled farmhand who brought up the rear, trailing a stick he never used other than to knock stinging flies off legs, or to stop a dominant cow shoving another. 'Sorry you had to do my job.'

'Well, it was my job for forty years, Mrs Devoran. Opening a gate and letting them out is all there is to it.' Ezra Jago pushed back his hat to scratch a thatch of grey hair. 'That was a bad do in town, that poor woman hit by the mail train.'

'You know, then?'

'Ah, they was talking of it in the Mermaid last night. I thought, that can't be the lady you went to fetch?'

'It was. It was Miryam Gittelman and it was dreadful.'

'And the little maid with her, her daughter?'

'She's in the house.' Gwenna wasn't ready to recount the details. Writing her witness statement at the police station had exhausted her powers on that score. Fortunately, Ezra had more sensitivity than his weathered face and half-closed eyes suggested and merely repeated, 'Ah.'

She said, 'You'll have had to do last evening's milking alone. I thought I'd be back.'

'Roddy and I got it done.' Roddy was her pig keeper and husband of the soup-making Hilda. Ezra nodded towards the milking parlour, meaning, 'Let's get on.' The cattle – all pure-bred Guernseys – threaded themselves into their stalls where they waited with heads lowered. Slipping into a well-practised pattern, Gwenna and Ezra put an armful of hay in front of each of them. Gwenna fetched the buckets Ezra had scoured out with boiling water the night before. Six metal churns stood ready, tagged with the farm's identity number.

She picked up her stool and her buckets, filling one with

water from a barrel before collecting clean washcloths. Milking at Colvennon was done by hand, and though it was repetitive work, it required concentration.

She put down her stool next to the first cow. Ezra did the same at the far end of the parlour. Yawning wide, she washed field dirt and grass stains off a bloated udder, murmuring softly as the animal shivered. The water came straight from the stream. Soon the predominant sound was of creamy jets hitting the base of a metal bucket. Colvennon was famous for its Guernsey milk.

'You're brim-full this morning.' Her fingers stroked the teats of the cow whose flank was an inch from her nose. Usually Gwenna sang as she milked, but today her throat felt full of stones. That hollow thud, the mail train's warning klaxon, repeated in her mind. How was she going to get through to Lotti? Clap her hands like that policewoman? Be brisk, smile like a vicar's wife? 'Well, well, life goes on, dear.'

No. She hated that approach. When her granny had died, she'd been sent to stay with her godmother in Devon so she wouldn't witness the old lady's body lying in state. The funeral had taken place in her absence. Result: confusion, followed by humiliation when she finally learned that Granny Bossinny had 'gone to heaven' and that there was to be no goodbye.

'No fairy stories for Lotti,' Gwenna murmured. 'She can ask as many questions as she likes.' It would be reassuring if the poor little child would ask just one.

When two of the churns were full of rich, yellow milk, Ezra came to lean against her stall. 'What's to become of the little maid now, then?'

'Her name's Charlotte, though she's always called Lotti. She's fast asleep in my bed.'

Ezra gave that some thought. 'I suppose there was nowhere else to bring her.'

'No, because she and her mother were going to live here, for as long as they needed.' Gwenna explained that having had distressing experiences in Berlin and Paris, Mrs Gittelman had found London too much for her nerves.

'She's no family here at all, this little maid?'

'Not a soul. They got here by boat, from the French coast, and my friend Mrs Fincham managed to wangle Lotti's mother a servant's work visa, otherwise she'd have been interned as an enemy alien. It was the only way they could be helped. I've no idea what Lotti's status is now, to be frank.'

'She's German, is that right?'

'She's German Jewish, Ezra, and if you know how the Germans treat their Jews—'

Running footsteps and an anxious 'Mrs Devoran?' interrupted her. Roddy Hoskens stood in the doorway. Younger than Ezra by about thirty years, he was breathing hard. 'Horses in the hay meadow; they've trampled a swathe of it and I saw...' Roddy tugged in a breath. 'I swear I saw it.'

'Saw what?' demanded Ezra. 'Spit it out, man.'

'The buck cheeld.'

Ezra rolled his eyes at Gwenna. The buck cheeld was a ghostly girl-child whose appearance foretold a death, and some round here still believed in her. Ezra, who believed implicitly in fairies, was convinced of her existence. He did not believe, however, that she would show herself to Roddy Hoskens, whom he considered lazy and stupid. Nor a true Cornishman, having come originally from Devon. 'Maybe you spent too long in the Mermaid after I left last night, my 'ansome.'

'I spied her,' Roddy insisted, 'edging out of the mist. All in white, with long yellow plaits.'

Oh, God. Gwenna made for the exit, pausing only to say to Roddy, 'Fetch head collars and get those horses off the grass.' With the onset of spring, the meadows were growing apace, full of sweetness.

She raced across the farmyard and wrestled open a gate. It

had dropped on its hinges – another job that needed doing. In the months before his death, her father had struggled with the aftermath of a mild stroke. With Ezra and Roddy to help him, and Hilda to cater to his domestic needs, he'd successfully hidden from Gwenna how badly affected he was. Living in Truro, visiting Colvennon every Sunday, she'd been aware that things were slipping but hadn't been overly concerned. His second, fatal, stroke just before Christmas 1940 had come as a devastating shock to her.

Leaving the gate open for Roddy, she ran towards a meadow set aside for haymaking. The two grey shires, Lady and Prince, were as Roddy had described, tearing hungrily at the grass. Like the cows, the plough horses spent the shortening nights outdoors, but on a well-grazed paddock so they didn't get fat. A bellyful of spring grass might give them colic or founder. Both horses raised their heads for no longer than it took to recognise her. They were making the most of their liberty.

Gwenna stopped to check that Roddy was behind her. More often than not, he ignored her instructions. He'd never accepted her right to take over the farm from her father. And indeed, it was Ezra plodding up the slope with head collars and lead-ropes over his shoulder. Perhaps Roddy was afraid of the cheeld jumping out at him, she thought contemptuously.

She ran on until her ribs were heaving, then paused to look back down over a quilting of fields and stone walls, to the grey-roofed farm and outbuildings. No figure in sight, but Roddy had seen something, she was certain. The possibility that Lotti could be heading for the sea pushed Gwenna on. Gasping out the child's name, she scaled a gate into a second hay field. This was Colvennon Glaze and it formed the boundary between the farm and the sea.

The ankle-high grass showed tracks of small feet. Gwenna ran the length of the Glaze and scrambled over the final wall. The ancient boundary was prickly with ferns and golden gorse, grasping her skirt. A squally wind dragged her hair across her eyes. She bunched it under her collar, but it blew free again. Beyond the curving cliff top, the sea glittered away to infinity. Rock faces shone purple, their crags hectic with birds and wind-blown plants. White gulls rode the bluster, skimming the breakers that crashed against the jawbones of Colvennon Cove.

A little girl in a billowing white nightdress stood barefoot in the tufty grass, staring down at the rocks sixty feet below.

4

Gwenna dared not move. Instead, she called, 'Lotti!' The child turned in surprise.

Still fearing to approach, or do anything that might cause Lotti to make a sudden, wrong move, Gwenna leaned against the wall. 'Lovely view, isn't it?'

The wind caught Lotti's nightdress, one of Gwenna's from her schooldays. The frail body bent with the buffeting force and Gwenna stepped forward, holding out her arms. There was a moment of agony when Lotti seemed to sway. Then she came slowly towards Gwenna, who took her in a firm grip.

'I don't mind saying, you gave me a fright. What were you looking for?' Gwenna was learning not to expect an answer. 'Never mind. Let's go and get some breakfast.'

She got herself and Lotti over a section of wall where the gorse was thinnest. The child was trembling and instead of putting her down, Gwenna hoisted her higher in her arms. 'You're chilled to the bone and you scared the wits out of poor Mr Hoskens. That's Roddy, who works for me. He thought he'd seen a wraith.'

The man himself watched their return to the yard, his

expression shuttered. Roddy Hoskens had once been the Romeo of St Wenna, a blow-in from Devon with a glint in his eye. Twenty years of marriage to Hilda had blunted his charisma, but Gwenna reckoned he still rated himself pretty highly. Seeing her straining under Lotti's weight, he seized back a little of his swagger.

'That the German maid, then?' he demanded.

'Well, it isn't the buck cheeld.'

'Uh, 'twas the mist confused me, swirling around, thick as milk.'

Gwenna kept walking. Lotti weighed almost nothing, but 'almost nothing' from the cliff edge to the house was considerable. She called impatiently, 'Roddy, is it too much to ask you to open the kitchen door for me?'

Roddy obliged in his usual, insolent style before following her inside. He watched Gwenna set Lotti on her feet, take off her own coat and lay it over the child's shoulders.

'She the one whose mother went under the train?'

'For pity's sake, imagine she was your child; would you like somebody saying a thing like that?'

'I only asked.'

'You were being spiteful, because she gave you a fright and now you're embarrassed. Are the cows milked?'

Roddy gave a sniff. 'Maybe.'

'Don't test my patience.'

'All but the last two.'

'Is Ezra finishing off?'

'No, he's bedding the horses in their stable, mollycoddling them I don't doubt, picking grass out of their teeth and singing songs to them.'

Yes, she could imagine that. Ezra treated the plough horses as massive children. He adored them. It occurred to her that she owed Roddy some credit for alerting her to their escape and moderated her anger. 'Please milk the remaining cows, then turn them out.'

'If you say so.' Roddy made no move.

Gwenna led Lotti to a chair. The little girl sat on its edge, her head sunk as if her salvation was to disappear inside herself. 'The cows?'

'I'm going.' Roddy unpeeled his shoulder from the door frame and jammed his hands in his pockets. He paused long enough to mutter, 'Germans at Tregallon, and now one in the house.'

She followed him outside. 'So it's definitely German POWs over at Tregallon? I saw the lights yesterday.'

'Blond hair and faces like granite, so least we'll recognise them if they break out.' Roddy threw the comment over his shoulder. 'Don't tell me there won't be trouble, sooner or later.'

Josephine padded inside with Gwenna and miaowed plaintively to be fed. 'I know, I know. Give me a moment.' Roddy's parting comment had hit its mark. Trouble had arrived already. One slip of a small, bare foot and she'd be reporting the loss of a child over the cliff. In the face of emergency, she'd acted calmly but now Gwenna felt sick. *I left her to wake alone, in a strange house. No mother would do that.* Freda's capable voice joined in:

'Honestly, Gwenna, what were you thinking of?'

Of the cows, being late for milking, the usual. She'd expected to welcome a child and mother, not a child alone. She couldn't abandon every other responsibility at no notice.

Lotti was shivering. Removing the coat, Gwenna took a soft shawl from a drawer and draped it around her narrow shoulders. Poor love, thin as a bundle of sticks. 'You need breakfast.' Colvennon's great blessing was its abundance of eggs, cream and milk. 'What's your opinion on porridge? Good, bad or indifferent?'

Josephine still mewed like a violin stuck on one note. Lotti stared at the cat, something wakening in her face. Saying nothing, Gwenna fetched cooked tripe from the pantry and poured milk into a saucer. She put it down on the floor and Josephine sniffed it and turned her back. 'Oh, honestly! I'm not giving you anything else. It's premium Guernsey milk and there's a war on.' She saw Lotti flinch. 'I'm sorry. I'm not cross, not at all. I chat to Josephine; she's come to expect it.'

Gwenna glanced at her parents' wedding photograph, which stood on a bookcase against a wall. Good, honest chapel people, Mary and Clive Bossinny would not have conversed with a cat. But then, they'd had each other for almost four decades, until Mary's death seven years past.

While the porridge cooked, Gwenna bathed Lotti's feet, which were grazed from the coarse clifftop. The child accepted the attention, but the blankness in her brown eyes worried Gwenna. Should she consult a doctor? What medicine was there for deep trauma and heartache? None, she suspected, other than love, rest, nourishment. She put plasters on the worst of the grazes then heated water on the Primus stove. Into the pan went two large eggs. 'Soft or hard-boiled?'

No answer.

Patience, patience. Gwenna pulled open a dresser drawer and took out Freda's last letter and re-read a particular passage: 'Mother and daughter are learning English, though naturally their mother tongue is German.' Last night, Lotti had reverted to that mother tongue.

Miryam Gittelman had found London difficult from the outset, Freda had written, having developed a terror of crowds after her experiences in Berlin and Paris. It hadn't been possible to relocate them immediately as the terms of Miryam's visa required her to work as Freda's domestic servant. 'Of course,'

Freda stated, 'I demanded no such thing of her, but we had to keep up the pretence. She wore a pinny and cap to answer the door, which she hated. Her nerves were always on edge and when things came to their inevitable head, I persuaded doctors to prescribe country air for her. You were my first thought as the person to provide sanctuary.'

Some sanctuary. Gwenna wondered what Freda meant by things coming to 'their inevitable head'? She skipped down to where Freda described Miryam as an educated woman who 'kept a milliner's studio in Berlin, alongside her husband's tailoring shop.' They'd been put out of business by the Nazis, but took up their trades again in Paris until the round-ups started when, for a second time, Miryam and Lotti were forced to escape at a moment's notice. Tellingly, Freda wrote, 'Miryam is convinced it is only a matter of time before the Germans invade Britain too.'

What would Freda make of the fact that a German POW camp had sprung up four miles from Colvennon?

With a quick miaow, Josephine jumped onto Lotti's knee. After some exploratory padding, she settled down and Lotti began stroking the patchwork back. Josephine purred and two words – they sounded like, 'Süße Miezekatze' – came from Lotti's lips. Gwenna's ears snatched them. Sweet pussycat.

'I learned a little German at school,' Gwenna said excitedly, thinking it would surely be all right to try using it, just until they'd built a bridge. As she ladled porridge into bowls, she asked Lotti in German if she thought it would rain later. She suspected her accent was off, but it was one of those stock phrases which stuck in the brain.

Lotti stared right through Gwenna. In a flash of inspiration, Gwenna repeated the question in French. Now Lotti looked distressed.

'I'm sorry, that was tactless but I'm going to keep on with German if you don't mind.' Gwenna put their bowls on the table and pulled out a chair for herself. 'Whenever you feel ready, just say something back.'

Lotti returned to stroking Josephine.

Sighing quietly, Gwenna sprinkled grains of sugar on her porridge, and a more generous amount on Lotti's, thinking, *If I were a mother, I'd know what to do. I'd have found the magic ingredient by now.* She picked up Lotti's spoon and tapped it playfully against the bowl. Persisting with her German, she said, 'Say goodbye to the sweet *Miezekatze*, and eat.'

There was a knock at the kitchen door. It was Ezra, reporting that the horses had taken no harm, and the cows were back in their pasture. Roddy had gone off to sort out the pigs, and Hilda was doing the chickens.

'All's well, then.' Gwenna smiled thinly, her spoon halfway to her lips.

'Not all, missus. I looked in on the heifers in Fairy Tump meadow.'

She lowered her spoon. 'They're all right, aren't they?' Heifers were young cows, those yet to have their first calf.

'They seem well,' Ezra said, 'but your grandfather never would put cattle on that field. He believed the small people would bring them a plague and so they did. In your father's day, we lost six of them, one after the other.'

'Yes and we know why. They arrived on the farm already suffering from bovine flu. You're going to mention that time we had to throw away the milk – that was because someone accidentally fed seaweed fertiliser to the herd. Nothing to do with fairies.'

Ezra answered, 'Hm. Speaking of little folk, how is the buck cheeld doing?'

'Lotti was on the cliff edge. I mean, right on the edge.'

'Seeking after her mother, I daresay. She doesn't want to believe what she saw yesterday.'

'No.' Gwenna didn't like speaking this way in front of Lotti, treating her as an object of pity. But Lotti gave no indication of minding or even hearing. 'You may be right, Ezra.'

'It would be cruel, missus, letting her go on thinking her mother will come back.'

'Except I don't know how to begin,' Gwenna admitted. 'I'll come out and cleanse the milking parlour once we've had breakfast. Then I must go into St Wenna, to the post office, to use the telephone.' Freda mustn't hear of Miryam's death from Sergeant Couch, who would at some point ring the number Gwenna had supplied to him. She'd take Lotti along, of course, and somehow make the call without the child overhearing.

'What's boiling dry over there?' Ezra nodded towards the Primus stove.

'Oh, crumbs.' She'd forgotten the eggs. Ezra chuckled, and said he'd see her presently. Gwenna fished the eggs out of the remaining inch of water, placed them in striped cups and put one in front of Lotti, along with a small spoon. She whacked the top of hers and was pleased when Lotti copied her.

'Slightly over-boiled,' she said then asked if she might cut Lotti's bread for her. '*Darf ich dein Brot schneiden?*' It was fifteen years since she'd spoken a word of German, and she added wryly, '*Mein Deutsch ist nicht so gut.*'

'Well, bless my soul! I never thought to hear that language in a Cornish kitchen.'

Gwenna swung round on her chair. Josephine sprang from Lotti's lap, making for the safety of the windowsill.

Roddy's wife, Hilda, had taken Ezra's place in the doorway and was switching her gaze from Gwenna to Lotti. A large woman with black-grey hair rolled like a ring doughnut, Hilda's presence always felt overbearing. It wasn't just her big features; it was the air of religious judgement she brought in with her. Gwenna's mother used to say of Hilda, 'She'd quote the Bible to the Almighty, but she's sly with it. What Hilda wants, she gets.' After Mary's premature death in 1936, Hilda had proved the truth of it, installing herself as the widowed Clive Bossinny's daily housekeeper. Gwenna suspected that for all her public virtue, Hilda had taken advantage of her father's grief and failing health. She still kept finding things missing from the house – small, valuable objects – and was often on the verge of dismissing the woman. But she needed Roddy for the pigs, and in a tight-knit community like St Wenna, you couldn't go round sacking people without extreme cause.

'Why is that child in her night things?' Hilda made it sound indecent.

'You know why, since I expect you've already had a conversation with your husband.'

'I'm glad I did. My Roddy said this little maid has already wreaked havoc, and now I walk in and hear German being talked! That's a criminal offence, Mrs Devoran.'

'No it isn't. Don't let me keep you from your work.'

Hilda huffed. 'I'm cleaning upstairs today, but don't expect me to make that maid's bed. I'm not tending to any German.'

'She isn't German. Not in the way you mean it and she's come here to be safe, Hilda, not bullied.'

'I can't take on more work,' Hilda replied. She wasn't paid to look after two.

When their porridge bowls were clean and the eggs eaten, Gwenna took Lotti upstairs to dress. She found thick socks and a sports shirt from her own schooldays. Digging out a pair of her dungarees, she cut the legs short. They hung rather on the skinny body, but by tying knots in the straps, she created a passable outfit.

'She looks a tinker's child,' was Hilda's observation when they passed her batting cobwebs from upstairs picture rails.

'I think she looks sweet. We're going out to help Ezra sluice the cowshed.'

. . .

To Gwenna's surprise, Lotti seemed content to push a broom. It was far too large for her, and she gripped it in the middle. But she got on with the job and even Ezra nodded in appreciation.

'She'll shape up, I don't doubt, then it'll be time to send her to school.'

School. That was something to chew on. Assuming Lotti stayed long enough, of course. Freda would have an opinion on that. Freda had opinions about everything. It was mid-morning before they set off for St Wenna. Gwenna oiled and dusted her mother's old bicycle, which had a seat at the back and which Mary Bossinny had used to get around when it was too much trouble to harness a donkey to a cart. With Lotti sitting behind, gripping round her waist, Gwenna felt that she was finally making some kind of headway.

She parked the bike outside St Wenna's little post office. Helping Lotti down, she explained, 'We're going to call Aunt Freda, to tell her the news about your mother. I know it will be hard, my love, and you don't have to listen. *Du brauchst nicht zuzuhören.*'

The elderly postmistress, hobbling out to empty a dustpan, gaped in astonishment. Gwenna cleared her throat. 'I need to make a telephone call, please, Mrs Andrews. To London.' She didn't resent the postmistress's blank nod. Mrs Andrews had lost her only son in the war. Not the present war, but the conflict of 1914 to '18. Nobody liked hearing German; that was understandable. On the other hand, Lotti shouldn't have to battle her way through the days in lonely incomprehension.

Inside the low-ceilinged post office, Mrs Andrews lifted up her counter and led the way to the back, where a pay telephone in a mahogany box hung in a cramped passage. She lingered while Gwenna asked the operator to connect her to Freda's west London number. The operator put her through straight away but there was no answer. Gwenna felt a rush of frustration as she counted twenty, then thirty, rings. Replacing the receiver, she said to Lotti, 'Your Aunt Freda is probably out at a meeting. I'll send a telegram.'

Mrs Andrews, hearing this, made her way back to her counter where she fumbled a form from a cubby hole. 'Write what you need to say. Has to be English, though.'

'Of course.' Gwenna frowned at the form. 'Uh, you've given me a dog licence application, Mrs Andrews.'

'Eh?' The postmistress peered through her spectacles. 'So I have.' She was so white-haired, her glasses so thick-lensed, Gwenna often wondered if the post office had forgotten to retire her.

'Telegram blanks are in that cubby hole there.' Gwenna pointed and the error was corrected. As Gwenna gathered her thoughts, Mrs Andrews stared down at Lotti, as if a child with corn-coloured plaits was not only a rare sight but a portent of something.

'Bad news, is it?'

'I'm afraid it is.' Gwenna wrote her message in one go: 'MG KILLED BY TRAIN AT TRURO. LOTTI WELL. WILL WRITE MORE. SO VERY SORRY.' She pushed the form towards Mrs Andrews. 'Can you send it right away?'

The postmistress read the words with agonising slowness. 'Bless me. I did hear there'd been a to-do at Truro.' She'd transmit it to London right away, and it would be at the recipient's home within a couple of hours. 'I've sent some sorry news in my time, but nothing like this. You were there when it happened?' she asked.

'I'd gone to meet them. This is Lotti, Mrs Andrews.'

'Lotti – I had a friend with that name, way back.' A thought trudged across the postmistress's cheeks. 'What kind of mother leaves her child and walks across a railway line?'

'We don't know what happened. Nobody knows.'

'I heard the German lady was on the line and left her girl on the platform. Put herself under the train on purpose, so they say.'

'Stop it. Don't.' How could such an idea have permeated to St Wenna, backwater of backwaters? Mrs Andrews told Gwenna that the postie, who came up from Truro to do his round hereabouts, had taken drink in a pub near the railway station where little else had been talked about. She peered at Lotti. 'She looks a pretty thing, but you'll be passing her on to a foster place, I daresay.'

Gwenna denied it emphatically. 'I'm looking after her, Mrs Andrews, and until a decision is made, *I* am her foster place.'

'I wouldn't rush into that, dear, for you'll soon find her a burden with all you have to do.'

'She is the opposite of a burden.' Why did everyone presume that Lotti was deaf, just because she didn't speak? 'And I can cope. I'm not half-witted.'

'All I'm saying, Mrs Devoran, is that the little maid would do best with a nice, motherly type after what she's been through. Someone with time to spare and other children to play with. Now then...' The postmistress totted up the number of words in Gwenna's message, along with Freda's address. 'That will be one shilling, one penny, please.'

Gwenna took coins from her purse. Mrs Andrews had always been pleasant in the past, having known Gwenna all her life. But right now, she could shake the woman. She caught Lotti's hand and left, giving a stiff goodbye.

It wasn't until nightfall that Gwenna broached the hardest one-sided conversation of her life. Lotti was again tucked up in the single bed that had been Gwenna's as a child. Sitting at its foot, Gwenna pressed her hands together. 'Lotti, you do know what happened yesterday?'

She waited. 'You understand that your darling mother was

killed?' She repeated herself in German. 'Your mother has gone...' *Don't say 'to heaven' or 'to a better place'. Stick to honest fact.* 'She is gone, Lotti. You have me to look after you, and Aunt Freda too, who loves you. You are not alone.'

The fair head turned away, denting the pillow. Lotti closed her eyes. Gwenna stayed until it seemed Lotti was asleep. Moonlight piercing a gap in the curtains illuminated tears on a rounded cheek.

Gwenna went downstairs and began a letter. Freda would have the telegram by now, and would no doubt have made many phone calls, seeking out details of how Miryam had met her death. And no doubt railing that Colvennon Farm was too isolated to have its own telephone connection. Gwenna began to write.

Wednesday, March 24th 1943

My dear friend,

I'm so sorry my dreadful news had to come by telegram, and I could not express in person how devastated, how responsible, I feel. I will tell you as much as I can. First, let me assure you that Lotti is safe—

Gwenna's pen hovered above the note paper. Saying that Lotti was safe was a little short of accurate, considering Gwenna had plucked the child from the edge of a cliff. She altered the last word so it read, 'Lotti is here, at Colvennon'.

She gave the best account she could of the tragedy, adding that there had been no actual witness to the moment Miryam had removed herself and her daughter from the Riviera Express. Mrs Andrews had implied that Miryam had abandoned Lotti and stood in front of a train to end her life, but Gwenna didn't accept that. Why come all the way to Cornwall, and only then choose such a desperate action? No mother would do that.

Except... Miryam had suffered a breakdown. She was terrified. And the Riviera Express had contained more than just holidaymakers and homecoming Cornish folk. An unpleasant thought hatched. German captives, German voices. Had Miryam—?

A weight landed in her lap. Josephine had come in from her hunting and padded on Gwenna's thighs, seeking a comfortable position. 'Thing is,' Gwenna said out loud, 'if I say too much, Freda will be on the next train down and will want to organise everything.' The words 'take charge' ran through Freda's veins like glittering mica in a Cornish rock face. 'I've only had Lotti a day, but I don't want to lose her.' Amid all the uncertainty, that fact shone out clear. *I may not be a mother, but I know how to love a child.*

So instead of describing Lotti's mute silence and that dash to the cliff top, Gwenna repeated her assertion that Lotti was coping. She requested that Freda tell her as much as she knew about Lotti's past – in Germany, in France. 'Anything that helps me be a good guardian.'

Caressing the cat, she murmured, 'I'll never replace Miryam, but why can't I be Lotti's protector, her dear friend. Not just for a short time, but forever?'

Josephine purred, and the question melted away unanswered.

5

Two days passed with Gwenna so reluctant to leave Lotti, her farmhands had to take over her work. Roddy muttered; Ezra shook his head.

'We'll need extra labour,' Ezra commented, 'if you're taken up with childminding.'

Gwenna agreed. A few months ago, she'd put in for Land Army girls to help out, but beyond a single line acknowledging her request, she'd heard nothing from the regional agricultural office.

Unused to being cooped up in the house all day, she buttoned Lotti into the red coat and showed her around the farm and its fields, avoiding the pigs and Roddy, explaining every sight and object – as far as she could in her rusty German. The end of this fractured week arrived, with Gwenna reeling from being a full-time childminder. Lotti was nowhere near ready to start school, that was glaringly obvious, but nor could she be left in the house. Something had to give. So, as Friday dawned, Gwenna informed Lotti that it was time she learned how to milk a cow.

Why not? Gwenna had started helping her father the day

after her eighth birthday, when she was considerably younger than Lotti was now. Her dad had looked at her across the breakfast table and said, 'Well, you're still no more 'an two jam pots high, but if you can sit on a stool and reach an udder you may as well learn the trade. If all I've got is a maid to hand on to, I'd best make a farmer of 'ee.'

In time, she had become an asset around the place and as her schooling came to an end, she'd been ready to join him in running Colvennon. However, her mother wouldn't hear of a farming life for her one child. 'You're only eighteen! I'd not forgive myself if you spent your existence looking at these same hills day after day. You've a decent brain, Gwenna, and you're a slight little thing. Leave the cows and the muck to the men.'

Her mind made up, Mary Bossinny had propelled Gwenna into secretarial school in Truro and, after that, to London where Gwenna had found a job she soon came to think of as the most boring on earth. In a room with twenty other typists, she'd bashed out correspondence and grown depressingly familiar with the head movements of the girl seated in front of her. She'd ached for Colvennon, the fields and the sea.

Edward Devoran's arrival on the scene had saved her the trouble of getting herself home by finding a job in Truro. He courted her in London and within six months, proposed. Gwenna had typed her last memo for the Institute of Canning and Packaging with feelings akin to uncorking a well-shaken bottle of champagne. A lesson there. Never open a shaken bottle, particularly when it lacks a label describing its contents.

Gwenna led Lotti into the milking parlour whose stone walls added a sharp chill to air that smelled sweetly of cows' breath. She placed two stools beside one of the more placid of the Guernseys and said good morning to Ezra, who had been at work since first light.

Returning the greeting, he told her he'd moved the heifer

herd from Fairy Tump field 'to Five Acres, which is healthier for them'.

She rolled her eyes but made no objection. Ezra had the right to make decisions. He'd received his first wage packet from her grandfather in the year 1882, as a lad of thirteen, and with his patched overalls tucked into leather boots and gaiters, he was as much a part of the texture of Colvennon as the buildings themselves. The metallic smell of the empty churns told her that he'd already scoured them with boiled water and borax. He might believe in fairies but he also understood the principle of sterilising.

She said, 'I hope you don't mind, Ezra, I've brought Lotti along.'

He'd already noticed the child. 'Indeed you have. Good morning, little maid.'

'You're the little maid,' Gwenna whispered to Lotti, and patted the stool beside her. 'It doesn't mean you wear an apron and cap. It's the way we talk, and if I ever call you "my lover" or "my 'ansome", it's a Cornish term of affection.'

Gwenna showed Lotti how to clean the cow's udders. 'Milking is simple when you know how, but it'll take time to build strength in your hands. Watch me.' Taking one of the cow's teats in both hands, she started to strip out the milk, drawing it out into the bucket beneath. 'We don't squeeze, and we don't pull as though we're ringing a bell. What I'm doing copies the way a calf suckles its mother. It brings out the milk, without hurting the cow. It's the nicest job on the farm.' She repeated that last phrase in German, hoping Lotti might respond.

Ezra, stumping up to empty a full pail into a churn, shook his head. 'I hope you're talking Guernsey to the cow.'

'You know it was German.'

'That's what I'm afeared of. You need to stop.'

'Lotti's from Berlin, Ezra, and I'm trying to bring her out of herself.'

'Doing it like that, you're making folks' tongues wag.'

Gwenna asked if he'd been gossiping with Mrs Andrews at the post office. 'Or with Hilda? She caught me testing out my German and read me a lecture.'

'I don't gossip, missus, but I have ears. You're setting people against the maid.'

'No! I'm trying to help Lotti.'

'How can it help her, making every soul hereabouts look on her as a stranger? An enemy.'

'That's so small-minded, Ezra.' Gwenna cast a stricken look downwards. Lotti sat on her stool, her hands folded in her lap, waiting for her next instruction. Gwenna almost wished the child would shriek at them to stop discussing her. Anything would be better than mute passivity. 'The moment she responds, I'll speak English.'

'If she's to live and thrive here, she needs to talk our language. You can harm a child with kindness.'

'Is that churn full?' Gwenna asked tightly. She asked Ezra to take it to the cooling shed, needing a moment to digest his comments. The painful part was, she suspected he was right.

Having said all he meant to say, Ezra hitched the churn onto a two-wheeled trolley and took it away. When the squeak of wheels could no longer be heard, Gwenna placed Lotti's hands on the cow's udder. Gwenna curled the small fingers around a teat and, with her own hands on top, began the stripping motion. Milk surged into the part-full bucket, creating rings of pearly bubbles. Its sweet-raw smell mingled with that of cow flesh.

'See? When you get the rhythm, it's really quite soothing.' This time, she spoke English. A decision had been made. There would be no more German. 'It helps to sing along to the rhythm.'

Gwenna began a Cornish favourite, 'The Sweet Nightingale'. It had several verses, and around verse three, something altered in Lotti's posture. A slight unbending? The weight against Gwenna's shoulder decreased as Lotti leaned forward until a strand of her escaped hair was tickling the cow's flank. Gwenna let Lotti take over the milking. The flow came slower, but it came. 'There,' she said. 'Now you're a milkmaid, my little one.'

Lotti turned her head, and for the first time squarely met Gwenna's eye. Something moved within them, a comment or a question. Gwenna held her breath. Lotti's lips opened.

'Mrs Devoran, am I disturbing you?' A well-modulated voice crushed the moment. Gwenna got to her feet as Lotti gazed in trepidation at the visitor.

'Mr Wormley!' Damn, damn, and damn again. It was the Ministry of Agriculture's local representative. 'Am I expecting you?' It wouldn't be the first time Gwenna had forgotten to put a meeting on her calendar, but she was sure he wasn't due here for another month at least. John Wormley was a decent man and a farmer himself – he owned a large estate a few miles inland – but something in his expression told her he was here in his official capacity.

'You're not expecting me, don't worry.' He reached out a hand to shake hers. He was wearing leather riding gloves and a belted coat, which, along with his top boots, gave off a healthy odour of horses. 'I was out this way and thought I'd save my office the bother of writing you a letter. I've tied my horse to one of your posts, hope you don't mind.'

'Not in the least. Um, a letter?' Letters from the ministry usually meant extra work.

'Colvennon Glaze, Mrs Devoran.'

'Oh.' A few weeks back, John Wormley had informed Gwenna that she was under-utilising her land and had instructed her to plough up the twenty-five acres of grass that formed Colvennon Glaze and plant potatoes instead.

The cow, sensing a dip in the mood, stamped a back hoof and swished her tail, catching Gwenna on the hip. Gwenna stroked her ridgy spine to calm her. 'As you see, I'm in the middle of morning milking. Could you come back a different day?'

'I see you have a little helper.' Mr Wormley smiled at Lotti, who stared back with brown, lollipop eyes. 'Why don't we toddle along there quickly, let me see your progress, then I can be out of your hair?'

Progress. There was the rub. Gwenna hadn't dug so much as a spade's depth of Colvennon Glaze. However, it was pretty obvious her visitor wasn't going to be fobbed off. 'All right,' she said heavily. 'Lotti, come with us.'

John Wormley looked puzzled when Lotti made no move. 'She doesn't have much to say for herself.'

'Lotti is from London and all this is very strange.'

'Ah, an evacuee?'

'Yes... pretty much.' If he hadn't yet learned the human drama of Lotti and her mother, he wouldn't get it from her. Gwenna had sensed fear crystallising around the child's small body from the moment John Wormley had appeared in the doorway. Perhaps Lotti associated all men with the brutality she'd encountered in Berlin and Paris. She laid a hand on Lotti's shoulder. 'Sweetheart, shall we show Mr Wormley Colvennon Glaze?'

6

LOTTI

She'd rather stay where it was warm, with the cow whose side rippled like water. Lotti knew the lady was scared of the man they were walking with. When a grown-up was scared, they held your hand too tightly.

He must be a policeman because his coat wasn't grey, or exactly brown, but a mixture of the two. It had buttons and a belt. Police had coats with belts. His trousers were pushed into shiny black leather boots. Men who came to hurt you always wore boots. He might still want to see her yellow star, and would he believe her if she told them that she'd lost it, that the train had come and Mutti had gone, leaving her hat on the railway line?

Lotti had done everything she could to keep her star. She had done everything Papa had told her to do: 'If ever you don't know what to say, say nothing.' And: 'If you ever lose sight of Mutti, stand where you last saw her.'

Lotti had gone back on the railway line, looking for Mutti. The straight-ahead rails had stuck in her eye and she couldn't blink, even when she felt a coming train in her bones. The lady had pulled her off the track.

Now the lady was talking to the man who was leading them uphill, sounding a bit like Papa talking to the policemen beside the truck that took him away. Talking too fast. You shouldn't ever talk fast to policemen because it showed them you were frightened.

She could hear the sea again. Papa had said there was a path over the sea, and she had gone in her nightie to find it. She'd seen it, gold with sunlight, chopped to pieces by the waves. Then the lady had come and talked and talked. The lady's words were like the coins in the money box she'd left behind, long, long ago in Berlin. You put coins in; aunties and uncles would put some in too, but you couldn't take them out. Aunties would say, 'When you turn twenty-one, Lottchen, your papa will saw off the lid and you will buy your wedding dress with the money.' Lotti had often rattled the money box, tumbling the coins inside. Clink, clink. That's how the lady's words sounded.

They'd reached another big field, and the policeman was pointing to each corner and saying a word over and over. Black birds with bright beaks flapped around them, making sounds like a bad cough, and the lady put her hands to the sides of her head the way Mutti used to when Lotti answered back. Lotti wanted to tell the lady, you can't make policemen listen to you. They made Papa put his hands in the air and get into the truck.

The policeman, who must be poor because his coat had leather patches on the elbows, was looking thoughtful. The lady turned Lotti around and then they were walking back the way they had come. She was speaking, but Lotti heard only clinking sounds because the words in her head had piled up, with no way to empty them out.

The last thing Mutti had said on the platform, before the train ran her down was, 'Stay where you are, say nothing to anybody, not a word till I come back.'

7

'Had Colvennon Glaze been ploughed for potatoes, it would be on its way to yielding eight tons per acre, Mrs Devoran.'

'As I've tried to explain...' The last half-hour had been most uncomfortable. '... there was no deliberate intention to defy your orders.'

'I daresay. But as Admiral Nelson saw no ships, I saw no potatoes and we have to feed the nation, don't we?'

'Yes, I know.' Flouting ministerial orders was serious. Until this moment, ploughing up the Glaze had been a job low down on her 'to-do' list. It was so labour intensive. Standing next to John Wormley, she knew she'd been weighed in the balance and found wanting. 'I try my absolute best, but there are only three of us here. Me, Ezra Jago, who is over seventy, and Mr Hoskens, who tends the pigs. Three pairs of hands on an eighty-acre farm. We simply haven't had time.'

John Wormley must surely understand, running his own two-hundred-acre concern at Perdew Manor. A mixed farm of Colvennon's size needed four able workers, minimum. Ideally, six. She wished he would do something other than frown.

Colvennon was hers, but that counted for little in wartime.

If the ministry told you to pull up your stair carpet and plant turnips all the way up to the bedrooms, you did that, and if you didn't, they could fine you. Ultimately, they could give your land to somebody who would do their bidding more efficiently. Imagine, if she were to lose all this... Her glance went where it so often did in moments of stress: to her parents' wedding photograph on the bookcase. Mary and Clive Bossinny outside St Wenna's chapel in 1899, blissfully unaware that within fifteen years the first of two world-engulfing wars would begin. Gwenna cleared her throat. Her mother would have had the kettle boiling by now. 'May I offer you a cup of tea, Mr Wormley?' She hoped he'd say that his horse had been waiting long enough, thank you. She needed to help Ezra finish the milking.

John Wormley said he would very much like a cup of something. 'Where has your little friend gone?'

'Lotti? She's in the room next door. Very shy, I'm afraid.' As the kettle wheezed on the Primus stove, Gwenna nipped out of the room. Lotti was curled up in an armchair. Josephine, who had darted out of the kitchen at the incursion of unfamiliar boots, was purring against the bib of Lotti's dungarees. Poor child must be worn out, a second uphill walk in two days.

In the kitchen, Gwenna laid a tray with sugar and milk, cups and teaspoons, cramming them on because she wanted to get this conference over with. 'The milk is yesterday evening's,' she said. 'I usually skim it for tea, or you can have it as it comes.' *Please have it as it comes.*

'Skimmed, please, Mrs Devoran. Though I shall turn my face away as you do it.' It was illegal, under wartime rationing laws, to take the cream off. The rule ensured that nutrient-rich milk was available to all. Farmhouse cheeses and clotted cream were banned for the duration too. Even giving a friend a pat of butter broke strict rationing rules. On the farm itself, things were a little more elastic. Butter and cream were perks that made the seven-day-a-week slog bearable and if some occasionally left under a coat for a needy neighbour, nobody told.

As they drank their tea, Gwenna had another stab at explaining her position. 'I don't have the labour to plough twenty-five acres. Besides, the grass on Colvennon Glaze is part of my hay crop. It's how I feed the cattle and horses over winter.'

'You can buy hay, Mrs Devoran. We can ensure you a supply.'

'That doesn't solve the labour issue. I don't work the plough; I'm not strong or fast enough to make it an efficient use of my time.'

'What about your fellow, Hoskens? He can't spend every waking hour with the pigs.'

'He helps his wife with the chickens, and does other jobs like ditch clearing, pruning, mending walls. He keeps the pigeons off the bean crop with his shotgun.' *If I ask him to plough, he'll pretend not to hear.* 'Last autumn, I asked for Land Army girls, Mr Wormley. Where are they?'

Wormley took a slug of his tea and smacked his lips. 'I'm sure we had two of them lined up for you. What happened?'

'I don't know. You tell me.'

He furrowed his brow. 'Hm. I have an idea that one got glandular fever and the other fell for an airman and found herself in the family way.'

'Surely, two healthy, non-pregnant replacements could have been found?'

'True.' Wormley stared into his tea for a moment, then said, 'Sounds like we mucked up. You'd accept help, then? You're willing to have strangers working alongside you?'

'They wouldn't be strangers for long, would they?' Gwenna welcomed the thought of new faces at Colvennon, just as she'd liked the idea of Miryam Gittelman and Lotti adding some fresh energy to the place. Thinking of Miryam brought a taste of sadness to her mouth. 'What I need is hands on ploughs and boots on spades.' Her guest was looking hopefully at the teapot. 'Refill, Mr Wormley?'

He accepted eagerly, then looked around. 'This farm was your late father's?'

'And his father's and *his* grandfather's all the way back to the reign of Queen Anne.' A date, 1710, was carved on a capstone above the front door.

'In the weeks up to your father's death, before you settled back here, Colvennon was run by a manager, I recall.'

'Not a manager. By Roddy Hoskens and unofficially.'

'The pig chappie? What gave you the notion of taking over, Mrs Devoran?'

Gwenna liked John Wormley, but tea-drinking and questions that hinted at her incompetence were growing stale. 'Would you ask that if I were a man?'

'If you were a man,' Wormley observed drily, 'I would be speaking a good deal more caustically of those twenty-five acres. I do not forget that you are a lady.'

'Ha, I often forget it.' Gwenna poured more hot water into the teapot. 'When the chickens go off-lay or the fox digs under the fence.' She couldn't resist a glance at the kitchen clock. 'I really have to get back to the milking parlour.'

John Wormley reminded Gwenna that feeding the nation was a little more important than one milking session. 'The old chap will hold the fort for now. Ezra Jago, yes?'

'Yes. But twenty-four cows are a lot for one man.'

'Homeland food production is a critical weapon of war, Mrs Devoran. Our role as farmers is to ensure that every acre of land fulfils its potential.'

'Yes, I know.' Masking her irritation, she poured fresh tea into John Wormley's cup.

'Every potato dug, every ear of wheat that falls under the scythe, takes the pressure off the sea convoys bringing food from other parts of the world.' He was warming to his subject. 'You might say that each acre tilled represents a merchant ship coming safe into port, and each potato a sailor saved from the waves.'

She suspected this was a speech he'd given to the local council or to the Townswomen's Guild. 'I do know this,' she said.

'Do you know how many of our vessels and their crews have perished since the start of war, torpedoed by Nazi warships and submarines?'

'Do I know?' Without another word, Gwenna strode into the sitting room and swiped a framed photograph off a side table. Lotti woke and Josephine sprang off her lap. 'Sorry,' Gwenna whispered.

Back in the kitchen, she laid the photograph in front of John Wormley and said with icy clarity, 'This is a picture of my late husband, Edward, whose corvette was sunk in the Atlantic by a German submarine. All on board were lost. So yes, I know the toll war has on our sailors.' The picture had been taken some time in 1939, at the naval base at Devonport, Plymouth. It was grainy, but his face was never far from her inner eye. He'd had deep-set eyes in a sensitively moulded face. Mid-brown hair that wanted to grow in a thick wave, flattened down with Brylcreem. Edward had been a musician when he'd proposed to her in London. He was happiest practising cello arpeggios, lost to the world, and so his decision to join the navy three years into their marriage had shocked his family, and her most of all. It seemed so inapt, yet he'd been promoted steadily, dying as the second-in-command of his ship.

Wormley was contrite. 'Forgive me, Mrs Devoran. I momentarily forgot your circumstances.'

'I don't have that luxury.' When her emotions were up, Gwenna found it hard to pull back. Her mother used to say, 'Gwenna-maid, you're like a cart running downhill, looking for a wall to crash into.' Reminded of this, she moderated her voice. 'I don't need to be told how important it is that we grow as much as we can, so fewer food and grain convoys need make that murderous sea crossing.'

'I apologise, madam, I spoke out of turn. I trampled on your grief. May we be friends again?'

Gwenna sat down. 'All right. I'm sorry too.' Wormley of course would assume her anger had sprung from grief at the loss of a beloved husband. He couldn't know how very complicated her feelings about Edward were. Or that along with true sorrow marched anger and a burning sense of betrayal.

At last, Wormley stood to go. He held out his hand, thanking Gwenna for the tea and saying, 'I now have to put on my official hat. While I have no desire to be heavy handed, I must make you aware that repeated failure to carry out ministry directives has serious consequences. So – Colvennon Glaze, one main crop of potatoes for the planting of. Yes?'

'Send me those land girls, Mr Wormley. That's all I ask.'

He left, and as though his exit created a change in the air pressure, Lotti stole into the kitchen. 'Shall we go back to the cows?' Gwenna asked. 'You were enjoying it before we got interrupted. Ezra won't have finished; we're still needed.'

As they walked to the milking parlour, male voices reached them. The sound was coming from the sunken lane. Gwenna suggested they see what was going on. 'Though I think I know.' Putting a finger to her lips, she added, 'Quiet as mice.'

Mr Wormley was a short way down the lane, his horse's reins in his hand. He'd use the milk churn stand at the bottom of the lane as a mounting block, most likely. Roddy Hoskens was holding him in conversation. Gwenna stopped at the iron gate. They would see her and Lotti if they turned, but they appeared wrapped up in conversation. She heard Roddy say, '... a strange child in the house too, Mr Wormley, sir. A blow-in from Germany. That's right. German. Leaving gates wide open, letting the horses into the hay field. It's a shambles here, since Mrs Devoran's father passed away. I'm not saying the missus don't do her best but a young widow running a place like this...' Roddy left the conclusion hanging.

Gwenna heard John Wormley's reply. 'I agree, it's a big job for a lady but Mrs Devoran has a lot of pluck.'

'Pluck don't lead a bull to the cows, nor plough five furrows an hour. What d'you say, sir, but that the ministry sets me in charge?' Roddy fired the suggestion with an energy that told Gwenna he'd spent time thinking it over. 'I ran this place after poor Mr Bossinny took ill, and until his daughter came home, full of ideas it weren't her place to have. I know Colvennon back to front. Put me in charge, I'd have those acres ploughed and teddies planted by Good Friday.'

'Teddies' was Cornish dialect for potatoes.

Good Friday was four weeks away. The shameless nerve of it! Whispering in Lotti's ear, 'Stay here,' Gwenna scaled the gate. As she jumped down the other side, the men turned. In a ringing voice, she declared, 'I'll have it done by April Fool's Day.' That was six days off, but she was furious enough to promise anything.

John Wormley gave a wry smile. 'May Day feels a little more realistic, Mrs Devoran. That gives you a full month, plus a little bit. I shall be back then to view your progress.'

'May Day it is.' She glared at Roddy. 'On your way home, Roddy, or did you happen to bump into Mr Wormley?'

'I saw his horse in the yard and thought to pass on my best respects.'

'So I heard.' She couldn't run things here without Roddy's help, but any remaining shred of trust had gone. 'Don't let me detain you.'

Roddy Hoskens touched his hat to Mr Wormley and shuffled past Gwenna with a faint smile. He unlatched and pushed open the gate, forcing Lotti to reverse quickly.

'Careful!' Gwenna admonished. Roddy strode on. 'Just you wait, my man,' she murmured under her breath. When the extra help arrived, Roddy Hoskens had better watch his step, because then she wouldn't need him.

Ezra, to whom she confided her resentment, sighed, 'What happened, see, was your father relied on Roddy and Hilda too much after your mother passed on. And when he had his first stroke, Roddy was always there.'

'But it's not as though Dad promised Roddy the farm!'

'No, but Roddy expected to run it after your father's death. At the time, you were a married woman, living in Truro.'

'And now I'm living right here. I am not a helpless lady, out of her depth as Roddy likes to think.'

Ezra gave her one of his long looks. 'Twenty-five acres ploughed and sprouting teddies in a shave more than a month?' Gwenna had mentioned her promise to have Colvennon Glaze ploughed by May 1st. 'I don't see it.'

'We have to, because I'm beginning to understand Roddy's game. He'll try to have me dispossessed. If necessary, I'll handle the plough myself. I'll build up my muscles.' Her father had taught her to plough. He and Ezra had taught her all she knew about horses. 'I can do it!'

Ezra's 'hm' was a marriage of sympathy and scepticism. 'You've skill, but not the strength for it, day after day. Nor have I, not now. I don't see how we'd manage the job anyhow, unless we plough by moonlight.'

'I will.'

'Moonlighting, with that little maid trailing along behind you in her nightshirt?' Ezra shot a quizzical look at Lotti, who was waiting patiently on her milking stool for Gwenna to join her.

'Then I'll wait for John Wormley to send me those land girls.'

Ezra wasn't impressed. 'They're doughty maids, I don't doubt, but ploughing is man's work.'

'So is war,' Gwenna came back, 'and that's where most of the adult men are.' The image of Lotti following behind her in her nightie had struck home. She felt stressed, her routine all over the place, and actually she needed to get Lotti into school. Though what school would accept a child who wouldn't speak?

Something caught Ezra's eye. Josephine was at the parlour door with her tail waving to and fro. Seeing her, Lotti jumped off her stool, startling the cows nearest. Ezra shook his head.

'The devil of it is, missus, you've got your hands full right at the time you most need them free.'

8

On Monday a package arrived from Truro police station. It contained Lotti's ration book, issued to her in London. A note from Sergeant Couch stated that it had been found beside the railway track, 'most likely spilled from the late Mrs Gittelman's handbag'. Gwenna was invited to come and collect other items.

What items? It was the worst kind of mystery. And another thing: the sergeant had referred to Mrs Gittelman, which suggested that a formal identification had taken place. Gwenna was surprised. If Freda had been to identify the body, why hadn't she made contact? Gwenna hadn't had an answer to her telegram, or to the letter she'd sent. The silence made her worry that Freda blamed her for the tragedy. She still hadn't got a word of English from Lotti, either.

Following her chat with Ezra, Gwenna had taken Lotti to the elementary school in St Wenna, and borrowed a stack of reading and maths books. The headmaster – who had taught Gwenna twenty-five years ago – had added a lined exercise book and one with squared paper for maths.

'Shall I put the child down to start here next term?' he'd asked.

'I'm not sure. I'll let you know, Mr Beecroft.'

Gwenna had begun lessons with Lotti the following day. Half an hour at lunchtime, an hour in the evening. So far, it was Gwenna reading out loud and Lotti listening. But she *was* listening. They hadn't ventured onto maths yet.

The rest of the time, Lotti accompanied Gwenna around the farm. She was now milking on her own. Slowly and hesitantly but seemingly at peace.

Though she had little appetite for a visit to the police station, events forced Gwenna's hand. The kerosene ran out as she boiled water for morning tea, and buying another can required a trip to town. As they waited for the country bus outside St Wenna's church, Gwenna felt her spirits rise. It was the last day of March, and the air was full of the coconut scent of gorse. Spring had brought a tide of yellow. Along with the saffron of the gorse, pale primroses and wild daffodils swelled in the hedgerows. Cultivated daffodils carpeted the churchyard and every front garden.

Women waiting for the same bus smiled at Lotti, though one of them got off on the wrong foot.

'That your little evacuee,' the woman asked, 'that Hilda Hoskens was talking of at chapel? She's mumchance, Hilda said.' Mumchance was dialect for mute.

Gwenna's hackles shot up. 'Hilda should keep her opinions to herself.'

Another woman made reference to Lotti's red coat. 'A cheery colour. You don't see much that's bright these days.'

Yet another stroked Lotti's hair, commenting on its shade. Lotti reared back at the touch. The woman tilted her head, as though inspecting a picture in a gallery. 'I always thought they were dark.'

'They?' Gwenna queried, coldly.

'The Jews. For that's what she is, isn't she? Mrs Andrews said as much and being postmistress she knows most things.'

'Yes, Lotti is Jewish.' Gwenna hated it when people spoke as though Lotti were invisible. Had they nothing else to gabble about?

'Come here on the Kindertransport, did she?' lisped a toothless old woman who, with her shawl knotted around her breast, looked as if she'd stepped out of a bygone photograph. 'I heard about that on the wireless. Those little children put on trains in Germany, sent here alone by their poor parents. I couldn't do it if she were mine, I'll tell you that for nothing.'

Gwenna appreciated that it was meant kindly. 'Lotti and her mother got to England by a different route. A dangerous one. One day, she will tell us her story. For now, she needs to feel accepted and safe.'

'Well, bless her, she's welcome here.' The toothless woman leaned in and said in an undertone, 'Best keep her away from Tregallon. She won't want to come face to face with those prisoners, bunch of nasty Nazis by the look of them. My old man says, give him a gun, he'd shoot the lot.'

When the bus came, Gwenna ushered Lotti to the back. It riled her that everyone was so free with their judgements, and prodded and poked as if Lotti were a plum on a market stall. As they trundled through the lanes, Gwenna distracted the child from the chatter around her by naming flowers, trees and the farm animals in the meadows. Did Lotti take any of it in? The journey dragged. The roads being too narrow for two vehicles to pass, the driver sounded his horn at every corner and a mile or so on from St Wenna, a broken-down butcher's van forced him to make a diversion. Gwenna's heart sank as she saw the straggling cottages of Tregallon. They were going to pass the POW camp.

They crawled around a tight double bend and a moment later, there was the old manor house, seat of a once-wealthy family. Where there should be a sweep of meadow dotted with ewes and new-born lambs, a village of brick and asbestos huts had sprouted up. A muttering rose from the passengers, reflecting Gwenna's feelings precisely.

The old woman leaned out of her seat. 'A sight to behold, isn't it, my 'ansome?' she lobbed at Gwenna. 'Fifty huts, they say, flung up like mushrooms to house Germans.' Her glance settled on the rim of Lotti's beret. Lotti sat at an angle, staring out of the window. 'I expect she don't like to see it, poor mite.'

Flung up like mushrooms... actually, the huts looked more like Swiss rolls cut in half lengthwise, laid out in lines, six rows deep. Curved roofs of ridged cement glistened in the sunlight. They looked basic as could be and they'd be damp inside too; Tregallon's meadows were low-lying.

Men were moving around the huts: men in tan-coloured boiler suits with clown-like yellow circles sewn on. Some wore forage caps, others woollen hats. The barbed wire that contained them was four feet higher than the hedge, loops and loops of it like a toddler's scribble. Guards in khaki, sub-machine guns in their hands, stood at corners. It looked pretty secure. Even so Gwenna's arms around Lotti became a protective wrapper.

First call was the ironmonger's where Gwenna handed in her empty kerosene can for a refill, paying two shillings extra for it to be delivered direct to the farm that day. It was costly, being forgetful. Then to the grocer's shop where she bought four ounces of hard cheese, the only choice. Its scratchy paper wrapping made it look a more generous chunk than it was. Three meals of cheese on toast would be squeezed from it, with a little left over for sandwiches. She passed over her buff ration book so the grocer could mark off the purchase, and then gave him Lotti's blue one to be registered by him. After that, they went to the butcher's where Gwenna asked for bacon, only to hastily backtrack. No pork, Freda had said. She bought neck-end of lamb instead and, after that, early rhubarb at the greengrocer before turning reluctantly in the direction of the police station.

She expected Lotti to show fear as they approached but the child padded alongside her, an uncomplaining ghost. To be fair, the police building on St Clement's Hill was a converted house and not intimidating at all. Perhaps Lotti had no memory of being here, as she'd arrived in the first flush of shock. Gwenna gave her name to the desk sergeant, saying she'd come to pick up a parcel. A poster on the wall behind warned 'Careless Talk Costs Lives'. If there were spies in Cornwall, she thought, they could do no better than ride around on a country bus full of gossips.

The desk sergeant frowned at her. 'Parcel? This is the police station, madam, not the post office.'

'I'm aware of that. Sergeant Couch wrote to me to say there's a package containing Miryam Gittelman's things.' Gwenna glanced at Lotti. 'She was the lady... you know.'

With a nod, the desk sergeant went out through a doorway. Gwenna heard him calling, 'Bob? That Mrs Devoran's here, for the big box.'

Sergeant Couch himself carried it through, and it looked large enough to hold a tea service. Gwenna took it, curling her fingers under the string. There wasn't much weight to it but her stomach clenched with anxiety. What would be revealed when she cut the string?

'How are we doing?' the sergeant asked.

'Not so good. Nightmares.' It intrigued Gwenna that Lotti could be in the presence of British bobbies and not seem to mind at all. There was no flinching, no fast blinking.

'Nightmares about what she saw?'

'I think so.' Gwenna took Lotti to a seat, saying, 'Sit here and guard our parcel. I won't be a moment.' Lotti assumed her habitual seated position. Perched on the edge, ankles together, head bent, looking at nothing.

Gwenna went back to the sergeant and confided, 'On her first night, she was shouting in German, of which I have too little knowledge.'

'Can anyone have too little knowledge of German, Mrs Devoran?'

'I tried speaking it to her. German, I mean. People thought it wasn't a good idea.'

'I suggest it probably wasn't.' He frowned towards Lotti in kindly concern. 'Perhaps what she witnessed sent her back.'

'Back where?'

'To her life before she and her mother left their home. You told me they'd escaped persecution in Germany.'

Gwenna slowly nodded. 'They left Berlin for Paris, where they thought they were safe. Until the Germans invaded. According to my friend Mrs Fincham, Lotti had learned French. In London, she was making strides in English too. Now it's back to German in her sleep and when she's awake, no language at all.'

'Well, now, WPC Roper, who you met last week, says it's not uncommon for children who've seen terrible things to go mute for a spell. They come out of it in time.'

'I can only pray that's so. Sergeant, has a formal identification of Mrs Gittelman been made?'

'It has.'

'And did my friend Mrs Fincham make the identification?'

The sergeant shook his head. 'We didn't need that lady's help in the end, being as we were provided with fingerprints.' He deflected her question. 'I don't see as it helps, you or the child to delve into official processes. Let it be, Mrs Devoran.'

It was a relief, in a way, to be given permission to remain ignorant. A relief too that Freda had been spared the ordeal of seeing the body. Gwenna had one more question. 'Has their luggage been found, apart from what was discovered on the track? The Gittelmans wouldn't have travelled empty-handed.'

'Ah, yes.' The sergeant thanked her for reminding him. A suitcase, a lady's vanity case and a school satchel had been picked off a rack in the carriage mother and daughter had sat in for the majority of the journey. 'But I'm afraid in all the confusion it all got sent back to London.'

Gwenna nodded, distracted by a new thought. 'Which carriage were they in, when they weren't having tea in the dining car?'

'One down from there, still in third class.'

Gwenna pictured her traipse through the train, first entering the smoky carriage littered with cigarette butts and indecent playing cards. Walking into the next carriage, she'd caught the attention of an elderly couple. They'd stared, perhaps because she'd looked so harassed. 'Why didn't I just ask that old couple if they'd seen a girl and her mother?'

Sergeant Couch blinked, confused by the swerve of her thoughts.

'Could you arrange for the luggage to be sent back here?' she asked. 'Lotti has no spare clothes, you see.'

'I took the liberty of having it sent on to the address you gave me, to Mrs Fincham.'

'Right.' Gwenna nodded, thinking it was fitting that Freda should be the one to sort through Miryam Gittelman's effects, having been her friend through difficult times. 'Sergeant – you realise, don't you, that Miryam and Lotti would have been sitting in the carriage next to those German prisoners?'

He did, he said. 'But only from Plymouth. Those boys were embarked from there.'

'You're saying, two frightened refugees listened to German being roared, sung and bellowed for a mere hour and a quarter?'

The sergeant cleared his throat. 'These questions are for the inquest.'

'Inquest?'

'The coroner will have to establish the cause of death, in

these circumstances. Excuse me.' A bustle in the lobby claimed his attention. A man, roaring out a vulgar sea shanty, came staggering in between two constables. Sergeant Couch turned on his heel, barking, 'Sounds like somebody's found a bottle and missed the boat. You cut your noise, m'lad.'

As the drunkard had reached the chorus of his shanty, and was now adding wild dance steps, Gwenna ushered Lotti out. They'd catch their bus home from Boscawen Street. Some of the St Wenna ladies were waiting for the return trip and they eyed the box Gwenna carried with interest. Perhaps they thought she was taking home contraband meat or an illegal turkey. She wished she was.

The refilled kerosene can was waiting at the end of the lane when they arrived home and Gwenna's first action was to top up the Primus stove and brew tea.

A note from Hilda informed Gwenna that she must do the second milking on her own. 'Ezra be up-along with the horses,' was explained in Hilda's blocky writing. 'Up-along' could mean anywhere on the farm that was higher than the house. Seizing the excuse to leave the parcel unopened, she suggested to Lotti that they go find him.

He was ploughing Colvennon Glaze, driving the grey shires, Lady and Prince, whose flanks gleamed waxily in the afternoon light. The creatures strained against their harness, heads bobbing as the plough blade carved into virgin grass. Moving closer, Gwenna and Lotti overheard Ezra talking in low whistles and song snatches. He was ploughing crosswise, corner to corner, so the rain would not create a bog at the bottom of the hill. Aged as he was, he still merited the title 'horseman', Gwenna thought. That wasn't a reference to any ability in the saddle – she'd never seen Ezra astride a horse. It was a farmer's term for a man who could handle these powerful creatures, earn their trust, keep them pulling in harmony with a straight furrow behind. When the land girls arrived, they'd have their work cut out, persuading him that it was anything other than a man's job.

The newly turned soil attracted a mob of gulls and some rare Cornish choughs, whose coral pink beaks shone like brooches against their black feathers. They swooped and hopped, feeding on grubs. Gwenna felt a choke in her throat. Colvennon Glaze had never seen the plough in a thousand years. And now, thanks to Hitler, it was being ripped open. It was a sacrifice they had to make, but it swelled her fury against every Nazi.

Getting the cows in, milking them with Lotti and manhandling the churns to the cooling shed used up the remaining day. 'You pop inside and rest,' Gwenna urged Lotti as she unhooked a broom to complete the final job. 'I'll light a lamp for you, and you can open your reading book. Do you understand?'

Lotti stepped past her and took down a smaller broom.

Gwenna thought: *You understand every word!*

They cleaned side by side, Lotti making neat, whisk-like strokes while Gwenna chivvied dirty water into the gulley. Such a sweet, kind child. She must have been her mother's joy.

As dusk fell, Gwenna located Roddy, who had shut his pigs in for the night and was washing his boots at the yard pump. Since she'd caught him conspiring against her, she hadn't exchanged more than a nod with him. Tonight, her disgust had to be set aside. She needed help taking the churns to the road.

Roddy looked pointedly at Ezra, who was bringing the horses in to groom and feed them. Their massive feet scraped on the yard cobbles. 'That's your job and his, missus. I'm through for the day.'

'Ezra's done a day's worth of ploughing, Roddy, and I can't lift the churns onto the stand single-handed.'

'Oh? Too much for a lady?'

'Far too much. My mother never did it. My father wouldn't have asked it of her.'

'I don't know what you and Ezra are trying to prove,' Roddy said curtly, 'but he won't turn all that land for you.' They watched Ezra tying the horses up outside their stables. He would brush them down before leading them to their overnight paddock. His movements were slow. Ploughing was hard on knees and hips. 'He'll be underneath the soil come summer if he goes on at this rate, and you know it, missus.'

Gwenna repeated her request for help in getting the churns to the road. Roddy might disagree with her – might even want the farm for himself – but she was still his employer.

He stamped away to the cooling shed where the churns were waiting in the dark. The shed was built over Colvennon's stream, which ran icy cold even in the height of summer, keeping the milk fresh until its collection early each morning. It was how they got by without electricity. Old-fashioned, but Colvennon's milk rarely went sour.

There were five full churns and a part-filled one – too many to load at once. They took two at a time on a trolley, Roddy pushing, Gwenna guiding the front wheels over the bumps of the sunken lane. Lotti plodded alongside. Roddy's ill-natured muttering was masked by the squeak of iron wheels, though when she turned, Gwenna saw his lips moving. Let him despise her. Size for size, she was stronger than most women she'd ever met.

At the lane end, they hefted each churn onto the stone stand. 'They'll be collected by lorry at four o'clock in the morning, while you're still fast asleep,' Gwenna explained to Lotti.

Roddy made a 'ft!' noise. 'She don't know what you're saying. Why bother?'

'They'll be taken to the railway station and on to a dairy in Exeter,' Gwenna continued calmly. 'The lorry driver will leave us empty churns in their place. That's how it goes, Lotti, every day. It's how people get fresh milk on their breakfast table.'

After manhandling the final two churns, Roddy set off for home, leaving Gwenna to push the trolley back along the lane. 'Hop on.' She gestured for Lotti to get on board, laughing when the child eased herself nervously onto the wooden slats.

A bright half-moon hung above the farmhouse. Before Edward's death, Gwenna had looked up every time there was a clear night and thought that wherever her husband was, he would be seeing the same stars and moon. She had sent out prayers for his well-being. All she had wanted was for him to come home safe, for the war to end, so they could dissolve the links between them with dignity. His death had left a ragged end to an unhappy story. Now she had no Edward, no children by him, and Colvennon was everything. Seeing the plough horses at work this afternoon had brought home to her how deeply this place lived in her heart and bones.

And there was Lotti now. Whatever it took, she must keep her.

'Send me those land girls, soon as you can,' she murmured to the moon. John Wormley had promised. She must try to be patient.

Right now, there was supper to cook and a parcel to unwrap.

9

Gwenna cut the string tying the box, winding it into a skein for re-use. Everything was in limited supply, with factories turned over to war production. The box had previously contained something issued by His Majesty's Stationery Office. Perhaps those posters, warning citizens to keep their lips sealed. The first thing out was a mustard-yellow beret, adult size. There was dirt on the crown. Oil or grease. The label inside was French: '*MiGi de Paris*'. A brown hair was attached to the inner band. Lotti was drying their dinner crockery – she had picked up a tea towel and begun the task, unasked – with her back to Gwenna. She'd shown no curiosity about the box and now didn't notice Gwenna quickly putting the hat in a drawer. Next out was an envelope containing a purse, the ration book that had helped identify Miryam, a handkerchief and comb. They went into the drawer alongside the beret.

A final item was wedged into the bottom. A teddy bear, instantly recognisable to Gwenna by its sailor suit and single, amber eye as the one she had seen abandoned in the railway dining car on her hunt for the Gittelmans. From its worn appearance, the bear must be many times Lotti's age. One ear was rubbed smooth, perhaps because successive owners had carried him around that way. There was time to stuff him back inside the box, but what if he brought comfort? Gwenna wavered, remembering how she used to take a stuffed elephant everywhere until he was removed from her clutches on her first day at school. The tears!

'Lotti, is this a friend of yours?' She repeated herself twice before Lotti turned.

Brown eyes opened wide. Lotti's lips moved, though no sound came out.

'Would you like to hold him?'

The cup Lotti had been drying fell to the floor, shattering on the slate slabs. It was one of the few surviving pieces of her mother's wedding-gift china and, without thinking, Gwenna cried, 'Oh no!' She went to pick up the pieces and Lotti, perhaps mistaking her urgency, jumped aside. Screams then poured from her throat. Gwenna tried to put the bear into her arms and the screams merged into one terrifying howl that racked the slight body.

It took a long time to soothe Lotti that night, and though she eventually fell asleep, Gwenna did not. Still in her work clothes, she went downstairs, seeing through the kitchen window the moon stuck firmly to the cowshed roof. Lighting the oil lamp, she stared at the one-eyed bear.

'You're going,' Gwenna muttered in anger towards this stuffed creature who had made Lotti's throat raw from screaming. She scorched her hand opening the stove door. Orange embers glowed within, the remains of a good fire she'd made earlier.

Throwing the bear inside, his blue cotton trousers caught at once and the sight of flames brought Gwenna to an instant panic. Before finally falling asleep, Lotti had sobbed out, 'Rumtopf, Rumtopf!'

Could that be the bear's name? She quickly pulled it out,

laid it on the draining board and doused the flames with a jug of water. The smell of scorched wool and cotton was most unpleasant. Now he looked a mess – his one beady eye staring out through blackened fur.

Wondering how she was going to explain this to Lotti, she sat him on the windowsill, as though to look out at the moon. He'd need a new suit of clothes and his burned fur to be clipped.

Her nerves rubbed raw, Gwenna poured herself a small glass of whisky and pulled a kitchen chair up to the stove. She wasn't ready for bed. Feeling alone with a stack of worries always cut into her sleep.

Josephine slipped in through the window which was always left open a few inches to allow her to come and go. She padded over to Gwenna and jumped onto her lap. Gwenna stroked her, but must have drifted off, because she was suddenly aware of a voice in her ear. Her father saying, 'They'll come. Help will come.'

Her eyes flew open. She knew she'd dreamed it, but it felt like an assurance that the land girls would arrive. She realised she'd slept in her chair for two hours when a rumbling sound from the direction of the road announced the milk lorry's arrival. The kitchen clock agreed. It was four a.m. After feeding Josephine, Gwenna put on her boots and stepped outside. The barns and the milking parlour were nebulous shapes, their slates misted with silver. The rumbling stopped, and the clank of metal on metal took its place. Gwenna counted a full minute before the engine started again. Part of the tapestry of sound on a dairy farm.

Back inside, she made tea and toast for herself, raked out and relit the stove. Josephine was on the drainer, batting the singed teddy with a challenging paw. 'We need a bear-repair service, Josephine, so don't make it worse.' After checking on Lotti and finding her fast asleep, Gwenna put on fresh work clothes and set off to walk around the farm, this time locking the kitchen door behind her. She couldn't risk Lotti ending up on the cliff again.

First, Gwenna checked the cattle. She then made a tour of her bean fields. They were doing well, Roddy's shotgun patrols keeping the pigeons at bay. They'd likely harvest them early this year. The horses trotted to their fence as she passed, their feathered feet stamping dew from the grass. They whickered and she fetched them some hay. The chickens were ready to be let out, and the pigs were slumbrous in their sties. As she walked back towards the farmhouse, she heard the throb of a truck out on the road. It could be the milk lorry, doubling back. Or a delivery lorry looking for one of her neighbours. As she entered the yard, she stopped dead.

A man was leaning on the gate that made a barrier between the yard and the house, his back to her. He was a well-built man with wide shoulders and as she walked closer, she saw an arrowhead of dark blond hair protruding from the back of his oilskin cap. He wore a brown boiler suit with a yellow circle in the middle of the back... Her heart stumbled. She'd seen overalls like this through the bus window, passing the POW camp at Tregallon.

There was a German in her farmyard.

10

He must have felt her presence as he turned and fixed her with eyes as piercingly light as the dawn mist.

'Who are you?' she croaked.

'This is your home?' He spoke with an accent, choosing words with deliberation. Unmistakably German. As he began to walk towards her, she raised her hand in a 'stop' gesture.

An escapee from Tregallon? And she'd thought those fences looked unclimbable. Fear trickled into every vein. She was completely on her own out here, and Lotti was alone in the house, asleep in bed.

A pitchfork hung against the stable wall, but Gwenna doubted she'd get to it before the man saw what she was up to. Perhaps he was seeking food or transport. Had he not realised this was the depths of the countryside, hidden lanes bounded by the sea? Josephine slunk under the gate and rubbed shoulder against the man's calf, her mouth opening and closing to emit supplicatory mews.

The man looked down with a faint smile. To Gwenna he said, 'You are to work very early. You care for the cows?'

She wasn't going to tell him that she owned the place. 'Just go. I won't try and stop you.'

'I cannot.'

That was when she realised she'd seen him before, on the platform at Truro station. He was the one she'd assumed to be the captain, an officer of some kind. His eyes were blue-grey, like sea glass, in a face that was tanned from exposure to the outdoors.

He said, 'Please do not be afraid of me. I am here now for all day.'

Oh no, you're not. 'There'll be a search party out—' She stopped as two more men walked into the yard from the sunken lane, both in identical brown all-in-ones. One wore a leather cap whose peak shaded a fading black eye and fresh-looking bruises to the brow. Gwenna recognised him too: he'd been the first off the train, bloody-faced, alongside another man. The one bringing up the rear triggered no recognition. He might have been one of the prisoners, but there was nothing memorable in his appearance. He looked nervous.

Gwenna's gaze jumped from man to man. The battered-faced one in the leather cap looked to be the most life-hardened, though he must be the youngest of the three. Around thirty, near Gwenna's age. He took out a cigarette, pushing it into the side of his mouth, and a hand reached into a pocket, for matches presumably.

Seeing it, she overcame her fear. 'Don't you dare!' she yelled. 'Not with barns full of straw and hay. Light up and I'll throw a bucket of water on you.'

His colleague, the officer, said something in German and reluctantly he put the cigarette back in his breast pocket. The nervous one, who had sandy, side-parted hair, blinked at her like a man who had mislaid his spectacles along with his purpose in life. If she'd managed to grab the pitchfork, she thought, she'd aim it at him. He wouldn't see it coming.

Lotti was alone, unprotected. A Jewish refugee and three German escapees...

'Go or you'll be caught.' Her voice trembled. 'If you're hungry, I keep hens.' She pointed towards a gate beside the stables, behind which were the chicken huts. They could fill their pockets with new-laid eggs, then disappear. Off a cliff, ideally.

'You give us chicken?' The officer, who looked nearer forty than thirty, frowned as if Gwenna showed signs of an intriguing medical condition. 'This is ordinary?'

'I mean, if you're hungry.'

The main gate clanged. Don't say there were more of them! Losing her nerve, Gwenna bolted for the house. None of the men tried to stop her and she was at the kitchen door before remembering she'd locked it. The key was in her breeches pocket but before she could retrieve it, she heard a woman's voice. Loud and unfamiliar.

'Hello, anybody there?' A tall young woman dressed in a green jumper and buff breeches strolled into sight. Seeing Gwenna, she gave a cheery wave. 'Morning, love. This is Colvennon?'

Gwenna gaped. None of the land girls she'd encountered since they'd been deployed in the countryside had looked like this one. The usual buff breeches, green jersey, thick socks, gaiters and boots but the figure was hourglass. Sausage-roll curls bleached to a Hollywood shine framed a boldly beautiful face. The young woman's mouth was pillar-box red. Moreover, she'd walked straight past the Germans, hardly sparing them a glance. Batting mascaraed lashes, she said, 'My directions were "Back of Beyond" so I've come to the right place, I hope?' Her accent was not local.

Gwenna flashed a glance at the men and hissed, 'Germans!'

'That's right, queen, every inch of them. Tell me who's in charge, 'cos I need someone to sign off on the delivery.'

'I'm in charge.'

'Then grab a pen, and squiggle on the sheet.' The girl took a clipboard from under her arm. 'Quick, if you don't mind, 'cos I've got to get off.'

Was the accent Liverpool? Whenever she had batteries for her wireless, Gwenna was a loyal listener to *ITMA* – *It's That Man Again* – with Liverpool comic Tommy Handley and he spoke the same way. 'Who are you?' Gwenna asked.

'Eileen McGuigan. Wiggy to friends, so bear that in mind 'cos you'll see a lot of me.' *A lorra me.* 'Wiggy' was now flanked by the men and still seemed unperturbed. Gwenna took the clipboard. At the top of the page, she read 'Ministry of Agriculture. Allocation of German prisoners of war for work'. 'Colvennon Farm' was typed below, with three other names.

Reiner, M.

Baumann, J.

Franz, W.

'Germans, for me?' Gwenna felt suddenly faint.

'That's right, pick of the bunch.'

'They can't come here. What's going on?'

'A war, last time I checked.' Eileen McGuigan was losing patience. 'Every hand to the plough and all that.'

'But... Germans?'

'Listen, love, can we not make this hard work because I've a truckload of their mates to drop off elsewhere.'

'Truckload? You're a driver?'

'Spot on, I'm Land Army seconded as a driver to the camp. As jobs go, it's a jammy one. Can you just sign, please?'

Gwenna shook her head. 'These men... this really is official?'

'One hundred per cent rubber-stamped by the Min of Ag. You wanted labour, queen, and you've got labour.'

'But I asked—'

'You've got Max, Jürgen and Walther.'

'Mr Wormley promised me land girls, not German rabble.'

'Hey, you'll hurt their feelings.'

The oldest one, the officer, had been regarding Eileen with open appreciation. He turned to Gwenna with a look of amusement, which raised her hackles.

'I doubt they have feelings,' she said. 'One of them looks as though he's just stepped out of a boxing ring. John Wormley would have warned if he was planning to send thugs.'

Eileen crossed her arms. 'They don't let thugs past the barbed wire. Honestly, these chaps are civilised.'

'Ha!'

'They know that if they cause trouble, or make a break for it, they'll spend the rest of the war in solitary confinement. Know how that feels?'

Gwenna shook her head. She'd experienced 'solitary' but not 'confinement'.

'Well, it takes twenty minutes to count the bricks in a cell, and once you've counted them, you go back to the start, for as long as this rotten war lasts. That's why they want to work; they're not fools. And they get paid.'

'Paid?' Gwenna's voice split with outrage. 'How much?'

'Cigarette money. They're not going to undermine the local economy. Now *please*, take my pencil and give us your signature. Or sign in cow muck. Or I can lend you my lippie. Just sign the docket, so I can go.'

Gwenna shook her head at the proffered pencil. She wasn't going be pressured into taking these men while Lotti's screams echoed in her head. 'I can't. It's too dangerous.'

'Give me strength.' Eileen McGuigan waved her leather-gloved fingers towards the officer, indicating the bright patches below his knees. 'Know what those yellow circles are for? There's another round the back between the shoulder blades. They're not decoration.'

Feeling cornered, Gwenna shrugged. 'To make them identifiable, should they try to escape?'

'They're for snipers to aim at if they go on the run. These lads know the rules and, like I said, they're not stupid. They want to go home eventually.'

'I still don't want them.'

'Tell that to the ministry.' Eileen snatched back the clipboard and dashed off some kind of signature, saying, 'I'm saving you from yourself, queen. My advice, make the best of them, don't get too friendly and remember they're entitled to knock off for dinner and a break in the afternoon.' She added that she'd return at dusk to pick them up.

'Please.' Gwenna opened the kitchen garden gate, behind which she'd felt marginally safer, edging out so no part of her would touch the men who stood on the other side. 'Miss McGuigan—'

'Eileen, if you can't manage Wiggy.'

'Take them away.'

But Eileen was on the move. She chucked a canvas bag to the officer. 'You forgot your scran, Kapitänleutnant. Make yourself useful and be a gentleman, right?' She flashed a crimson smile at Gwenna. 'Ta-rah, love. See you later.'

A minute later, a truck engine fired. Gwenna was left to deal with this disaster alone.

11

Max extended his hand. 'My name is Ernst-Maximilian Reiner. Max to most. Your name is, please?'

She glared. No German was going to first-name her.

Max indicated his bruised companion. 'Here is Jürgen Baumann.' Then the mild-mannered one. 'And here, Walther Franz.'

All she could think of was how Lotti would react, hearing real German being spoken by captured soldiers. And what about Ezra, Roddy and Hilda and her other neighbours, who had roundly judged her for trying out a few words of German with Lotti? And there was Edward's family in Truro who would sooner or later hear of this turn of events. At the station, Gwenna had judged the prisoners to be sailors. Faded uniforms and the salt stains on oilskin and leather had pointed that way. But if so, men like these had sent Edward – a husband, son and brother – to his death.

As Gwenna and the men stared at each other, the air vibrated with the noise of contented lowing. Ezra was bringing in the cows. He wouldn't have seen Wiggy's truck as he always took a shortcut across the fields from his home. A moment later, the yard filled with undulating, pale-gold backs and broad, glistening noses. Gwenna beckoned Max, Jürgen and Walther to come through the open gate, into the kitchen garden. 'Move, don't get knocked over. They won't stop for you.' She wondered if they'd ever seen a cow before. Germans, and incompetent too. Thank you, Mr Wormley!

Throaty bellows acknowledged the presence of strangers, but the cows filed into the parlour in their habitual ranking order. Ezra followed behind, whistling. The tune ceased abruptly as he saw the men. He came over, giving Gwenna one of his tilted looks. 'What have we got here, then?'

'Prisoners of war,' Gwenna said tightly. 'Sent to work on the land. I had no idea.'

'Ah.' Ezra glanced at them in turn. 'Ah.'

'Ah what, Ezra?'

He dug his hand inside his waistcoat and handed Gwenna a small brown envelope. 'Beg pardon, missus, I shoulda given this over yesterday. Postman come late morning, while I was sluicing out the parlour and I clean forgot.'

Sparing Ezra a dark look, she inserted a fingernail under the flap. The thin, wartime paper ripped easily. Inside, a quarter-size sheet stated formally what Eileen McGuigan had already told Gwenna.

Understanding your plight, I have expedited the allocation of three POWs from the newly established camp at Tregallon. All have outdoors experience. I hope you will find them good fellows, and willing.

Your obedient servant,

J. Wormley

'How could you forget to give me a letter like this? I'd have had a day's warning.'

'You was in town, missus, on your errands. But I beg pardon. I shoulda remembered to.'

'How do you think it felt, to see them in front of me?'

'I bad shock, I should say. Been sent to help, have they?'

'Yes, when I asked for land girls!'

'By the looks of them, you've got the better deal.' Ezra treated the men to a full inspection. Each bore his scrutiny in a different way, each to their character. 'Best thing would be to split them up and take one man each. One for milking, one for the land, one for the pigs.'

'I'm having nothing to do with them.'

'We can't send them away, not without the devil of a fuss.' Ezra raised his voice the way he did when it was noisy in the milking parlour. 'Are you boys able-handed at milking a cow?'

The men stared back.

'I don't think they have much English, Ezra. What a headache, having to translate the simplest instruction.'

'Milking.' Ezra mimed the stripping out of a cow's udder, adding a convincing imitation of mooing. The one called Max burst out laughing and shook his head.

'Not me. Never.'

'Then what can you do, my 'ansome?' Ezra wanted to know.

Max extended his arms, implying, 'Whatever you like.'

'Ploughing,' said Ezra. 'That's where we're short-handed.'

Gwenna shot back, 'You always tell me it takes five seasons for a man to learn to plough a straight furrow.'

'That's when there isn't a war on.'

'I'm not risking our horses with rank amateurs.'

'Then let 'em turn their hand to milking,' Ezra came back patiently. 'They can take the churns to the cooling shed, and down to the road at the day's end. You'll be glad to be spared that, missus. One of them might help Roddy with the pigs.'

'He won't have them. I can tell you that already.'

'And with them to help you, I can get on with ploughing the Glaze.'

'You'd leave me alone with Germans?'

Ezra's patience remained undaunted. 'You'll have Roddy about the place, and Hilda.'

Three Germans and the Hoskenses. Perfect. 'It takes more than a day to teach someone to milk a cow.'

'Not if they're a natural, like the little maid is.' Ezra noticed then that Lotti was absent. 'Where is she?'

'Asleep, and what am I going to tell her?'

'The truth. That you've got no choice.'

With a groan, Gwenna said, 'Take them to the milking parlour, then, start your lessons. Watch them like a hawk. I'll join you when I've got Lotti's breakfast.'

She found Lotti already up, trying to reach the bear on the windowsill. A kitchen chair had been dragged across the floor. Lotti had got herself dressed in the clothes she'd arrived in, but must have trodden on her hem, because the dress's skirt had torn away from its waistband.

'Careful, let me help you down.' Gwenna held out her hand and Lotti took it. She fetched the bear off the sill. 'Is he called Rumtopf? I need to explain, he's a little bit singed.' Lotti's dress looked a nice-quality garment to Gwenna's eyes, cotton with a pattern of blue and orange cherries. A quick mend would sort it out. Hilda might oblige, though more likely, she'd sigh as though she'd been asked to donate an eye to science. 'Lotti dearest, we must find you other things to wear.'

Seeming to understand, Lotti touched the ragged tear in her skirt and hung her head.

'It's not your fault.' Gwenna gave her a squeeze. 'Unfortunately, the clothes you brought with you have been sent back to

London, so for now, let's repair this lovely dress with a couple of safety pins.'

When that was done and breakfast over, Gwenna washed her hands in preparation for milking. 'Lotti, I think you should stay in and read your schoolbook. Just for today.' How to explain that the farm was suddenly out of bounds? 'Or I could find you a picture book, one of my old ones. Would you like that?'

Ignoring the lack of an answer, Gwenna found an illustrated book of animal rhymes. Lotti folded her hands behind her back. Gwenna felt a rending sympathy. 'Darling, I can't take you out with me. Not today.'

Lotti began to weep.

Oh, heavens. Jürgen, Walther and Max. How had it happened, and how would Miryam have felt, if she'd seen this situation? Hardening her heart, Gwenna installed Lotti in the sitting room. 'I'll be as quick as I can. Please, please, don't leave the house. Hilda's coming in, so you won't be alone.'

You're failing her. The thought, sharp as lemon juice, ran through Gwenna's mind as she shoved her feet back into her work boots and shut the door behind her.

12

In the milking parlour, she found Ezra standing with Max and Jürgen, watching Walther milking one of the larger cows. The cow's tail swished in agitation.

'Don't squeeze, lad,' Ezra admonished. 'You aren't wringing out a flannel. Do like I showed 'ee, draw out the milk gently.'

'I don't think he understands,' Gwenna said.

'If we can't teach 'em, they're no use.'

'Exactly.'

Walther must have picked up their exasperation, because he got off the low stool and muttered something.

Max translated. 'He says "Sorry". You hold *Schweine?*'

It took Gwenna a moment to realise she was being asked if they kept pigs.

Max added, 'I hear them, and smell.'

'We do,' she said.

'Walther good for pigs,' Max said. There followed an exchange in German. Max translated. 'Home in Germany, he keeps pig.'

'One pig? We have twelve breeding sows and their young,' Gwenna said crossly.

'Don't forget our two fine boars.' Ezra gave an impression of a grunting male pig. The men laughed. Gwenna did not. Her last sight of Lotti, dwarfed by the chair, holding a book more suited to a child of five than of ten, left her feeling helpless. It was hard not to blame these men for making the task of acclimatising Lotti to her new home all but impossible.

'It won't work,' she said. The pigs were Roddy's kingdom, and it was unlikely he'd consent to work alongside prisoners of war. If these men couldn't milk or plough, there was only one job she could put them to. 'The ditch between Colvennon Glaze and Fairy Tump needs digging out,' she told Ezra. It should have been done last winter. Roddy had never found the time. 'Give them shovels, get them started,' she said. 'I'll push on with the milking.'

Ezra thought about it. 'I'll take the shy fella and the bruiser.' He meant Jürgen. 'You hold on to the one who finds us so funny. You need cheering up, missus.'

Gwenna had no desire to be left alone with Max – she couldn't recall his longer name. Behind the twitch of a smile was something she couldn't put her finger on. Not a threat, but certainly a challenge. 'I'm not going to sit next to a strange man and teach him to milk a cow.'

'I've a fancy he'd be wasted digging sludge,' Ezra said with his methodical logic. 'I'd put half a crown on the fact that he's read a book in his life.'

'So what?'

'Hands that read books can milk cows.'

'You don't read books, Ezra.'

'I read my Bible,' Ezra fired back, visibly offended.

'Yes. Sorry.' And he was right; Max seemed intelligent and spoke enough English to make teaching him feel worth the effort. 'As ever, you know best.'

'I know men,' Ezra agreed as he signalled Walther and Jürgen to come with him. 'Young, old and all stages in between.

You only ever knew one that wasn't your father, Mrs Devoran, and most of the time you were married, he was at sea.'

Gwenna felt herself deflate. Ezra didn't speak the truth, he hammered it to the wall. Turning to Max, she indicated the milking stool vacated by Walther. 'Sit down.' She added 'please' as an afterthought.

Max faintly raised an eyebrow and surveyed the narrow stool. Gwenna fetched hers, murmuring to the restless cows as she passed. She perched next to Max. 'Come on. Sit.'

It was clear he didn't know where to put his legs. *He must be six foot.* His knee nudged hers, and she jumped. Soothing the cow, who was twitching impatiently, Gwenna opened out her left hand, palm flat, thumb raised. 'This is the shape we use. Not this.' She clenched her fists and shook her head. 'You understand?'

'*Ja, ja.*'

'First, we cleanse the udders and teats, but this one's already been cleaned. There must never be dirt in the milk. Then we relax our girl by stroking.' She demonstrated, and glanced at Max.

Amusement darted through his eyes, but he nodded.

She swallowed. 'See? Like this.' She massaged the cow's udder. It was warm, veiny and very full. Walther hadn't stripped out more than a cupful. 'The first part is called "letting down the milk". Basically, we're relaxing her. If her calf wanted to suckle, it would butt gently against the udders and that's what our hands... Do you understand anything I'm saying?'

Max was looking at her, not at the cow's udder. She suspected he was lip-reading, and it made her uncomfortable. 'Please pay attention.'

'Pardon.' He fixed his gaze on the udder, and on her hands as she began to release milk into the bucket.

'When you get into a rhythm, it's eight to ten minutes per cow.' She continued until the bucket was two thirds full of frothy, butter-yellow milk. 'That's her done. She's yielded about twelve pints, which considering she's been poked and spoken to in German isn't bad.' Gwenna strained the milk into the churn. 'Your turn now. Bring our stools on to the next lady.'

Wordlessly, he picked up the stools, one in each hand. She took him to the top end of the parlour where Ezra would normally work. Cows liked routine and so she would alternate ends. She cleaned the udder, then pushed back her stool. 'Show me what you've learned.' Wiggy had addressed Max as Kapitän-leutnant. That sounded officer-class. *Let's see how quickly he picks up new skills.*

He copied her action, gently stroking the cow's bloated udder. His hands were strong, tanned on top as Edward's had been. The hair on the backs was golden. Life on board ship was not conducive to soft whiteness, and it had been upsetting to see Edward's cellist's fingers coarsen after a few months. He'd joined up before war was even a shadow on the horizon, and only Gwenna knew why he'd done it.

She snuffed out the memory.

'I do good?' Max asked.

'You're fine.' Gwenna acknowledged a sensitivity in the way he worked. Not wringing out a flannel like Walther. The cow turned a curious nose towards him, perfectly relaxed. At one point, Gwenna leaned forward and stopped his hand curving into a 'C' shape. 'Keep it straight.' Her brow grazed his cheek, and she flinched at the roughness of it. He was more or less clean-shaven, but she could imagine that shaving soap was in short supply at the camp. She thought of those brick-and-cement huts and wondered if the guards let the inmates have razor blades.

Credit where it was due, though. 'You aren't the worst dairyman I've met.'

Max greeted the compliment with a slight smile. She pointed to the milk pail. 'Time to empty it.' She showed him the steel churn, making it ring with a tap of her knuckles. 'This is a churn. *Churn*,' she repeated with a teacher's clarity.

As Max emptied his bucket, something slipped from behind his collar. An angular black and silver cross hanging by a salt-stained ribbon.

Reeling back, Gwenna stared in horror. She found her voice. 'You can't wear that here. Take it off!'

Without pulling his eyes from hers, Max dropped the medal back inside his brown collar. 'I make my choice; I take no orders. Not with this.'

'Then leave my farm!'

He stared at her, pale eyes unblinking, then shrugged. 'I cannot, until lorry comes.'

She knew he was right. They were stuck with each other but she wasn't going to sit next to a man wearing a German military cross. 'Go to the other end of the parlour, then, and I don't ever want to see that vile object again. Go!' Her heart pumped. Propaganda leaflets depicted German soldiers as savage barbarians sporting death's head skulls and crossbones. Max's cross was simple. Black with four arms rimmed with silver, but she doubted you got that medal without having killed.

She fretted through the next few pails of milk, half her mind on Lotti abandoned in the house. Eventually, she went over to Max and said, 'You must promise never to show that thing here.' She nodded towards his throat and he touched the shape beneath his overalls.

'I promise. I do not mean to frighten you.'

'I'm not frightened. It makes me feel sick and so angry. You shouldn't be allowed to wear it.'

Again, he gave her a level stare. 'I am an officer; some things I may do.' It was said with a hint of arrogance.

Swallowing her fury, Gwenna showed Max how to latch a full milk churn to the trolley, then walked ahead of him to the cooling shed. It was useful, she admitted privately, having someone literally take the burden from her. Farms were designed for men. From the weight of a full churn to the size of the working horses, everything was on a masculine scale. Except for milking stools, but then, milking had always been women's work. That girl, Eileen... Wiggy... had said Max wanted to work. As an officer, presumably he could have chosen an easier life than this.

He unlatched the churn from its frame, working out the screws and levers without her intervention. 'It stands in here?' He pointed to the gully that channelled the stream.

'Yes, lift it gently so it doesn't fall over.'

'*Ja, ja.*'

That switch from arrogance to reasonableness confused her. How could such an obliging character be a fighting man? *Kriegsmarine* was what the Germans called their navy. Edward had written to her once, saying, 'All eyes on the horizon, we daren't blink looking out for the bally *Kriegs-heil-marine* who in their polite and well-ordered fashion only want to kill us.' Her late husband had developed a respect for the German navy. Feared, hated but never underestimated them. He'd probably have enjoyed chatting with this man, now.

Max settled the churn in the cold water then arched his back. 'Ow-ah.'

Gwenna nodded. 'Milking's easier if you're a bit on the short side, like me.' She didn't wait for a reply and walked out into the weak sunshine. Two mallard ducks, colourful males, quacked where the stream gushed out from the cooling shed. The arrival of wildfowl heralded a change of season, and Gwenna had spied a nest of green-blue eggs where the water pooled among the rushes. You'd have to be hard to witness spring arriving in this corner of north Cornwall and not feel uplifted. *Mustn't let anger dull the beauty.* A movement made her turn. 'Lotti! I asked you to stay inside.' Gwenna strode forward. She'd spent longer nurse-maiding Max than she'd intended. 'Come back into the house. Now, please.'

Lotti side-stepped her. Rumtopf the bear was tucked into her cardigan, scorched head and paws poking out. This, and her dress being held together with safety pins, made her look less the tidy little girl from London and more like a beggar maid. *I'm sending her backwards*, Gwenna thought, thoroughly ashamed. Lotti headed towards the cooling shed.

Gwenna caught her. 'Darling, why won't you listen? You can't go in there.'

But Lotti had seen a movement inside. Perhaps she was looking for Josephine.

Instead it was Max who came out, pushing the trolley. After a moment's surprise, he smiled in pleasure. 'Hallo, who are you?'

Lotti did not flinch at the strong accent, but made a puzzled face. It seemed the outfit confused her, rather than the man. Gwenna was glad when Max walked on, pushing the squeaky trolley back to the parlour. Lotti's eyes followed him and Gwenna gave up on the idea of dragging her back into the house. She'd only find a way out again. 'All right. Come on. Milkmaid duties call.'

They completed the morning's work between them and walked the herd back to their meadow, though the cows could easily have taken themselves and only needed humans to open the gates.

Max paused on their way back to the yard to view a separate group of cows, grazing along the edge of a field. He asked, 'What is bad with those deer?'

Gwenna remembered that *Tier* in German meant 'animal'. 'You mean, why aren't they being milked? They're too young. They are heifers. Some will have their first calves later this spring, and those that aren't in calf will keep company with the bull. If you understand my meaning.'

Max looked impressed. 'You have bull?'

'No, too much trouble. We rent one.'

Gwenna sent Max to join Ezra and the others. Later, as distant chimes rolled across the valley announcing one o'clock and lunchtime, the men returned to the yard, their overalls dirty up to the knees. Max had left his ration bag by the wall that separated the kitchen garden from the farmyard and, finding a place to sit, he took out a thin package wrapped in greaseproof paper.

It looked like bread and margarine. It seemed insubstantial for a working man. 'Would you like tea?' Gwenna asked, before she'd stopped to consider that hospitality might break down the boundaries she intended to erect between these men, herself and Lotti.

Max shook his head. '*Nein, danke. Wasser?*'

Gwenna glanced nervously at Lotti, whose only reaction to the sound of German being spoken was to gaze even more curiously at Max. Still, Gwenna wasn't taking any chances and steered Lotti towards the house, pointing to the pump from which she drew her drinking water and telling Max to help himself. As she ushered Lotti inside, she turned to see if Max was availing himself.

He was still sitting on the wall, stroking Josephine, who had jumped up beside him. Gwenna had the idea he was talking to the cat, who stretched her back, purring in pleasure.

'I'm making it a rule,' Gwenna muttered, 'no German unless they're out in the fields, out of earshot. No German on my yard.'

Gwenna gave Lotti the task of spreading butter on bread. 'Hilda churns it by hand, from our own cream.' Hilda must be somewhere about, because a familiar string bag was slung over a chair and a pair of low-heeled boots stood by the mat. She'd better go and explain the arrival of the POWs before Hilda found herself face to face with one or all of them.

Gwenna located her sweeping dust off the stairs. In a wraparound apron, wool stockings, her hair bundled under a scarf, Hilda gave the impression that she'd armoured herself against work she resented. 'We need a quick chat,' Gwenna said.

Hilda gave a grunt that meant, 'What about?'

Gwenna felt the news ought to be delivered sitting down. 'Kettle's on. Come and join us in the kitchen.'

Hilda whacked the stairs a couple more times before putting down her brush. Following Gwenna down the corridor, she observed, 'You're teaching that German child to read, I take it? There's a picture book on a chair.'

'I'm encouraging Lotti in her English.'

'I had a look at they schoolbooks on the table.'

'I'm starting a regime while I decide which school Lotti should go to.'

'Isn't St Wenna's good enough for her? It's where I went, and my children.'

'It's where I went too, but Lotti needs extra coaching.'

'Huh, special is she?'

Gwenna stopped. 'Hilda, be kind. Lotti is coping the best she can and she's endured so much.'

Hilda seemed mildly chastened, so Gwenna pushed her luck. 'If you've a bit of time spare, I was hoping you might mend her dress. It's torn.'

It was a push too far, as was instantly clear. Hilda's eyebrows knit in a single line. 'I don't think the day has come when I'm skivvy to a German.'

'She isn't— Oh, for heaven's sake!' How many times must she take a breath and swallow Hilda's downright unpleasantness? The fact was, she could get by without the woman. Rise an hour earlier in the morning, clean, churn butter and do the chickens herself. But, as she kept reminding herself, she needed Roddy, and if she sacked Hilda, Roddy would walk out.

In the kitchen, her heart did a sideways slide. Lotti had gone again.

She was outside, sitting on the low wall, an arm's width away from Max. Josephine was batting a paw as Lotti circled a finger to create a moving target. Max was holding Rumtopf and saying something. Jürgen sat a distance away, eating an apple. Being a head taller than Gwenna, and standing behind her, Hilda had a perfect view of the scene.

'Who the devil?' she muttered. Then, 'Mercy me. I know those uniforms. I've seen men like that from the bus, going past Tregallon. Germans. You've fetched Germans here, Gwenna Devoran!'

'I didn't "fetch" them, they were sent—'

Violent shouting curtailed her explanation. Roddy appeared round the side of a barn, from the pig sheds, and he was manhandling meek Walther by the scruff of the neck.

Max and Jürgen leapt off the wall, shouting.

Gwenna started forward as Roddy pushed Walther first to his knees, then onto his face. 'Don't,' she cried. 'Roddy, don't!'

Ignoring her, Roddy Hoskens stood over the prone man. The shotgun he used on the pigeons pointed into the back of his victim's brown, prisoner-issue collar.

13

Max and Jürgen roared, in urgent German, for their companion to be left alone. Roddy's finger only tensed on the trigger. Gwenna felt the ground beneath her feet shiver and tilt. 'Roddy, put down the gun.'

He took no notice. His face was brick red, perspiration slick on his forehead. Gwenna turned to Hilda. 'Make him.'

But Hilda shook her head. 'I'm fetching the police.' She didn't move, however.

'What's all this?' Ezra's voice cut through the harsh panting that came from Walther, squashed up against the cobbles. Gwenna hadn't seen him arrive, but the smell of horse and stable told her where Ezra had eaten his lunch.

Ezra addressed Roddy. 'Calm down, lad, and explain to me, kindly, why you're pointing a gun at a man as isn't armed.'

'I found this bastard sneaking round my hog sheds,' Roddy snarled.

My hogs, thought Gwenna. *Not yours.*

Roddy aimed his loathing at Max and Jürgen. 'We'll lock the three of them in a storeroom and you' – he swung his anger at Gwenna – 'bring the police.'

'This is my fault, Roddy.' Gwenna knew she ought to have explained the men's presence the minute Roddy arrived that morning. 'They're here to work. It's official.'

Roddy spat on the ground. Walther, getting the edge of it, babbled incoherently.

'He is saying, he only went to see pigs,' Max told them. He looked pale, eyes moving fast between Walther and the gun.

'I won't have Germans near my hogs,' Roddy bellowed. He now pointed the gun at Max. 'Stand back, put your hands up.'

Max linked his hands behind his back.

'I said, hands up. Him too.' Roddy included Jürgen in the order.

Jürgen made no move either.

Gwenna knew she must assert her authority or these men would never respect her. *Never...* was she coming round to keeping them? 'They've been sent as extra help. They're not escapees or criminals.'

'You asked for them?' Roddy swung round, the shotgun travelling until it pointed at Gwenna's chest.

Ezra swiftly put himself in front of her. 'Don't you aim a gun at the missus! Set the damn thing down, Roddy, afore you commit murder. She's explained, hasn't she? These men are here to work and if you kill them, you won't get a medal.'

Roddy slowly lowered the shotgun. 'What's she doing, asking for Germans with her husband not two years drowned!'

'Leave my husband out of this.' Lights burst behind Gwenna's eyes. 'And don't you call me "she" on my own farm!'

Roddy curled his lip. 'It sickens me, Mrs Devoran, seeing our country's enemy treated like they're our friends. I was in Truro the day these bastards bombed the hospital.'

'These men didn't bomb anything,' Gwenna retaliated wearily. 'They're sailors.'

It cut no ice with Roddy. 'I helped dig out the dead. You

didn't see the bodies brought out or hear the cries of the little children caught under the rubble.'

'I know.' Bombs had fallen on the town last summer, hitting the Royal Cornwall hospital. She'd been in the fields, bringing in the last of the hay and the explosions had echoed like dull thunderclaps. She sympathised with Roddy more than he imagined, but she wouldn't tolerate insolence. 'Lock that gun up, Roddy, or I'll report you for threatening behaviour.'

'You would,' Roddy jeered. 'Turn in a patriot and coddle a German.' His gaze went to Lotti, who was cradling her bear, wide-eyed and her mouth drawn tight in distress. 'Let's invite them all over, why don't we, give them bread and jam.'

Gwenna passionately wished that Lotti could be anywhere but here. The child was staring at the shotgun with an expression that was not exactly fear. More bitter resignation, as if she lived in hourly expectation of death. God forgive Roddy Hoskens if he'd added another grain of trauma to the child's unbearable quota. She strode up to him, intent on taking the shotgun off him.

Roddy gripped it all the tighter. 'Back off, woman!'

'Don't you call me "woman" either! Give me that gun.' They grappled, the metal barrel drawing circles in the air.

Max ran between them, using his momentum to drive his fist into Roddy's stomach. As Roddy doubled over, Max twisted one of his arms behind his back and as the gun clattered from Roddy's grasp, Gwenna seized it, shoving it barrel-downwards among the late Brussels sprouts in the kitchen garden. Ezra followed and pulled it out, broke it at the breach, and Gwenna heard something patter on the ground. Straightening the gun out, Ezra pushed it back into the earth.

'He's gone too far this time, missus. You need to stand your ground.'

Roddy was trying to punch and kick his way out of Max's hold, and Max was keeping up the pressure. The pain.

Gwenna knew what Ezra was implying. She should order Roddy off the farm. Dismiss him. And her name would be mud in the village: the woman who had sent off a local man in favour of Germans. She couldn't do it but at least she could help Walther to his feet. Jürgen got there first. Gwenna noticed that the moment Walther was upright, Jürgen stepped away. No tenderness there, it seemed. She passed Walther a handkerchief, for the dirt on his cheek.

Max let Roddy go, dodging a wild swipe. He shook himself, flexing his wrists and fingers as Roddy staggered to the vegetable patch to retrieve his gun. When he had it in his hands again, he turned it towards Max.

'I'm not having Germans running free on this farm, not with my Hilda in the house.'

Hilda was still watching from the kitchen doorway, seeming anything but fragile. It didn't stop Roddy advancing towards Max, pointing the gun at him.

Gwenna pulled Lotti into her arms, shielding her with her body. Roddy, when he was six feet away from Max and without provocation, pulled his trigger.

The gun fired; Gwenna screamed. Max shuddered, but did not fall. Roddy looked incredulous. Dirt spattered Max's breast, but no blood.

'Daft beggar, did he suppose I'd leave the cartridges in?' Ezra muttered. 'Lucky he didn't aim for the lad's eyes.'

Gwenna could feel Lotti sobbing silently against her. In a voice she did not recognise as her own, she said, 'Roddy Hoskens, leave my farm and don't come back.'

Roddy stared at her. The last moments were catching up with him and he seemed to physically shrink. He stared down at the gun in his hands as if it was somehow to blame for his attempt at murder. He nodded, turned and walked away towards the pig sties.

Hilda, by contrast, had plenty to say. Gwenna was a collaborator, a German-lover, a no-use fancy piece playing at being a farmer and ruining a good living for honest men. 'I wouldn't work another hour here if you owned the last field on earth.' She pulled off her apron and flung it down, then went inside for her things. Coming out again, she strode up to Gwenna, standing with her face pushed up close.

'What's the use of you, Gwenna Devoran? You've no husband and they say you were barren as an acre of flint.' Hilda pointed at her belly. 'Five children I have borne, and you have none. Lady you might be, but who is the better woman?'

'I have no answer to that,' Gwenna answered coldly. 'Follow your husband, and don't come back.'

14

'So, they'll be staying, then, they Germans?' It was late afternoon, the same day, and Ezra had come from the back fields to help with second milking. Gwenna muttered a reply.

Ezra cupped a hand to his ear. 'Say again, missus.'

'I said, "I suppose I've no choice" because who will tend the pigs in place of Roddy and the chickens in lieu of Hilda?'

'I daresay you could always get them back.'

'By grovelling? You don't expect me to.'

'No, and your father would have done the same. We can't have murder at Colvennon.'

'Nor did we, thanks to you, Ezra.' Gwenna smiled encouragingly at Lotti, who had finished scrubbing out her milking pail. The bear was tucked into the belt of Lotti's dress, but he looked rather unstable. 'Make sure Rumtopf doesn't fall into the milk, Lotti.'

'Is that his name, Rumpot?' Ezra frowned.

'Rum-*topf*,' Gwenna said.

'What does that mean, then?'

'Lotti will you tell because I don't know either.' For a heartbeat, Gwenna thought Lotti might answer. Instead, she picked up her milking stool and went to the next cow.

'I will possess my soul in patience,' Ezra declared, and stumped away to the other end of the parlour. Gwenna watched Lotti delicately washing her cow's udder. After which, the small hands began stripping creamy milk into her pail.

She's a miracle of nature. Lotti had been dreadfully shaken by Roddy's display of rage earlier, and it was obvious she'd seen guns before and that they frightened her. Yet she seemed to grasp that they'd witnessed a man beside himself with fury. What had upset her most was the bullying of Walther and the targeting of Max... Gwenna relived the moment of absolute horror as Roddy fired his gun. Had it been loaded, her future here would have been blotted out. Not to mention Lotti's. She wondered if Lotti's unnatural calm was due to shock. Yet the little girl was absorbed in her task. Perhaps that was the key. Activity, good as any medicine.

Evening milking was completed. Ezra asked Max and Jürgen to wheel the churns down to the road, but explaining the task defeated him. Both men were uncommunicative, which was not surprising, and in the end, Gwenna said, 'I'll come with you and show you.'

Which meant Lotti must come too, and where did that leave Gwenna's determined insistence on keeping the child at a safe distance from these men? Up in the air and round the bend, it would seem.

Gwenna noticed Max looking from side to side as he helped Jürgen push the trolley along the sunken lane, taking in the play of late afternoon light on lichen-crusted walls. She felt he was grateful to be out in the fresh air. Grateful to still be alive?

At the end of the lane, Max touched the cratered standing stone.

'It marks the boundary,' she told him. 'Nobody knows when it was raised, but probably over two thousand years ago.' She indicated the concrete stand, saying, 'This, my father built in 1928.'

After lifting the last of the churns onto the stand, Max pointed across the lane where Colvennon's stream gurgled into a gully. Among the gorse and spindle trees that overhung a wall, a bird made a flash of coral pink. '*Was ist das?*'

'Bullfinch,' Gwenna answered.

'Bull. Finch.' Max nodded as though filing the information. 'In German, "*Dompfaff*".' He smiled at Lotti, whose attention was fully on him. '*Verstehst du Deutsch?*' he asked.

Lotti's eyes opened. Her lips too, seemingly in pleasure at being spoken to in her mother tongue. Gwenna moved fast, stepping between them. 'I forbid it!'

Forbid what? Max's face asked. 'I think she is not English. I hear you call her name Lotti. Where comes she from?'

'It's not your business. And don't speak to her in German. I mean it.'

He looked chastened. '*Einverstanden.*' I agree.

An olive-green Leyland truck rounded the corner and pulled up. Its canvas roof was strewn with twigs, suggesting it had trundled up overgrown lanes with insufficient headroom. Eileen 'Wiggy' McGuigan leaned out of the doorless cab. She caught sight of Max and Jürgen and jerked her head. 'Get on board, lads. Where's your mate?' To Gwenna, she said, 'Got to get the scallies back to base. They dine at six, you know.'

Gwenna caught a whiff of cigarette smoke and realised there were POWs in the back of the truck. A head peering round the canvas proved it. Ice-blue eyes regarded Gwenna with interest before shifting to Lotti, their expression marrying recognition with twisted pleasure. He shouted something that Gwenna translated as, 'Hey, sweetheart!'

Lotti began to breathe fast.

Gwenna stepped in, steering Lotti away towards the sunken lane. *Hey, sweetheart.* It had sounded more like an insult than an endearment, and she was sure the man who had flung it was the stocky German who had come off the train the same time as Jürgen, blood bright on his face. He'd been under heavy guard then. She looked back and found him still watching them. With his injuries healing, he was handsome in a chilling way. Features carved with an arrogant hand. This is what she most feared, the enemy around every corner and unable to protect Lotti because she didn't have eyes on every side of her head. Max called to her. He'd followed them and she heard him ask if all was well.

In her distress, she rounded on him. 'Get in the truck, will you, so you can go? I don't want that man near us.'

Max glanced back at the vehicle. 'Kurt Fuhrman? He is not trouble. All is show.'

'Not the way he looked at us just now.'

Eileen had turned off her engine and came to talk. She over-heard the last comment. 'Looked at you? Blimey, who have thought it? Listen, they're men, they're locked up and you're cute with your little waist and baggy breeches. Brunette locks tied up under a duster really does it for some men.'

It was a headscarf knotted on top of Gwenna's head, but she let it pass. 'It's not a joke, Miss McGuigan. I don't want that Kurt individual anywhere near.'

'I said, call me Wiggy. I've been that since I signed up.' Wiggy peered up the sunken lane, which was criss-crossed with shadows. 'Is that Friend Walther trudging towards us?'

It was indeed Walther Franz, silhouetted in the fading light.

'They're all harmless,' Wiggy insisted. 'Just bored, mostly. The fanatical ones are sent elsewhere.'

'This is not always true,' Max corrected her. Gwenna demanded to know what he meant.

He shrugged as Kurt Fuhrman jumped down from the rear of the truck and stretched his arms in a leisurely, insolent way. He took up a stance with his legs apart, and watched them as though mentally recording their conversation, posture and the degree of familiarity between them. His eyes finally rested on Lotti, and there they remained.

Gwenna yanked Wiggy's sleeve. 'Take my three back to camp and don't bring them tomorrow. I can't have this.'

Wiggy laid a conciliatory hand on her arm. 'Sorry, queen, I'm under orders and there's nothing I can do about it. At least yours are prime specimens.' Walther shuffled past at that moment. 'Well, two of them are at any rate.'

Max followed Walther towards the truck. Gwenna saw Walther speak to Kurt Fuhrman as he got close, and Fuhrman either laughed or sneered in reply. It was difficult to tell which. Max, right behind, rapped out something and Fuhrman answered back. Gwenna recognised a silent clash in the way the two men faced each other. A tense moment.

Then Fuhrman spat on the ground and walked backwards several paces without taking his eyes off Max. He turned only when he reached the truck, to climb inside.

Max gave Gwenna a final, unsmiling nod.

'Harmless?' she growled at Wiggy.

Wiggy sighed. 'See you tomorrow, queen.' Getting back behind the wheel of her truck, she pipped goodbye on her hooter, and reversed into the sunken lane to turn round and head back the way she'd come.

Gwenna shouted over the grind of the engine, 'Lotti can't have Germans around her; she's already escaped the Nazis twice.'

Wiggy heard not a word. As the truck drove off, Gwenna saw Max looking back at her. The heel of one hand was pressed against his mouth, and when he lowered it she saw a splash of fresh blood across his lower lip.

15

Flat 12, Orme Mansions,
  Bayswater,
  London
  March 30th 1943

My dearest Gwenna

Thank you for writing so candidly of poor Miryam's last minutes. How did she get onto the railway track? It's not as though she'd never been on a train before. It's too awful. Hardly had I digested your telegram than I received a call from Truro police station which put paid to any hope that your news was some kind of misunderstanding. My heart breaks for Lotti. In your letter you said she still has not spoken and has nightmares. If these persist, she may need some kind of therapeutic treatment. With this in mind, I telephoned an acquaintance, Dr Kleinman, who believes a mute response is not unusual in cases of extreme shock. If it has not resolved within a couple of weeks from now, you must bring Lotti to see him.

No. Gwenna didn't say it out loud but refusal jolted through her. Freda was kind, but taking Lotti away from Colvennon would only unsettle her. Too much change in too short a time. Gwenna read on.

> Lotti is welcome back in Orme Mansions any time. Norbert and I would love to see you too, if you can ever release yourself from the grip of the good earth.

Norbert was Freda's husband, who wrote books on early-years education. Freda went on to explain how she'd helped with the identification of Miryam Gittelman's body.

> I was able to direct the sergeant in charge to fingerprint records taken at the time of Miryam and Lotti's arrival in Britain. I admit, Gwenna, I was relieved to be spared the ordeal of identifying what remained of my poor friend.

What remained. What does a train do to a human body and what images was Lotti carrying around in her mind? Tucking the letter into her pocket, Gwenna boiled water. It was late morning, the second post just delivered. This was day two without Hilda and Gwenna had risen at four. The chickens were cleaned out and pecking in their orchard. The eggs were collected, milking was done, the cows back in their pasture. Max and Jürgen were learning to plough under Ezra's tutelage. Walther, who had fed and mucked out the pigs, was now digging his way around the farm's ditches. Gwenna felt flaked out and reckoned she could safely take half an hour off for a mid-morning snack. While she made cocoa for herself and Lotti, she turned over a page of her calendar. It was the 1st of April, when she'd rashly promised to have all twenty-five acres of Colvennon Glaze ploughed.

'The 1st of April, some do say, is set aside for All Fool's Day.'

John Wormley had saved her from becoming a public fool, allowing her an extra month. Would Max and Jürgen master the art of ploughing fast enough? Folding away Freda's letter, she admitted to herself that her feelings towards her Germans were contrary and unstable. Mostly, she wanted them gone. Then she'd look at the jobs they were taking on and feel nothing but relief.

Contradictory emotions were part of human nature, she told herself. 'Lotti, cocoa's ready.'

Lotti came in from the sitting room with Rumtopf under one arm. She'd trimmed his fur of all the scorched fibres and the bear looked bald, but clean. He urgently needed a new sailor suit, however. Lotti slid into her seat at the kitchen table and put her hands around her cup. No nightmares last night, nor the night before, despite horrible Kurt Fuhrman doing his best to intimidate them. Gwenna felt more than ever that Colvennon was where Lotti must stay, and where she would heal. Very soon, it would mean attending school. Mr Beecroft from St Wenna's elementary had left a note for her on the milk stand at the bottom of the lane, weighted down with a stone. He wanted confirmation that 'the young lady under your care' would enter his class at the start of the summer term.

Gwenna wished it could be so. Mixing with others, making friends, homework and hobbies would do Lotti a power of good, but Gwenna only had to picture her sitting wide-eyed in a class full of gawping village children to know it was impossible just yet. Private tuition was what Lotti needed.

Freda would have formulated a plan by now. Gwenna unfolded her letter again and picked up from where she'd stopped earlier.

You asked me about Lotti's life before she came to England. I've a meeting shortly, so I will limit myself to a potted history. Born on the east side of Berlin, August 23rd 1932,

father and mother in the apparel trades. Lived over the shop
with a grandmother and an uncle and aunt. The tailoring
shop destroyed November 1938, during the Kristallnacht
attacks. Grandmother, uncle and aunt left Berlin,
making for—

Where? Gwenna tried to read the scrawl. It looked like
'nowhere'. Was Freda saying that Lotti's extended family had
vanished?

There was no more, Freda presumably flying off to her
meeting at that point. A scribbled coda, added before the
letter was posted, gave Gwenna something extra to worry
about.

A summons has arrived for Miryam's inquest in Truro. You
will be there too, no doubt.

Gwenna would indeed. A formal letter had arrived yesterday. The inquest into the death of M. Gittelman was set for
Tuesday, April 13th, at Truro City Hall. Gwenna's presence, as
a witness, was required.

Freda would expect to see Lotti. *Better smarten her up*,
Gwenna thought. Today, Lotti had on a dress that Gwenna had
worn aged twelve. Woefully out of style with its drop waist and
square collar, it swamped the child. Lotti's cherry-print dress
was drying on the line, sleeves billowing in a breeze that
smelled of new grass. Even in a world where everyone's clothes
were worn out, Lotti's looked sorry. *She needs something pretty*,
Gwenna thought, though as she had so little time for home-
sewing, any new clothes would require a shopping trip to Truro.
And as yet, Gwenna had no clothing coupons for Lotti, so it
would have to be something second-hand. A face, a name, came
into her mind, of someone who would help if she but asked. It
was Camilla Devoran, Gwenna's mother-in-law and known

within the family as Mill. Gwenna had not called on her for far too long.

'Please, hot water?'

Gwenna hadn't heard Max Reiner approaching. Lotti looked up in expectation.

He smiled at the child. '*Hallo, Mausi.*'

'Water for what?' Gwenna's abject failure to keep Lotti and the Germans separate was bordering on farcical. But she could hardly lock and bar the kitchen door.

Max held up a billycan. 'Coffee. We take now our break.'

'Coffee... you get given the real stuff?' Gwenna had discovered a taste for good coffee when she'd worked in London before her marriage but all she could buy now were bitter chicory grains. 'I only get rotten imitation,' she said, to make a point.

Max's unspoken response was amusement and something else. Heavens... a flicker of admiration? And why now particularly? She'd dressed in the dark, as she almost always did, tucking a blue and white check blouse into the waistband of her well-worn riding breeches. The blouse was soft from over-washing and maybe too tight across the bust. What was that Americanism Wiggy had used? *Cute.* Gwenna wasn't quite sure if being cute was a good thing for a widow whose living companions were a child and a cat.

'We too drink bad coffee.' Max's eyes were still on her. He had a swelling on his lower lip and an obvious split. She remembered him wiping away blood in the back of Wiggy's truck. Confined men fought, she supposed, but it had been only too obvious that Kurt Fuhrman held some kind of grudge towards Max. Or perhaps it was mutual.

She put a pan of water on the Primus and stared into the blue ring of flame. Hilda would have ordered Max outside. 'No Germans in my kitchen!' The problem with being high-handed was that his behaviour was always the right side of correct, giving her no excuse for excluding him. The water began to bubble and bead. Reaching for the billycan, she grasped only thin air. Turning, she gave a gasp. Max had Rumtopf and was examining the bear, shaking his head. Lotti seemed to be waiting for him to say something.

Gwenna hurried over, a protective hand going to the back of Lotti's chair. 'What are you doing?' she demanded of Max.

'I have interest,' Max said. 'What is his name?'

Gwenna shook her head. This must not happen. This was crossing the line.

'He must have a German name. He is German. See?' Max stretched out the bear's ear to show a metal button. 'It says "Steiff".' He passed the bear to her.

He was right. This bear must have travelled every mile with Lotti on her journey to freedom.

Max addressed Lotti. '*Wie heißt er?*' What's his name?

'No German,' Gwenna said furiously. 'I told you.'

'But the child does not speak English,' Max pointed out. 'She says nothing, ever.'

Lotti glanced at Gwenna, making a rosebud of her lips as though the act of speaking might be dangerous. Gwenna wavered between an overwhelming desire for Lotti to finally break her silence, and fear that if she did, she would swim away on a tide of German.

Max, understanding none of the sensitivities, repeated his question.

Lotti took a breath and said, '*Er heißt Rumtopf.*' Her voice was clear and bell-like.

Behind her, the water was furiously boiling but Gwenna was fixed to the spot. She should be dancing with joy at Lotti's first proper sentence. But it had been given not to her, but to a stranger. 'Please,' she rasped as Max spoke again, 'don't encourage her to speak German.'

Max had chuckled at the name 'Rumtopf' but now he looked grave. 'I must be still?'

Silent, he meant. She nodded. 'Everything depends on Lotti learning English. She has to fit in.'

'But you wish her to speak, yes?'

'Of course I do, just not German. You surely don't need me to explain why?'

Max said nothing at first, and she expected some counter argument. She was floored when he said, 'You have not ever had a child.'

'How do you know?'

'You are slim, like a girl. I have sisters, older than me. I am uncle five times. My sisters are not slim.' He spoke again to Lotti, something about 'looking after Rumtopf'.

'What did I just say?' Gwenna demanded.

'*Ja, ja.*' Max tapped the billycan, to remind Gwenna about the hot water.

Filling the can and watching him saunter out with it, fury blossomed. Either he was having fun at her expense, or he just didn't get it. Suspecting the former, she picked up an enamel bowl containing last night's kitchen scraps that were destined for the chickens. If he wouldn't respect her rules, and put Lotti's future in jeopardy, she'd find a way to get through to him. 'From now on,' she called to him outside, 'you're not to come to the kitchen. No kitchen. I will bring hot water to you in the field.'

He stopped and she caught up with him. She was aware she looked like an outraged fishwife, brandishing potato and carrot peelings. She might have backed off, had Max's expression not slipped into that mask of barely concealed amusement. Fury came to a head. 'Just because I'm forced to have you here doesn't mean you're welcome. I hate you, more than you will ever know!'

He absorbed the insult. 'We can all hate, no?'

'Yes, we can hate.' Gwenna carried an image of Edward's last minutes of life, built from the scant facts she'd received about the sinking of his ship. Always the same scene of a tarry sea, flames reaching up to a star-studded night sky. Her husband's corvette had been torpedoed in the early hours of a frozen November morning. 'Don't!' Max had picked a curl of potato skin off her blouse.

He dropped it into her bowl. He was wearing his prisoner-issue boiler suit, as always, undone at the front to display a V-necked undershirt that revealed a smattering of dark-gold chest hair. He had rolled his sleeves to the elbows, no doubt to free his arms to handle the plough. He was a well-muscled man, with a narrow waist and broad shoulders. *A fine specimen of Nazi manhood, so don't you go admiring him. Don't start comparing him to—* 'Look at you,' she said, deliberately whisking up her prejudice, 'shorn of rank, an unpaid farmhand.' Her gaze stopped at his throat and she noted the iron cross was missing. 'Not so proud of yourself now, hm?'

Quietly he said, 'You are shouting always, Mrs Devoran.'

He'd pronounced her name correctly. Dev'ran. Ezra must have taught him. For a moment, she was flummoxed. Colour spread across her cheeks. 'Are you always so rude?'

His shrug gave nothing away. Probably, he wanted to get back to the others. She must let him have his coffee; ploughing was physical work. The horses pulled but the man behind guided the ploughshare through the earth. Until your hands hardened, blisters were the norm. She hadn't registered it until now, but he'd wrapped a handkerchief around his right hand and there was blood on the white cotton.

'Off you go,' she said tartly, unsettled by that dart of sympathy. With anyone else, she'd have fetched down the first aid box and spread salve on his palms. She wasn't expecting him to laugh, that's what he did. As though months and months of pent-up tension was being unleashed.

16

In her astonishment, she dropped the bowl of peelings, which rolled, spilling its contents. 'Stop it,' she ordered him. 'There's nothing to laugh about.'

'*Ja, das stimmt.*' Unwrapping the bloodied handkerchief, he mopped his streaming eyes and his laughter stopped. 'You ask if I am proud. I am. You too. We both have too much of him.'

'Of pride?'

'So we should be kind to each other, maybe?'

She recognised the bid for mutual tolerance, but he had no idea what lay in her past. He must, however, know the mass misery and despair his country was causing the world over. And to Jewish people in particular. Thanks to Freda, she knew more than her neighbours of the fate of Jews across Europe. British newspapers kept silence, as did the BBC, and Freda railed against them.

'Only the American and Canadian press dare speak the truth,' Freda had told Gwenna. 'Jewish people are being sent not to work in healthy surroundings, but to die.' Others through their race or from being labelled 'degenerate' were also being seized and transported, deemed unfit to live by the Nazis. What gave one lot of people the right to say who should be allowed to breath the air, and who not? Fury brought thudding pain to Gwenna's temples. Be kind? You might as well ask the rocks in Colvennon Bay to be friends with the bludgeoning waves. 'Just go,' she told Max.

With a formal bow of the head, he did so.

'*Rumtopf weint.*' It was spoken softly behind her. Gwenna turned.

'Lotti!' The child had finally spoken directly to her. Not to Josephine, not to Max Reiner but to *her*. 'What are you telling me?'

The bell voice repeated, '*Rumtopf weint.*'

Pointing at the bear tucked into Lotti's cardigan, Gwenna shook her head in frustration. 'What does that mean?'

Lotti bit her lip, then said, '*Er weint. Sie streitet Euch, so wie Mutti und Papa.*'

It was the most beautiful thing Gwenna had ever heard – and the most painful because she didn't understand. 'Wait here, darling.' She ran after Max, calling him to a stop. He'd reached the gate that opened into the meadows and he waited as she hurtled up to him. She repeated Lotti's words. 'Tell me what she said.'

For a moment she thought Max would refuse. 'Please?' she begged. 'I have to know.'

He answered with sadness in his voice, 'She says Rumtopf is crying because we argue, like her mama and papa.' He watched her reaction, then said quietly, 'We must stop, you and I, yes?'

She nodded. 'Yes, we must. But it will help if you keep away from me.'

Next day they did the morning milking together, nothing passing between them beyond the most basic yes and no. Afterwards Max made his way to the Glaze to take a hand at ploughing. Ezra had found an old Primus stove at home and boiled water for his tea, and the men's coffee, in the field, so there was no need for Max to come to the kitchen.

Had Lotti sensed the constrained atmosphere? She hadn't spoken again.

We argue, like her mama and papa.

Gwenna couldn't recall a single angry outburst at home between her parents. Clive and Mary Bossinny had been chapel-going Methodists though not severe or over-religious. Farming life rarely bred outright hilarity but there had been love in plenty. Happy home, happy school days. That could be her motto, Gwenna thought, hung above her bed in cross stitch. Lotti's words yesterday were a plea for peace. 'Stop quarrelling!'

But Lotti could not know Gwenna's dilemma. Max was an enemy combatant whose sole mission for months and months had been to destroy lives like her husband's. Until Gwenna could forget her husband and the deep pity she still felt for Edward, she could not forgive. Frustratingly, Ezra was growing to like the man.

On Sunday, Gwenna decided she ought to attend chapel as missing too many Sundays made people gossip. Dreading the inevitable meeting with the Hoskenses, who were chapel folk, she took Lotti, having repaired the child's cotton dress to a level of respectability. She bound Lotti's plaits with blue ribbons. To her profound relief, none of the Hoskens family were present in the pews and on their way home, they fell in with Ezra, his wife and their twin granddaughters, Becky and Penny.

The girls, well-grown fifteen-year-olds, glanced curiously at Lotti and giggled. Their grandmother silenced them. The girls were orphans, their grandparents having raised them with a mix of chapel strictness and understated love, as was the way of things.

Ezra, who was holding his prayer book against his waistcoat

buttons, said to Gwenna, 'You'll be thanking John Wormley, missus.'

'Will I?'

'They German lads have a knack for the work. Nice manners, too.'

'What a relief. Imagine, if they hadn't washed their hands before tea, or said please and thank you. Have you learned their life stories?'

'Ha! That Jürgen says hardly a word, 'cept in a whisper to Max. Walther mutters German and I don't heed him,' Ezra said. 'Max has English enough for us to talk on farm matters. Nothing more. We agreed that at the start. As for manners, they go a long way, even in a field.' Ezra directed the comment to his granddaughters, one of whom had undone the bow-tie belt at the back of Lotti's dress.

'We'll come and work for you, Mrs Devoran,' Penny offered. 'Becky and I want to be land girls, now we've left school.'

Her grandfather had plenty to say about that. 'You'd do better taking jobs in Truro, in a shop or such. Land girls are too pert for their own good, striding round in breeches. That Wiggle-maid, for one.'

'Wiggy, not Wiggle.' Gwenna chuckled. 'You're just not used to modern women, Ezra.'

'Strong lads are more use behind a horse than any red-lipstick maid in a man's boots.'

'Ignore him,' Mrs Jago said, shaking her head at her husband.

Gwenna pointed out that Wiggy McGuigan handled a truck as competently as any man. 'She'd probably drive the horses equally well.'

Ezra wasn't having it. 'I won't say she's not a fine figure of a woman, Mrs Devoran, but handling a team is a man's job. You come up to the Glaze tomorrow and watch Max and Jürgen at work, you'll see what I mean.'

'Can we come and watch too?' Penny and Becky Jago nudged each other, swapped whispers and giggled.

In unison, Ezra and his wife answered, 'No you can't.' Mrs Jago shot a glance at Gwenna, rolling her eyes in a way that said, 'We know where that kind of thing leads.'

This conversation piqued Gwenna's curiosity to see the men's work, but pride stopped her until the following Monday evening. Only then, as the horses clopped home to be rubbed down and fed, did she nod to Lotti. 'Come on, let's judge their brilliance with our own eyes.'

Venus twinkled, a diamond in the purple twilight. As they plodded uphill, larks surged up from the grass, trailing notes in upward spirals. Gwenna felt a tug. Once the Glaze was ploughed, the larks that nested there would move on. War, the relentless need for home-produced food, meant much was being lost. It was nothing compared to the sacrifice of men like Edward, and she would smile her way through the process, but it tripled her determination to hold on to Colvennon. Her home, her reason for being, and in time, Lotti's too?

'I was born here.' They were crossing a pasture grazed by cows with calves at foot, and some of the youngsters were following them. Gwenna had no fear, but she took Lotti's hand. 'I don't mean in this field. In the farmhouse, in the bed where I sleep. I came back when I needed purpose in my life. This was where I had to be.' There was no sign Lotti understood, but Gwenna suspected she did. More or less, anyway. 'Not everyone approved of my coming back. "A woman can't run a farm single-handed" they said. My mother-in-law pleaded with me to stay in Truro and my sister-in-law... her name's Angela... let's say that judgement was passed. As for Roddy Hoskens, he scowled so hard, his face turned inside out.' She gave Lotti's hand a squeeze. 'Now he can scowl from a distance.' They were approaching the gate to the Glaze. 'Let's see how much Ezra's fine lads have done.'

Against the green, a swathe of newly ploughed land shone like molten chocolate. A bittersweet sight. Gwenna calculated that two thirds of an acre had been turned, less than she'd hoped though it was bound to be slow to begin with, as Ezra would not encourage haste. By May Day, less than a month off, all twenty-five acres had to be done.

Lotti let go of Gwenna's hand and dipped down. When she stood up, something glinted in her palm. It was an iron cross on a frayed ribbon. Lotti knew whose it was, and after a two-day-long wait, she finally spoke again. 'Max.'

'Yes!' Gwenna laughed out loud. 'Yes, it's his, you clever girl!' Gwenna held out her hand. She didn't want to touch it, but she supposed she ought to give it back to him.

'*Nein.*' Lotti tied the cross around Rumtopf's neck.

'No, sweetheart.' Gwenna removed it. 'I'm not angry, but you don't understand. We show them respect, but we cannot cross the line.' She was putting it wrongly. Too complicated. She tried again. 'Lotti, Max can't be your friend.'

Lotti's expression closed and Gwenna's joy faded. Damn and blast Max. Had she been alone, she'd have flung the cross into the furrows. How come he'd been allowed to keep it anyway? She didn't suppose British prisoners in Germany were permitted to flaunt their military honours. Actually, she couldn't imagine how British prisoners were treated in Germany. Many had been captured. Did they work the land, like Max or the Italian POWs, of which there were hundreds in Cornwall? Was there a German equivalent of herself, a Frau Devoran, hating a blue-eyed Englishman? That kind of information never came over on the wireless or in the newspapers. Stuffing the medal into her breeches pocket, she said, 'Race you to the top. We'll go and stare out to sea.'

She set off, trusting Lotti would follow, but after a few paces she looked back and saw Lotti hurrying in the opposite direction. Running towards a man.

It was Max.

He seemed to be holding something out. Gwenna found a burst of speed and caught them up.

'What is that?' she demanded.

Max inclined his head as if they were meeting outside church or in a bank. 'Walther finds this and thinks you will be interested.' He showed her a broken piece of a horseshoe. It was rusted to orange, and soil encrusted.

She took it, held it up to the fading light. 'Dug out of the ditch? It came off a plough horse's hoof, from the size of it.' Gwenna laid the fragment across her palm so Lotti could see. 'My great-grandfather introduced the first shires here, in the 1860s.' Before that, the ploughing had been done by men – one pushing, the other pulling – and Colvennon had been a mere thirty acres across. Heavy horses had allowed for expansion and greater yields. 'It could be eighty years old.' She offered it back to Max.

'You keep. What can I do with it?'

'I'm not sure what the luck quota is with a broken horseshoe. But fair exchange...' Gwenna took the iron cross from her pocket. 'It's shinier than what you've given me. I expect the ribbon snapped.'

She was struck at the alteration in Max's eyes as he closed his fist around the cross. His expression was of undiluted anger and then he strode away, uphill towards the sea. Lotti called, 'Max, Max,' and followed, giving Gwenna little choice but to go along too. The sky was violet now, Venus a clear orb to the west above a distant headland.

Max helped them over the boundary wall and Gwenna gripped Lotti's arm as they walked to the cliff, stopping well short of the edge. The tide was in, surf creaming around the rocks. The dying sun made a wide scorch on the sea's surface. It was a serene view, and even the black-backed guillemots searching for nesting sites along the cliff face flew unhurriedly. Max went right to the lip of the cliff, and turned when Gwenna urged him to step back. He regarded her through his lashes. 'I am too close? But you tell me, keep away.'

'From the house. That's different. The cliff edge can crumble suddenly.'

'Keep away, you are telling me always.' Eyes pale as steel cut into her. 'Not friends, *ja?*'

'Yes. No, I mean – I don't want you to fall to your death. Please, step back.'

He did so, throwing a smile. 'We keep distant, good ladies and bad POWs. Then we are all lucky.'

'Happy. We're all happy.' Gwenna tried to sound amused, but her voice found its habitual rut of anxiety. 'We're not going to quarrel because it upsets Lotti. I – I admit I was insensitive.'

'Of?' Max asked.

'Your thing... your iron cross. I don't claim to approve, why should I? I know what it implies. "Heroism in the field of combat". Isn't that a polite way of describing violence?'

He looked at her and then at the cross. Bending at the waist, he drew back his elbow. A rapid overarm swing, and the cross was cutting through the evening light. Moments later, the waves swallowed it. They rolled over the sand and shrugged back out again.

'Why, Max?'

'Because you are right.'

'About what, exactly?'

His answer was a rise and fall of the shoulders and a stare that offered no clues. She could make of it what she wished, he seemed to say. He owed her no explanations.

.   .   .

Supper that night was macaroni cheese. Gwenna and Lotti passed the evening listening to the BBC Orchestra and a recital of songs on the wireless, and were nodding off before the end. At some indistinct hour of the night, Gwenna was woken by panicked screams slicing through the bedroom walls. Lotti's nightmares were back.

17

In the early hours, having got Lotti to back to sleep but finding herself again wide-eyed and wakeful, Gwenna penned another letter to Freda, thanking her for fleshing out details of Lotti's wider family and how they made their living in Germany before being forced out. Of Lotti, she wrote:

'By day, she seems unable to articulate the loss of her parents. By night, it all floods out and it's heart-rending. Lest you think I'm struggling, I have positive news too. Lotti spoke for the first time the other day.'

Rumtopf weint.

'I'm sure you know all about Rumtopf, Freda, but it was a breakthrough for me when she confided her bear's name.' Her pen jerked. Lotti had offered her first words not to her, but to Max Reiner. Shame at lying led Gwenna to a confession:

'Lotti is so far only speaking German. My belief is that shock has thrown her back to childhood, clouding though not erasing her knowledge of English. We will work through it, and I am convinced Cornwall is doing her good. Her colour is better, her cheeks fuller. You will see for yourself—'

On the day of the inquest, was what Gwenna intended to write, but she laid her pen down. She hadn't yet worked out what she'd do with Lotti that day. It wouldn't be fair to drag her into court.

The question hung like a dark cloud as she walked with Lotti to post the letter later that morning. St Wenna was a one-street village, but as well as the Mermaid pub and post office, it had a grocer's shop and a butcher's. Stone cottages clustered around a church dedicated to the martyred fifth-century saint for whom Gwenna had been named. Opposite was the Methodist chapel and the school, a single-roomed building with a stubby bell tower. A dairy farm, tenanted by kinsfolk of Ezra's, abutted the chapel graveyard. The farm's matriarch, Nancy Jago, hailed Gwenna from her gate.

Auntie Nancy, as she was known to all, carved a glance at Rumtopf, who peered out from the neck of Lotti's cardigan. It was a sapphire-blue cable-knit that Gwenna had found in a trunk, which Lotti was wearing with a grey school skirt that had also been one of Gwenna's.

'I recognise they buttons,' Nancy said, pointing to Lotti's chest. 'Your mother knitted that cardie for you, but they mother-of-pearl buttons came off one of my girls' Sunday frocks. I cut them off and gave them to your ma.'

'Waste not, want not. Lotti' – Gwenna smiled down – 'this is Mrs Jago, a relation of Ezra's.'

'She may call me Auntie Nancy.'

An idea crept up on Gwenna. Would this good woman look after Lotti on the inquest day? 'Lotti, did you hear that?'

After waiting in vain for a response, Nancy Jago shook her head. 'Ezra did say, the little maid's all mumchance.'

'She's not. Just overwhelmed and shy. She needs time.' And

not to be stared at like a stuffed owl in a glass case. Thoughts of asking Nancy to take Lotti in for a day were shelved.

Auntie Nancy asked how things were at Colvennon, 'Now Roddy Hoskens is out on his ear, and Hilda.'

'Ezra told you why?'

'He did, and Hilda has been blaring off in the village ever since.' Auntie Nancy extracted a barley sugar from her apron pocket and held it towards Lotti. 'You have this, maidie.'

Lotti looked at Gwenna, unsure.

Gwenna smiled encouragingly. 'Take it. Thank you, Auntie Nancy.'

'You're welcome. I don't blame you for giving Roddy his marching orders, waving a loaded gun. I never knew what Hilda saw in him. Except I *do* know.' She tapped her nose conspiratorially. 'A loudmouth, and not from these parts.' Which, in Nancy's opinion, accounted for everything. 'Only – you've got Germans parading round the place instead.'

'They don't parade, Auntie. They work. Didn't Ezra tell you that?'

'Oh, he rates them all right, but you be careful, Gwenna. You have no mother to whisper in your ear. A sharp tongue and an angry heart make enemies.'

'I wouldn't call my POWs particularly angry.' Introverted, hard to read. Gwenna entertained a brief memory of Max hurling his iron cross into the sea. Who was that defiance aimed at? At his country? At her? Or at himself?

Nancy Jago wasn't referring to the Germans, but to Hilda Hoskens. 'She was saying how you started wearing your blouses tighter and curling your hair after they arrived.'

'What?' Poleaxed by this absurd insinuation, Gwenna stared at the old lady. 'She said that?'

'She do say it.' Auntie Nancy narrowed her eyes, inspecting Gwenna's hair, which, for this trip out, she'd brushed to a shine and pinned so it fell behind her ears in natural waves. 'You're some 'ansome maid, Gwenna, and with a farm to your name you're a catch. You don't want to dress up and look too fetching, if you get my meaning.'

'I'm not looking to marry. Or take a lover, as I suppose Hilda's implying.'

Auntie Nancy laughed heartily at Gwenna's outrage. 'Take care, all the same. A jealous woman's anger is a dangerous weapon, and Hilda's mighty enraged with you.'

On the green outside the post office, Gwenna and Lotti admired a clump of primroses. Hilda's spiteful gossip was not going to spoil this little outing. 'They smell sweet, if you bend down close,' she said and demonstrated. To her pleasure, Lotti bent too, putting Rumtopf's nose against the petals.

Gwenna chuckled. 'Is he growing to be a country bear, do you think?'

Sucking her barley sugar, Lotti couldn't have answered even if she'd wished.

The postman pulled up beside them. He got off his bicycle to hand over a large letter, saying, 'That'll save me a pedal up your lane.'

From the crest on the envelope, Gwenna guessed it contained the quarterly magazine of her old school, St Morgan's in Truro. Gwenna always looked forward to the *Morganite*, though with wartime paper shortages it had shrunk to a few folded sheets of news and youthful poetry. Opening it, an idea blossomed. She was fully resolved that the local school would not meet Lotti's needs – she really must reply to the headmaster's note – but what about St Morgan's, with its emphasis on learning and public service?

She found what she was looking for. 'Applications for entry to Year 1 this coming September will close on April 30th.'

The entrance examination was on June 24th. It didn't give much time.

'Not bad news?' asked the postie.

Gwenna explained the situation. Lotti turned eleven this August, just of an age to start at St Morgan's in September. 'But I'd have to get my skates on and apply.' She turned to Lotti, conscious she was talking about her, not to her. 'For St Morgan's, my old school. You'd have to sit an exam. It's not all that hard – after all, I passed it – but it's at the end of June and you'd have to catch up on your English by then.'

The postman smiled at Lotti. 'And say goodbye to Teddy, too, maidie?'

'All in good time,' Gwenna said quickly, seeing Lotti's hand close protectively around Rumtopf's head. As she posted the letter and they turned for home, Gwenna reflected that it was all well and good for Lotti to follow her around at Colvennon, recovering from her ordeal, but sooner or later the school inspector would ask questions.

Freda too would want to know her plans for Lotti's education when they met next week. Realistically, there was little hope of her passing the entrance exam. Which meant a year at St Wenna's. They walked by the school in time to witness the boys' door being flung open for morning playtime. 'Bear pit' described it perfectly, and she recognised two of Hilda and Roddy's lads, scabby-kneed, pushing other boys out of the way as they hurtled towards a climbing frame. Gwenna shuddered. No. Lotti wouldn't thrive. It would have to be private tuition, and then Lotti might try for St Morgan's in a year's time. If she was still in Cornwall, if Freda didn't rule Gwenna an unfit guardian and sweep Lotti back to London.

Worries over Lotti's schooling remained a background irritation, like the crackling of a badly tuned wireless. Gwenna knew she must act, but she couldn't think who to approach for private tuition. Meanwhile, the pressing issue of who would look after Lotti on the day of Miryam's inquest was solved when Ezra offered his wife and granddaughters as child-minders.

'They'll be kind and not tease her, I do promise.'

It took a load off Gwenna's mind. April 13th arrived and relief turned to disaster when one of Ezra's grandsons knocked at the kitchen door.

'Grandad's laid down with a stomach gripe,' the lad told her. 'Up all night, and grandma has it too, and Penny and Becky are worse. Auntie Nancy too. Doctor's been and says they have to stay abed.'

Gwenna's initial reaction was to think, *I can't go to the inquest.* Until the voice of her conscience told her, *You have to.* There was no help for it: Max would have to take Ezra's place. He'd have to give his companions a swift milking lesson and turn his hand to the pigs as well. As for Lotti, she must come to Truro. Sit in the gallery out of sight, and not listen when the coroner announced, 'We are here to determine the cause of death...'

She and Lotti had time to cover the morning milking. Max, who came to help, picked up on her mood and she caught him glancing at her. He was probably wondering why she'd put on one of her father's old waistcoats that morning. Hilda's snide comments had hit home: nobody would look at her now and accuse her of wearing her blouses tighter or dressing provocatively.

'You are upset, Mrs Devoran.'

'No. Well, yes.'

'I may help?'

Gwenna glanced down the parlour to check that Lotti was not listening. Lowering her voice, she told Max that she was due at the inquest for Lotti's mother in a few hours.

He didn't understand 'inquest'.

'A hearing, to discover how somebody died. You do know that Lotti's mother was killed by a train?'

He nodded. Ezra had told him. 'She and Lotti were on the same train as me. As all of us. I did not care to speak of it.'

'No, well, the inquest decides if it was accident or foul play. Or...' Their glances locked and, momentarily, she was seeing the other German. The one named Kurt Fuhrman with eyes blue as a china saucer and cruelty nestling in their depths. 'Or if it was provoked in some way,' she said, 'or even self-induced.'

'Self...' Max frowned. 'Ah, self-killing? You think this of Lotti's mother?' He got up from his stool and Gwenna was sure he wanted to add something, but Lotti was coming towards them, bringing her bucket. Lotti only ever filled her pail halfway, otherwise she struggled to tip the milk into the churn. Max said, '*Guten Morgen, Lotti, guten Morgen, Rumtopf. Wie geht es Euch?*'

Lotti answered, '*Sehr gut, danke schön.*' Well, thank you.

Gwenna felt her insistence on 'English only' wither away. She couldn't leap up waving a flag every time a word of German was exchanged.

Max said to her, 'You will not take Lotti to this *Anfrage*, this...'

'Inquest. I have to; there's nobody to look after her.' She hoped he wouldn't offer himself as a childminder, because she would refuse. He did not offer. He frowned.

'You have not relatives here? It is just only you?'

The way he said it, as if something in her inspired pity, made her snap back, 'I'm not alone in the world. I have my mother-in-law, living in Truro.'

'Cannot she look after Lotti?'

'Well, yes, but...'

'But?'

Let it go.

'You do not like her?'

'I like her very much, for your information.'

He raised his hands, implying, 'Problem solved, then.'

He didn't understand that while she loved her mother-in-law, going back to the house she had shared with Camilla Devoran and Camilla's son was an ordeal. A return to a scene of humiliation where secrets, carefully hidden, waited for her.

18

By a quarter to eleven, Gwenna was buttoning Lotti into her red coat. It was time to leave. She frowned, her hands stilling. 'What was sewn here?'

Light through the landing window showed needle marks on the coat's left-hand breast. Gwenna pulled a wisp of yellow thread from one of the holes.

Lotti wriggled free and went downstairs. Gwenna found her in the kitchen with Rumtopf clamped to her lapel to hide the marks. Had it been a school badge? Was red a school-coat colour on the Continent? Because it wasn't a usual choice over here. From the look on Lotti's face, Gwenna suspected she'd unintentionally probed a scar.

And now she was going to do it again. 'Lotti, I don't think Rumtopf ought to come with us.' Taking a child into court would be questionable enough. 'Let's leave him at home.'

Lotti stared back in a way that always made Gwenna feel helpless. What went on in Lotti's mind at these moments?

At any rate, the child's grip on the bear was unyielding. With a sigh, Gwenna said, 'Very well, let's go.' She was already wearing her best coat, hat and uncomfortable town shoes, scuffed from their encounter with the railway track. She checked there were clean handkerchiefs in her bag, and money too. There would be tea afterwards with Freda, if time permitted. Tea with Freda, Lotti and Rumtopf. It promised to be interesting.

Max was opening the gate to the kitchen yard as they left the house. 'Go in and boil water for yourself,' she invited. He might not feel entitled to use the absent Ezra's Primus stove.

'I do not wish water,' Max said, 'but to speak with you. Before, I could not.' He cast a significant glance at Lotti.

'No time.' Gwenna tapped her watch. 'The bus waits for no man, or woman.'

'Then I walk with you to the road.' He said something in German to Lotti which sounded like: 'Run ahead of us, I need to speak with this lady.'

Lotti did as she was asked. Gwenna sighed yet again. 'Will it make any difference if I say "No German" for the fiftieth time?' Probably not. 'What do you need to tell me?'

'I know a reason why Lotti's mother is killed on the railway track. And I must tell you, so you can tell the court.'

When they arrived at the City Hall on Truro's Boscawen Street, a clerk informed Gwenna that children were not allowed into the courtroom, unless they were part of the formal proceedings.

'I take it she isn't giving evidence, madam?'

'No.' Thank goodness, nobody had suggested that.

'The little maid can sit out here,' said the clerk, indicating the lobby. 'Looks like she's got company.' He winked at the bear in its customary hammock, which was Lotti's cardigan.

'Very well. Would you keep an eye on her?' Max's confession as they walked along the lane had left her shaken, and Gwenna was secretly relieved at the ban on children in court.

At the same time she disliked the thought of Lotti being left alone in unfamiliar surroundings.

'I'll do my best, madam.'

While the clerk wrote her name down on his clipboard, Gwenna looked around in the hope of spotting Freda. Freda arrived early, whatever the occasion. But there was no sign of her. People were starting to arrive, Sergeant Couch among them. He was followed in by WPC Roper.

As Gwenna recognised the dour figure, so did Lotti. Frightened eyes went to the WPC's shin-length skirt and the stout black boots beneath. She reached for Gwenna's hand with trembling fingers. Gwenna thought, *That's it, she can't stay here.*

There was another option and Max had already waved it at her. 'Lotti? We have to find you a safe haven for a few hours and there's only one person I can ask.'

Gwenna's mother-in-law, Camilla Devoran, lived on Lemon Street, which had been raised to elegance in the Georgian era by merchants and seafarers who had made their wealth from Truro's river port.

'You're going to meet Mill,' Gwenna said as they approached a handsome, cream stuccoed house. 'Everyone close to her calls her that and you'll like her.' She spoke through gritted teeth because her shoes had rubbed the skin off the back of her heels in the short walk from City Hall. Vanity again. She should have worn her mid-heel, go-to-chapel shoes today.

She opened an ornate iron gate, hoping Lotti wouldn't be overwhelmed by the proportions of Fendynick House, as she had been the first time she stepped inside. It stood within its own walls, over which spilled an ancient vine. Edward had brought her here as his bride and they'd shared the home with his mother and sister.

'Isn't that the pip in the grape?' Freda had asked at the time.

'Young marrieds ought to have their own space.' Freda's opinion carried some force, as she'd been engaged to Edward before Gwenna, and had broken it off. At the time, Gwenna had taken the comment to be a sign that Freda regretted her decision, only coming to realise later that it was relief at a narrow escape.

That Fendynick still unnerved her showed in the way she hurried Lotti to the front door, and rapped with the brass knocker in nervous Morse code.

The door was opened by an elderly maid who wasn't quick enough to hide her displeasure at the surprise. 'Mrs Devoran! We wasn't expecting you.'

'Hello, Janet. Is my mother-in-law at home?'

'She's in the vegetable garden, planting shallots.' As though that ruled out the possibility of interruption. Janet was a member of what Gwenna privately called the 'Disapprovers' Club', which also included Gwenna's sister-in-law, Angela. The club was formed of those who considered Gwenna Bossinny, farmer's daughter, to have been not good enough to have joined the Devoran clan. Gwenna inquired if Angela was at home.

'Miss Angela is at work, it being a Tuesday, and not expected back until tomorrow.'

Perfect. 'Janet, please tell my mother-in-law I'm here, and in a tearing rush.'

'If you'd care to wait...' Janet's glance fell on Lotti, whose arms were crossed protectively across Rumtopf. 'I'll see if madam is at liberty.'

No time. Gwenna ushered Lotti across the threshold, sweeping past Janet and through to the back of the house. As she went, she saw that hers and Edward's wedding photograph had been removed from a table of family portraits. Remembering how she'd left this house on a miserable winter's day in 1940, twenty-four hours after her father's death, she tightened her mouth.

'Mill, I'm so sorry to impose.' Gwenna hesitated at the

conservatory door, then walked forward to greet the thin woman who had obviously been coming back into the house, stopping to ease off a pair of wellingtons.

Camilla Devoran hopped a moment on one foot. 'Goodness, Gwenna. I thought I heard someone knock. How lovely to see you. Give me a hug.'

Their embrace was onion-scented. Mill removed handfuls of shallot sets from her pinafore pockets, laying them on a metal table. She peeled off her gardening gloves but seemed to have forgotten her hat. Ash-grey hair poked through the crochet and Gwenna recalled Edward saying of this hat, 'Mother, there's a scarecrow somewhere, scratching his bald patch.' At the time, Mill had answered, 'A gardener should never try to outshine her plants.' The comment had summed her up. A gentle matriarch with no pretensions, but also half blind to truths within her own family.

Mill stepped back to look at Gwenna. 'My, you're smart. Have you come for lunch? And who is this wearing such a gorgeous shade of red?'

'Um, this is Lotti. Lotti Gittelman. I wouldn't be asking but I have to be somewhere and, well, I've nobody to look after her.'

'Gittelman? Ah. And you're needed at her mother's... *ahem*.' Mill mouthed the word 'inquest'. 'I read about it in the paper.'

'I can't take her in with me.' Gwenna lowered her voice. 'Anyway, what I'm going to say... she can't hear it.'

'Indeed, no. Let me take off this pinny, then I'm all yours.'

Gwenna glanced upwards, at oblong panes of glass. The grapevine ran through the conservatory, reaching in and out of the top vents. The last time she'd stood under its gnarled arms, she'd been reeling from the news of her father's death from a stroke. Angela had found her in here, distractedly writing a note to Mill. Being Angela, she'd unashamedly read it over Gwenna's shoulder.

'You're leaving us? To see to things at Colvennon, of course. To arrange the funeral, that's understandable, but you're coming back afterwards. Gwenna? It sounds like you're not coming back at all.'

She was not returning, Gwenna had made up her mind. 'I'm needed at Colvennon. It's where I want to be. Actually, I'm leaving Edward.'

Angela's fury had erupted. 'What a pitiful bolter you are, quitting my brother while he's at sea, serving his country. You're not getting away with a cowardly note. Mother!' Angela had called Mill in from another room.

Nothing, not even Mill's pleading that Gwenna take time to think, to see things in perspective, had changed her mind. She should have gone weeks or months ago. Then she'd have been with her father when he needed her. A scouring wind had harried her as she dragged her suitcases to the bus stop. Home to Colvennon to spend her first ever Christmas alone. When she'd grown a little calmer, she had written a second letter to her mother-in-law. An explanation: 'Edward has someone else. I cannot remain married, living a life I no longer believe in.' She'd posted that letter from St Wenna and had heard nothing from Fendynick House for eleven months. Not a word, until news arrived of Edward's death.

'There. Now I'm presentable.' Mill's voice dragged Gwenna back to the present. The pain of rubbed-raw heels flooded in, as well as consciousness of the time.

'Mill, sorry, I really have to run—'

'And you need somebody to take care of this little one?' Mill completed Gwenna's sentence. 'We'd be delighted. Isn't that right, Janet?'

The maid had found them and said grudgingly, 'Yes, madam.'

'We'll begin with tea and crumpets.'

That was too much for Janet. 'They're for later, madam.'

'The sky won't fall in if we eat crumpets at lunchtime and save carrot soup for supper.' Camilla crouched to speak to Lotti. 'Hello, little flower.' To Gwenna she said, 'Off you go, or they might not let you in.'

They embraced again and the hug felt fragile. Camilla had aged in the months since losing her only son. A doubling of guilt made Gwenna blurt out, 'I've no right, barging in after staying away so long.'

'You're a farmer, dear. We understand.'

If 'we' included Angela, Gwenna doubted it. Her sister-in-law hadn't delivered the news of Edward's death to Colvennon but had forwarded the stark Admiralty telegram to the post office in St Wenna. Gwenna had learned she was a widow a day after everyone else, and from the hands of a messenger boy. She gave Lotti a cuddle and promised to be as quick as she could.

'I wish Angela's motor car were here, so I could give you a lift,' Mill said. 'She's driving her employer today, on constituency business. Always busy, if it's not being hand-maiden to our revered member of parliament, it's her "Make Do and Mend" club. Have you heard of it? Don't answer that. Off you trot, Gwenna darling, we'll do fabulously.'

Mill said to Lotti in credible German, 'What a lovely coat, and what is this handsome fellow's name... did you say "Rum-topf"? Isn't that a kind of dessert? Let's see if he likes crumpets.'

Gwenna cried silently as she hurried back to Boscawen Street, and not because of the agony of tight shoes.

19

To Gwenna's relief, the inquest had been slightly delayed. A clerk directed her to a seat at the back of the court as the bespectacled coroner concluded his opening remarks. They were gathered 'to ascertain the circumstances leading to the tragic death of Miryam Gittelman, aged thirty-four. To determine whether death was caused by accident or was, in some way, intentional.'

I know how it happened. Max Reiner told me. He should be here, giving evidence. Taking a handkerchief from her bag, Gwenna blotted her cheeks. She looked for Freda and saw a plain hat and a coil of netted black hair. Otherwise, it was a sea of men's suits and nearly white collars. An all-male jury exuded an air of solemn anticipation and the air was sticky with the smell of hair cream.

After a police surgeon had given his evidence, Freda was next to be sworn in at the witness stand. Gwenna recognised her friend's 'utility suit'. It was the one Freda had got married in. Gwenna, as chief bridesmaid, had walked into Chelsea Town Hall behind that angular, grey ensemble. She remembered Norbert turning, his face a mixed platter of adoration and awe. Mind you, Freda could wear a horse blanket and make it look like Paris couture.

Having asked Freda to state her full name and address, the coroner invited her to explain her relationship to the deceased.

'Friend and protector,' came the clear reply. 'I am a Quaker, a member of the Society of Friends, and trustee of an organisation with links in Europe. Over the past five years, we have helped endangered people escape Germany and other occupied territories.' Freda detailed Miryam Gittelman's personal history, some of which Gwenna already knew. But not all. Soon, she too was leaning forward intently.

'Like her husband, Miryam was born and raised in Berlin,' Freda said in her mezzo voice. 'She married Leopold Gittelman, whose family ran a men's outfitters in the Jewish quarter. They had one child, a daughter, Lotti. In November 1938, their shop was vandalised, along with others. On the same night, their local synagogue was destroyed.' Freda paused, composing herself. 'Afterwards, some Gittelman family members fled to Norway, which at the time was a safe haven.'

Norway? That's what Freda had put in her hurried letter. Gwenna had read it as 'nowhere'.

Freda was asked if the deceased had also taken refuge in Norway. Her answer was, 'No. Miryam and Leopold stayed behind in Berlin as the tailoring business was their only source of income. They regretted it in the weeks before war broke out. Herr Gittelman was attacked while out delivering a suit to a customer. He was beaten so badly, he lost the sight of an eye and couldn't work after that. Miryam, who had a millinery business, lost her customers. They were afraid, hungry, with no choice but to leave.'

German Quakers acquired visas for them, Freda explained, and the family fled to Paris, 'Where they re-established their business, from their flat. Their daughter went to school but I need not tell anybody what happened next.' She did have to tell them. The coroner requested it. 'In June 1940, the Germans occupied northern France and the Gittelmans were again in desperate peril.'

They survived two years, keeping their heads down. But in the spring of 1942, it became law for all Jews, whether French citizens or immigrants, to wear a yellow star on their clothing. From that moment, they were targets. Herr Gittelman was arrested on his way home from visiting a cloth merchant. His whereabouts and fate were still unknown, Freda said. 'His wife and young daughter saw him dragged away.'

Papa, nein! Papa, nein!

The nightmare shrieks made absolute sense to Gwenna now. Poor little girl, still calling him back.

Freda continued: 'The following day, Miryam was warned by a neighbour that the Gestapo was in the street. Rounding up the stragglers.' She said it with angry contempt. 'They got out with moments to spare.' Freda's charity had already supplied Miryam with the name of a sympathiser who kept a safe house on the Brittany coast. 'They got there, though it took them a month. From the safe house, Miryam and her child were taken by van to a remote cove and put on a fishing boat. That's how they reached our shores and eventually arrived in London, at my door.'

The coroner asked her to explain how Miryam Gittelman came to be in Cornwall as a passenger from London on the Riviera Express.

'That was my doing,' Freda acknowledged. 'When she came into my care, Miryam was in a dreadful state. Their escape from the Breton safe house had been traumatic, as they'd been pulled up at a German roadblock and the van driver had to race away in a hail of bullets. One of their rescuers was killed in front of them. Miryam and her daughter were then horribly seasick on the crossing. We muddled on, me teaching them English. Lotti enrolled in a local school. Things seemed to be improving, until one day they were strolling in a park near where I live and were accosted by a man who heard Miryam speaking and picked up on her accent. He shouted and in panic she answered in German.' Within moments, Miryam and Lotti were surrounded by a mob, and the police fetched. 'Miryam believed the Gestapo had come to take her. She had a breakdown. I felt that both would thrive better as far from London as could be managed. I wrote to a good friend, Mrs Devoran.' Freda located Gwenna in her seat, and gave a slight nod.

'You asked this friend to take in mother and daughter?' the coroner prompted.

'Yes, and Gwenna – Mrs Devoran – readily agreed. I made the arrangements.' Freda's voice lost its confident ring. 'I should have travelled with them. I should never have sent Miryam alone with her child and a mere letter of introduction. It was a mistake.'

'You could not have foreseen events, Mrs Fincham,' the coroner said kindly.

'But I should have. What's the point of doing good works if you forget the people you're meant to be helping? I am so very busy, but it is no excuse.'

Freda then answered questions intended to establish Miryam Gittelman's state of mind on the day of her death. She was adamant. The Miryam she knew was delicate and prone to panic, but she was of sound mind and not, categorically *not*, suicidal.

Next up was Sergeant Couch, who described the telephone call to the police station at four fifty on the afternoon of March 23rd. 'Person struck by a train at Truro, on the up-line.' He had sent a young constable to follow up, and now wished heartily that he'd gone himself.

The court fell silent as that constable haltingly described what had been found of the person named later as Miryam

Gittelman. Gwenna closed her eyes and pictured Lotti safe at Fendynick House. Thank God she was spared this.

When the mail train driver's turn came, Gwenna pitied him. He recounted the moment he'd seen Miryam Gittelman on the track, apparently heading back to the Riviera Express. Her shoe had caught in a rail, he believed, and she'd frozen in fear. He'd applied the brakes, 'Hard as I could, and sounded my horn. I keep seeing her face.' He broke down and Gwenna fumbled for her handkerchief.

Next, a man who had been travelling that day stated that he had witnessed a woman and a girl in a red coat jump from the stationary Riviera Express, and recalled shouting, 'Get off the line!' The pair had leapt directly onto the tracks, he said, struggling across to the platform opposite. The child had followed the adult woman, who appeared to be fleeing something. After a minute or so, the woman had climbed back down onto the track, leaving the child behind.

Gwenna listened with fierce attention. This reflected what Mrs Andrews, the postmistress, had said about Miryam abandoning Lotti on the platform. The gossips had implied that Miryam had deliberately jumped back onto the rails to put herself "under the train" which Gwenna had not believed then, and now had even stronger reason to refute.

The witness on the stand suggested that, from her strange behaviour, the deceased must have left something behind on the London train.

The coroner wanted clarification. 'She was definitely heading back towards the train she'd exited moments before?'

'Absolutely, sir,' the man replied. 'I saw her. It was on her return trip across the line that she was struck. She appeared to falter, and perhaps her shoe had indeed got stuck. But in my opinion, she didn't stand and wait for the oncoming train. I suspect she did not hear it until too late.'

Gwenna twisted her fingers. Though she was dreading her

moment on the stand, she knew it was vital that she speak clearly and calmly. Miryam and Lotti had escaped the Riviera Express for a reason. Max had told her what that reason was. Would she be able to get her words out succinctly and factually like Freda?

Somebody was tapping her arm.

'Madam, you're being called.'

Gwenna rose, her heart colliding with her ribs. Her hand on the Bible, she gave her name and address, and at the coroner's invitation explained her reason for being at Truro railway station at the time of Miryam Gittelman's death. 'To meet them. As Mrs Fincham has stated, I had offered her and her daughter a home. I—' She swallowed. 'I was going to take them back to Colvennon Farm.'

'And did you meet them?' she was asked.

'No. The first I saw of either of them was when I spotted Lotti on the railway track. I jumped down to fetch her off.'

'You rescued the child, Mrs Devoran, in the teeth of an oncoming train.'

Gwenna stared at the coroner. 'I don't know, sir.'

'It says so in the stationmaster's report of the incident. You may be in line for a medal, Mrs Devoran.'

'I don't want one.' Gwenna jerked in revulsion as, for some reason, Max Reiner's iron cross came to mind. 'I acted... You would have done the same, anyone would.'

'But you saw neither Mrs Gittelman nor her child on the London Riviera Express.'

Gwenna described her search. 'I couldn't understand why they hadn't got off, and I was allowed on board to look. I ended up in the third-class dining car, which has no through-corridor. There was no way for them to go further up the train, so I thought they might be hiding in the lavatories.'

'Hiding, why?'

'Because...' Gwenna paused. Not for effect but because she

couldn't control her voice.

'Mrs Devoran?'

'Because a little bit of Nazi Germany came to Cornwall that day.'

The coroner invited her to go on.

'There were German POWs on the same train, being brought to the camp at Tregallon. I suspect the men had been fighting. Some had blood on their faces.'

'How was this relevant to Mrs Gittelman's situation?' the coroner wanted to know.

'I believe that Miryam Gittelman jumped with her daughter onto the tracks because of them. The prisoners had boarded at Plymouth, the carriage next to hers, and I think she took her daughter to the dining car when their voices reached them. You heard Mrs Fincham say how Miryam secretly feared the Germans would invade Britain as they had France? I think there came a moment when she believed they had.'

There was a buzz around the court. Gwenna caught Freda's eye, saw the astonishment in the arch of her friend's brow. The coroner was less impressed.

'This edges towards speculation, Mrs Devoran,' he said. 'You cannot know the deceased's state of mind and you have already stated that you did not meet her. No conversation took place.'

'No,' Gwenna acknowledged. 'But I have been given facts. From one of those POWs.'

The rumble around the room made the coroner call for silence. Gwenna was invited to explain. She told the court that three POWs had been assigned to her farm, as labourers, and that one of them, an officer, had passed on something vital.

'They were escorted off the train shortly after it pulled in at Truro and were marched a little way up the platform. Then they were brought to a stop as policemen cleared a path to ensure they passed unmolested to the exit.'

Or to protect your citizens from us, Max had said to her earlier, a sardonic twist to his mouth.

Gwenna told the court, 'My informant then realised that one of his comrades, a lower-ranking officer by the name of Fuhrman, was staring into the dining car at a woman within, and at her child.'

Max had noticed how frightened both the woman and child had appeared. Later, he'd recognised Lotti as the child. Gwenna related this.

'Mrs Gittelman and her daughter appeared visibly distressed?' asked the coroner.

'The word my informant used was *starr*. He couldn't think of the English equivalent, but I believe it to mean "still". In other words, paralysed with fear. He ordered his subordinate to turn around. To leave them alone.'

'How very gracious of your informant,' offered the coroner, heavily. 'Did he see Mrs Gittelman leave her seat and attempt to escape this unpleasant scrutiny?'

'No. He was marched off at that point, but it's obvious, isn't it? It was that man Fuhrman staring at them from a couple of feet away that pushed Miryam over the edge. She had to escape. I don't know why, when she reached the safety of the opposite platform, she then turned back. But I am convinced she abandoned the Riviera Express to escape those she had learned to fear most.'

The coroner chewed over her evidence, eyes lowered. He came to a decision. 'You offer us a reasonable explanation for Mrs Gittelman's impulsive action in leaving the train, putting herself and her child in lethal danger. I am afraid that what you have told us is only hearsay. Unprovable and, without corroboration, inadmissible. However, I believe that every person present will acknowledge your brave conduct in rescuing Mrs Gittelman's daughter, to whom this court extends its deepest sympathy.'

20

The café by the cathedral served tea from a pot made to commemorate Queen Victoria's diamond jubilee forty-six years earlier. The sight of it was mildly comforting to Gwenna, who was still shaking from her public ordeal. It reminded her that life trudged on, that all tragedies eventually sank under the weight of time.

Freda ordered scones whose speckled appearance suggested they'd been baked with grated carrot to make up for a lack of sugar and sultanas. A curl of margarine replaced the local butter they'd have enjoyed before the war.

'I wonder if we'll ever taste clotted cream again,' Freda sighed.

'One day. No war lasts forever.' The café was a little chilly, the nearby cathedral throwing its shadow at the window.

'What about the Hundred Years War?' Freda said.

'Who was that between?'

Freda couldn't remember.

'We weren't great scholars, were we?' Gwenna kept the banter going, delaying the moment they discussed the revelations she'd put before the court. '"Effortlessly middling" was the summing-up on my report one year. We added scant lustre to St Morgan's.'

Freda added milk to her tea. 'Still, we've done all right.'

'You have. You're one of the "great and the good", married to a rising academic star and heading for the honours list, I shouldn't wonder. What do I do? Run a very small farm, and bash heads with the Min of Ag. No children—'

'You're not alone in that.'

'You still have a chance at motherhood, whereas mine is blown.'

Freda reached across the table and touched Gwenna's wedding ring. 'Widowhood isn't a life sentence. What happened to you has happened to thousands of other women. You married a seafarer.'

'No – I married a professional musician who was not suited to the rigors of matrimony and joined the navy to get away from me. Or so I grew to suspect.'

'You wouldn't have married him had you known?'

That was a loaded question, from Freda. 'If I had known,' Gwenna said carefully, 'I would have made different choices. As you did.'

Freda either did not hear, or chose to ignore, the subtext. 'You're in your early thirties. There'll be someone else, bound to be.'

'I don't see how and I'm not sure I want another husband. I wanted a baby, Freda. Whenever Edward came home on leave, which wasn't often, I was a woman on a mission, doomed to fail.'

Freda couldn't ignore the cry of pain, but offered no comfort beyond a quick headshake. 'Perhaps this is a discussion for a more private location.'

Gwenna wasn't ready to be silenced. 'Farming fills my life but doesn't fill my heart. Lotti does, though.'

'How can she? You've known her such a short time.'

'Cows lick their calves the moment they're born. Within seconds, they're inseparable.'

'Calves... I hardly think... really, Gwenna.'

Telling herself to hold back on the farming imagery, Gwenna hacked her scone in half, spreading margarine followed by jam so pale in colour, its principal ingredient had to be turnip. 'I want to make up for what has happened to her.'

'That's a tall order, though nobody doubts your good intent.'

'By loving her, Freda.' By a knife-twist of fate, Miryam and Lotti had been confronted by their worst nightmare in what was supposed to be a safe haven. A Nazi had stared unblinking at them from the other side of a train window. She'd not informed the court of the insults that Fuhrman had mouthed through the glass. In his stilted way, Max had told her.

'He knows somehow that she is Jewish.' Fuhrman had been born and raised in Berlin, so perhaps he'd met Miryam before. He might even have ordered suits from her husband, Max had suggested. Unlikely, but possible. Gwenna had repeated none of this in court, fearing it might draw Lotti into the frame. The police might ask her to identify Fuhrman. Gwenna's voice shook as she told Freda, 'I'll do anything to give Lotti the life she deserves.'

'You want a child, I understand. But she's not yours, Gwenna.'

'Then whose child is she, Freda?' Other customers glanced their way. Gwenna moderated her tone. 'She has no parents, unless her father is alive somewhere.'

'It's impossible to say. Jews arrested in France were almost all deported.'

'To Germany?'

'And other countries where the Germans are in charge, such as Poland and Czechoslovakia.'

'What happens to them then?'

'Most are never heard of again,' Freda said flatly. 'The able-bodied are worked to death in labour camps. The weak, the old and very young are allowed to die, or killed in mass executions. From the information that reaches me, I know that thousands of Jews like Leopold Gittelman have been murdered.'

'Murdered,' Gwenna echoed. 'How do you know?'

Mostly from Americans allowed out of Germany in prisoner-swaps, Freda explained. 'The American press reports what's going on more freely than our newspapers, though our politicians know the truth. For the most part, they suppress it.'

'You said so in your letter.'

'Yes. Hundreds of thousands killed. I dread to think what we'll discover when news flows across Europe again, Gwenna.'

Freda's eyes glistened with such fierce pain, Gwenna looked away. She felt so ignorant, tucked safely in her peaceful corner of the world. Was one of the murdered 'weak ones' Lotti's father? She asked, 'Do you think all of Lotti's family are dead?'

Freda couldn't say. 'Remember, her grandmother, aunt and uncle made it to Norway.'

Which the Germans had occupied since 1940, Gwenna said miserably. 'Wherever they are, alive or not, right now, Lotti has only me.'

'And me.'

'You said in court, your work consumes you. You save many lives, Freda, while I have this one precious life to care for. Don't take her from me.'

'We have to think what's best for Lotti.' Freda bit sparingly into her scone. She was one of those people who ate only from bodily necessity. 'In your letter, you mentioned her mute state. Nightmares every night. Perhaps Cornwall simply isn't the answer.'

'Not nightmares every night. Not since...' Gwenna searched back in her mind. 'Not since the 5th of April, nearly ten days ago.'

'Eight days. You were never strong at maths. Gwenna, dear,

all we asked was that you give two refugees a home. Nobody expected you to be plunged into this horror. It's too much.'

'It's not. I can cope...' Gwenna heard her voice rising again and lowered it. 'Lotti's settled at Colvennon and I know where I want to send her to school.'

'Oh?'

'Our old haunt. St Morgan's.'

'They've offered a place?'

Gwenna shook her head. 'Not yet. I'm going to get private tuition for her.'

'How will that work, if she won't speak?'

Gwenna waved this away. 'Honestly, Freda, if you could only see her around the farm. She's firm friends with Josephine.'

'Josephine?'

'My cat.'

'Cat. I see.'

Gwenna pressed on, feverishly itemising Lotti's progress, feeling Freda's growing cynicism. 'She loves the cows, and they love her.' Damn. She'd mentioned cows again. 'They're at ease with her and she's learning to milk. Not everyone can do that.'

'No.' Freda shuddered.

'And doing it beautifully. She's a sensitive, loving child.'

'Cows are dangerous.'

'Mine aren't.'

'No? I well remember the dear creatures following us across the field once. We were going for a picnic and they decided to join in. You ordered me not to run.'

'One should never run near cows.'

'It didn't matter how often you told me they only wanted to be friends, they scared me.'

'Lotti isn't scared.'

'I envied your bravery.'

'You envied me?' That was unexpected.

'I'm glad Lotti has "the touch".' Freda finally smiled. 'I

wanted her to thrive with you. Nothing was further from my hopes than this awful tragedy. But it happened and we have to deal with reality.'

Gwenna wouldn't allow the past tense to take hold. 'She *is* thriving. Lotti's speaking now.' Honesty forced Gwenna to add, 'A word here and there. And mostly in German.'

This was not something Freda wanted to hear. 'Her mother wouldn't allow a word of German to pass between them. I'm disturbed to think Miryam's wishes are being flouted.'

'I wouldn't dream... You said in court that Miryam spoke German under stress.' Gwenna felt under cross-examination, and doing badly. 'It got her into trouble, you said.'

'Yes...' Freda paused, taken back to an uncomfortable moment in the past. 'That is rather my point. Miryam lapsed into German – and sometimes Yiddish – when she was badly frightened. That's why she was so determined Lotti shouldn't copy her. She'd tell Lotti to be silent, rather than give her origins away—' Something in Gwenna's face made her break off. 'What have I said?'

'Yiddish, that's it!' Gwenna explained. 'When that horrible man, Fuhrman, stared through the train window at her, Miryam might have blurted out something in Yiddish, in fear. If he could lip-read, or heard through the glass, it explains how he knew she was Jewish.'

'Poor Miryam.' Freda sighed. 'The fact that Lotti's speaking German now suggests that she too is afraid. Dr Kleinman must get to the bottom of it. We'll get her an appointment, soon as we can.'

This was Gwenna's greatest fear, that Freda and her army of professionals would crush her hopes. What claim did she have to Lotti, other than good intentions and messy yearnings of motherhood? She asked, 'Who exactly is this doctor?'

Albert Kleinman, it transpired, was a leading child psychologist.

'He has worked with many war-scarred children,' Freda said, 'with excellent results.'

Gwenna had lifted her scone to her mouth but couldn't take a bite. 'You mustn't take her away, Freda. I need her as much as she needs me.'

'Too much sentiment is not always best.' Freda touched Gwenna's wrist, a tender gesture that stung like a burn.

Tears sprang to Gwenna's eyes. 'Neither you nor I have been blessed with children, but it doesn't mean we have no capacity to care.'

The way Freda withdrew her hand told Gwenna she'd touched a raw spot. *Freda wants a child as badly as I do.*

Freda spoke. 'She's in trauma and that's an area which, with the best will in the world, you have no experience.'

Gwenna couldn't argue.

'Locked in this state, one clever little girl could grow up to be a damaged woman. You could end up with an accomplished milkmaid, Gwenna, when the world might have had a surgeon, a lawyer or an inspiring teacher. This "informant" of yours, this POW – did I hear right, that he's one of your farm labourers?'

Having stated as much in court, Gwenna couldn't avoid full disclosure. 'Yes. They were provided by the powers that be. I couldn't send them back.'

'No doubt, but how can Lotti thrive surrounded by the very people she fears most?'

What could Gwenna say? Explain that Lotti appeared to like Max Reiner and sought him out? Freda wouldn't understand. Gwenna didn't understand it herself. She said weakly, 'I try to keep them at a distance.'

'Try? Do you succeed?'

'Not always. It's difficult when we're all outdoors. It'll be different when Lotti starts her lessons.'

'When. If. Should, could.' Freda glanced at her watch. 'Ah – the court session will be over by now.' She asked the waitress if the café owned a telephone. Could she pay to use it? She went into a back room, leaving Gwenna staring out of the window, wondering how Lotti was getting on. The cathedral spires reminded her of ice cream cones, glazed with sunlight. Ice creams in the park, a walk along a beach, gathering seashells for necklaces. That was the way to build trust with a child. Simple joys. The rest would follow. Max, Jürgen and Walther were less of a threat to Lotti than an abrupt relocation to London. In her opinion, but who listened to that?

Gwenna slipped off her shoes and massaged her sore heels. The blood had dried, fastening her stockings to her flesh.

Freda returned. 'Verdict is in. Death by misadventure.'

'Who did you call?'

'The local paper. I wrote articles for them in my last year at school. Remember? Moral opinion and nature notes. Anyway, I saw their court reporter in the room.'

Freda had obviously kept her connections in the town. Gwenna asked, 'What exactly does "misadventure" mean?'

'That Miryam took a risk in crossing the tracks and was in part responsible for her own death.'

'It wasn't her fault! She was intimidated by Fuhrman. Didn't anyone listen?'

'They listened, but proving it would take resources the court and the police don't have. Not with war raging and half the manpower elsewhere. It's over, Gwenna, and the important thing is, there is no implication Miryam deliberately harmed herself. Finally, she can be decently buried.'

The waitress brought their bill. When the woman had returned to her counter, Freda said, 'That's something I wish to be involved in.'

'The funeral?' Gwenna nodded. Of course. She was dissatisfied with the inquest verdict. It left questions unanswered.

Freda picked up the bill, saying, 'This is on me.'

Gwenna took out her own purse. 'You're my guest while in

Cornwall.' She placed silver and copper coins on a plate. It was time to leave. The need to be with Lotti was suddenly all-consuming. As she got up to go, her blood-crusted stockings tore loose from her heels. Hearing her intake of breath, Freda looked up. She'd been putting down a tip.

'What's the matter, monthly pains?'

'Tight shoes. I had to run this morning in irrational footwear. When are you travelling back to London, Freda?'

'Not tonight. Tonight, I'm only going as far as Exeter, visiting Norbert's sister who lives there, and insisted on it. I'd have preferred to stay with you, then I could see Lotti for myself and assess her well-being. Actually...' Freda gave Gwenna a speculative look. 'Shall I pop back to the farm with you? I expect someone's taking care of her while you're here.'

'Um... somebody is taking care of her, yes.'

'And I don't have to get an Exeter train much before half six as Norbert's sister keeps very late hours. There's time for a flying visit to see the little one.' Freda must have felt Gwenna's confusion because she prompted, 'Lotti *is* at Colvennon?'

'No. She's with my mother-in-law.' The admission was dragged out of her.

'In Lemon Street? That's only a couple of minutes away. Why didn't you say?' Freda tucked her arm through Gwenna's as they left the café. 'It'll be lovely to see dear Mill again. Will Angela be there?'

'I don't think so. She's being chauffeur to her employer and isn't expected back till tomorrow.'

'Good. I can assess Lotti's emotional state without interruption. Does she have a change of clothes with her?'

'Lotti? No, why?'

'In case I decide to take her away with me this evening.'

21

At the door of Fendynick House, Janet beamed at Freda. 'Why, Miss Helyer, how very nice to see you.'

'I'm Mrs Fincham now,' Freda replied. 'Janet, you've hardly changed.'

'Nonsense, but it's nice to be flattered. How smart you look. I can always tell when a lady has shopped in London.'

'It's all "utility", I'm afraid. This outfit could have been bought anywhere.'

'Ah, but you always did know how to make a simple thing look special. Not everyone can do that.' Janet frowned as Gwenna kicked off her shoes in the hallway. 'I've just polished the floors, Mrs Devoran.'

'Sorry.' Gwenna twisted round, assessing the damage to her hose.

'Lordy, look at those silk stockings, all spoiled at the heel.' Janet was scandalised.

'It's divine punishment for vanity,' Gwenna told her. 'Freda, stay here. I'll find Mill and Lotti.' She feared the first meeting. What if Lotti screamed or stared silently? Or worse, ran sobbing into Freda's arms, begging to be rescued? 'You might wait for us in the drawing room.'

Janet ruined things by saying, 'Madam is in the conservatory with the child. She'll be bowled over to see you Miss Hel— Mrs Fincham, sorry.'

Freda set off. She needed no directions, having been a frequent guest at Fendynick as Edward's fiancée.

Trying not to slip in her stockinged feet, Gwenna indulged in a bitter smile. How was it that Freda had broken off her engagement to Edward, yet remained a favourite with Janet? It came down to timing, of course. Freda had made her bolt before the big day. She'd seen what Gwenna had not.

The conservatory was a bowl of late afternoon sunshine. The bombing of the hospital the previous August had damaged buildings throughout the town, and this time Gwenna noticed cracks in some of the side panes. They had been repaired with criss-cross tape. The grapevine was coming into sappy bud. Mill and Lotti sat bathed in the greenish light it cast, chairs drawn up to the metal table. They were sewing, heads bent over their work.

It took Camilla Devoran several seconds to realise they were there, and who was standing next to Gwenna. She blinked. 'Freda, well I never. You were in court, I suppose. How went it?'

Freda looked at Lotti. 'It will be in the papers, but today draws a line. I hope you're well, Mill.'

'Oh, passing fair. Old age is wonderful, I've yet to hear anyone say.'

Giving a faint smile, Freda regarded Lotti. Rumtopf, on his back on the table, was wearing new red trousers. 'Lotti, dearest, how are you? I'm sure you recognise me.'

Lotti continued stitching, her hand moving up and down in placid rhythm.

Mill said in German, 'Look up and see who's here, Lotti.'

Freda cleared her throat. 'English, please, Mill. It's our rule.'

'*Our* rule?' Mill wordlessly consulted Gwenna.

Caught in cross-currents she didn't much like, Gwenna explained. 'I banned German at home, Mill. I know I didn't say so earlier, but it's hard to insist on it when German is all Lotti will speak.' She gave Freda a nervous grin. 'As I already mentioned, sometimes I have to allow it for practical reasons. Though definitely not outside in the street. Never in public.'

'You shouldn't allow it at all.' Freda was stern. 'Children need clear, consistent boundaries. All the studies say so.'

Chastened, Gwenna agreed while silently adding, *Try standing in my shoes for a day. Then talk about your consistent boundaries.*

All this time, Lotti's gaze moved from Gwenna to Freda. Without warning, she dropped the fabric she was stitching and pushed back her chair. Slowly, she came towards them.

'Sweetheart.' Freda bent her knees and opened her arms. But at the last moment, Lotti changed direction and threw herself against Gwenna's waist.

'*Tante Gwenna, wo warst Du?*'

'Oh, darling.' Gwenna crouched down and pulled Lotti into her arms. 'I had to go to an important place but I knew you'd be all right here.' She hugged Lotti, then led her to the table, picking up the discarded needlework. 'You did this?' It was a sailor shirt, cut from petticoat cotton. 'I love Rumtopf's cherry-red trousers too.'

Freda watched them, her expression untranslatable.

The bear's missing eye was now disguised by a piratical black velvet disc. 'How clever of you.'

Lotti outlined the patch with her finger. '*Ja, genau wie Papa.*'

'Like your daddy?'

Freda had told the court that Lotti's father had lost the sight of an eye after being attacked. Was Lotti attached to Rumtopf because he reminded her of her father? Certainly, she guarded the bear like a treasure. And yet she'd left him on the train at the moment of crisis.

Freda approached and took the sailor shirt from Gwenna. She inspected the stitching. 'Very neat. Mill, is this Lotti's work?'

'It is indeed. This girl is a genius. I was assembling this little item' – Mill showed Freda and Gwenna a waistcoat she was making from black and yellow tweed – 'and Lotti indicated that I'd attached the facings to the wrong side.'

'Her parents were craftspeople, so it's no surprise.' Freda held out her hand to Lotti. 'Do you remember me?'

Lotti nodded. She stepped back a pace and dropped a neat curtsey. '*Guten Abend, Tante Freda.*'

A flush touched Freda's smooth cheeks. 'Aunt, not *Tante*. And no need to be so formal, my dear.' She added for Gwenna and Mill's benefit, 'Her mother taught her to be mannerly. I never demanded curtsies, I assure you.'

'I know you wouldn't,' said Gwenna. 'It seems Lotti has regressed to an earlier phase of her life. Perhaps to when all seemed safe and normal.'

'And we must bring her out of it.' Freda regained her poise. 'It's clear that you and she have formed a bond, but I'm not convinced it's to her advantage.'

'But why not?' Gwenna just wanted to get Lotti home to Colvennon, away from Freda's appraisal. When Mill invited them to take tea, she hastily explained they'd just drunk a potful.

Freda, with time in hand before her train, was happy to retire to the drawing room. 'I need to have a proper chat with Lotti, after all.'

'In English?' Mill asked mischievously.

'In English,' Freda replied firmly.

Sitting at one end of a sofa, Gwenna tried not to fidget or look at the clock. Janet brought in the tea tray, then pulled down the blinds against the lowering sun.

'I'll pour, Janet,' Mill said. 'Don't wait on us.' When the maid had gone, she turned to Gwenna. 'Lotti was bereft when you left.'

'So was I,' Gwenna admitted. 'Yet she seemed so content when I came back.'

'Well, I took her for a walk around the garden and showed her the toad who lives under a bucket, and the frogspawn in the pond. I couldn't remember the German for either frog or toad, but I do a very passable croak, and I jumped around pretending to be an amphibian.' Mill addressed the next comment to Freda. 'No child can resist an adult making a fool of herself. After that, we went inside for tea and crumpets. Golden syrup on top, and that cheered her up.'

'It would.' Gwenna smiled.

'I insisted Janet lay a place for Rumtopf and that's when I noticed his dolorous state.'

'He got singed and had to be clipped out, like an old pony at the end of winter.'

'Singed how?' Freda had said little since they'd sat down. She now looked distinctly alarmed.

'By accident.' Gwenna wasn't going to explain that she'd thrown Rumtopf into the stove, then dragged him out again.

Mill cut in. 'He's been through the wars, no doubt of it. After we'd been frogs again in the garden, I fetched my sewing chest and cut out new clothes from scraps. Lotti quickly took over. The afternoon sun comes in very low through these windows so we retired to the conservatory. We chatted as we worked and Lotti was good enough to overlook the shortcomings in my German.'

'I must point out the danger of encouraging Lotti to speak that language.' Freda's complexion was still high.

'Surely, any language is better than no language,' Mill suggested.

'I'm really not sure that's true.'

'Oh, come off it.' Gwenna had reached her limit. Freda might be married to a child educationalist, and be a thoroughly good person, but she didn't know everything. 'Once Lotti's found her tongue, her English will flow again. I'm convinced of it.'

'I really would like Dr Kleinman to see her.' Freda leaned forward in her chair. 'Lotti dearest, would you like to come back to London with me and sleep in your old bedroom?' Lotti did not reply. Lowering her voice to coaxing sweetness, Freda repeated the offer.

Lotti's head slowly moved side to side. '*Nein, danke, Tante Freda.*'

Mill chuckled. 'You cannot argue with that.'

'She's saying what she thinks we want to hear.' Freda's cheeks were now carnation pink.

'Balderdash,' was Mill's opinion. 'One shining attribute of this child is that she says exactly what she thinks. Lotti doesn't need to be taken away to be poked and analysed. She needs occupation. She needs school. She needs friends.'

Gwenna agreed eagerly.

Freda kept her voice reasonable. 'With the greatest respect, Mill, I am responsible for this child's welfare.'

'Are you? With the loss of her mother, it would seem to me that the child is somewhat in limbo. A ward of state, most likely.'

'I am her guardian.'

'All right.' Mill smiled placidly. 'I still say Lotti made her choice when she ran to Gwenna. Our choices deserve respect, don't you think?'

'Not always—' Freda began but Mill ploughed over her.

'Whether it's the choice of a child who wants to feel safe, or a grown woman who has decided she's in love with another man.'

Freda gasped. 'I won't pretend not to know what you mean.'

'No, you won't. What I always admired most in you, Freda, was your unswerving honesty. This moment calls for a little more of it. Don't upend this child's life merely so you can stamp your authority on the situation. Stop being jealous of Gwenna.'

'Jealous? I'm not!'

'No? After all, she went through with her marriage to my son.'

Freda looked as though she was about to say something long stored-up, but Gwenna put a stop to it by jumping to her feet. 'Freda, will you give me until summer to prove I can provide a wonderful home for Lotti?'

'Summer?'

'Yes. If by August Lotti is failing to thrive, I will bring her back to London myself. I have plans – I think I said. Private tuition and language lessons. I agree with you wholeheartedly, she must begin speaking English again. Let me try, please.'

Freda pulled herself together. She turned over Gwenna's offer with agonising slowness. 'August?'

'Say, by her birthday, which is on the 23rd.'

'July.' Freda was still visibly upset. That accusation of jealousy had hit its mark but she had never been given to malice, and this showed itself now. 'My birthday's July 3rd and it's on a Saturday. Bring Lotti to London and we'll have a tea party. Then we will decide how to proceed.'

Gwenna expressed her gratitude. In her haste to thank Mill for her hospitality, and get Lotti away before Freda changed her mind, she failed to check they had everything they'd come with.

·　·　·

Walking with Lotti to the garden gate, her feet swollen from sitting an hour in her stockings, Gwenna wished there were black cabs in Truro. A ride home would be a blessing. She jumped as Lotti gave a scream so piercing, birds shot up from the trees.

'Rumtopf!' Lotti tore back towards the house, Gwenna in pursuit.

Mill was at the front door, holding the bear. Lotti seized him so hard the stuffing inside him creaked. Freda came to the door. She and Gwenna exchanged a glance and while Mill calmed Lotti down, Gwenna went up to her friend and whispered, 'Friends again?'

'Of course. We both want the best for Lotti, only we see it differently.' Freda's gaze went to Lotti. 'Will she ever let go of that bear? Gwenna, what is bothering you now?'

'It's just come to me.' Gwenna shot a glance at Lotti, who was clutching her bear as if defying the world to take him. 'Lotti left Rumtopf in the dining car of the Riviera Express in their panic to escape, and when they reached the opposite platform, she realised it. Miryam went back across the railway track to fetch him and caught the heel of her shoe in the stones, or between the rails. Maybe she didn't hear the oncoming train, or perhaps she did and couldn't do a thing about it.'

Freda looked shocked, then doubtful. 'Miryam had more sense than to risk her life for a stuffed toy.'

'Something sent her back towards a railway carriage she'd fled from. It wouldn't be anything trivial – a glove or a half-read novel.' Mill was helping Lotti button Rumtopf inside her coat. Tears on Lotti's cheek spoke of raw distress. 'Look at her, Freda. Can't you just hear her shrieking, "If you don't fetch Rumtopf, Mutti, I will"?'

Freda gnawed her lip. She was clearly fighting against the idea. 'That would make Miryam's death Lotti's doing.'

'In a way, and Lotti must never think it,' Gwenna said hoarsely. 'Let it haunt me, and you, but on this point I will lie my heart out if necessary.'

'And so will I,' Freda said fervently. 'Take care of her, Gwenna. I will see you both in July.'

22

Max wanted to know the outcome of the inquest and during milking next morning, Gwenna told him – 'misadventure' – and left him to work out the meaning. Perhaps one of the guards at the camp would explain it to him.

'Did you say my words, what I tell you about Fuhrman?' he asked.

'Yes, but it was inadmissible. Nobody can prove it.'

He took that in, made a motion of the lips. 'I would swear it, if they ask me.'

'They won't. It's over and done with, verdict given.'

'The police will not come to the camp, to speak with Fuhrman?'

'Do you want them to?'

'Maybe. Maybe not.' Max looked resigned. 'Oberleutnant Fuhrman and I do not watch eye to eye.'

'I'm glad to hear it. I don't like the verdict much either, but I've come to the conclusion that the kindest thing will be to allow Lotti to live her life. We have a phrase, "Let sleeping dogs lie".'

'You wish me not to wake dogs.'

'Exactly.'

Max got on with his work, leaving Gwenna certain that things would never sleep easily between him and Fuhrman. The inquest had added a disturbing dimension to the horror of Miryam's death, and she was more than ever reluctant to allow friendship between Lotti and Max.

Days passed. Ezra came to find her one morning a week or so after the inquest, while she was grading and washing eggs destined for the village shop. Lotti was in the house, colouring in a map of the world that Gwenna had found among her old schoolbooks. She'd begun setting daily projects for Lotti to ease her into the habit of lessons. Soon as she could take an afternoon off, Gwenna intended to take Lotti into Truro again. To call on Mill, and also to drop in at St Morgan's and see if someone there could recommend a private tutor.

Ezra cleared his throat. 'There's a heifer in Fairy Tump field looking a mite lame. I'll bring her down later.'

Gwenna nodded. 'Please do and I'll take a look.' She waited. Ezra was staring at the eggs, but without seeing them. Or so she judged. She was right.

'Why are you ignoring the boys, missus?'

'What, Max and co.? I'm not. I speak to Max every morning, in the parlour.'

Ezra narrowed his eyes. 'I seen you glaring at him.'

'I don't.'

'If looks was blades, he'd be spread out on the cobbles.'

'Looks are not blades, Ezra.'

'Well, I wouldn't want to read your thoughts, missus. 'Tain't his fault. He don't have no more choice where he's sent to work than any prisoner. They're doing a rare good job of ploughing Colvennon Glaze, so why won't you take a pride and come and look?'

'Because I'd have to bring Lotti.'

'Then bring the maid.'

'I can't. I have to keep her away from them. Don't you understand? It jeopardises her recovery if I allow her to fraternise with Germans. If I had land girls, it'd be no problem.'

'If you had land girls, the Glaze wouldn't be ploughed, and you'd have John Wormley on your tail.'

'All right.' She plonked an egg down too hard. 'Damn. I know it's not Max's fault, any of this. It's just I've so much to work out. Lotti's schooling, and where her mother should be laid to rest.' Gwenna's initial idea for Miryam's funeral had been slammed. 'She can't be interred in St Wenna's churchyard because of her Jewish faith. The vicar was utterly unhelpful. He suggested a public cemetery, the bit put aside for Nonconformists. It's enough to make one an atheist.'

Ezra nodded, understanding her outrage. 'The buryin' must be in hallowed ground, of course.'

'Yes and close to here. Partly for practical reasons, and so Lotti knows where her mother is. I'm half minded to ask the elders if we might bury Miryam at our chapel.'

'I don't think so.' Ezra shook his head.

'You'd reject her too?'

'No,' Ezra answered steadily, 'because the graveyard's full, missus. I've booked my plot, and one for my good lady, and unless you've booked yours next-along your parents, even you won't get in when your time comes.'

'Oh.' This was news. Perhaps the answer was to be Truro's public cemetery, though it felt random and impersonal. 'I want somewhere Lotti can lay flowers, but not pushed into a corner, out of sight.'

'Your friend Freda Helyer's a Quaker, that right?'

'Freda Fincham now.' But yes, Freda's family had been among the first of the Cornish Quakers, tracing back almost three hundred years.

'They're a broad-minded lot,' Ezra went on. 'I'm surprised she hasn't thought of Come-to-Good.'

Come-to-Good – the old Quaker meeting house a mile or two outside Truro. She'd visited once with Freda and, walking through the graveyard carpeted with spring flowers, had felt herself drawn into the gentle soul of the place. 'Oh, Ezra, you are a scholar and a sage.'

Ezra mumbled something about liking sage and onion, and not knowing much about things scholarly. 'You go write a letter, have your friend Freda make the arrangements. Do it quick, though.'

'In case the authorities take it on themselves to put Mrs Gittelman in a public plot?'

'Hey? No, I mean get writing, 'cos those German boys are expecting you to inspect their ploughing.'

'Ezra, I just explained—'

'Just a glimpse, five minutes. No more.'

She inclined her head. 'All right.'

The letter to Freda was written and Gwenna took Lotti with her to post it. With her promise to Ezra in mind, she took Lotti back home by the cliff path. The wind off the sea was blustery, bunching Gwenna's hair around her ears and turning Lotti's hair ribbons into streamers. Lotti seemed happy walking alongside, sucking a toffee which the assistant in the grocer's shop had given her. Gwenna had taken a box of eggs with her, and shillings clinked in her pocket.

She'd noticed before that Lotti ate her sweets in one go, never saving them for later. Perhaps she'd been deprived of treats in Germany and France. Lotti's gaze sought the horizon as she hugged Rumtopf to her chest. The only time she put him down was at mealtimes, when he sat propped up against a flower vase on the table. He now sported a complete set of clothes as Mill had posted the finished waistcoat.

'This way.' Gwenna opened a tumbledown sheep gate set in

the cliff-top wall. They'd reached Colvennon land and the gate took them into the Glaze at its highest point.

An astonishing sight greeted them. A slope of rich, dark earth disappeared into the distance. Her father, and Ezra in his prime, had ploughed two acres a day with good horses. Max and Jürgen, learning from scratch, weren't that much slower. 'Well, well,' she murmured into the wind.

So long as the dry weather held, they'd finish a week ahead of May Day.

Like a spontaneous round of applause, seagulls rose up and the cause of their flight were the shire horses, Lady and Prince, white as galleon sails, led by Max and Jürgen, emerging from a fold in the land. It was almost eleven, so they were likely coming in for their morning break.

Lotti set off at a run, calling, 'Max, Max!'

Gwenna followed, stumbling in the ploughed ruts. The backs of her ankles were still sore from last week's expedition in tight shoes but she caught up with Lotti. Grabbed her. 'Darling, you'll scare the horses. Stay with me.'

Seeing them, perhaps reading her intentions, Max signalled to Jürgen and turned the horses in a different direction. Gwenna said to Lotti, 'We'll have a chance to pat Lady and Prince later, when they've finished for the day. Come on, we'll go round the edge. It's exhausting striding over ploughed land.'

At the bottom of Colvennon Glaze, she found Ezra lifting a blackened kettle off the Primus stove. His rudimentary field kitchen consisted of a pallet of wood, a large biscuit tin and four tin mugs. 'I'm impressed with what the men have done, Ezra,' she said. 'What you've done. It's extraordinary.'

'Stay and have a cup of something hot, then you can tell them yourself, missus.'

'No. It's time for Lotti's lessons.'

'*Guten Tag, Frau Devoran.*'

Gwenna hadn't noticed Walther coming, and she instinctively held Lotti more closely. Brambles clung to his trouser hems. He had happily taken over the care of the pigs since Roddy's departure, and when he was not needed there, he could be seen wheel-barrowing ditch silt to the muck heaps, whistling as he went. There was a lot of ditch on an eighty-acre farm, which meant that a man of such simple pleasures was destined to be happy forever. Without making eye contact, Walther took a bottle of coffee essence from the biscuit tin and measured a little into three of the tin mugs.

'Make an extra one for the missus,' Ezra instructed him.

'No, please don't.' Gwenna tugged Lotti's hand, but the horses were close and Lotti was straining to get to them. Gwenna felt a crossfire of emotions. Two men in rippling shirt-sleeves leading shining, eighteen-hand horses across the furrows. Men in their prime, audibly chatting to each other in German. Lotti didn't seem to mind a jot, but Freda would be aghast.

Gwenna plucked her gaze from the men and studied Lady's powerful forequarters. Shires had a particular way of treading the ploughed earth, picking their feet up in exaggerated style, arching their necks like war horses to aid their balance. Taken with the mare's beauty, she relaxed her grip on Lotti, who seized her chance and ran towards the advancing men. She too stumbled on the rough earth. London shoes weren't suitable for this terrain.

Get her some sturdy boots. Freda hadn't mentioned the Gittelmans' luggage, which must have arrived by now from railway Lost Property. Odd that she hadn't, Gwenna thought. Oh! Max had swung Lotti up to sit astride Lady's back.

Don't shriek, Gwenna ordered herself. She used to ride Lady's mother back from the field as a child with no bridle, just a rope halter and her father or Ezra trudging behind, smoking their pipes and oblivious to risk. Nobody had taught her to be scared and she'd gained a confident seat. Lotti looked astounded at being up so high. Her fingers threaded into Lady's flaxen mane.

Leading the horse onto the strip of grass, Max wished Gwenna good afternoon. 'We have done good work?'

Her reply was less than gracious. 'Not bad.'

'"Not bad" means "good"?'

'Yes,' she conceded. 'You have done well.'

With a flick of an eyebrow, Max translated for Jürgen, who led Prince a little way off without making a comment. Perhaps he was the life and soul when it was all men together, but Gwenna had hardly heard a word from Jürgen in all the time he'd been coming to Colvennon. It struck her – perhaps he resented her as much as she resented his presence here.

Max invited her to join them for coffee, which she again declined. 'I have to get Lotti back to the house for her lessons.' She smiled up at the child and held out her arms. 'Slither down; we need to leave these men to their work.'

Disappointment clouded Lotti's face.

'Soon we lead the horses to their paddock,' Max said. 'To rest, they have worked five hours. You will let Lotti sit on the back?'

Gwenna hesitated. Yet again, she was being turned into the party wrecker, the miserable spoiler of fun. Nobody seeing Lotti's grin would say that she was intimidated by the proximity of these men, yet the world would judge Gwenna all the same. 'I'm sorry, but her lessons are important.'

'Of course,' Max agreed earnestly. 'So we take the horses now. Jürgen?' He jerked his head, summoning his colleague. 'Bring Prince.'

Gwenna looked to Ezra, who surely was in charge here. But Ezra was filling his pipe with tobacco and merely nodded. 'You boys do that. We'll keep your coffee hot.'

Out-manoeuvred, Gwenna played the only card left to her.

'If Lotti's to ride, I'll find her a pony.' She'd fall six feet if she slipped off Lady's back.

'Then you get up behind her, missus.'

Gwenna glared at Ezra. Much more of this, and she'd imagine he was trying to sabotage her authority. 'I can't. I've no mounting block.'

'You've got a strong man there can you lift you up.'

A glance into Max's face told her that he understood every word. 'You wish?' he asked.

'All right.' She knew when she was beaten. Lotti was obviously thrilled to be on horseback, but her ankles barely reached to Lady's girth. 'Give me a handclasp.' She meant Max to make a platform of his hands, but he handed the lead-rope to Jürgen, seized Gwenna around the middle and hoisted her up. After a squeak of surprise, she threw her leg over, settled herself on Lady's back and placed her arms either side of Lotti. 'Hold tightly to the mane. That's her hair, darling. Tight, tight.'

As they made their way from the field, Jürgen and Max leading the horses, Lady turned her head and nibbled Gwenna's foot. 'Cheeky.' She couldn't help laughing. Lady liked to do that, she remembered. Before she'd left for London, before Edward had entered her life, she'd often ridden to the beach with her father, she on Lady, he on Prince's predecessor, a massive shire named Duke. The sweet, sweaty scent of a hard-working horse gave Gwenna a longing to gallop across Colvennon Cove. My, that would blow some cobwebs free! Eight massive hooves hitting sand was like a cavalry charge and it had been one of the few times she ever heard her father laugh out loud. It was like being rolled up inside the wind. Wading birds would take off ahead of them.

There wasn't time for pleasure riding any more and if she rode Lady out alone, even for an hour, there would be mayhem in the stables. Prince could not bear being by left by himself and there was nobody to ride him.

They reached the paddock where the horses would be turned loose for a couple of hours.

Lotti slithered down into Max's arms. He set the child down, then reached up for Gwenna.

'It's all right, I can get down on my own.'

'I know, Mrs Devoran. But here am I. You do not have to.'

She swung her left leg over and tumbled into a secure hold which lasted a moment longer than it needed. Brushing white hairs off herself, she looked into Max's blue-grey eyes. 'You should not have put Lotti on the horse without asking me,' she said.

'But you would say no. Always you say no.'

'Because I have to protect her.'

In reply, Max looked towards Lotti, who was holding open the paddock gate for Jürgen. She looked happy, carrying out her little task. As Jürgen passed, leading Prince, Lotti giggled.

'What did he say?' Gwenna demanded.

'He said, "Thank you, dear gracious young lady." I know.' Max widened his eyes. 'No German. I will explain to Jürgen why he must be only silent.'

'You think I'm a rotten, curmudgeonly spoilsport, don't you?'

'I have no answer,' was his reply, 'as I do not understand. On a horse back, Mrs Devoran, you are very beautiful.'

She stepped away, disturbed because he had spoken as if he'd come to a conclusion any man would share, and was merely passing on his opinion. Gwenna wasn't used to compliments, or being thought of as out of the ordinary. She bore Lotti away but couldn't resist glancing back. Max had led Lady into the field, and the two horses were playing like foals, bucking and galloping side by side in a circuit of the small field. He was leaning on the gate, watching. The sight of him in shirtsleeves, bathed in sunlight, a buttery sheen to his hair, gave her a feeling of unbearable regret. In that moment, she wished desperately she could copy Ezra and like Max for what he was now, and not hate him for what he had been. The feeling took her back to a conversation she'd had with Wiggy a few days before.

They'd been waiting for the men to come from the field. Wiggy had driven into the yard and popped her head round the kitchen door where Gwenna was mixing up chicken feed, saying, 'Permission to use your lav, queen. I could have ducked into a hedge but modesty prevails.'

Pointing out the stone-built privy to the side of the house, Gwenna had poured tea from a pot simmering on the stove. Wiggy never said no to a cuppa. Gaps between meals were long.

'Bless you.' Wiggy had taken the mug gratefully. 'Strong, just how I like it. Have you time for a bit of gossip?'

'I can spare a moment.' Gwenna had learned to look forward to Wiggy's visits. The girl was a window into the world beyond.

'This'll make you laugh, then. You know there's an Italian POW camp over at St Columb?'

Gwenna knew about it, yes.

'Well, there's an outbreak of German measles there. How's that for irony?'

Max, Ezra and Jürgen bringing the horses home had interrupted them at that point. Wiggy had watched their approach, then murmured behind her hand, 'I'd take a tumble with him in the haystack.'

'With Ezra?'

'Crikey, queen, I'm not that short-sighted! The one on the left.'

'That's Jürgen.'

'I mean my left, not... Never mind.'

'You mean Max.'

'Well, wouldn't you? Course you would! You don't get a pair of shoulders like that in half a pound.'

'He's German, Wiggy.' Gwenna hadn't kept the indignation from her voice. 'He's the enemy.'

Wiggy had drained the last of her tea and rubbed lipstick off the rim with her cuff. 'Enemy or not, the mattress doesn't care. Nor the haystack.'

The idea was grotesque. To offer your body or heart to a German, a Nazi, you'd be betraying everything you stood for. You'd have to have something wrong with you.

The horses were still in high spirits, perhaps performing a little for the watching men? They came close to the gate and Gwenna shouted, 'Watch yourselves, step back, they're quite capable—' She got no further. Prince did exactly what she'd feared, made a massive, corkscrew buck, his hind legs flashing high in the air. With a hideous shout of pain, Max flew backwards and landed hard on the beaten-earth path.

Gwenna ran and dropped down beside him. Jürgen did the same and laid his hands either side of Max's head.

'*Max? Mein Kapitänleutnant?*' He was almost crying, his blunt features contorted.

'Careful, don't turn his neck.' She laid fingers against Max's temple, searching for a pulse. She found it, to her immeasurable relief. He had a nasty contusion to the side of his head, below the hairline, probably from striking the ground. Prince's hoof had got him plum on the shoulder. A dusty horseshoe mark was the evidence.

'Lotti?' Gwenna could hear agitated breathing behind her. 'He's all right but please, go and fetch Ezra and Walther, because we need two men to carry him to the house.'

Lotti began to whimper.

'Please, Lotti, go and find them. He's going to be all right.'

Max was stirring, his palms struggling for a purchase on the ground. He was muttering in German. She had an idea he was saying, 'Damned horse.'

She should have warned him earlier, made him stand back.

Had she allowed dislike and prejudice to blur her responsibility?

Though how often had she leaned on a rail, watching spell-bound as those amiable giants thundered around, raising joyous dust? Prince and Lady stood at the fence now, whickering in agitation, sensing, as they did so acutely, that something was wrong with their humans. Lotti was crying – small, snatched sobs. 'It looks worse than it is,' Gwenna assured her, though with more certainty than she felt. Max had struck the ground very hard.

'*Blut, so viel Blut.*'

'Yes, darling, I know but head wounds bleed very badly. Please fetch Ezra.'

'*Papa, so viel Blut.*'

'I know you saw your papa hurt. And you're frightened. But would you give Max your cardigan?' Gwenna stood up and tentatively unbuttoned Lotti's cardigan. Rumtopf fell to the ground. Gwenna picked him up and said, 'He can wait here with me, but Max needs a pillow.' She made a pad of the cardigan and slipped it under Max's head. His eyes were unfo-cused. Concussion? That meant a doctor. With a final sob, Lotti sped off.

She understands everything I say, Gwenna thought. *Every word. I can only hope that one day soon, I'll find the key to unlock her voice.*

23

They got Max into the sitting room and onto a couch. Gwenna fetched a rug and laid it over him. He was conscious but was shivering though it was a balmy day.

'You whacked your head,' she said softly. 'And you'll have a bruise the size of a plate on your shoulder.'

Ezra fetched the first aid box. Jürgen and Walther stood at the side of the room, their hands awkwardly at their sides, watching Gwenna as she cleaned the cut to his head. It was an inch long and full of dirt. Afterwards, she applied Dettol and castor oil against infection. 'Sorry,' she said as Max clenched his eyes tight. Ezra fetched a glass of water.

'Can you sit up, lad,' he said, 'and show you're in the land of the living?'

Gwenna gave Max her forearm and with a groan that indicated pain, he pulled himself up.

'You are thinking, if I die, it will be one German less and that horse should get a medal.'

'Of course I don't think that. I'm blaming myself for letting you stand against the fence.'

'It is punishment perhaps that I disobey your commands to

me. I do not do so again. Hey, *Mausi*.' Lotti, who had been sitting cross-legged on the floor, crept forward to the end of the couch. She gave Max a woeful smile and he said to her, 'Mrs Devoran is right and horses are not so good for health.'

Gwenna looked at the mantelpiece clock. Wiggy wouldn't be along for hours. 'Ezra, would you be good enough to brew a cup of strong, sweet tea?'

'Righto. Jürgen, Walther, you get outside and see to the pigs. You and I can get back to ploughing later, Jürgen, and after that, we'll bring the cows in together.'

Hearing this, Max tried to get off the couch. Gwenna stopped him. 'You're in no fit state. Lie down, I mean it.' She asked him if he'd like her to draw the curtains. 'If your eyes are hurting.'

'No, I do not need, but I would like this sofa to be longer.'

The couch was a Regency heirloom, designed for a lady to repose on, and a foot too short for Max. Gwenna pulled up a stool to extend the length. 'Better?'

'*Ja, ja.*' He looked around when she'd finished, a glance that took in the oak beams above his head, the two armchairs drawn up to the clean-swept fireplace, the basket piled with logs. He said, 'I like this room.'

'It hasn't changed in years.'

'That picture, you and your man?' His eye stopped at a formal photograph on the mantelpiece. Gwenna had placed it there after her recent visit to Fendynick House. Though she'd said nothing at the time to her mother-in-law, the removal of her and Edward's wedding picture from the hallway had upset her. She and he had failed on many levels but nobody had the right to erase their history. So, on coming home, in tit-for-tat, she'd put her copy of their wedding photo on display.

For the same reason, she'd put a picture of Edward on top of the kitchen bookcase. It was the one she'd angrily shown to John Wormley, of Edward posing on the bridge of his ship, HMS *Bee*

Orchid. The message to any visitors was clear. She was not a runaway wife, but a widow who, for a time, had believed in true love.

Ezra brought Max's tea, and announced he would quickly check on the horses. 'I shall tell Prince there's no real harm done.'

'We don't know that yet,' Gwenna muttered.

'I shall tell him all the same, missus. Horses mind more than we think.'

'Are you going to drink your tea?' Gwenna asked when Ezra had left. It was on a table next to the couch. Max hadn't reached for it.

'I do not understand all this tea,' Max sighed. 'I would like beer.'

'Can't oblige, I'm afraid, and I'm not sure you should drink alcohol after a shock. Brandy maybe, but I don't have any.' She had a nip of whisky, but water would do best. She'd offered aspirin earlier, but he'd declined. 'I'll leave you to rest. Shout if you need me.'

Gwenna took Lotti into the kitchen and resolutely got out her lesson books. 'We can start doing sums,' she said, opening a maths book at page one. Lotti's mouth set in a stubborn line.

Gwenna sighed. Then an idea presented itself. 'Or... you might like to read to Max. He might enjoy it.' She picked up a book, *Adventures in Reading,* that St Wenna's headmaster had lent her. It contained short passages designed to extend pupils' vocabulary. Some of the stories were quite fun. Gwenna had read a few of them out loud to Lotti.

Lotti cautiously took the book. Gwenna felt she liked the idea and needed only a little coaxing.

'There's a story in there about a polar bear rescuing a fisherman from the waters. Max might rather like that, being a sailor.'

They found Max asleep. 'Oh, well. It was a thought.' Before

Gwenna could persuade Lotti to retreat, he opened an eye and mumbled something.

'Lotti was going to read you a story,' she said, 'but I think you need to be left alone.'

He replied in a dragging voice, 'She is a sweet child who speaks only bad German.'

'What do you mean, bad? Don't say that!'

'She speaks *Berlinerisch* and also, sometimes, Yiddish. She should not; it is dangerous.'

Sympathy for Max drained away on the spot. He was rambling, but he'd reminded her of why Lotti was here without her mother, suffering and silent. Without bothering to temper her disgust, she said, 'She's in Britain now, and has nothing to fear from you and your kind. She needn't worry about your friend Fuhrman, either.'

'Not my friend.' Max touched the almost-healed cut on his lip then pressed his temple. 'Have you aspirin for my head?'

'You didn't want it a moment ago.' A small hand creeping into hers made her pull back from anger. Gwenna all but heard Lotti say, 'Don't be hard on him.' She imagined it, of course, but after handing him his tea, her voice found a kinder note. 'Drink up; I'll fetch you some tablets. Are you all right? I mean, your vision's not blurred or anything?'

Max told her he felt a bit sick. 'Like I drink.'

'You mean, as though you're drunk?' She really should call the doctor, only that would mean a trip to the post office to use the telephone, and by the time the doctor got the message, Wiggy would have arrived and taken Max away. 'Is there a medic at your camp?' She could send a note with Max, detailing his accident.

'There is medic who inspects us for disease, also a doctor who was with my crew. Him I trust more. I will talk to him.'

As Gwenna rifled in the medicine cabinet for aspirin, she had a conversation with an imaginary Hilda. Though the incident with Roddy and the shotgun was almost three weeks in the past, the woman's presence still lingered in the farmhouse.

'*You oughta be careful, Mrs Devoran,*' the spectral Hilda muttered. '*Hanging about that man, chatting away.*'

'I was asking if he has concussion, in case I should notify the camp's doctor.'

'*Camp doctor! And we have to trudge halfway to Truro if we want to see ours. That devil's not your responsibility.*'

'But he is, Hilda. I don't like or trust him, but he was hurt on my farm.'

'*You can be too nice. He's a good-looking man and people gossip.*'

'Don't they just.' Closing the cabinet with a hard click, Gwenna filled a glass with water from the ewer and returned to Max. Lotti had tucked Rumtopf under his blanket and was sitting on the edge of an armchair, perhaps waiting for him to notice.

Seeing Gwenna, Max wriggled into a sitting position, and, seeing Rumtopf on his chest, gave a grimace of amusement. A shaft of sunlight threw every hollow of his face into sharp relief and gilded the impatient growth of an afternoon beard. The old scar running beneath his cheekbone was bone-white against his developing tan. He touched it, as though Gwenna had mentioned it.

'At least they missed my eye,' he said in the tone of a man unwrapping a familiar joke. 'I prefer to see than to be handsome.'

'Who is "they"?' she asked.

He dismissed that with a blink. 'Aspirin?'

She offered the pills in the palm of her hand and, in taking them, his gaze skimmed her wedding ring, which, in spite of everything, she had never removed.

'Where is your husband, Mrs Devoran?'

'Ezra hasn't told you?'

'Ezra speaks only work.' He swallowed the pills and gulped water.

'My husband was a Royal Navy sub-lieutenant. His ship went down.' Max must have heard her voice icing over. She felt the chill of it in her mouth.

It didn't stop him asking, 'Where did he die?'

'The Atlantic, the South West Approaches. Would you like to know how many miles off the coast of Ireland?'

'No.'

'It was too many to swim.'

Max absorbed the bitter reproof. 'What kind of ship – battleship, destroyer, escort vessel?'

'Something like that,' she said vaguely. Loose talk cost lives. Nobody revealed details of that kind to anybody. 'What was your ship?'

'Mine?' He hesitated.

'Yes. What kind was it?'

'Large. Grey.'

The same rules applied, so it seemed. 'What was her name?' Gwenna persisted. He'd started it, after all.

'*Der Kriegswolf.*'

War Wolf.

Taking the water glass from him, she said, 'I'll let you know when the truck comes. Lotti, let's see if Ezra has a job for us.'

But Lotti was immovable. She peered at Max's injured face and spoke. Gwenna recognised the word *Wunde*, wound. And *Blut*, blood. And then, '*Mein Papa.*'

'Is she comparing your injury to what happened to her father?' Gwenna wanted to know.

'She has worry,' Max answered, 'that something bad will happen to me now.'

'I would imagine the worst is over for you.' *War Wolf.* A massive warship sailed across Gwenna's mental horizon.

Smoky-hulled and bristling with turrets and guns. 'Reassure her, then.'

'I thought it was "no German".'

'I'll allow it just once.'

He took Lotti's hand and said something that Gwenna couldn't follow. 'I am telling her, I will only get better when she talks to you, like a big girl, in English.'

'That's blackmail!'

'But you wish it, yes? You say to me that you are afraid for Lotti, and how she goes on here.'

'You shouldn't ever lie to children.'

He asked, how did she know it was a lie? Perhaps his good health was in the hands of Lotti.

'Rubbish.' Gwenna told Lotti it was time to let Max rest. 'Bring Rumtopf.'

Ignoring her, Lotti spoke to Max, in German. Max turned his head away.

Lotti tried again, her voice agitated. Again with no response. She began to cry.

'At least look at her, Max,' Gwenna begged. She couldn't bear to see the child so confused.

Max closed his eyes. How long this would have continued, Gwenna never discovered because a figure peered in at the sitting room window, and, discerning figures within, tapped on the glass.

24

It was Mr Beecroft, headmaster of St Wenna's elementary school, who had come to enquire after Gwenna's 'young evac- uee'. 'Did you receive my query, asking if she would be attending school after Easter?'

Gwenna reddened, conscious of her omission in not replying to the well-meaning note. She invited the headmaster into the kitchen, where he loomed over her. He was very tall and, to Gwenna's eye, had hardly changed since he'd taught her, other than to grow whiter on top and bushier of eyebrow.

'You know it is the law that all children attend school if well enough to do so. Shall I expect her?'

'No.' Gwenna outlined her alternate plan. 'Lotti has no English; she'd be out of her depth even in the infants' class. I need to find her a private tutor. She's bright, you see.'

'Mm.' Mr Beecroft glanced at the world map, open on the kitchen table, which had been meticulously coloured in. 'I already have six evacuees who are doing very well with me. Two in the top class, four in the infants'.'

'But what you don't have is a traumatised refugee.' Every child there would have heard about the 'little mumchance

German'. Gwenna was adamant. 'She is recovering from a personal tragedy, Mr Beecroft. She's not ready.'

Lotti was standing slightly behind Gwenna, Rumtopf held close. Max must have handed him back. Mr Beecroft looked past Gwenna and addressed the child. 'Would you like to come to school, my dear?'

Lotti tightened her grip on Rumtopf and clamped her lips.

Mr Beecroft's shaggy eyebrows interrogated Gwenna, who felt nine years old again.

Many years ago, he'd stopped Roddy Hoskens's younger brothers bullying her in the playground, though not before she'd run away from school and triggered a frantic search of the countryside. He had caned both boys, ten strikes each, for pushing her down some steps and giving her concussion. *Ah-ha*, she thought. *That's why I'm worried for Max. I know how concussion feels.* 'You mean well, Mr Beecroft,' she said, 'but Lotti and I are making progress at our own pace.'

A crash from the sitting-room made Gwenna dash out. Max lay on the floor. He must have rolled off the couch and overturned the little table next to it. He was muttering in German – swearing, she suspected – with a hand pressed to his left shoulder.

Lotti had run in with Gwenna and Mr Beecroft came too. Gwenna heard him say, 'Good God. A German.'

Gwenna glanced round at him. 'Can you help me get him back on the couch? He got booted by one of my horses. A heck of a kick.'

'Then he ought to be in hospital, surely.'

'I would imagine that Truro hospital would not be ideal,' Gwenna said crisply.

'After the bombing? No, quite,' Mr Beecroft conceded.

Gwenna got her hands under Max's shoulder blades, feeling him wince. 'Can you take his feet? On the count of three...'

Max bellowed a raw expletive as they heaved him back onto the couch. He then apologised.

Lotti hung over him, repeating a question Gwenna understood to be, 'Does it hurt?'

Teeth clenched, Max didn't answer.

Lotti persisted. '*Max, sag es mir, bitte!*'

'Do you encourage German conversation in your home?' Mr Beecroft looked perturbed.

'No. I don't,' Gwenna replied. 'In fact, I've banned it but this is not a normal occasion.' It could be worse, she reflected. Max might still have been wearing his iron cross. 'He's my POW farmhand, and I can't just leave him in the hay store.'

'I understand, but am I right in saying that Lotti is Jewish?'

Gwenna gave a nod.

'Then to have close contact with a German POW seems at the very least to be misguided.'

'On a farm, we're thrown close together.'

'Do you understand the meaning of *Judenstern*, Gwenna?'

'I think so.'

A teacher to his bones, Mr Beecroft assumed that meant no. 'It means "the Jews' star", yellow in colour, which they have been obliged to wear all over occupied Europe. It is a way of identifying and marking them out. I find it astonishing that you should fear Lotti coming to school to mix with children of her own age, yet allow her to converse with one of her persecutors.'

Gwenna felt the criticism like a whip. 'I know how it looks. There's much I don't understand in Lotti's past, Mr Beecroft, but I'm trying every day to make her happy, healthy and part of this community.'

Mr Beecroft stooped to look into Lotti's eyes. 'Are you scared, young lady? Do you want to leave this house? You may tell me.'

Gwenna had to bite her tongue to stop herself intervening. Meanwhile Lotti stared up into the fiercely earnest face above hers. She seemed to be drawing in and holding her breath and Gwenna waited for the screams to start.

Lotti didn't scream. She said, 'No.'

Gwenna gasped. Had she heard right? Had Lotti spoken her first English word? 'Lotti, did you understand that Mr Beecroft is asking if you like it here? You can tell him the truth.'

The following seconds lasted an age. Gwenna could see that Lotti was wavering between the desire to speak and a habit of closing in on herself. *Please, please*, she begged silently. If emotion could travel, Lotti would feel it like a hailstorm.

'Speak, *Mausi*. It is time.' Max's voice was deep, full of pain.

Lotti lifted her chin. 'I like it here. I like Max and my Aunt Gwenna. I love Josephine too.'

'Who is Josephine?' Mr Beecroft asked.

'Aunt Gwenna's calico cat. She is calico because she is made of three colours: white, black and brown.'

'And this is your true answer, Lotti? Nobody has made you say this?' Mr Beecroft's voice was like a fine-bladed chisel, practised at levering out lies.

Lotti nodded. 'It is.'

'Mrs Devoran said you spoke only German.'

'Until now, I spoke only German.'

'Why?'

Lotti made a familiar movement of the mouth, drawing her lower lip under her top teeth. 'Because of what Mutti told me.'

'And what was that?'

'At the railway station.' Lotti looked down, as if a promise lay at her feet. 'I tried to obey. I always try.'

Mr Beecroft straightened up and addressed Gwenna. 'It's not for me to prise that secret from the child. You are best placed to do it. If private tuition is your determined choice, then act, Mrs Devoran. Children of Lotti's age forget their learning quickly and it's hard to catch up.' He bid her good day, and Lotti too. For Max, he had only a slight headshake, and a frown at the lemon-yellow circles on Max's prison uniform.

Gwenna accompanied him outside. The tears streaming from her eyes were of gratitude. Lotti had finally broken into English. In the conservatory at Fendynick House, she'd run into Gwenna's arms. *Why do I doubt her?* She cleared her throat. 'Mr Beecroft.'

He waited while she rubbed her face with her sleeve.

'Will you report me for fraternisation?'

Mr Beecroft considered the question, then glanced towards the sitting-room window. 'Is that what it is, fraternisation?'

'No. But Lotti likes Max. I haven't encouraged it, not ever, but she does.'

A groove appeared between the white brows. 'Could it be that he makes her feel safe? I would imagine that is her first priority.'

'It could be.'

'Whereas your longings, your tears, have the opposite effect.'

Ouch. She rubbed her eyes harder.

He asked, 'Which school do you favour, once she's had some coaching?'

'St Morgan's. As I said, she's bright.'

'Then here is my tuppence-worth.' Mr Beecroft whipped a notebook and pencil from his jacket pocket, scribbled something, and handed her the page.

Gwenna read 'Verity Linley, Cathedral Row, T/O'. Shorthand for Truro. 'Who is this lady?'

'The best teacher in Cornwall, retired. A telephone call from me might persuade her to make an exception. You'll be wanting your little ward to sit the June examination for St Morgan's?'

'Oh no. This year's too soon.'

'A sad lack of ambition, in my view.'

Gwenna escorted Mr Beecroft to the footpath that would take him the shorter way back to St Wenna. 'You don't think much of me, do you? You think I'm failing Lotti. That I'm lax and uncommitted, whereas nothing could be further from the truth.'

'Not at all, Mrs Devoran. I was doing my job with my probing questions. I'm convinced that little girl loves you.'

'She *likes* me, if we're being honest.'

He tutted impatiently. 'She loves Josephine *too*. What does that tell you?'

'More than one object of love.'

'Exactly, and therein lies a problem. It will not serve her to see a German POW as a father figure.'

'You think that's how Lotti sees Max?'

Mr Beecroft's answer was unsatisfactory. 'I have taught more children than I will ever remember, Gwenna, and in their way they are all a mystery. Give me a few days to make a telephone call, then visit Miss Linley in Truro. If you won't bring Lotti to St Wenna's, then that is my best suggestion. At any rate, the child needs to be away from this farm.'

'Away?' A little axe struck at Gwenna's heart. What was he implying?

He elucidated. 'Out during the day, so you aren't all thrown together. That gentleman in your sitting room is the product of a vicious and remorseless regime. He is not fit company for a child of Lotti's background.'

'He was injured. That's the only reason he's in the house.'

Mr Beecroft's left eyebrow rose in crafted contradiction. 'As I remember, Gwenna, you always cared for hurt creatures. You nursed the school tortoise for weeks after it was obvious to everyone else he wasn't going to emerge from hibernation. But this is serious. You're a young woman with a child to care for and not everyone is good. Remember that.'

25

Max did not come to work the next day, nor the next. Wiggy told Gwenna, 'He's in the sanatorium.'

'Badly hurt, then?' Gwenna had feared he'd been hiding some serious damage.

'Your daft dobbin gave him a right nasty bruise and he won't be lifting his left arm for a week,' Wiggy confirmed, 'but that wasn't the worst of it. There was a kerfuffle in the mess hut later, so I heard. Fighting. Military police got called in.'

'Max wasn't in any shape for a fight.'

'He got punched and kicked all right. Jürgen knows, but if you can unlock his gob, you're a better woman than me.'

Gwenna cornered Jürgen later that morning. She needed answers, because Lotti was asking where Max was. Having discovered the power of speech, all she wanted to know was, is he hurt, is he dead? For two days in a row, she left her breakfast to stand in the doorway, waiting for Wiggy's truck. When only Jürgen and Walther jumped out, she crumpled. For Gwenna, the radiant joy of Lotti finally talking was tempered by a new anxiety. Was Max turning into Lotti's father figure? If so, the mirage would have to be destroyed, which would be Gwenna's unenviable task.

Jürgen indicated his shoulder, arm and upper ribs. 'He is hurt here. And here.' He tapped the bridge of his nose. When Gwenna asked about the incident in the mess hut, he made a vague face. He knew nothing of that. From Walther, Gwenna got even less information but an added reason to worry. Giving a furtive shake of the head, Walther muttered, 'Too much is said.'

Gwenna tried Ezra. 'Jürgen talks to you,' she said. 'I need to know if Max is coming back.'

'He'll be back, missus. He likes being here more than he likes being in his compound.'

'But when?'

'When he's ready, I suppose.'

That wasn't until the following Tuesday, the week after Easter. Gwenna had delivered eggs to the village shop, leaving Lotti to prepare breakfast, and she returned to find them together, sitting on the kitchen garden wall with Josephine. Max had lost a little weight, and there were healing cuts across the bridge of his nose. He seemed cheerful enough and held up the billycan to tell her that he wanted hot water.

'I need coffee, but Lotti cannot make.'

'No. I forbid her to use the Primus stove. She's so capable, one forgets she's not quite eleven.' After a pause in which she assessed her own feelings at seeing Max back in one piece, she said, 'I'm glad you're back. We learned how much we required your... um, your contribution.'

That amused him, her sounding like a mayoress presenting a gold watch to a retiring janitor.

Lotti was impatient with this grown-up talk. 'Max can have breakfast with us? I laid three places. I knew he was coming back today. I did.'

'You did?' That did little to put Gwenna's mind at rest.

Max picked up on her reluctance. 'I will stay outside but if you have bread, Mrs Devoran? I sleep too late for breakfast.'

Lotti wasn't giving up. Clutching Max's hand, she tried to drag him off the wall.

He got down under his own steam and in a low voice said, 'You must make decision, Mrs Devoran, or Lotti will think she is the captain of the house. I know well, there can only be one captain.'

He was right, of course. She said, 'I'll bring you out some coffee and toast. Go sit on the mounting block.'

Lotti had gone inside, but when she saw Gwenna come in alone, she made a dash for the door. Gwenna closed it, stopping her. 'Get the bread and butter from the pantry, please, Lotti. Max isn't coming in.'

'Why?'

All the times she'd wished for Lotti to speak, Gwenna had not imagined she'd be on the receiving end of a challenge like this. The truth was too complicated to parcel up for a child of Lotti's age, so she said, 'Max agrees that if he came in for breakfast, I'd have to invite Jürgen and Walther as well, and I simply don't have the rations. Bread, please, Lotti.'

Lotti lowered her head in angry defiance. Gwenna feared she'd sent the child back into her mute state. 'Lotti?'

No answer.

'Darling, we have to have breakfast.'

Still nothing.

She knew how Hilda Hoskens would deal with this: a cuff to the side of the head and 'Do as you're bid.' Gwenna's own mother had exercised quiet authority in the home. As a child, had she ever dug her heels in, as Lotti was doing now? Gwenna couldn't remember, but if she had, she had a feeling she'd have been left to come to herself in her own time. Glancing at her parents' wedding photo, Gwenna summoned her mother's voice. 'I'm sorry you disagree with me, Lotti, and that you're upset, but my decision is final.'

She made toast on a skillet, buttered two slices and then brewed her substitute coffee. She poured a mug out for Max and took him his breakfast, handing it to him over the wall. 'It's Colvennon butter. It's very yellow, but completely natural.' She'd noticed him eyeing it in surprise.

'Thank you. You look sad,' he said.

'I'm perplexed. We're at loggerheads in the house.' Without waiting to see if Max understood the phrase, she returned to the kitchen. Lotti had not moved. Gwenna made more toast and cocoa. She took the food to the table and was about to clear away the extra place setting when a moment's empathy stalled her. Rumtopf was sitting up against a glass flower vase, and feeling this was a make-or-break moment in her relationship with Lotti, Gwenna went to the bookshelf. She removed five or six old recipe books, piled them on a chair and sat Rumtopf on top, placing his arms so he looked as though he was ready to tuck in.

'Lotti?' She cleared her throat and said in a deep, bear's growl, 'I'm hungry. Come and sit by me.'

Lotti jerked around. She stared with astonishment and a dash of outrage. Gwenna sat down and casually cut her toast into four pieces, putting two of them on Rumtopf's plate. 'You'd better hurry, or he'll have yours for himself.'

There was a scuff of feet. A chair scraped. Lotti sat down. She wouldn't meet Gwenna's eye.

'Honey on your toast?' Gwenna asked.

'No thank you.'

'Just butter, then. I would imagine Rumtopf likes honey.'

'It makes his whiskers sticky.'

Their eyes met and Lotti began to giggle. Gwenna giggled too. 'What a pair we are.'

'We are three,' Lotti said.

'Three? Are you including—'

'Rumtopf. You, me and Rumtopf. But I like Max too,' Lotti said, with stubborn emphasis.

'I know you do.'

Lotti curled her knife through the yellow butter, cool from the pantry shelf. 'I wish you liked him like I do, Aunt Gwenna. Do you not like him because he's German?'

'Max is here to work, Lotti. Liking him isn't necessary.'

'But is it because he's German?'

'No.' What else could she say? 'We have nothing in common, that's all.'

'But he likes you.'

'Don't be silly.'

'He does! He watches you when you aren't looking.'

'Then he should not. He has no business doing that, and it's the last thing I—'

A throat cleared, cutting through Gwenna's annoyance. Max stood in the doorway, holding his mug and plate. 'I will leave them on the step?'

Gwenna could have cut her tongue out. Her heart had skipped at the revelation that Max admired her, and her pettiness had been partly shock, but mostly to conceal a guilty pleasure. Max had no business liking her. He was a threat to her peace, and her guardianship of Lotti, yet she'd counted every day of his absence, and missed him. He had brought Lotti out of her shell, encouraging her to speak. Yes, first of all in German, but *he* had done it. And now he was going off to fetch the cows down, his ears filled with her rejection.

As the working day came to its close, Gwenna tracked Max down. Lotti was in the house, doing sums, and Gwenna had said, 'I'm going to find Max, to say sorry.'

Lotti had given her a considering look, then nodded. 'All

right.'

'And if you finish your sums, I'll make us jam and clotted cream for later, as a secret treat,' Gwenna promised. She had done the first three sums in the book to show Lotti, saying, 'Do the next six yourself. They're simple additions and subtractions. We'll see how you get on.'

Max was in Fairy Tump field, checking the heifers on Ezra's instructions. Four of them were heavily in calf. The others would be put with a bull later in the month and produce their first calves at the end of winter. 'Ezra thinks this field is unlucky,' Gwenna said, walking up to him. 'He doesn't like me putting pregnant cows in here, in case the fairies curse them and they lose their calves.'

Max shot her an uncertain look. 'Fairies?'

'I don't know what they are in German.'

'*Elfen*. They make the cows unwell?'

'Ezra is a believer,' Gwenna said. 'He says this field is bad for their feet, and he is sometimes right. I don't mock him.'

'I will not dream of it, though I am a scientist.'

'Are you?' This was new information. A glimpse of Max before the war, before the brown boiler suit obscured personality and history? It was an invitation for him to say more, but he did not. Everything in his manner said that she had hurt him.

'Shall I give you the tour?' Gwenna walked around the cows, leaving Max to decide if he wanted to follow her or not. Left ungrazed most of the year, Fairy Tump was a useful field to put cows on after the long winter months. The grass was studded with yellow bird's-foot trefoil and cowslips and nodding purple snake's head fritillary. Brown butterflies danced and the air had that special, extra brightness that came off the sea.

Max caught up with her. 'You have a beautiful home, Mrs Devoran. I cannot think of another place so peaceful.'

'I know.' And because he'd broken the ice, she asked,

'Where do you come from?'

'Dresden, in the east of Germany.' He added, because that meant little to her, 'A big city, and my family live in the centre. But my grandparents, from my mother, live in the countryside.'

'Are they safe?'

His shrug suggested he didn't know and that bothered him. 'I hope it goes good with them, *natürlich*.'

They reached the Colvennon brook which cut off a corner of the field. Gwenna led Max around a series of low grass mounds, the 'tumps' that gave the field its name. Here, Ezra was convinced, the fairies gathered. Or he liked to pretend. Gwenna was never sure. They were obviously man-made, and of great antiquity. She'd never heard any logical explanation for the twenty or so that clustered along the brook's edge, interspersed with small, shallow ponds.

Max was equally curious and peered in one of the pits. 'What are these for?'

'They might be dew ponds, ancient ones, for sheep or cattle,' Gwenna said. 'They've always been here.'

'And the small hills?'

'They're the fairy tumps. Tump means a tumulus, an ancient barrow or grave. There may be bodies buried under them, from as far back as the Iron Age, but nobody would dare dig to find out.'

'Graves?' Max looked unconvinced. 'They are too small.'

'Not if they're for fairies.'

'And you believe?'

'I'm Cornish and I know there is more to the world than we see.' She didn't believe it one jot, but teasing a self-declared scientist was irresistible.

Max said, 'Near my grandparents' home are long graves, also very old. It is where we bury our giants.' He pointed at a set of hoof prints sparkling with rainfall. 'Your cows stand here in the wet; this is why their feet get illness. Not fairies.'

'I think you're right.' Gwenna explained that Candlemas, the 2nd of February, was the traditional day for bringing the cows out to permanent pasture. 'The ground can be a bit soggy.'

'In Saxony, my home province, it would be hard with ice in February.'

'This is Cornwall. We pick snowdrops at Candlemas and daffodils on St Piran's Day. That's the 5th of March. Piran's our patron saint.'

'I am learning more all day. *Each* day,' Max corrected himself. He leaned over one of the pits and scooped water in the palm of his hand and let it filter through his fingers. 'From my eyes, your water has iron, see the colour?' He showed her his palm, wet and orange-brown.

'That's the soil getting into it,' Gwenna said.

'No.' Max scooped up more and let it filter into her palm. 'It is heavy with iron. My job before now is water for cities, make clean for drinking.'

She took that to mean 'a water engineer'. 'Is iron in water good or bad?'

'Your cows are looking well to me, but it is perhaps good to check they have not too much iron in their blood.'

'Oh. Right. I'll ask Mr Wormley how to do that. He's the man from the ministry office.'

As they walked away, Max sniffed the air. 'I smell the sea always when I am working on this hill.'

'Yes, its breath rolls over us and the sound is always there. Do you miss being at sea – captaining your *Kriegswolf*?'

A faraway look came to his eyes. 'I miss being with the men, having work. But if you have been at sea, in danger always, the love is not so great afterwards.'

She knew nothing of how he came to be a prisoner. There would be a story, of course. A disaster. Death, fear, surrender. She always imagined Edward abandoning ship, along with those of his crewmates who had survived the initial attack on the HMS *Bee Orchid*. Had Max done the same, waiting till last, like a good captain, before hurling himself over the rail? She imagined waves breaking over his shoulders, the numbing cold entering his bones.

Max was speaking. 'Are the fairies here always angry, wishing to harm the cows?'

'Not if you pay the correct fine to them.'

He shook his head, not following.

'Every year, at midsummer, you have to leave something of value to make them happy.'

'Such as a ring, a watch?'

'Nothing that expensive. A bowl of cream is the usual tariff, and I've usually got plenty of that, but don't tell anyone because I'm not supposed to keep any beyond our own ration.'

Max had been serious all this time, but now a smile broke through. A sad smile, but it was welcome. 'Ezra will give the fairies his cup of morning tea, I think.'

Gwenna laughed. 'Now that would be a serious sacrifice! He and my father used to argue about the old superstitions, but you know what? My dad always paid his tribute too. The one year he didn't, there was a disaster.'

Max looked intrigued and without any particular destination in mind, they continued walking, over a stile into another field which ran alongside the Glaze, and took them onto the cliff top, where Gwenna checked her watch. Wiggy would be along in twenty minutes. She mustn't keep Max. In Colvennon Cove, silvery-apricot mist rose off the sea and the sinking sun coloured the surf. Guillemots had colonised the cliffs and their busy heads made the rock face appear alive with movement. Seagulls waded in the shallows. The tide was out quite a distance, leaving stranded shellfish for those great beaks to pick over.

Max and Gwenna stood side by side, not close but sharing the same view.

'The disaster with the cows that I mentioned happened in

1921,' she said, raising her voice over the wind and the birds' jabber. It was the year she'd turned eleven. Pretty much the same age as Lotti was now, expect that she had a winter birthday. 'It was Good Friday. I remember because my mother was dressing a goose for Easter Sunday dinner. Easter was early that year and I helped my dad bring the cows from the barn for early milking, because they were still inside at that point. So, I pulled my stool up to milk my first cow and, just as now, I smelled the sea. That isn't a good thing in a milking parlour. I called Dad over, and he was perplexed. The cow he was milking had smelled fishy too. We tried another cow, and her milk also smelled and tasted of fish. I remember a sort of dread falling over my father. Course, we had to throw all the milk away.'

'The cows are ill?'

'Well, we supposed it was some hideous infection, and I know exactly what flashed across my father's mind. "We'll lose the whole herd, and the farm with it." Then he suddenly strode off.'

Max turned to face her, and now he stepped closer, to hear her over the clamour of the birds and the whip of the wind. His eyes rested on her lips, as if they were a source of mysterious knowledge. Gwenna felt suddenly tongue-tied. 'What does your father find?' Max prompted.

'You saying you could smell the sea brought it back. The day before, we'd taken a delivery of seaweed.' Raked off the rocks and dried, it was to be spread on the land as fertiliser. 'After a storm, the rocks down below are thick with seaweed and local lads collect it.' She leaned towards the edge and pointed. A gust caught her, ballooning her blouse and making her take a step sideways. Instinctively, she gripped Max's arm and their hips touched. 'The lads brought the weed up from the beach on the back of a cart, and they unloaded it too close to where the cows were housed. Our cows must have stretched their necks through the railing and nibbled a quantity of it before someone moved it. Anyway, the flavour of raw seaweed got into the milk.'

'But you did not lose the farm?'

'We lost a week's milk production and everything had to be cleaned out and sterilised ten times over. The thing was, before we brought them inside for winter, the herd had been put on Fairy Tump field and that was the one year that my father didn't pay his tribute at midsummer. He didn't go because he'd sprained his ankle stepping into a rabbit hole. Ezra blamed that on the fairies, too.'

'Afterwards, your father did make tribute?' Max asked. The wind tugging his hair revealed small scars at the apex of his cheekbones which Gwenna hadn't seen before.

Her hand lifted. She quickly lowered it. What had made her want to touch them, to ask how they'd got there? Flustered, she answered his question. 'After that, to his very last summer, my dad took a bottle of beer to the field and poured it out over the tumps. Ezra doesn't approve of me putting cows there, but imagine me trying to explain to the Ministry of Agriculture why I'm letting a whole field go to waste.' She looked up at him. His expression was locked in intensity, his thoughts closed to her, but Lotti's surprising comment was still fresh. *He watches you sometimes.*

'I'm sorry I was so rude about you, earlier,' she said quickly. 'Saying you were just a farmhand.'

'I am so. In Cornwall, it is all I am.'

'I don't think that is true.'

'Then what am I?'

'A puzzle. I didn't want you here, but when you were hurt, a slice was carved out of the farm. I don't want to feel like this.'

'You like to hate me.'

She nodded. It was so much easier. Their gazes locked. Max's eyes had always seemed the lightest grey, but the evening light revealed a halo around the iris of amber-gold dots. While her eyes tracked the circle, reading them like the numbers on a clock face, he lowered his head and kissed her.

The woman who kissed him back was not the contemptuous or reluctant employer, but lonely Gwenna who had been waiting thirteen years for arms around her. When she opened her lips to Max's kiss, his mouth became harder, more demanding, and Gwenna's thoughts sped to a hotel bedroom. In London, spring 1930, she and Edward just married. She'd been wearing her going-away suit. Edward had been staring out of their window, his shadow jutting onto the carpet, and she'd stepped into it, putting her arms around his waist, her head against the back of his shoulder. *Hello, husband.*

Edward's response had been a kind of embarrassed dance as he tried to escape her arms. By contrast, Max's hands moved restlessly against her back, her waist. His body against hers was ardent.

He raised his mouth from hers to say, 'You do not mind?'

'No.' And then the implications of what they were doing struck, and she said hoarsely, 'This is a mistake.'

He removed his hands from her waist. She missed his touch immediately.

'I'm sorry.' He cupped her face. 'Not a mistake but perhaps a danger, *ja?*'

'Yes.' Mrs Devoran, a naval officer's widow, with a German. Gwenna was thankful she'd gathered her wits in time, though it was like having nectar and ambrosia pulled out of a hungry mouth. She turned away and gave a horrified gasp.

Disaster stood on the path a few feet away.

Staring at Gwenna and Max was a woman in good tweeds and a brown hat which was in peril of being ripped away by the wind.

'Angela!' Gwenna gasped.

Her sister-in-law looked as horrified as Gwenna felt.

26

'*Lieber Gott*,' Max muttered, 'who is this?'

Without replying, Gwenna pulled away and walked towards the tweed-clad figure. 'How long have you been here?'

Angela Devoran's features assumed their customary chiselled arrogance. 'Long enough. Would you like to explain yourself?'

'No,' said Gwenna. 'How did you get here?' A foolish question. There was only one way and that was to walk.

'I was at Tregallon, on constituency business with Sir Henry.' She meant Sir Henry Copping MP, her employer. 'I thought I'd come to call, see how you were doing.'

'And you walked up the fields?' Gwenna glanced at Angela's shoes. They were low-heeled but not really suitable for striding over fields.

'Actually, I came from the village, along the cliff path.'

'You fancied a stroll by the sea?' Really? Her sister-in-law was not a great lover of nature.

'I didn't want to risk my car tyres on your execrable lane, so I parked by the church and came on foot. What do you think you're doing, Gwenna?' Max had taken a couple of strides towards them and Angela looked him up and down, taking in the work boots, pitted and scuffed from days of ploughing. The cap and boiler suit with its target-patches on the knees. 'This person is from Tregallon. I've seen his compatriots behind the barbed wire.'

'I'm sure someone told you I have German workers now.'

'She told me but I hardly imagined I'd stumble on you playing birds and bees. So much for grieving widowhood.'

'Angela, stop it.' Gwenna passed her hand across her lips, displacing the kiss. 'Be shocked if you like, but I'm not going to grovel or apologise. What's the point?'

Max waited at a distance, clearly aware that he could do nothing to help. At a slight signal from Gwenna, he walked to the wall, climbed it and was soon out of sight.

'Oh, Gwenna.' Angela wrung the name through her teeth. 'A German farmhand. Do you know what that man is, what he's done, what he stands for?'

'Of course I know. He was a captain in the German navy.' Fed up with having her hair blown in every direction, and of Angela's disdain, Gwenna took the same direction as Max. Straddling the wall, she shouted to her sister-in-law, 'Do you want tea in the house, or to go back to your car?'

'I was intending to come to the house, but under the circumstances, I won't. I've seen enough Germans for one day.'

'Then shout your reason for visiting – or come to the other side of the wall, where there's less wind.'

After a moment standing with her fists clenched, Angela came to the wall. She struggled to clamber over the rough stones and her skirt caught in the gorse. She muttered and sucked her teeth. Gwenna could have directed her to the sheep gate, of course.

When they were out of the wind, Angela said, 'I'm astonished Edward's poor face does not haunt you.'

It did haunt Gwenna, but there was little point explaining

to Angela the nightmares she suffered when her brain conjured Edward's death in close detail. Instead, she told her sister-in-law that she didn't believe in hauntings.

'But you believe in responsibility. Respectability and duty, or one would hope. Your conduct is unpatriotic. It may even be unlawful.'

'Heavens to Betsy, Angela, are you a police informant now? Max Reiner has been sent by the Ministry of Agriculture to work, along with two colleagues.'

'That was work I witnessed?'

'It was a kiss. Very human, and actually rather nice. Now I need to get back to the house so say why you're here.'

'To bring a message from Mother. I understand you called the other day and palmed the child off on her.'

'"The child" has a name. She is Lotti and I left her with Mill to their mutual delight.' Gwenna saw a pinprick of jealousy appear in Angela's face and couldn't resist pressing her point. 'Mill urged me to visit with Lotti any time I was in town.'

'That's the kind of thing Mummy would say. People take advantage.'

During her marriage and residence at Fendynick House, Gwenna had had plenty of opportunity to study Angela's verbal tics. When Angela was being overbearing, she had a mother. When she was being possessive, or commencing the slide towards martyrdom, it was 'Mummy'.

'What is the message, Angela?' Gwenna really wanted to get back to Lotti. To see if she was struggling with her maths, or worried at being left.

'I'm not sure now I wish to pass it on. How many months did you stay hunkered away here, not deigning even to visit us at Fendynick?'

'Thanks to you painting me in the worst possible colours when I left, I didn't go back at all, until I had to. For which I'm sorry,' Gwenna said. 'Try as you might, you cannot make your mother hate me, nor I her. If you won't give me the message, I'll say good evening.' She started to walk away.

'Oh, all right. It's simply to say that Mummy very kindly noticed that your young charge was woefully dressed on her visit.'

Gwenna swung round, riled despite her desire not to react to Angela's punches. 'Those are not Mill's words and there was nothing wrong with Lotti's appearance.'

'Mummy has asked me to sort out some clothes for her. I'm chairlady of the Truro Make Do and Mend Society.'

'So I understand. Save your efforts; I'll worry about Lotti's clothes.'

'But you don't even worry about your own.' Angela gave Gwenna's blouse and breeches a skimming glance.

Gwenna withstood it. She wouldn't waste her breath pointing out that she was dressed for outdoor labour. 'Why are you here, really? I don't believe you went to all this effort to bring a message Mill could have put in a note and posted. You're being nosy, aren't you?'

Angela discovered a beetle on her skirt and batted it off with a shudder. 'I was trying to help, see if there was anything I could do to help your evacuee.'

'You want to inspect Lotti, see how we're muddling on? Come and meet her, though you'll have to walk across a ploughed field.'

Angela bunched her lips. 'And ruin my shoes?'

'Probably. Once, I could have gone and fetched a donkey and cart for you, but when the donkey died, I didn't replace him.'

'I don't know how you manage, so remote and no vehicle of any sort.'

In reply, Gwenna struck her thighs like a pantomime principal boy. 'Good legs, Angela.'

'Oh, honestly.' Angela gave a scandalised roll of the eyes.

She had never been beautiful. Edward had owned all the family looks, but when Gwenna had first met her, she'd been attractive with neat features and brown hair that swept effortlessly up in an elegant bun. Gwenna had always envied Angela's hair. As a sister-in-law, Angela had been bossy and critical, but the malice had come later, as if her life's disappointments had matured like a bad cheese, adding a bitter vein to her character. Gwenna knew there had been a fiancé some twenty years ago, but he was never alluded to except once, by Edward, who had said, 'Him? Oh, he slipped the leash.' Other marriage prospects had perished in the war before this one, and so Angela's world was her work, her charities and, in Gwenna's opinion, the routine crushing of other people's simple joys. Angela's mouth had acquired a pinch and Gwenna braced herself for a fresh attack. It came.

'I ought to see this child, Lotti,' Angela said, 'as there is some concern about her in town.'

Gwenna felt suddenly cold. 'What do you mean?'

'Within the educational department, and social services.'

For a moment, Gwenna could hardly breathe. 'Why do you say that?'

Now on stronger ground, Angela's chin went up. 'I meet many officials in my role as Sir Henry's secretary. The circumstances of the child's arrival naturally made her a talking point. May I be completely honest, Gwenna?'

'No.'

'The thinking is, you don't have the time or the experience to properly nurture a difficult child.'

'You mean, *you* don't think it.'

'You never wanted children with my brother, so why now?'

Gwenna held back a furious riposte. This wasn't the time. It never was the time. Roughly, she beckoned Angela to follow her, led her to the sheep gate, opened it and gestured for her to go through, back onto the cliff path. 'Take care where you tread. Keep away from the edge.'

She then walked towards home, across the brown furrows of Colvennon Glaze.

She found Lotti at the farmyard gate, waving goodbye to Max and the others as they bumped away in the back of Wiggy's truck. 'Finished your maths?' Gwenna asked, expecting an evasive reply. If she'd been left to work her way through sums at Lotti's age, she'd have quickly found an excuse to give up. A dog or a cat needing attention, or a chicken straying out of its pen.

Lotti said she had finished, thank you. But clearly, her mind was elsewhere. 'Max looks happy now.'

'Oh, really?' Not even Angela's transparent threats had taken the imprint of Max's mouth from Gwenna's lips. 'You thought him very happy?'

'Well... not so sad.'

'That's good. Let's see how you've done.'

Inside, Gwenna picked up the maths book, turned a page and then another. 'When I said, have you finished, I meant the six sums I set you. Not the whole book.'

Every single sum was filled in. 'And Lotti, you are meant to copy them into your maths book, not fill in the textbook. Did I not say? Not that it matters.' The work was all in pencil, which could be rubbed out. 'You have been busy, but it's going to take me quite a while to check your answers.'

'You don't need to check, Aunt Gwenna. They're all correct. I went through them, so I know.'

Gwenna turned back to the first page, and saw that Lotti had changed the answers to the sums she'd filled in as examples. 'Why have you done that?'

'You got them wrong, I'm afraid.'

'Wrong – are you sure?'

'Yes. But not very wrong,' Lotti said kindly.

That night, after Lotti was in bed and Gwenna was tidying up, she found the atlas Lotti was colouring in page by page. It was open at Scandinavia. Running her finger across, Gwenna located Norway. Had Lotti been looking for the place her relations had escaped to? One of her grandmothers, an aunt and uncle had made it to Norway. 'They should have been safe,' Gwenna said, 'but then it was invaded.'

'You wish me to say sorry?' She could almost hear Max's weary answer.

'It wouldn't mean much if you did,' she muttered and felt a glimmer of the shock Angela must have experienced, seeing her in Max's arms. They'd been kissing. Passionately. A German. Where on earth had that wild desire come from?

Not from the earth, Gwenna told herself, but out of the air. When Max had looked at her in his particular way, prejudice and memories of past hurts had flown and she'd given in to the moment. Returning to the kitchen, checking Lotti's work by oil light, Gwenna was forced to admit that the only mistakes on the pages were the ones she'd made.

It was obvious this level of mathematics was way beneath Lotti's ability.

By happy coincidence, a note had arrived from Mr Beecroft during the day to say that Miss Linley would be pleased to meet Lotti and give a first lesson tomorrow afternoon, four sharp. Gwenna found the address the headmaster had written out for her. The die was cast.

Get to bed. As she mounted the stairs, the day she'd just lived through fell away behind her. She wished she had someone to share her weariness, her bed. One face only came to mind.

27

LOTTI

She liked this cow who swished her tail in time to the spritz of the milk into the pail.

The old gentleman, who called her 'little maid', had pointed at this one and said, 'You take her to be going on with.' Lotti had seen him bringing the herd into the yard and had gone to help, because it needed two to do the milking and Aunt Gwenna was still fast asleep.

'You got your stool?' Ezra had smiled, showing his funny teeth. 'We oughta make a little stool for Mr Bear to sit on, alongside 'ee.' He'd asked her if she understood and she had said, 'Yes, sir.'

'I'm Ezra Jago, Uncle Ezra if you prefer.' It had taken time to learn his way of speaking, as he talked sort of growly, not in the least like Aunt Gwenna. To Lotti's ears, his English was worse even than Max's.

Lotti called this cow Uma, after one of Papa's very old aunts who had been soft with cuddles and who had died when Lotti was quite little. She had gone to kindergarten one day, kissing the old lady in her chair, and when she came home, the chair was empty. It was some time before Lotti had realised what a grown-up meant when they said somebody had been 'gathered to her rest'. It didn't mean the person was on holiday.

When Lotti had peered round the bedroom door, Aunt Gwenna had been lying on her front, her face in her pillow. For a moment, Lotti had thought she wasn't breathing and had opened her mouth to scream. And then she saw a little thread on the collar of Aunt Gwenna's nightdress, rising and falling, and Lotti had felt her world come down to rest again, like an egg on an egg cup. She had got dressed and gone outside on her own to find the day being born, sparkling and smelling of coconut ice.

Lotti liked all of the cows with their pushy, cold noses and eyes of liquid kindness. The calves were just lovely, and Lotti did not know why some of them would have to leave the farm. Aunt Gwenna said the boy calves had to go, but why? There were lots of fields and some were empty. Uma, cow-Uma, had a scar on her udder where Lotti's eye rested when she was milking. The old gentleman had said it was because she'd been bitten once by a nasty fly, and it left a lump.

On the kitchen table, Lotti had noticed a piece of paper, with a name and address on it. Verity Linley, Cathedral Row, T/O. She'd thought T/O might mean 'turn over' but the page had been blank on the back.

Poor Aunt Gwenna had wanted Lotti to speak for ages and ages, but Lotti hadn't said a word because she'd kept her promise to Mutti who had told her after they ran across the railway tracks, 'If anybody speaks to you, Lottchen, say nothing, because if you do, they will know we are German and they will hurt us.'

Lotti had promised. Now she did speak, her head had some room in it again. The words inside were no longer pressing against the sides.

'My Lotti only ever listened to her papa,' Mutti had said when they'd been escaping from Madame's house in France. They'd held on tight because the van driver was taking side roads and 'doubling back' – whatever that meant. The man who smelled of cigarettes, who Lotti was supposed to call Oncle Gael, had told them to hunch down. 'We're going to crash a roadblock.'

The man, Gael, had been cross when Mutti started whimpering in German. He had told her, 'Stop, Madame, be quiet,' and when she didn't, told her to 'Shut your mouth. We've got police chasing us.'

Lotti knew it was because he was scared. In that part of France, the police scared everyone because they were sometimes the Milice, who liked Germans, or the Gestapo who *were* German. Papa had whispered about the Gestapo to Mutti when he thought Lotti couldn't hear. 'They have no feelings; they forget how to be human.'

The golden milk spurted into the pail. Spritz, spritz, spritz and Uma-cow munched on hay.

'My Lotti only ever listened to her papa.' Mutti had spoken of Papa as though he was gone and Lotti knew it was so as she had seen him being caught. His eye patch had come off, and he had looked for them with his good eye. Mutti had made them walk away, but Lotti had seen tears in Papa's broken eye.

Before he was caught by the police, Papa had told her, 'If ever you don't know what to say, *bubbeleh*, say nothing.' In the van when they escaped from Madame's house, she'd been ordered only to speak French. At the station when they jumped from the train, Mutti had said, 'You mustn't speak at all.'

Grown-ups were a muddle.

Yesterday, when Lotti was saying goodbye to the men at the farmyard gate, Walther had whispered, in German, 'I am sorry about your mother.'

Max had told Walther to get in the truck. Jürgen had hissed at Walther, 'She doesn't know her mother is dead, you idiot.'

But Lotti did know. She had known from very soon after it happened and then Aunt Gwenna had told her too. Lotti did not speak of it because she knew it was all her fault. Hers and Rumtopf's.

She knew her papa was dead too, because she heard him in her sleep. She had no parents now, but she did have Aunt Gwenna, the cows and Josephine, Rumtopf and Max.

'There you are!' Gwenna could hardly form the words, her throat clenched round the ragged lump in her throat. She'd woken late – horribly late – and found Lotti's bed empty. She'd sprinted to the cliff, fuelled by terror, then back to the house having found the cliff path deserted. She'd dragged on dungarees over her nightie and then taken a moment to work out that Lotti would probably be with the cows. 'I'm glad you're safe, but I wish you'd woken me.'

'You were lost in sleep and catching your snores in your teeth, Aunt Gwenna.'

'Was I?' Gwenna smiled, forgiving Lotti everything in the undiluted joy of hearing her speak. 'I'm glad you're the only one to have witnessed that. Shall I take over from you?'

'No. I am happy here.'

Gwenna walked over to Ezra, who paused the motion of his hands and told her, 'Now Walther hasn't come to work. He got a bad punching at the camp, I'm told. His nose is broken. I don't know, missus.'

Gwenna didn't know what to make of it either. 'Sounds to me as though they need more guards on duty at Tregallon. Who did the punching?'

Ezra hadn't asked. 'All I'm thinking is, there's nobody to tend to the pigs.'

'Then one of us had better see to them right away.'

Ezra shot her a grin. 'One of us is already sitting down quite comfortably.'

'I get to do the pigs? I've got to go into Truro later.' Gwenna was taking Lotti for her first coaching session. 'I can't smell of the piggery.'

'Don't you worry about that. By the time you've done the chickens, missus, you won't smell so much of pig.'

Her father had always said that people either liked cows or pigs or they liked neither. Gwenna's affinities had established themselves in childhood, but it didn't mean she didn't appreciate the friendly creatures who pushed their snouts between the rails as she approached with a swill can.

'*Bon appétit.*' She tilted the can over the fence, filling the trough. Snouts went in, back ends swung and wiggled. All the sows were in pig, bellies swollen, and they'd farrow by the middle of the month. Having scratched every head in greeting, she fetched another feed bucket and made her way over to the farm's two boars. Pendragon and Sir Galahad lived separate from the sows in bachelor quarters. Pendragon was a heavy-weight Cornish Black while Sir Galahad was an Old Spot sire, a prize-winner at the Royal Cornwall Show. Not recently, as the war had put a stop to such frivolity. As they saw her coming, the boars stuck their snouts through the bars of their pen and made sounds like builders' trowels scooping sand and cement.

'Ready?' Potato peelings, carrot tops and Yorkshire puddings that looked as though they could be fired from a small cannon tumbled into the trough. The swill came from Gwenna's kitchen, mostly peelings and apple cores, from the Mermaid pub and also from Tregallon. Some indescribable stodge plopped into the trough. 'Looks like the cook burned the POWs' porridge.'

Was that what made the men in the camp aggressive: bad food, awful accommodation? Max had thrown his iron cross off the cliff edge in a fit of either despair or rage. Men who had been inculcated with a burning mission to conquer would not sit comfortably behind fences, being fed swill.

Once they'd cleaned their trough, she let the boars out and they ambled into an abandoned orchard behind their pen. Here, they'd spend the day rootling and dozing. She then released the sows into their paddock, which was a quarter-acre of churned turf, cratered with wallow holes. Taking a moment to watch them, she retied her headscarf. With April two-thirds over, and the hedgerows greening, flies were becoming abundant. The warming days brought them from wherever they spent the winter. Now for the job she'd so happily left to Roddy Hoskens, and, more recently, Walther.

She fetched a shovel and a high-sided barrow from a shed and began attacking the muck in the sows' pen. The tools were too big for her, and her first few shovelfuls landed on the ground, but with the sun on her shoulders she discarded her cardigan and found her rhythm. A song bubbled up to her lips. 'Kiss me goodnight, Mr Churchill, I'm tired and I'm ready for my bed...'

'Mrs Devoran, you sing so sweetly.'

She lowered her spade and ran her forearm across her face. She didn't have to turn to know whose teasing voice had cut short her song. 'You've never finished the Glaze this early, Max.'

'We stop because the plough blade is dull and Jürgen...' Max mimed a sharpening motion. 'While he does this, I am wondering if you need help.'

'I wouldn't say no. I heard what happened to Walther. Was it that monster Fuhrman who broke his nose?'

'No. They are not enemies, Walther and Fuhrman.'

That was a surprise. 'Then who socked him?' Max gave an

impenetrable shrug, which annoyed her. 'You're his superior officer; you're meant to protect him.'

A chill light awoke in Max's eyes. 'You pity Walther?'

'I do. A broken nose is awful.'

'But you sing so you cannot be too unhappy. He is only another German farmhand.'

'That's not fair. I apologised for saying that yesterday.'

That brought back a smile. 'And you said much more besides.'

Last night, tired as she was, she'd lain awake imagining Max alongside her and indulging in ideas that she would reveal to nobody. 'If you must know, the song I was singing used to make my husband laugh and I was thinking of the last time he was ashore.' Nothing like summoning up a lost husband to put a dangerous new obsession back in its place.

Max looked briefly away, then back at her. 'You loved him very greatly, I think.'

She'd walked into this, and she didn't want to lie or fob him off with something trite. 'He and every man on board his ship was lost when it was sunk. I dream often that I'm on another ship, sailing to their rescue, but the waves keep pushing me back. I can hear them in the dark but cannot reach them. I hope they went quickly and weren't burned. It doesn't matter whether I loved him or not; his death torments me.'

Max seemed intent on outstaring her, and she needed to know he'd heard her. 'They were torpedoed; the ship blew up. It didn't say that in the official telegram but I know what happens when a vessel is engulfed, and the sea burns with spilled oil. I *know* what happens.'

'I too know what happens, Mrs Devoran. The sea is as cruel to Germans as it is to good Englishmen.'

Months of repressed emotion took her over and she strode up to him and thrust her hand against his breast, where the iron cross would have lain. 'The difference is, he went to sea because you started a war. You invaded a neutral country. You were the aggressor; he responded. I think you know that, otherwise I'd feel the outline of that medal under your clothes.'

He caught her wrist and held it against his heart. 'I understand what you say – it might as well be me who killed him and his fellows. But he would try to kill me in the same way, if we were in the same waters. We are all like the fish in the barrel, waiting for the gun.'

'You're not listening. Edward didn't ask to go to sea to fight. He didn't create the war.'

'Nor I, Mrs Devoran.'

'But you did, all you Germans! You let evil grow in your country. You might as well have fired the torpedo yourself and turned my husband's ship into a burning hell.'

His eyes released hers, and he pulled out a handkerchief and wiped her tears which had sprung from emotion. It was an unexpected touch that jerked her to stillness. He said, 'I might as well have killed him, but I am not evil. If you want to meet a fanatical Nazi, look for Kurt Fuhrman.'

'No thank you.'

'If you want to meet a Nazi who hides in the shadows, look at Walther Franz.'

'You're all Nazis.'

'No, we are not all so; Jürgen is not. I am not. But those who are come in all shapes, Mrs Devoran.'

'You're saying Walther is like Kurt Fuhrman? He seems so meek and harmless.'

'He is not and he will not come back to work here, I make sure of it.'

She took in his words. 'You broke his nose!'

Max admitted it. 'It is a thing I wait a long time to do. I have known Walther Franz much time, since he is one of my crew.'

'And you always wanted to hit him?'

'I ask to have him removed because he makes bad feeling on

board, but the answer is always no. He is expert signal operator; he must stay. You say we are all Nazis, but in truth we are different men, with many ideas. We are ruled by Nazis, which is why in every crew is placed some of their men.'

'Hardliners, you mean? They put them among you to keep you in order.'

'Yes. Men like Kurt Fuhrman, who measures everybody's salute to see if we make it sharp and high enough, and rats like Walther. They report on those of us who are not enough Nazi to the security police, to the Gestapo.'

'They can't now, though, can they?'

'Still they spy, and save their reports for later.'

'When you're all back home?' Gwenna recalled Fuhrman watching Max, herself and Wiggy talking at the end of the sunken lane. Had Fuhrman been filing a mental report on his captain's fraternisation with two English women?

'They believe one day they will lay their stories at the feet of the Gestapo and have reward,' Max said.

'And you allowed Walther to work here, and said nothing?' Her hand still lay against his chest and she felt the bump of buttons, the lines of stitching. She sensed the pump of blood deep in his chest.

'I tried to say that Walther Franz must not come but I might as well shout to the wall. I am sorry for not telling you, but I know you can do nothing also. I promise I have watched Walther every day, and Jürgen has watched too. Last night, as we leave, we see Walther speak to Lotti.'

'He talked to her, alone?'

Max nodded. 'About her mother, and now he lies in the sanatorium, with broken bones.'

Gwenna felt shaken. She had left Lotti unattended and a devious and dangerous man had approached her. Max ought to be admonished for attacking someone weaker than himself, but all she could think was, *The rat won't come back now.* She didn't blame Max. Only herself. Walther had seemed so inoffensive.

'*Not everyone is good.*' Thank you, Mr Beecroft.

There was a question that could not be avoided. She asked Max, 'Are you telling the truth when you say you're not a Nazi?'

'You will believe me?'

'I'll try.'

'I do not join the Nazi Party.'

What did that mean? Gwenna had never joined a political party, but she voted at elections. She had political affiliations. 'That sounds like a fudge. An excuse.'

'If you know Germany, you will understand it is not fudge.' He pronounced it *futch*.

'All right. I believe you.'

'And do you hate me still, Mrs Devoran?'

'I don't. I did – well, yesterday must have shown you that I've changed. I'm reeling from what you've told me. The thought of Walther creeping around, speaking to Lotti about her mother of all things – it makes my skin crawl. I wish I'd let Roddy shoot him that first day.'

'No, that does not go well. You will see Walther never again.'

'I'd better not. If he dares show his face—' The creak of poorly oiled wheels told Gwenna that someone was about to join them. She reached for her shovel.

'I have not changed, Mrs Devoran.' Max took the implement from her. 'I think about you all night, and all the nights before, though I should not.'

'Anybody at home?' came a cheerful, nasal voice.

Gwenna seized back her shovel and began thumping down the muck in her barrow. If they'd had another ten minutes, she knew she would have kissed Max again.

28

It was Wiggy, her curls only a few shades lighter than her duster-turban. She was bringing a swill can, one of those sent up from Tregallon, and it was lashed to a sack barrow. They were usually left at the lane end. 'Thought I'd bring this up to you, since you're a man down.' She grinned at Max, who had put a careful distance between himself and Gwenna. Nobody would guess that moments before they had been touching. 'Go on, Hercules, ram it on your shoulder. I've done my bit.'

Gwenna pointed to the feed store and Max strode away, lugging the vessel against his chest.

'I like a strong man who doesn't answer back.' Wiggy peered into Gwenna's face. 'There's something different about you today.'

'Lotti's talking. It was a wonderful moment, and I feel I'm finally seeing the wood for the trees.' She told Wiggy that, later, she was taking Lotti to Truro, for her first lesson with a proper tutor.

'Oh, my.' Wiggy turned her eyes to Max. 'D'you realise, queen, your man doesn't have to do a day's work if he doesn't want to. As an officer, he could sit around in the camp and sketch the scenery. The Geneva Convention says so.'

'He likes to be busy.'

'He needn't wear those godawful clothes either. Officers are entitled to have uniforms made, copies of their real ones. Medals and all.'

'So why doesn't he?' Gwenna bounced the question off Max's back. What drove him to volunteer for back-breaking labour if he could sit around in his camp, enjoying the privileges of rank? Something had made him put his name down for work, and then stick at it. A desire to get out of a place populated with ideological enemies? Had he stayed to keep watch on Walther Franz, to protect her and Lotti? Gwenna had noticed early on that Jürgen and Max didn't really like Walther. Now she knew why.

Wiggy flicked up an eyebrow. 'Did I barge in on something?'

'Not at all.' Gwenna fluttered a hand at the half-cleaned pen. 'I'm doing the pigs and Max came to see if I needed a hand.'

Wiggy sniffed. 'And there's me thinking you'd doused yourself in Chanel No. 5.' She picked a piece of straw from Gwenna's hair. 'I know you two have a thing.'

'We don't. Please don't say such a thing.'

'I'm the eldest of seven including four boys who were lying little toads growing up, so I can always winkle out an untruth. Besides' – Wiggy licked a finger, held it in the air – 'it's mating season.'

'For heaven's sake! We were talking about something serious.'

'Like, a creepy POW with a broken nose?' As Gwenna gave a cautious nod, Wiggy checked nobody was nearby. 'Not a word, right? I always let a couple of POWS sit up alongside me when I'm driving back of an evening. They take it in turns, very Germanic. It relieves overcrowding in the back of the truck and lets them practise their English. I pride myself that after this war's over, I'll send them back home fluent in Scouse. So, in consequence, I know more about Camp Tregallon than the guards. Such as, why Walther got nobbled.'

'He's a Nazi and was infiltrated into Max's crew along with that man, Fuhrman. The one you insisted was all hot air. They're paid-up, fanatical Nazis, riding around the countryside in your truck with nothing to stop them making a run for it. I doubt Walther's got the courage, but what if Fuhrman decides to fight his war here, on our ground?'

'He'll get shot,' Wiggy said in a matter-of-fact way. 'By the way, Walther Franz suffered more than a broken hooter. His thumb and two fingers of his right hand were fractured as well.'

It seemed to Gwenna that Max had done a thorough job. Had he gone too far? She commented to Wiggy, 'You'd think the guards would stop the men harming each other.'

'Guards don't sleep in the huts, and they're not behind every tree. There's two teams at Tregallon. Team one is boggle-eyed Nazis and team two are those who'd give a cheer if they heard Adolf Hitler had fallen down a well. I mean, they're all bastard Germans but some still think they're fighting the war, while the ones like Max have embraced reality. The two factions are getting closer to each other's throats.' Wiggy followed Max's progress as she spoke. He was closing the feed store, brushing down his overalls. 'He's respected, and popular with most of his crew, but a few of them blame him for getting them taken prisoner. They think he should never have surrendered.'

'He says he's not a Nazi, Wiggy. I think I believe him.'

'You want to, and why not?' Wiggy shrugged. 'Max doesn't strike me as a man who thinks the answer to every question is "Heil Hitler!" Men of his age were funnelled into one service or the other, whether they liked it or not. I can't see him falling for that "blood and glory" nonsense.'

'No. It was never like that for Edward,' Gwenna agreed. 'My late husband believed it was a fight for good over evil; otherwise, he couldn't have done it.'

'I believe in evil,' Wiggy said. 'And the worse the war goes for the Germans, the nastier the atmosphere turns at Tregallon. They see British newspapers, so they know it's not all going their way. Our bombers are flattening their industrial zones, and they all have families back home.'

'Does Max have a wife?' The question shot out.

Wiggy gave her a searching look. 'Ask him yourself. Everyone has someone they care about.'

'He has sisters, he told me. In Dresden, in the east.'

'Far as I know, we haven't bombed Dresden yet.' Something was gnawing at Wiggy. 'When did you lose your Edward?'

'A year last November.'

'Nineteen forty-one, then. Out of interest, how much do you know about Max's naval career?'

The question surprised Gwenna. Did Wiggy assume she and Max relaxed after the day's work was done and compared life experiences? 'All I know is he's *Kriegsmarine* and that he won the Iron Cross. That's for gallantry, isn't it?'

'Gallantry – or a good aim. I hope you don't think I'm speaking out of turn—' Wiggy stopped. Max was coming back towards them. He paused as if some subtle change in the women's posture inhibited him.

He called to Gwenna, 'I finish the pigs for you?'

'She says yes,' Wiggy shouted back. Whatever else she'd been about to say, the moment had passed. 'Any chance of a quick cuppa? And I need your facilities again.'

They drank their tea sitting on the kitchen garden wall, Wiggy blowing on hers. She needed to be on her way but was held back by things left unsaid. 'Sure I haven't upset you, talking about Tregallon?'

Gwenna reassured her. 'It's important I know what kind of men are coming onto my land every day.'

'And you'll keep quiet about what I said? I'll be in heaps of trouble if anyone finds out I chat with the POWs.'

Gwenna promised, then voiced her thoughts. 'I suppose I imagined every man in a POW camp would be on the same side. The opposite side to us. I am naive,' she added resignedly. 'I was quite sheltered, growing up here.'

'You don't say.' Wiggy regarded the squat farmhouse and its yard hemmed about by barns and old stone buildings.

'Edward said I always thought the best of people until proved otherwise.'

'That's fair enough.' Wiggy looked down at her fingers, the short nails with their illicit shine of clear polish. 'Your Edward died at sea, right?'

Gwenna nodded. She didn't mind talking about it to Wiggy, who could be trusted not to trot out polite sympathy, or ask the dreaded question: 'Don't you wish you had children to remember him by?'

'He was sub-lieutenant of a "Flower class" corvette, the *Bee Orchid*. They were on convoy escort; they'd come from South Africa and were almost home. His ship was the second of five to be torpedoed in one night.'

'God love you, queen.'

'Yes. I often wake at night, thinking, "This must be the time it happened." He was a few miles off the coast of Ireland.' Gwenna managed a kind of smile. 'A day from home.'

'I've two brothers at sea.' Wiggy shuffled her shoulders. 'Where I come from, the sea sucks the lads in. It's either navy, merchant or royal, or get on your bike to Birkenhead and work at the yard, making the ships. My youngest brother, Mikey, is a rating on a destroyer and Vince is an ASDIC operator on another. ASDIC is the anti-submarine thingummy.'

Gwenna knew slightly more of that than Wiggy did. It was echo detection equipment that located German submarines by picking up underwater sound waves. Edward had described the wonders of it once, in her hearing, saying how strangely soothing it was to sit in the ASDIC tent at the back of the ship, lulled by its rhythmic pinging. Listening for enemy subs slinking deep below, finding and destroying them.

Sometimes, detection failed, as the *Bee Orchid* and other ships in Edward's convoy had found to their calamitous cost. 'You're afraid for your brothers,' Gwenna said. It hardly merited saying. Something was sending Wiggy's gaze away into the distance.

'Only every night and most days.' Wiggy drank down her tea and flicked a smile. 'Specially Mikey. He's only seventeen, cocky little arse.' She wedged her tea mug in a cleft between the stones of the wall and jumped down. 'Can't chew the cud all day, queen. See you later. Don't do anything I wouldn't do.'

'That's a fair bet,' Gwenna answered, as her mind ranged over the rest of the morning's task sheet. She'd learned a lot in a day that wasn't many hours old. Walther Franz would not work on a farm again.

'Kiss Me Goodnight, Mr Churchill' was a very silly song.

Max Reiner thought about her at night and if Wiggy hadn't butted in, she'd probably have told him that she, too, hated an empty bed.

Miss Linley's terraced cottage was part of a row that had once housed cathedral clerics. It had arched, lattice windows and hanging baskets each side of the door. These were packed with drooping tendrils of strawberries. Miss Linley clearly took her duty to grow her own food seriously.

'Here we are.' Gwenna knocked at a knotty pine door. 'Ready?'

Lotti was wearing her cherry-pattern dress and the blue cardigan with the pearl buttons. Both garments now looked tight on the child, and Angela's disparaging comments came back. 'Your young charge was woefully dressed...'

Still, Lotti looked healthy, her complexion bright, and with plaits neatly braided, she looked the picture of a schoolgirl on her way to extra lessons. Except that she had refused to leave Rumtopf behind.

The door opened and a small, white-haired woman filled the space with her smile. Inhabiting her late sixties, grey cardigan, spectacles, stockings and shoes, Miss Linley made Gwenna think of a squab pigeon. Her tone was fittingly soft. 'This is Lotti, yes? And you are Mrs Devoran. And this?' She pushed her spectacles down her nose to inspect Rumtopf.

Gwenna let Lotti answer. Lotti whispered the name.

'Oh, a German gentleman. A sailor, by the looks of things. Come along in. Will you sit in today, Mrs Devoran?'

Gwenna had anticipated the question. 'I'll settle Lotti with you, then pop out.' On the bus, she had reached a decision. 'I'm going to drop in at St Morgan's and hopefully see the headmistress about Lotti doing the examination next year.'

'Why next year?' Miss Linley looked down at Lotti. 'You've still time this year; it's not till the end of June.'

'I just don't think Lotti is ready.'

'Shall we wait and see? I'll tell you if she's not, but there's no harm putting her down for the exam now and cancelling if we feel that's best.'

Gwenna digested this. It made sense. 'All right. Nothing ventured, after all.'

Miss Linley advised her to speak to the school secretary, not the headmistress. 'She's generally there till five. I'll see you back here at six, if that's all right.' As Gwenna made to leave, Miss

Linley said in an altered voice, 'I remember you from school, by the way.'

'You taught at St Morgan's? I'm sorry, I don't—'

'You wouldn't. I've changed since 1924. I stood in for the geography mistress who was ill for a term. You were Freda Helyer's quiet friend.'

'What an extraordinary memory, Miss Linley.'

'I remember because you correctly named all the countries in Africa, the only child who ever managed it.'

'Yes!' Gwenna had swotted for hours. Her mother had tested her over and over. 'I got a gold star!'

'You wouldn't have done if I hadn't been sharp-eyed. Your friend Freda swapped your paper with hers at the end of the lesson. She was the monitor and collected them all in.' Seeing Gwenna's expression, Miss Linley snorted. 'Did you never realise?'

'No.'

'Don't worry. I swapped them back. The first attribute of a good teacher is eyes on all sides of the head.'

Walking the short distance to Old Bridge Street, where St Morgan's commanded a central position, Gwenna mulled on what she'd just heard. Freda Helyer's shy friend. Ha. *I am still her friend,* Gwenna told herself, *but stealing my answers? And her a good Quaker!*

As Gwenna aimed her feet towards a white pillared entrance, she felt a new resolve. After the inquest, she and Freda had wrestled for possession of Lotti, which felt wickedly unethical. But love was not ethical. It made you ready to rip off an arm to have and to hold. Freda – she had suspected and was now certain – cared for Lotti but also wanted to prove a point. To win, in other words.

But would Freda sit cross-legged by Lotti's bed in the early hours, listening for the first sounds of a nightmare? Or put Lotti down for a school entrance exam she had little chance of passing, because it was worth a mad try? No. Freda would deem it irrational and march the child to Dr Kleinman. Love was selfish but was also the most generous of emotions. Freda had not always acted generously towards Gwenna, and Miss Linley's revelation was the latest proof.

They were due to go to London at the beginning of July. Gwenna hoped desperately she'd have something solid on which to hang her claim to Lotti. A place at St Morgan's would be a very good beginning. Sixty-three days for Gwenna to prove to Freda that life in Cornwall was Lotti's best hope. She rang the front doorbell of the school.

A brisk fifteen minutes later, Gwenna walked out again with wilting confidence. The school secretary had warned that, owing to high demand for places at the school, only those girls who excelled in the examination would be considered. Would Charlotte – St Morgan's Girls School shied away from pet names – be intending to enter as a full boarder, weekly boarder or day girl? Gwenna hadn't been at all sure. Day or weekly, one or the other. It depended...

'On the level of fees? There are bursaries, if Charlotte does particularly well in her examination.'

That felt very unlikely. Nevertheless, Gwenna had formally entered Lotti's name on the exam roster.

29

Colvennon Glaze was now ploughed edge to edge, and it was still only the 28th of April. They'd finished ahead of the May Day deadline. Gwenna had baked a cake with grated carrot and apples from the storehouse, and it was waiting in the pantry. Ezra had put stone jars of beer in the cooling shed, and they would have a mid-morning celebration. All of them. The 'no fraternisation' rule had well and truly expired, Gwenna reflected. On a working farm, you couldn't patrol and keep people separate. Truth was, she trusted Max and Jürgen. 'Lotti, please get the cake out, and if you like, cut it into portions.'

Miss Linley had told Gwenna that the first lesson had gone well, that Lotti was adept at fractions. 'I suspect she's rather clever and the only thing holding her back is the many disruptions to her schooling.' Miss Linley had suggested three coaching sessions a week, as the exam was less than two months away.

When Gwenna came downstairs, having washed and changed for their little party, she found Lotti marking the cake out in five large, equal slices.

'Uncle Ezra, Max, Jürgen, you, Aunt Gwenna, and me.'

Looking at the meticulous angles scored on top of the cake, Gwenna felt a surge of optimism. In Lotti, intelligence was married to precise hand control. Of course, she was the daughter of a tailor and a milliner.

'Where is Walther?' Lotti suddenly asked. 'Shall I save him a slice of cake?'

'Um, no. Walther's unwell.' Gwenna searched the child's face, scanning for signs of distress. She found none and shed a few lurking fears. Apart from that one last approach which Max had quickly shut down, she was confident Walther had not imposed himself on Lotti. 'Let's set the table, shall we?'

'Has he got sick, then?'

'Er, yes. Quite badly. He won't come back.' Gwenna hated lying. Years on, it still hurt that her parents had concealed her grandmother's death from her, judging her too young to know. And of course, Edward had built a lie the size of a castle keep. She told herself that on this occasion, false information was justified. Lotti's newfound happiness was fragile.

Outside, a late-April shower had come and gone, and a rainbow that warned of a second one was being absorbed by darting cloud. Still, it was too damp to sit outside. Seeing Max and Jürgen enter the yard, Gwenna called to them. 'We're having food inside.'

The men hesitated in the doorway. 'We smell of pig,' Max said. Her nose had already told her that they'd been round the back, doing Walther's job.

'Take your boots off at the door,' Gwenna answered. 'My nose is used to it. Over time, one adjusts.'

'Adjusts.' Max repeated the word, stowing it away. At her invitation, he and Jürgen took their places at the table.

Jürgen watched Lotti propping Rumtopf in his usual place against a vase containing the last daffodils of the season. '*Hey, Mausi, wie gehts?*'

'*Sehr gut, danke,*' Lotti replied. 'But we have to speak English now.'

'*Ach, ja.*' Jürgen nodded.

Ezra came in, taking his boots off at the door and revealing a pair of neatly darned woollen socks. He had the beer, and Gwenna fetched a stoppered bottle of ginger beer for Lotti. As she poured the drinks, she listened to Lotti saying, 'When I am scared, I forget poor Rumtopf, and he has nobody to look after him. I sometimes think I deserve to lose him. Do you feel scared sometimes?'

The question was for Max. who considered it seriously. He said, 'I used to, often. All us men did because there were times we were in the mightiest danger.'

'Did you run away?' That was Ezra, tongue in cheek, but with an edge of gravity.

'There is nowhere to run when you are in a U-boat. You may dive, or surface, or surrender. This is all the choice you have but as captain, the first job is not to have fear.'

Gwenna stared at him. Had she heard correctly? Max had captained a U-boat? A submarine. *Der Kriegswolf.* She'd assumed it was a surface vessel, a ship. He'd let her think it... or she had made the assumption. She slowly looked from Max to Jürgen. Submariners. Seeing them for the first time at Truro station in salt-stained leather jackets, she'd assumed them to be ordinary German sailors.

Max was looking perplexed. 'Mrs Devoran, you do not join us to celebrate? This beer is very good.'

'Best Cornish,' Ezra agreed and raised his glass. 'To speed the plough and ask God's blessing on the land.'

Gwenna caught hold of herself. She wanted to run. Like Lotti when afraid, she needed to scream. Edward's ship had been sunk by a torpedo fired from a submarine. A captain just like Max Reiner had given the order to fire.

'Aunt Gwenna?' Lotti plucked at Gwenna's sleeve. 'You aren't eating your cake. It's lovely.'

'Yes.' Gwenna tried to smile. Happiness, a fragile bubble. She must not prick it. With all her willpower, she pulled the threads of herself together, ate a corner of her apple and carrot cake, raised her glass, pushed the bitter beer down her throat. She must have chatted, even laughed, because nobody guessed that she wanted to snatch Edward's photograph off the bookcase and run with it to the cliff edge and howl into the wind.

When the proximity of Max and Jürgen grew too much, she retreated to stand against the stove, like a good wife surveying her feast. The beer was drunk, Jürgen and Ezra rose to go, some job in mind. Neither man was a sitter-at-table. They had what Gwenna's mother would have called 'fidgets in their bones'.

Max and Lotti remained. They were talking, Max using his careful English, Lotti chattering back. To Gwenna, they might as well have been speaking Greek. Her head pounded with a nightmare image. A dark, dark sea, a ship ablaze. Explosions against the pitch-black sky. Two ships ablaze, then others. Men, their faces lit by the unnatural glow, bobbing and gasping in the broiling sea.

'Mrs Devoran.' She had the impression Max had spoken her name three or four times. He was holding Lotti's hand across the table. Lotti's shoulders were drawn inward, bunching the collar of her cardigan.

Instantly, Gwenna slid onto the chair beside Lotti. She sought Max's eyes and discovered that his face was a tremulous blur, viewed through an oppressive pain in her temples. 'What did you say, what's brought this on?'

'She asks me about my papa,' Max said. 'Is he in Germany? I tell her I lose my father when I have eight years. Lotti tells me she loses her papa when she has nearly ten years. This is what makes her sad. I say to her she cannot know where her papa is but one day she will know.'

'That's all? You didn't offer any opinion about where he might be?'

'Of course not. For now, she must live the life he would like for her, is all I said.'

Lotti spoke. 'When I told Ezra my papa was dead when we were milking, he said, "Your papa's in heaven, looking down."'

'That is what Ezra believes. He believes that heaven is a place, and we go to it. Lotti, do you believe it?' Gwenna asked.

Lotti nodded. 'I do. Papa is with me some days and at night. If he was still in France, where the policemen took him, I would not feel him. I know I have lost Papa and Mutti and they are together with Tante Uma and my Grandpapa Jakob and my other grandparents who died before I was born. One day I will see them.' Her eyes blazed at Gwenna, daring her to contradict her. 'I have only you now, Aunt Gwenna, and you, Max.'

Oh, heaven help the child. Gwenna folded Lotti's small hand in hers. Max's hand enclosed Gwenna's. Or perhaps hers slipped inside his as into a glove. A submariner. How could he have concealed it? As the room slowly whirled around her, they sat, their joined hands completing a triangle. Untouched cake on her plate reminded Gwenna of a scone left uneaten in a railway dining car.

Into this emotional vortex came voices. At first they seemed disembodied, as if squeezed out of the wireless.

'Careful how you step, and where you step. The state of the yard, Mummy. You might mention it to Gwenna.'

And the reply: 'I'm perfectly well-shod for this adventure, Angela, and why should I add anything to poor Gwenna's list of worries?'

Oh, no, please not now. If Gwenna could have run, she would. But she was locked in a three-way handclasp, and all she could do was steel herself and wait.

.   .   .

The kitchen door was thrust open and Angela Devoran pitched a brusque 'Hello?' into the room. 'Oh, you're here...' Her voice petered out as her gaze fell on the three people at the table. Her attention switched next to the empty glasses whose insides were laced with froth. 'Beer at eleven twenty in the morning?'

'Gwenna, dear.' Camilla Devoran came in carrying two large parcels. 'I hope you don't mind, but I've brought Lotti—' The look of absolute horror as she took in the scene at the table would stay with Gwenna. Mill stared at Max's hair, which had still to fully grow out of the severe crop given him by the camp barber, and at his hard-hewn profile. When he stood politely, letting go of Gwenna's hand, she visibly flinched. She opened her lips but found no words.

Lotti wriggled off her chair and went to her, saying, 'Aunt Mill!'

'Lotti, dearest.' Mill cuddled Lotti against her cardigan, while holding Gwenna's gaze.

Max showed no embarrassment, and addressed the visitors. 'Good day, *gnädige Frauen*. Forgive me, I have work to do.' He left, with 'gracious ladies' suspended in the air like a bad smell. He'd spoken German purposely, Gwenna was sure.

'Mill,' she said, her voice catching like toast crumbs in her throat, 'I wasn't expecting you but how lovely to see you.'

'What on God's green earth were you doing with that man, your hand in his?'

'I warned you, Mummy.' Angela's Judas tones throbbed with vindication. 'I told you she had German workers and fraternisation was taking place.'

Mill told Angela to kindly allow her the use of her own voice. 'Actually, you told me that Gwenna was in need of guidance and that Lotti was desperately short of clothes. You said nothing of German POWs. I imagine you hoped I'd stumble on such a tableau. Well, your hopes are met.'

Gwenna was contrite. 'Please believe me, I didn't ask for

Max to come here. He and the others were forced on me by the Ministry.'

'I don't suppose you did go out to find them.' Mill indicated the empty glasses, the cake platter with its buttery residue. 'Is Edward's death so much in the past?'

'No. Forgive me.'

Mill gently unlatched Lotti. 'We've brought clothes we think will fit her – Angela, take these parcels from me. Lotti dear, go with Miss Devoran and pick the items you like.'

Lotti looked at Gwenna. In her face the clearest 'Don't make me' Gwenna had ever seen.

'Put them on the dining-room table,' Gwenna told Angela. 'We'll look at them together.' The stubborn will that had driven Gwenna from Fendynick House to solitude at Colvennon came to her aid. She turned back to her mother-in-law. 'If you wish to scold me, Mill, do it in front of every-one.' This domestic drama with a coldly triumphant Angela and a distressed Camilla was wearyingly familiar. She was having none of it here, in her sanctuary. 'Say what you want to say.'

Mill went to the bookcase, drawn there by a mother's instinct. She brought the photograph of Edward in his naval uniform to the table, placing it face down.

Gwenna turned it over. 'They say that you never know the inside of a marriage unless you're the one inside it.'

'What does that mean?' Mill was momentarily distracted by Josephine, who had leapt up onto the window sill outside and was batting the glass to catch a fly on this side.

'It means that you should be cautious with whatever repri-mand you have in mind. There is a child present.'

Mill shook her head. 'You're a widow, entitled to do as you wish, but imagine the scandal, the social cost, Gwenna, if you were to compromise yourself. You haven't thought it through.'

'Of course she hasn't. She's the one who ran away from

Fendynick, stockings trailing out of her suitcase.' Angela used the voice that cut through paper.

Gwenna saw Lotti flinch at the harsh tone and said, 'Darling, take Rumtopf up to your bedroom. Why don't you read for a little while?' Lotti was out of the room before Gwenna had finished the sentence.

'What about the clothes?' Angela indicated the brown paper parcels.

'Take them into the dining room and your mother and I will join you in a moment.'

Angela stalked out with the parcels. Two doors opened and slammed behind her. When she and Mill were alone, Gwenna folded her arms. 'This visit feels like an ambush dressed up as being helpful.'

'Angela felt you needed advice on Lotti's clothes.'

'Angela told me that *you* raised the subject of Lotti's clothes.'

'Well, I didn't. Angela mentioned the child has only one dress to her name.'

'How on earth would Angela know?'

Mill sat down. 'Sir Henry has taken his wife to London, leaving her at a loose end. She's been busily acquiring things for Lotti, and suggested we seize the moment. I had no idea that coming would cause such an upset.'

'What do they say about unannounced visits?'

Mill managed a faint smile. 'That uninvited guests are most welcome when they leave.'

Gwenna wasn't yet ready to smile. 'I had in mind something about "Beware what you discover".'

'What have I discovered, Gwenna?'

Gwenna settled on the truth. 'Nothing much. I'm lonely. I have been for years. Max is interesting. Attractive.'

'War makes many women lonely, my dear.'

'I've been lonely since long before the war started.' Gwenna ran her fingertips across the glass of Edward's photograph. His features at this range were dots of grey and charcoal. 'I've been on my own, largely untouched, since the 18th of August 1930.'

The date's significance soaked in. 'That was your wedding day,' Mill exclaimed. 'You're saying you were neglected? It isn't true! We made you part of our family.'

'I said "untouched". There were days I longed for a little benign neglect.'

Mill looked bewildered. She'd made an effort for this visit, Gwenna realised. The untidy hair was brushed and secured with a mock-tortoiseshell band Gwenna had bought her one Christmas. For a moment, Gwenna was tempted to appease. To ask forgiveness again. And then she thought – *No. I've chewed on thistles for too many years. It's time Mill knew.* 'August 19th, my first full day as a married woman, was the most miserable of my life. Had you any idea?'

Mill picked up Edward's photograph and held it away from her, her expression folding into agony at the sight of her son in dress uniform at a ship's rail. 'It makes no sense for you to say you were unhappy. Gwenna. I know I'm his mother but Edward was such a catch! Handsome, well connected. Girls swooned.'

Gwenna knew that her reality clashed with what Mill had chosen to see, which was the myth of a sensitive Edward who married on the rebound of rejection by Freda. Edward, enduringly good-natured, plumping for Freda's unspectacular friend, making the best of things, and without the solace of children to comfort him. She opened her mouth to speak, but Angela reappeared just then.

She'd got bored waiting for them in the dining room. 'I wouldn't say no to a little refreshment.' Her eye alighted on the teapot.

With a buried sigh, Gwenna lit the Primus and filled the kettle.

'Is that your own butter?' Angela lifted the cow's head dish which Gwenna hadn't returned to the pantry. It held a generous pat of butter striped with knife marks.

'It is,' Gwenna said, detecting a hint. 'Would you like some?'

Angela's tongue made a dart to her top lip. 'Only if you can spare it.'

Gwenna parcelled the butter in greaseproof paper and passed it to Angela. She then replaced the photograph of Edward on the bookcase.

'Before you came in, Gwenna was telling me how very unhappy she was, married to Edward,' Mill blurted out.

Angela's expression tightened, showing a hint of alarm. 'Why?'

'Why was I saying it, or why was I unhappy?' Gwenna didn't want this conversation with Angela. She doubted her mother-in-law was ready for it at all. 'I explained in the letter I wrote after I came back here. Edward had someone else. A lover. I was tired of being second best. His rejection of me began hours after we walked from the altar.'

'Rubbish,' said Angela.

Gwenna ignored the comment. 'Mill, your son married me because he wanted a wife. I "did the job" but it took me some painful months to realise that I could have been inter-changeable with any compliant, moderately intelligent female.'

Mill was shaking her head. 'He was awfully fond of you.'

'"Awfully fond"? Pardon me for wanting more. Such as, "madly in love" or "dizzy with passion". Awfully fond is how I feel towards the older cows in my herd.'

'Is your German dizzy with passion? One cannot imagine it somehow.' Angela had relaxed, as she sensed Gwenna pulling back from more intimate revelations. 'Has he a name, rank and number?'

'He is Kapitänleutnant Max Reiner...' The next words

required a hard breath. 'Of the *Kriegsmarine*. The German navy.'

With a hard laugh and an 'I told you so' look at her mother, Angela left the room, saying, 'I'll sort out some of those clothes myself, as Gwenna obviously hasn't the inclination. Then we'll go.' Clearly, she'd given up on the idea of tea.

Mill, meanwhile, sank down again onto a chair. She breathed deeply, trying to regain her poise. 'I'm glad your German friend isn't a stoker or a rating. Not that one is a snob, but it helps to think that you've gone up the ranks, Gwenna. My son would appreciate the irony as he'd hoped to be one day given command of a ship.'

'This isn't fair, Mill.'

'Life isn't, but it is a constant source of astonishment and wry humour, if one has the taste for it. You may be a captain's lady yet. What was his ship called? Something appropriately aggressive, I suppose.'

'*Kriegswolf.*' Only it wasn't a ship—

'*Wolf of War*. I couldn't somehow imagine the Germans naming their ships after flowers.' Mill suggested it might be interesting to plot the course of the *War Wolf* and discover what havoc she had wreaked among Allied shipping. 'For instance, did your captain ever fire at our troop carriers, or at ships taking civilians to Canada and America?'

Nothing would now induce Gwenna to admit that Max Reiner had commanded one of the feared German U-boats.

A thump from the floor above made them look up. Gwenna went quickly through to the dining room. Summer dresses, jerseys and blouses covered the long table, arms thrown back in an attitude of surrender. Of Angela there was no sign.

30

In Lotti's bedroom, there were clothes on the bed. Clothes Gwenna recognised. The wardrobe door was open and Angela was reaching in.

'What are you doing? Where's Lotti?'

Angela straightened up, gripping a coat hanger from which hung the outdated dress Gwenna had shortened for Lotti. She told Angela to put it back.

'I'm removing whatever the child must soon grow out of,' Angela said without a trace of embarrassment. 'Another child somewhere can make use of this. We have to reuse our precious resources. There's a war on, you know.'

If Gwenna had been a goose or turkey, she'd have struck at Angela with her beak. She made do with narrowing her nostrils and saying quietly, 'Leave Lotti's clothes alone.' Taking the hanger from Angela, she returned the dress to the wardrobe. 'This is Lotti's private space.'

'Children don't have private spaces.'

'Where is she?'

'I haven't seen her. I heard her as I came up the stairs, so I presume she's hiding.' Angela pulled out Lotti's red coat and cast it onto the bed. 'Did you glance into the dining room?'

'Yes.'

'Then you will have seen what I've acquired for her. Making room in the wardrobe is good management. Hoarding is unpatriotic.'

'So is driving around, burning fuel, on social calls.'

That passed right over Angela's head. 'The clothes are things Lady Copping's daughters have grown out of, and some are handmade. You know who Lady Copping is?'

'Your employer's wife.'

'Of Tredorcas Manor. Are you turning your nose up at clothes donated by the wife of Cornwall's most popular member of parliament?'

'I wasn't turning up my nose until you demanded Lotti's possessions in exchange.' Gwenna took the red coat, clamping it over her arm.

'Red is such an unsuitable colour, and it's no kindness to make the girl stand out.'

'Then why would you want to pass it on to another child?'

Angela responded with an exasperated sigh. Gwenna said, 'Take Lady Copping's cast-offs away and kiss her bottom while you're at it.'

An argument flowed, ending with Angela blaming Gwenna for Edward's unhappy life, not least breaking the engagement between him and Freda Helyer. 'Who would have suited him perfectly.'

'And my pigs might fly. And don't do your usual, blaming me for inciting him to join the Royal Navy. Somebody else had a hand in that.' Gwenna watched her sister-in-law's reaction closely.

It was classic Angela. 'We're a naval family; going to sea is traditional for our menfolk. Or perhaps he joined up to escape a disappointing marriage.'

'He joined up to gain his freedom, but I didn't drive him into it.' Edward had adored being a musician, the long days of rehearsal when, in his own words, he could escape the leaden ties of being human in a stifling age. 'We both know the truth. Perhaps it's time to speak it.'

Something of the cornered animal came over Angela, but she battled on. 'This, from the woman fornicating with the German enemy in front of a child?'

A movement at their feet made them both look down. The quilted coverlet hanging in folds at the base of the bed shifted. A small face peered out at them.

'Come out at once,' Angela ordered.

Lotti slithered out and stood by Gwenna. Angela, meanwhile, took the red coat from Gwenna and held it up, measuring it with her eye against Lotti.

'It's too heavy for the summer and she'll have grown out of it by October. There's a smart gaberdine with a tartan lining downstairs, belted and side vented. A little large to start with, but she'll grow into it. Lady Copping says it came from Walton's in Exeter. She takes a strong interest in Lotti's well-being.'

Lotti lunged for her coat but Angela was too quick. 'Don't be a baby.' She removed Rumtopf from the end of the bed and tried to leave but Lotti clutched at her jacket.

'*Nein, nein!*'

Gwenna also blocked the door. 'Angela, put him down.'

'The child's too old for a toy.'

'Put him back.'

'*It.* It's an it.'

The unearthly screams that poured from Lotti paralysed both women, and brought Mill up the stairs.

'What in heaven's name?'

Gwenna hissed, 'Tell your daughter to give those things back. I mean it, Mill. I'm an inch from murder.'

In a voice Gwenna had never before heard her use, Mill shouted, 'Angela, do it.'

Quite pale in the cheeks, Angela hurled the coat and bear at Gwenna, snatched her jacket hem from Lotti's grip and stalked to the stairs, informing her mother she would wait for her in the car. Mill apologised, sounding and looking stricken.

'You know how it is – Angela never can allow anyone else the last word, or the last action.'

'She went too far, Mill.' Lotti's screams had subsided, but their return had torn into Gwenna's self-possession. 'Please take her away, and the stuff she brought.'

'Gwenna... I have a feeling this is about more than Angela's blundering. That man you were with – do you love him?'

'No.' *Yes.* She didn't know.

'Just remember that lust can disguise itself as love.' Mill urged her not to reject the clothes in the dining room. 'Lotti is growing out of her things; even I can see that. She can't go out into the world in skirts above her knee.'

'How can Lotti go into a world where adults behave like Angela?'

'Because they don't all behave like that, and Lotti is resilient. She's proved it.' Mill hugged herself, as if something ice-cold had passed through her. 'You have to launch the child, not wrap her in cotton wool.'

Gwenna turned to Lotti, who was sitting on the bed, hugging Rumtopf. 'Do you want to stay here a little while?'

Lotti didn't answer. Gwenna took it as yes. 'I'll come and fetch you in a bit.'

Downstairs, there was no sign of Angela. The butter was gone from the table and after Gwenna returned from escorting Mill to the car, she sensed something else had gone too. It took a moment to work out that the photograph of Edward on his ship was missing. 'To shield his eyes from my wanton lusts, Angela?'

'What are wanton lusts, Aunt Gwenna?' She hadn't realised that Lotti had padded quietly down the stairs to join her.

31

Looking at Lotti in the red coat, Gwenna had to concede that it was short on her. 'You've made another stealthy growth spurt. All the rich milk.' Gwenna lifted the coat away from Lotti's shoulders. 'With a bit of letting out here and at the hem, you might get another winter's wear out of it. Let's try that coat Angela brought.' Mill had been right; she oughtn't in conscience reject good clothes, whatever their source.

The gaberdine hung to Lotti's ankles. 'Not for another year, at least, but it's a lovely cut.'

'Yes, it is,' Lotti agreed. 'But it's not quite as well sewn as my red one. Papa made that.'

Gwenna thought – *I should have guessed.* 'How's Rumtopf?'

'Shaken.'

Gwenna smiled properly for the first time in hours and held out the red coat. 'Let's try this on again.' She watched Lotti eagerly unbutton the gaberdine and stick out her arms for her familiar coat. 'Mm. Give me a pirouette. Slower than that.' Gwenna tilted her head. 'There's a seamstress in St Wenna who'll alter it for us. One more season for the red, then.' She removed a wisp of yellow thread from beneath the lapel, and once again noticed a constellation of needle holes. 'Was there a school badge here?' The distress that ran for cover in Lotti's eyes was not staged. 'Darling, you don't have to tell me, but you can.'

'*Der Judenstern*.' Lotti covered the place with her hand. 'Mutti was wrong and so was Madame, telling me to take it off.'

'Who's Madame?'

'The lady who owned the hidden house, and let us stay until Oncle Gael fetched us away. Only he wasn't my real uncle.'

'You wore a yellow star on your coat in France?'

'Only in Paris.'

'And in Germany too?'

'I can't remember. I don't think so.'

Mr Beecroft had spoken of the *Judenstern*, the yellow emblem which marked out Jews in occupied Europe for persecution. 'I can understand now why it made you so upset, Angela trying to take this coat.'

'I don't want another little girl to have it.'

'Of course not.'

'Your sister doesn't like us.'

'She's my sister-in-law. That means my late husband's sister.'

'I won't have to call her Aunt Angela?'

'You won't. And nobody will take your red coat from you, ever.'

That night, Gwenna dreamed she was desperately trying to pull Max from Angela's grasp, while Mill screamed from under a nearby bed.

The final day of April was one of rainbows and rinsing showers. After the morning milking, Gwenna got on with a task that always fell at this time of the year: cleaning, sharpening and oiling the blades of the 'Briscow's patented potato seed cutting machine'. In obedience to the Ministry of Agriculture, she'd ordered her seed potatoes, tons of them, and they had to be cut in two for planting. They were due to arrive any day.

Lotti sat on a straw bale, knitting a cherry-red beret she'd found half finished in Gwenna's sewing chest. Her needles clacked, her small hands interpreting the pattern without looking at instructions. She'd already had her third lesson with Miss Linley, and would go again after the weekend. Gwenna had asked Lotti if she was worried about sitting the exam for St Morgan's. Lotti had replied, 'If I fail, will you be cross?'

'Not remotely.'

'Then I won't be worried.'

Later, Gwenna and Lotti walked to the post office, to post a letter to Freda. For the first time, Lotti had written her news, and Gwenna was confident Freda would be as impressed and overjoyed as she was. For her part, she'd sketched an update of Lotti's progress and her growth spurt. She'd mentioned the red coat, with its traces of yellow thread, adding, 'I'm ashamed, because I don't read newspapers often enough. Tell me more of what Lotti went through, Freda. Help me understand.'

She was cautiously oiling a narrow blade when the sound of boots outside brought her head up. It was Max.

'Have you please sugar?' He held out an empty jam jar. 'We have gone out. I mean, we run out. Ezra asks.' He sounded unsure of the reception he'd get. They hadn't seen each other since Angela and Mill had driven him out of the kitchen.

'I will get it.' Lotti put down her knitting.

'No, I will.' Gwenna eased herself off her stool and left the shed. As she passed Max, her shoulder brushed his arm. She walked on, refusing to meet his eye. Mill's question, 'Do you love him?' had turned over and over in her head. She'd said no, which had reflected her sense of being put on the spot. The answer was neither yes nor no, but a painful hybrid of the two.

Yesterday's fracas with Angela had obscured the real conflict: how to be with a man who represented all Gwenna hated and feared. Or, if she was going to be philosophical, to what extent could one man be blamed for the actions of his country? Gwenna was groping for answers. Meanwhile, her emotions switched sides with dizzying regularity. In the kitchen, she emptied half of what was in the sugar bowl into the jar, spilling some and sweeping it up with the side of her hand. 'There.' Max, who had come in with her, took the jar but didn't move.

'The ladies who are here before do not like to see me at your table.'

'They were my mother- and sister-in-law,' Gwenna answered curtly. 'Edward's mother and sister. So, no. They weren't pleased to catch us holding hands. And Max, I don't blame them. Why didn't you tell me what you were?'

She'd spoken too quickly. Max shook his head. 'What is it I do not tell?'

'That you were a submariner.'

He slowly nodded. 'It was not for you to know. At first. We were strangers. Then, when I learned your husband is killed at sea, sunk by a U-boat most probably, I could not say it.'

'When you slipped up yesterday, said it without thinking, I had to pretend nothing was wrong. It *is* wrong.'

'Please, listen – *ach*, sorry.' Max had collided with Lotti's red coat, which Gwenna had hung from one of the ceiling beams. She'd sponged and pressed it in preparation for alteration and it was drying. It fell and Max caught it and passed it to Gwenna.

'Look at this.' She spread her hand under the fabric, displaying where the yellow star had been attached.

He came close. 'What should I see?'

'See where there was stitching?' In the watery sunlight through the window, a six-pointed star-shape of tiny holes was clear to see. 'Lotti was forced to wear the *Judenstern* in Paris. It meant she could be seized off the street at any time, sent God knows where. To die, Max. It's probably what happened to her father. Don't you have anything to say?'

'The *Judenstern* I know.' Her attack had caught him off guard. 'After war started, it becomes the law in Germany and other territory that all Jews wear the star. I see it myself, in my own town of Dresden. I know it.'

'And that is the extent of your insight?'

'What do you want me to say, Mrs Devoran?'

'My friend Freda, who has contacts, thinks Lotti's father would have been deported back to Germany to work, but he may not have survived. He wasn't all that fit, you see, probably not considered ideal for forced labour, having lost an eye through an earlier assault in Berlin. What does that say to you, Max?' She expected a denial, or evasion, but his answer took their conversation in a new direction.

'Hitler warned the world's governments for years that he meant to rid Europe of its Jewish population. Your government heard and took no action.'

'Oh – we're to blame?'

'That is not what I am saying.'

'Then what are you saying?'

'Do I know that Jewish people are taken prisoner, perhaps murdered? Yes. I know that for ten years, Jews in Germany are pushed from their life, it is made hard for them. Many have to leave for America and other places. That I know and I do not like.'

'You fight for the regime that does it.'

'I do not fight civilians. I do not hurt children, or their mothers and fathers.'

'You do. You're German.'

He dipped his head. 'Then I am guilty.' He walked out.

Gwenna caught up with him and found him watching a pair of house martins darting under the eaves of the cooling shed. They were flying to their hidden, chirruping nests. They stood in silence until first one bird, then another, made an outward dash for more food in a blur of black tail feathers. Finally, Max spoke. 'Five years ago, I am in east Germany, working to bring clean water for my town. I am water engineer. In 1938, I know war will come and I join the *Kriegsmarine*.'

'And made it your job to kill people. Only not out in the open, on top of the waves. Underneath where nobody could see you.'

This slight to his courage made him stiffen his shoulders. 'Today I am tilling your soil, Mrs Devoran, driving your horses over ground I have ploughed to make ready for planting.' Max opened his hands, showing Gwenna the dirt-ingrained lines of his palm. 'Not long past, you take this hand as a friend, perhaps more, and today I am a hated man.'

'I don't hate you, only what you stand for.'

'Then you hate me. I cannot escape.'

'You lied to me.'

He rejected that. 'I did not tell you a whole story, which is not the same.'

It felt the same. 'You were part of Hitler's war machine and would be still if you hadn't been caught.'

'You are right.' He relaxed, a kind of surrender. 'A soldier or sailor or pilot cannot say "No, I have done enough, I would like now to stop."' With a move she didn't expect, he took her hand in a grip that was not quite gentle. She felt the pulse beating in the crease of his thumb, the calluses caused by the handles of the plough. His sleeves were rolled halfway, revealing the tanned and sinewy forearms created by long, physical hours. 'Do you wish me to leave Colvennon?'

'No. You can't. You have a job and I need you here.'

'Then what do you want me to be, Mrs Devoran? Perhaps the Max Reiner who builds water pipes and has never thought of war, or the captain of submarine with death on his hands?'

'I want to hear that you'd do anything not to be German.'

'Not to be German? That is not possible. Nor my wish.' He released her hand. 'I go back now to my work.'

'Aunt Gwenna, Max!' Lotti came out of the shed where she and Gwenna had been working to show them a tiny white egg. It was broken, and empty. 'A bird came from it.'

'It's a house martin egg,' Gwenna said. 'There'll be lots of them in the barn and on the shed floors.'

Lotti showed it to Max. 'It must be a very small bird to come out of it.'

Delicately, he took the shell between finger and thumb. 'You should keep, *Mausi*, and make a little museum of all the interesting things you find.' To Gwenna he said, 'I must go back; Ezra needs his tea. We make with the harrow now you are ordering the potatoes.'

Nobody moved, and Gwenna realised they were standing in the same triangular formation as yesterday. Martins zipped back and forth, locked in the restless relay of feeding their young. Josephine slunk out of the cooling shed. When birds were nesting, she prowled, a habit Gwenna deplored but could not prevent.

Lotti called, 'Josephine, puss-puss,' and when the cat paced towards the hay barn, she followed.

Max and Gwenna seized this last private moment. They stood so close his collar grazed her forehead and her hair caught in his front pocket buttons. He said, 'I had one choice. To fight for my country, with heart. Or like a coward, looking for a way out. I choose to fight. I choose the *Kriegsmarine* which is the most free of the services.'

'Free?' She disentangled her hair, leaving some of it behind.

'In the *Kriegsmarine*, it is not so important to be like Fuhrman and praise Hitler all day.' He unravelled the chestnut hair from his button and wound it around a finger. 'I wanted to sail on ships, but I am asked to join the U-boat section because I am an engineer. I do not love it but I am thinking that every day is my last chance to help my country win the war.'

'Sinking ships, killing men like my husband. Men like yourself. And you feel no shame?'

'No shame, but I have a conscience. This is why I fight.'

He left the statement hanging. Lotti came running back. 'I saw Ezra and he says, "Ask missus where is the noggin sugar." What does "noggin" mean?'

'It means he's impatient.'

'Come on, then.' Lotti sped away. With a roll of the eyes, Gwenna said, 'Let's go,' and they walked together in silence. In Colvennon Glaze, they found Ezra waiting impatiently, and Jürgen lying on the grass, the guttering Primus sending blue flame from the base of a steaming kettle. A toothed harrow the horses had been pulling over the soil to break up the lumps was unhitched.

Lady and Prince grazed in an elm tree's shade, their harnesses looped up under their neck collars. Lotti went to stroke Lady and waft the flies off her.

'What took you, man?' Ezra took the sugar from Max. 'My throat is parched.'

Max turned to Gwenna and pointed at the horses. 'Lady and Prince work good together.'

She nodded. 'My father trained Prince to work alongside his dam from when he was three years old.'

'Ah, but Prince takes sometimes advantage by letting his dam do more of the work. When she is tired of this, she will bite his shoulder. If one horse will not pull his weight, the work takes longer.'

'Yes. Why are you telling me?'

'So it is for me, when I command my *Kriegswolf*.'

Gwenna was aware of Ezra and Jürgen watching them, doubtless asking themselves why she'd chosen this morning to join them, and with such a serious face. So serious, it brought Jürgen to his feet.

At his approach, Max muttered in an urgent undervoice, 'I fight for my country, not for Nazism.' Though meant for Gwenna's ears only, the breeze carried his words. Jürgen said something and Gwenna was sure it contained a warning to Max to shut up. Wiggy had told her about divisions at Camp Tregallon, that some of Max's crew blamed him for their capture. Nazi versus not-Nazi, as Wiggy had described it in her unique style.

Clearly, Jürgen felt his captain was saying too much. He glared at both Max and Gwenna, then uttered a sigh she took to mean, 'You're wading in dangerous waters, Captain, sir.' He walked away.

Gwenna stopped Max from following him. 'Was the *Kriegswolf* part of those wolf packs that trail our ships and destroy them where there's no hope of rescue?'

'What do you think? The wolf is always a hunter, and stalks the prey.'

To hide her distress at this, Gwenna picked a sprig of the yellow bird's-foot trefoil from the grass. She twisted it in her fingers. 'Edward went to sea on a flower. Not this kind. His was named for a rare bloom.'

She put the trefoil in Max's buttonhole, patting his chest as if to say, 'Now you're properly turned out.' His gaze cut through her, and she wondered if her words had taken him back to his life in a steel tube, a thousand feet under the sea. His *War Wolf* might be rusting on the seabed or slewing around on the currents as burned pieces of hulk. It might have been captured and pulled into a British port. Their talk this morning felt unfinished.

A distant rumble made her glance up. The sky had darkened, anvil clouds gathering on the horizon. It would rain hard at some point, and that would be it for the harrowing until things dried off. She should let Max go.

She didn't want to let him go. 'Since you've told me your vessel's name, I'll tell you the name of Edward's.' She paused, so he had to look at her. 'His ship was called the *Bee Orchid.*'

She felt Max flinch. Behind the tan, his face turned ashen.

'The *Bee Orchid?*'

'Yes. He thought it a silly name.' A Flower-class corvette, one of hundreds of similar ships performing escort duties. Sunk in the Atlantic Ocean, south of Ireland. Lost with all eighty-three men aboard. Why would Max react to the name? Yet he had.

For a moment, she'd thought he was going to vomit.

32

The change in Max's face haunted Gwenna all through that day and only the predicted downpour arriving at the same time as twelve tons of seed potatoes shifted her mind from it.

She was in the milking parlour, giving it an extra clean while Lotti was in the house, doing homework for Miss Linley.

Gwenna didn't hear the potato truck arrive over the rasp of her broom and the rain on the parlour roof. It was Lotti who alerted her, running from the house, Rumtopf jiggling in her waistband.

'A truck comes!' In her excitement she sounded very German. 'Kartoffeln! Vielen Kartoffeln!'

'What? Potatoes? Oh.' She shouted to Ezra, who was sweeping the other end. 'The seed teddies have arrived!'

Gwenna went outside into a sunlit downpour and discovered a brown mountain in the middle of the yard. The truck was leaving.

Ezra grumbled behind her. 'What made them dozy lummocks bring them in Noah's flood? They'll be ruined.'

'We have to move them.' The cows would be walking across this yard in a couple of hours. The rain was easing off, the sky a brisk picture of blue and white cloud, but unless the wind shifted course, there'd be more later.

'All it would have taken was a quick word with the driver, missus, to tell him to tumble them off into the barn.'

'Yes, and next time, I'll keep my crystal ball on hand, so I can predict the exact moment of his arrival.'

'No need to snap. The lads will be bringing the horses in any moment, and it's all hands to the pump.'

Within ten minutes, Gwenna, Ezra, Max and Jürgen were filling barrows, wheeling damp seed potatoes to the barn where a canvas covered in thick straw had been laid. Lotti was helping, filling a hessian bag whose ends were tied over the handles of a sack barrow. At one point Ezra pointed at Rumtopf, buttoned into the neck of her dress as she wielded the barrow, which was nearly as tall as she was. She had declined a rain mac and had taken off her cardigan to work in her cotton dress. 'I'm already wet, Aunt Gwenna, and it isn't cold. Rumtopf doesn't mind either.'

'He ought to lend us a hand,' Ezra said. 'Teddy shifting teddies.' He chuckled at his own joke. 'I'll tell that to my good lady, for she likes word games.'

'If they are wet, they will rot?' Max asked, meaning the potatoes. He had said little since coming down from the field. Colour had returned to his face, but Gwenna felt he was re-living something. It didn't escape her that Jürgen kept glancing grimly at his captain. Naming the *Bee Orchid* had caused this alteration in Max's demeanour.

She answered, 'If they get a soaking, they'll rot from the bottom of the heap. It's why we're spreading them out, to let the air to them.'

'You've never smelled a stink like a heap of rotting teddies,' Ezra put in. He was kneading his lower back with his fists, and Gwenna knew that he'd pay sorely for this over the coming days. It was a new source of guilt, because now she thought about it, the seed merchant had told her to expect a delivery today. She'd even put it in her diary, but with all the upset yesterday, it had slipped her mind.

The last barrow was emptied into the barn as the rain came down again in an unseasonable deluge. 'Into the kitchen,' Gwenna said. 'Kettle on. Thanks, everyone. Lotti, go and change into dry things.'

Gwenna buttered scones she'd baked two days ago, definitely past their best, and the atmosphere in the kitchen felt similarly heavy. Drinking her tea, she felt she was presiding at one of those gatherings where there has been a rift in the family but everyone is putting on a good face. She'd been brought up to tell the truth and expect the truth, but in doing so she feared she'd erased the best part of Max. As she might cut the rot out of a seed teddy, she'd thrown away the friendship and was left only with the enemy.

The 1st of May fell on a Saturday, which Gwenna had not taken into account when she'd struck her deal with John Wormley to get the Glaze ready for planting. She doubted he'd check up on her before Monday. So, that evening, once the churns were in the cooling shed and the cows returned to their meadow, she and Lotti went up to the Glaze to check how it would look to the eyes of the ministry man.

The answer was 'unready'. Being a farmer, Wormley would instantly see the line between the ploughed soil and that which had been harrowed to a finer tilth. Only seven or eight acres would be ready for planting by Monday.

'Still,' she told Lotti as they walked away in search of Ezra, 'I said I'd have it ploughed by May Day so we're on the side of right. His Majesty's Government cannot find fault.'

Ezra was in the calving shed, where two of the heifers lay in straw. One was in the latter stages of labour, her swollen sides heaving. Ezra was crouched beside her, and Max was on his knees, lifting the animal's tail. He wasn't obliged to work at the weekend, but had chosen to.

'I see a front foot!' Max noticed Gwenna and gave a screwed-up smile. 'This is first time for me as birth helper.'

'There'll be a calf for you by supper time,' Ezra said confidently. 'Something for the little maid to look forward to. Do you take her for her schooling again today, missus?'

'Into Truro? Not till Monday. I can help, if you like.'

Ezra grunted. 'If you're taking the maid to her lessons four or five times a week—'

'Three times a week,' Gwenna corrected.

'—we need another hand round the place. Someone to do Walther's work. What do you think, Max?'

'When harvest comes, we will need more,' Max agreed, then asked Gwenna, 'You wish me to ask the camp commandant for more men?'

Irritated that they'd obviously discussed manpower without her, Gwenna said, 'I need to think about that. Lotti?' The child hadn't come right into the shed. Gwenna had rammed home many times not to approach the cows, and it appeared Lotti had heeded the lesson. 'You may stay and watch from a corner, or go and do your lessons inside. Where's Rumtopf?' Unusually, the bear's face was not peering out over Lotti's neckline.

'Inside, he's still damp from yesterday. I have to finish a story for Miss Linley, and then I could peel some carrots for dinner?'

'You're a love. I'll call you when the calf is coming.'

Lotti skipped away. Gwenna squatted at the heifer's shoulder. She was a beautiful caramel girl, two years old and obviously bemused by this new experience, her eyes wide like a deer's. 'You'll be grand, sweetheart.' Gwenna stroked the dished face. 'When you're done, you get a special mash to build your strength.'

'Aunt Gwenna, Aunt Gwenna!' Lotti was returning at a run, shouting as she came. The heifer threw up her head in alarm.

'Watch out in case she rolls,' Gwenna warned Max. 'What is it, Lotti?' The little girl was framed in the shed doorway.

'They've hurt Rumtopf!'

'Who has?' Gwenna went to her. Ezra, meanwhile, laid his hand on the heifer's poll, the bony promontory of the head, and murmured soothing words in some magical language grown in these parts. Gwenna took Lotti's hand and said, 'You mustn't shout and yell near animals. It scares them.'

'They've hung Rumtopf up!'

'Let's go and see.' They went, Lotti setting the pace as Gwenna thought, *If this is Angela, wreaking vengeance, I'll throttle her.*

The kitchen was deserted, but the pantry door was wide open, which it never usually was in order to conserve the cool air inside. There were two steps down to the narrow room, and Gwenna stood on the top step looking at a crown-shaped game hook suspended from the ceiling. In days gone by, pheasants, hare and duck would have hung from it. Gwenna used it for strings of onions in the autumn. Someone had impaled Rumtopf on one of the hooks. A kitchen chair had been dragged to stand beneath it. 'Did you try to get him down?' Gwenna asked.

'Yes, but I can't reach.'

'But did you bring the chair?'

'No, it was already there.'

Gwenna instantly discounted Angela as the culprit. Her sister-in-law was tall enough to have reached up unaided, and besides, dislike her as she did, this did not have the Angela stamp to it. Gwenna climbed up and unhooked Rumtopf. He felt damp still from yesterday's rain, and insubstantial. Thinner. His arms, which usually stuck out stiffly, were limp. She saw then that his belly was split and somebody had emptied out half his stuffing. Lotti was sobbing now, her hands full of wood wool scooped up from the pantry floor. It resembled a tangled bird's nest.

'Who did it, Aunt Gwenna?'

'I don't know.' Children, she was pretty sure. It had the flavour of a nasty child's prank. As she got down from the chair, her foot struck something. It was her carving knife which she kept on a shelf in here. So that's how he'd been opened up.

'Did you see anyone, or hear anything?'

Lotti shook her head. She was about to speak when the heavy clash of a door out in the yard offered the possibility of there being someone nearby. Handing what remained of Rumtopf to Lotti, Gwenna rushed outside. She was in time to see two thickset lads emerging from the barn, each dragging a hessian sack. She knew them at once and, with a roar, ran at them. One boy dropped his sack and seed potatoes rolled out. The larger lad attempted to swing his onto his shoulder, but he'd overfilled it. Gwenna caught a corner of the sack and heaved on it to overbalance him. The first lad caught her round the waist and tugged likewise. For a while, they heaved back and forth and she thought they must resemble a pantomime elephant. She gritted her teeth. She wasn't letting go.

Into this melee strode Max. He rapped out an order in German, and instantly Gwenna was released and found herself hugging a heavy sack. She dropped it. Max seized one boy by his collar as the other made a dash for the gate.

'Who are these?'

'Two of Hilda and Roddy Hoskens's lads. How dare they steal my crops!'

'You wish that I lock them up, and you call police?'

The boy Max held struggled ferociously as Gwenna thought about the consequences of making this official. 'Not the police, but I'll inform John Wormley. Robbing seed affects production. It's serious. You hear that, lad?' To Max: 'Let him go.'

Max released the collar and the boy stumbled away, shouting 'Nazi!' when he was safely over the yard gate.

'I pick up the potatoes,' Max said impassively. 'The calf, she is born.'

'Healthy?'

'Ezra says so. She is very – I don't know the word. Sticky?'

Gwenna managed a smile. 'Congratulations on your first birth. It is your first?'

'*Ja, ja.* No children for me.'

'I'd better go to Lotti. Those little tykes did something rather mean.'

Lotti was sitting on the kitchen floor with Rumtopf beside her, sorting among the strands of wood wool. 'It's not all here,' she said dolefully. 'It won't make him fat again.'

'We'll restuff him, don't you worry,' Gwenna said. 'I'll get some lambswool and he'll be right as rain.'

'No, it has to be the same inside.'

'All right, we'll ask Ezra. He'll know where we can get wood shavings, then I'll stitch your boy up again. Or you can; you're good at that.'

Tearfully, Lotti nodded. 'I shouldn't have left him alone.'

On a sudden hunch, Gwenna went to the cupboard where her best tea set was kept and checked the silver teaspoons were still in their box. They were. Those lads had probably come with the intention of taking seed potatoes, and slipped into the house in the spirit of mischief. Or because they were hungry.

Yes, six hard-boiled eggs Gwenna had intended to mash for sandwiches later were gone. They'd be in the lads' pockets. She was most angry at the hurt done to Lotti. She could imagine Hilda going home and saying at the tea table, 'That mumchance maid, she carries that bear around like a baby. It isn't natural.' Or something of the sort, and her boys, discovering Rumtopf on the kitchen table, hadn't been able to resist a vile practical joke. It proved that cruelty was universal.

Lotti pulled something from the tangle of wood wool. She held out her palm and showed Gwenna a frayed scrap of yellow fabric.

It took Gwenna some moments to realise what she was seeing. 'Your star,' she breathed. 'Is this what you had to wear in France?'

Lotti nodded.

'And you kept it all this time.'

'I hid it. Will I ever have to wear it here? I can stitch it back onto my red coat.'

'No, no, darling. It isn't the rule here and it never will be.' Gwenna sat down on the cold kitchen floor, her knee nudging Lotti's. 'You haven't seen anybody in England wearing a star.'

'Auntie Freda said so, but I don't know.' Lotti seemed unsure, as if the word of adults was simply not enough.

Gwenna touched one of the star's ragged points. 'We can throw this away, light the fire, get rid of it.'

'*Nein, nein!*' Lotti clamped her fingers around it. When Gwenna tried again to explain, she rocked and repeated, '*Nein, nein.*' It was obvious there was something she desperately wanted to say, but she'd fallen back into German. Interspersed with sobs and gasps, it made no sense.

Gwenna felt there was no choice but to fetch Max.

He crouched and spoke softly and Lotti opened her palm, revealing the crumpled shape.

'*Darf ich?*' Max took it with an expression Gwenna couldn't decipher. Lotti touched the yellow circle on his overalls, over his heart. He went still and Gwenna held her breath. He allowed Lotti to trace around the circle before gently removing her fingers.

'I must wear this because I am a prisoner. You understand, Lotti?' He spoke English, and very slowly. 'For me it is the rules. But for you now, there is no such law.'

After a minute's intense listening, Lotti nodded.

'May I throw the star away?' Gwenna asked.

'No.' The response was adamant.

Before he left them, Max gave a curious glance across the kitchen. 'The picture of your husband, it is gone.'

Gwenna explained that it had been removed, without her permission.

'You should bring it back,' Max said. 'Only you may decide if his picture is there.'

'You're right,' she said. 'Would you like tea, Max?'

Saying ruefully that he'd much prefer a cold beer, he suggested she take a cup out to Ezra. He accepted plain water, then returned to the shed, where the second heifer had begun her labour. The calf was still unborn when Wiggy arrived to take him and Jürgen back to camp. Gwenna could see how frustrated he was, to leave before the birth. A clear sign, she thought, that he was turning bit by bit into a farmer.

Ezra directed Gwenna to a farm outside the village where the family kept rabbits and used wood wool for their bedding. She and Lotti walked over and bought a bagful and, that evening, they put Rumtopf back together. Watching Lotti suture up his stomach, Gwenna said, 'Did you put your star inside him when you were in France?'

'Yes, on the boat after we left Madame's house. She tried to cut it off, and Mutti helped her, but there wasn't time. I pulled it off in the van and kept it in my hand. I know now that was dangerous because it would have given us away, if we'd been caught. On the boat, I hid it inside Rumtopf and not even Mutti knew.'

'And that's why you are so fearful of ever losing sight of him?' It was a loaded question. Essentially, she was asking Lotti if Miryam had made the disastrous decision to cross a busy railway line to retrieve this bear.

Lotti returned an innocent look. 'I look after Rumtopf because he knows things.'

'Course he does. Where's the star now?'

'Gone.'

Gwenna glanced at Rumtopf, but asked no more.

33

On Monday, having delivered Lotti to Miss Linley's, Gwenna waited for the door of Fendynick House to be opened to her. She'd rehearsed what she was going to say to her mother-in-law. 'I would like my wedding picture, which Angela stole. Whatever you both think of me, I was his wife and I won't be browbeaten or judged.' In truth, she dreaded the meeting. So much so that after dropping Lotti off, she'd walked twice round the cathedral grounds, summoning courage.

Why was she afraid of a woman who was so invariably kind to her? The answer was that she wasn't frightened of Mill, but of the immense secret that had dominated her marriage.

Janet opened the door and, to Gwenna's surprise, gave what could pass for a gasp of pleasure. 'Oh, Mrs Devoran, I'm glad you've come.'

'You are? Don't tell me, my mother-in-law's in the garden.'

'She is.'

'I suppose the surprise would be to find her in the house. Shall I walk round, save you the bother?'

'No, come in if you please and I'll fetch her.' The way Janet said it suggested Mill would appreciate a moment's warning.

With a sense of foreboding, Gwenna entered the house and waited in the hall while Janet bustled away. It allowed her a moment to discover that her and Edward's wedding photograph had been replaced by one of Angela receiving a plaque for something or other from the lord mayor, which left no doubt as to who had made the switch. Mill might not even have noticed yet.

Janet returned. 'Madam says, would you go and sit with her in the rose arbour and I will bring tea out. You won't be sharp with her, now, will you?'

'Sharp – of course not.' Now thoroughly unsettled, Gwenna found her mother-in-law in a part of the garden hidden behind shrub roses that were full of tight green buds. Mill was sitting on a wrought-iron sofa and Gwenna's immediate impression was that she'd lost even more weight.

'May I sit down?'

Mill looked up. She must have been deep in thought because Gwenna had approached anything but silently. 'Of course, dear. I think Janet's bringing tea.'

She hasn't slept, either, Gwenna realised. 'I've come to ask for something,' she said, 'but first, I need to apologise.'

Mill looked taken aback. 'What for?'

'For being caught holding the hand of one of my German workers.'

'I presume it's only one whose hand you hold?'

'Yes.'

'Mm.' Mill scraped lichen from the bench with a squared-off thumbnail. 'Are you falling for him? I think I asked you that before.'

'No.' And though she hadn't come to Fendynick to make confessions, the worrying change in Mill loosened Gwenna's tongue. 'No... because I already have.'

Mill gave a start – not of surprise but pain. It made Gwenna add, 'I know nothing can come of it. I'm not stupid.'

'No, and I won't insult you by saying that love conquers all. It doesn't. People would be very angry with you, Gwenna.'

'They already are.' Gwenna managed a parody of a smile. 'You included.'

'For Edward. I'm angry for him. My darling boy, my clever, sensitive son is lost, and the manner of his death is my constant nightmare.' Mill turned to face Gwenna, who saw the recent trace of tears in garden dust on the lined face. 'If it were different, I might understand,' Mill said. 'Sympathise even. But I cannot imagine how you look into those ice-chip eyes and see a man fit to be loved.'

'Because they aren't ice chips. Max has a soul too.'

'Which is sold to Nazism.' Mill shook her head. Janet was bringing tea. Mill asked her to please bring the objects from the dining room table. 'Both, if you don't mind.'

Both? Gwenna was expecting to leave only with a picture.

When Janet was gone, Mill asked how Lotti was getting on with Miss Linley. 'I know Verity Linley quite well. We belong to the same gardening society and she can't stop talking about her new pupil.'

'Lotti's doing well, but I'm keeping my hopes in check because it's a big task, prepping her for St Morgan's.'

'They'll suit each other very well, Lotti and dear old St Mogs. She has a lot to overcome, though, I do see that.'

'And whatever you think of me, Mill, I would do nothing to hamper Lotti's chances.'

A mistle thrush hopped nearby, its speckled waistcoat flashing in and out of the grass. Gwenna wondered if Mill had forgotten about their tea. She'd always been vague where mealtimes were concerned. Angela, Janet and Gwenna had often had to fetch her in from some gardening task as the light faded and soup went cold on the table.

Reminiscing, Gwenna wasn't prepared for Mill to say abruptly, 'Would that include giving Lotti up?' Seeing Gwenna's face fall like a shutter, she sighed. 'If there were relations wanting her back, would you let her go?'

'If I believed they were kind,' Gwenna said slowly, 'and in a position to take care of her.'

'That is a lot of "if".'

'We don't know anything of Lotti's family or her wider relations. We don't know where they are or if they're alive.'

'"We"? This is about you, dearest. You were so desperate for a child in the early years with Edward, I saw need bleeding through your flesh. Now you have a child, but she isn't yours. I ask again, could you give her up if other relations came forward?'

'I'd have to.'

'But you hope it won't come to that.' Mill poured tea for them and picked up a plate of plain biscuits, urging Gwenna to take one. 'You look famished; take two.'

Janet returned just then and passed over a square parcel secured with string. Mill gave it to Gwenna. 'This was removed from your house.'

It was the picture; a quick feel confirmed it. Gwenna said, 'I was cross when I saw it was missing. Angela shouldn't have taken it.'

'No,' Mill agreed. 'Angela somehow grew up believing herself to be the guardian of the world's morals. My mother was the same, so I suppose the habit jumped a generation. I have a confession, though. Angela didn't take the picture. I did.'

'You?'

'When you were upstairs, tussling with my daughter, I put it in one of the bags we brought in with us. I was so angry, seeing you with your German, I thought, she doesn't deserve any part of my son.'

Conscious that Janet could hear every word, Gwenna said nothing. Mill had spoken of two objects and she saw now that Janet held a letter. Mill extended her hand to take it.

'Janet, you can finish for the day. I'll bring in the tea things and I shan't have supper. Dry crackers will do fine.'

With a shake of the head, Janet left. For a full five minutes, Gwenna and her mother-in-law watched the thrush take a snail to a flat stone and smash it in a flurry of drumming. Another thrush, its mate perhaps, sang lustily on the chimney pot, summoning the evening.

Finally, Mill said, 'Angela never forgave you marrying her brother. In her mind, you replaced Freda.'

'Except I didn't, as I reminded Angela the other day.' Gwenna repeated: Edward and Freda had split weeks before he first asked Gwenna out. He'd invited her to join him for drinks at the Savoy. She'd been homesick, in a job she hated and was only doing because her mother had wanted her to experience some life outside Cornwall. Edward had been an up-and-coming cellist with an elite orchestra and she'd been stunned that he should remember 'Freda Helyer's shy friend'. For all that, she hadn't been blinded by romance. The first thing she'd asked as he ordered White Ladies for them at the Savoy bar was, 'It really is over between you and Freda?'

'As over as the fossils in the Natural History Museum,' had been his answer. Gwenna repeated this to his mother now. She went on, 'Angela must have thought me qualified to be her brother's wife because she took over organising the wedding, remember? My poor mother was pushed right out. I think Angela welcomed me as the solution to an intractable problem.' A glance at her mother-in-law showed the swim of new tears. Gwenna had always believed some things should never be told but Mill's silence seemed a kind of invitation. 'Do you want me to shut up?'

'You mentioned an intractable problem, relating to Edward, I presume. You'd better finish. I don't much like cliff-hangers.'

Invitation accepted. 'I loved Edward, you do know that? Passionately and increasingly desperately.' The thrush, alarmed by something undetectable to their ears, flew up into a clipped bay tree. Mill was still guarding the letter. Gwenna, needing a moment's respite, opened her handbag and took out a sealed jar. 'Butter for you. Did Angela like hers?'

'She passed it on to her employer's wife. Apparently, Lady Copping can't abide margarine.'

'I hope Angela didn't mention it came from me. It's illegal contraband, you know. Mill, I'll have to go shortly and you've not even half drunk your tea. I'm worried about you, and so is Janet.'

'Janet fusses.'

'She's so anxious, she was actually nice to me today.'

Mill appeared not to have heard and when she finally answered, it confirmed Gwenna's suspicion that today was a day for secrets to be told. Mill said shakily, 'I know about Edward. Why you left him.'

Gwenna's instant response was – *She can't know, not really.* 'He had someone else. I told you that at the time.'

'I know why you left him,' Mill repeated and passed the letter across. 'I found this when I and Janet were spring-cleaning the bedrooms. It was under Angela's mattress and I don't know why...' Mill ran out of explanations. 'Read it at home, not here.'

'I— yes. All right. How long ago did you find it?' The letter was addressed to Edward, and had obviously travelled between lodging houses in search of him, from the number of crossings-out on the envelope. In the months before the outbreak of war, Edward had been living in Plymouth when ashore, and had moved house several times. In October 1939, the date on the postmark, he'd been made second-in-command of The *Bee Orchid* and had perhaps been able to afford better rooms.

Seeing Gwenna trying to make sense of the various different scrawls, Mill said, 'It made its way here, in the end, and Angela must have picked it up. I found it after you left,

Gwenna. Some time in March 1941. I read it and immediately wished I hadn't. It told me why you'd had to go.'

'You said not a word, Mill. I thought you blamed me.'

'I have spent a long while avoiding the obvious.' Mill drew in a harsh breath. 'Seeing you at Colvennon with another man, hearing you declare that you'd been miserable from the first day of your marriage, ripped away a curtain. I was left exposed in all my nakedness, nothing to reach for but the truth. Edward was at fault, not you. Still, I was hard on you that day.'

'You were hurt, seeing me with Max.'

'I was rude and unkind. Scraping the barrel of sarcasm, for heaven's sake.'

Gwenna gave a faint smile. 'That wasn't like you, I admit.'

'I was desperate to retain the mirage I'd created around Edward. But listening to Angela defend the indefensible in that battering way of hers, cured my self-delusion. If there was a shred of it left, being driven home by my daughter ranting the whole way completely finished it.'

Gwenna could imagine.

'But I left Colvennon in an ungracious spirit, my dear, for which I apologise.'

'There's no need, Mill.'

Mill waved a hand. 'Let me say it. I'm sorry. Sorry you were deceived by my son, neglected by me and denied the solace of children. Forgive us both.'

Gwenna felt a lump swell in her throat. She couldn't form words. She nodded.

Mill greeted it with a look of relief. 'Thank you. I still love my son and miss him every minute, and Gwenna, I don't want to speak of this matter again. Read what's inside the letter and when you're ready, destroy it.'

Gwenna stared at the crossed-out directions and Mill gave a bent smile.

'I don't imagine the original sender ever thought this correspondence would end up here.'

When Miss Linley opened her door to Gwenna at six p.m., Gwenna was still reeling. The letter was in her handbag, unopened.

'Thank you for arriving promptly,' Miss Linley said. 'It's always appreciated.' She held out a folded note, clearing her throat as Gwenna simply stared at it. 'I invoice at the beginning of each month in arrears.'

'Yes, of course.' Gwenna fumbled for her purse. 'Was Lotti all right today?'

'She was fine. We continued our written work. Of course, she writes in a non-standard hand, a cocktail of French and German, so we will concentrate on that. For the last hour, we chatted about her favourite subjects.'

About Rumtopf, no doubt. Lotti's spirits had been rather up and down following the assault on her beloved bear. 'I expect she mentioned sewing, too?'

'Sewing? No.' When Miss Linley frowned, her spectacles went up on one side. 'Physics and history. Lotti knows all about the Sun King of France, Louis Quatorze, and we talked about his wigs and shoes, then moved on to the valency of atoms.'

'The... right. Gosh. It sounds rather ambitious.'

'That's the point, isn't it, to get Lotti moving ahead?'

'It is, but—'

'I have instituted a rule, Mrs Devoran. Once Lotti is over my threshold I make no concessions to her age, background or experiences. Coddling won't get her into St Morgan's. It is English only during our lessons. When she's at school, she can take modern languages and win the German and French cups every year.' Miss Linley turned her gaze on Lotti who had come to the door in her coat and beret. 'Back tomorrow, same time, yes?'

Dropping a small curtsey, Lotti answered, 'Yes, Miss Linley.'

'Your curtsey is charming, Lotti, but not necessary.'

There was nobody about when they reached Colvennon and walked through the long shadows of the sunken lane. In the house, they changed into work clothes and together, they checked the animals. Two heifer calves suckled their dams, on unsteady legs on a deep straw bed. Their mothers munched hay from a manger. Ezra must only just have left.

Lotti named them Maria and Teresa, after Louis Quatorze's queen. Gwenna made no objection, though she anticipated that Ezra's reaction would be, 'What's wrong with Buttercup and Daisy?' She still hadn't opened the letter Mill had put in her hand and was glad that closing down the farm for the night gave plenty of reason not to. But night-time came, and Lotti went to bed. Josephine slid out into the night.

Gwenna took the envelope from her handbag and pulled the oil lamp closer.

34

This letter had started its life in London. The postmark said Whitehall SW1A, and was dated October 12th 1939, when Edward would have been at sea, taking part in his first convoy duty under wartime conditions. She fetched whisky from the pantry and poured a measure. Letting the liquor run across her tongue, she plunged in.

> When you write to say how it tortures you, my darling Edward, living your fake and imitation life, you mirror my own tormented thoughts. If you would leave your little country mouse, and I would throw in my miserable lot with the Admiralty, we might find ourselves an island. We'd make it our paradise, my wonderful boy. A shack and one generous hammock would suit us well enough. We could make music that would outvoice the war. Because I must see you or die, I will take the train to Plymouth and be waiting when your ship comes into port.
>
> Ever yours,

Charles

Charles Avril-Whiting had been a long-time friend of Edward's, working in Naval Intelligence. Friend and, as Gwenna had come to realise, much more. They had met at Oxford, playing in a college orchestra, which explained why Charles cast her as the interloper in *his* relationship with Edward.

Avril-Whiting wrote in a slanted script, casual confidence in the shape of the letters. It was ironic, Gwenna thought, that this letter had been sent when she had been planning to sit down with Edward and talk about their future. He'd been expecting some Christmas leave that year, and she'd been going to say, 'I know you have someone else. Is this person always going to eclipse me?' Being conventionally minded, she had assumed that Edward's aloofness towards her meant he was involved with another woman.

Edward had spent Christmas and Boxing Day 1939 at Fendynick House, avoiding her and sleeping in a separate room on the grounds that he had a bad cold. He'd found the time to visit London afterwards, when Freda Fincham had spotted him walking with a man along the Embankment. Freda had written to Gwenna, 'Saw Edward with Charlie A-W, locked in conversation. Did you know they were still such very close friends?'

Of course she did. Charles Avril-Whiting had always been around. Once, during their engagement, when Gwenna had called on Edward unannounced, Charles had emerged from the bathroom, a towel knotted around his loins.

God, how naive and credulous she'd been, swallowing Edward's red-faced explanation that Charles's flat was being redecorated, and he'd needed a sofa to sleep on.

'What about a hammock?' Gwenna said bitterly now, taking a slug of her drink.

During his last, flying visit to Fendynick House in June

1940, Gwenna had overheard Edward on the telephone, inviting someone to join him in Plymouth. 'Come tomorrow, yes?' He'd mentioned an address in Basing Road and had then spoken of her. 'Done my duty to the little woman. God, I can't wait to see you.' He'd added something that only made sense later: 'You can get away without some birdwatcher tailing you, I hope?'

Gwenna had listened as he helpfully repeated the address. 'Near the docks. Don't expect classical architecture.' The following afternoon, Edward had left Fendynick House and she had followed on a later train, and spent two hours watching a mean-fronted terrace in smelling distance of the docks, and being ogled by sailors on leave. She'd seen Charles Avril-Whiting alight from a taxi, knock at the door and be swiftly admitted. She'd seen Edward drawing the curtains across the front window.

"A birdwatcher" was presumably a slang word used in intelligence circles, meaning a snooper.

As dusk fell, she'd crept round the back of the terrace and located Edward's house. Scaling a wall, she'd peered through a window that hadn't yet had its blackout curtains closed and watched them embracing. Everything had fallen into place: an unaccountably chaste courtship culminating in a wedding day when Edward had hardly glanced at her. His hopeless, sometimes angry, attempts at lovemaking, and his sudden decision to join the Navy, abandoning his musical career because, in his own words, he felt 'stifled'. Had he joined up because the man he loved worked in Naval Intelligence, and it would bring their worlds closer together?

Too mortified to confront him that day, she'd slunk back to Fendynick House, and waited. After nearly a decade of marriage, she wasn't going to be cast off like an embarrassing choice of jacket or necktie. *The little woman.*

She'd had no plan then for actually divorcing. That was

unthinkable in a small town, and besides, she had a secretarial job in a solicitor's office. It was interesting work, and she was well thought of there. As a divorcee, she would have to leave. And there was Mill to consider, and her father who was so proud that she'd married 'up in the world', and who was not well though she had no insight at that point quite how unwell. Her plan was for a discreet separation. She would make Edward agree terms... But he hadn't come, his voyages to the southern hemisphere taking him away for weeks on end. And when he was ashore, he stayed either in Plymouth or took the train to London.

When her father suffered his first stroke, the farm had drawn her back. Clive Bossinny's sudden death the following December was the catalyst for permanent change. The morning after it happened, when a distraught Ezra telephoned her from St Wenna's post office, all notions of respectability and sacrifice fell away. She'd packed her bags and written a brief, farewell note to Mill. She'd left Fendynick House for good on December 22nd 1940, two days before her thirtieth birthday.

Angela had called her a 'pitiful bolter', deserting a husband serving his country. And yet... Angela had since read the letter Gwenna was now staring at, and unless she'd persuaded herself that 'Charles' was a woman, she must at some point have concluded that her adult brother loved another man.

There had been no confrontation with Edward. He had written her a surprisingly fulsome and emotional letter of condolence over the death of her father, when the news finally reached him, but he hadn't come to find her. The following November, the war had claimed him. It was strange, Gwenna thought, allowing herself a small, second dram, how she still loved Edward in her fashion. Perhaps it made her unusual, but she respected his right to love somebody else. It was the lying and humiliation that hurt. Edward had drawn her into his life, then stepped out of hers without setting her free, denying her the chance to meet someone else or to be a mother.

And as this letter showed, the two men had discussed her. Laughed at her. *Little woman. Little country mouse.*

'Let it rest,' she whispered to herself. Edward's awful death had evened the score. As she took the letter to the stove, intending it for the embers, her mind switched to Max, and how he'd looked when she'd given him the name of Edward's ship.

Max had looked as though he wanted to be sick. If she were brave, she'd ask him straight out. 'What do you know about HMS *Bee Orchid*?'

Perhaps she should start being brave. Instead of burning the letter, she tucked it behind Edward's photo, then finished the last dribble of whisky in her glass and pondered how much she wanted to know about war. Specifically, in what way Max's war might have intersected with Edward's.

35

The new-born calves were suckling well and Gwenna brought a third pregnant heifer into a pen next morning.

A bull calf was born at eleven o'clock. After which, Gwenna set to with the potato cutter, the mind-numbing task of slicing every seed potato in two, to double the number for planting. Gwenna cut. And cut. And cut. Lotti placed the cut pieces into boxes, laying them edge to edge as if they were eclairs in a Parisian patisserie. At two, Ezra located her by the machine's sound and stood in the doorway, watching.

'How many years are you planning to sit there, Mrs Devoran? The boys can help, and don't you have to take the maidie for her schooling?'

Gwenna nodded, but let the sound of the cutting blades fill her mind. Nicely sharpened, they sliced through potato flesh. Last night's resolve for a heart-to-heart with Max now felt like an idea born of whisky, and she was glad Lotti's visit to Miss Linley would take her away from the farm as he came down to help with the milking. 'I'll carry on here for another half-hour,' she said without looking up. 'Just let me get on with it, please.'

Gwenna's mother had often asserted that Ezra Jago heard

only those words he wanted to hear. 'What does he do with the rest?' Mary had asked rhetorically. 'Store them in his boots?'

Minutes later, Max came into the shed, saying, 'Ezra says, he and Jürgen will take over now, and you and I are to milk early.'

Gwenna huffed, 'Does nobody bother with what I say?'

Her irritation slid off Max. 'I get the cows in, *ja*?'

'Oh, very well.' Somehow, these men always had her beaten, though privately she wasn't sorry to hand over to Jürgen and Ezra. She was seeing potatoes when she closed her eyes. She popped into the house where Lotti was finishing her prep, and said, 'Will you get yourself tidied up for Miss Linley? Find a snack from the pantry. We'll need to leave at three thirty prompt.'

As the cows filed into the parlour, she expected Max to go to the far end but they ended up in adjacent stalls.

He said nothing for at least half an hour, and Gwenna was happy to let mutual silence set in. However, when she sat back and rolled her shoulders to let go some tension, he looked directly at her. 'I know why we cannot talk.'

'I'm tired, Max. That's all.'

'No, it is more than that. We do not finish our before conversation.'

'Yes, well. That's water under the bridge.'

He disagreed with her again. 'I know the name. I hear it.'

She chose to misunderstand. 'Your cow's name? Whatever Lotti likes to think, you're milking cow number eight.'

'The *Bee Orchid*. I hear this name.'

It felt like the moment of hitting the ground after a long fall. The end of the scream in the stomach. 'I thought as much.'

'When I know your husband dies from attack by German U-boat, what can I say?' He asked when her husband had been reported missing.

Her voice hardened. 'Missing presumed dead. I got the

news on November 27th 1941, hand delivered by the post-mistress's grandson.' The boy had knocked at her front door, in darkness and a rainstorm. The wood had warped; Gwenna had to wrestle the door open and there he stood, bathed in his own torchlight, rain cascading off his sou'wester. All unprepared, Gwenna had read the news that Angela had sent on a couple of days prior. Gwenna told Max, 'Edward's ship had been sunk on the 23rd.'

She could see Max digesting this information as milk flowed into the pail at his feet. She'd fallen into a pit, at the bottom of which was the possibility that his submarine had been involved in the *Bee Orchid*'s destruction. 'There were five losses in the convoy that night,' she said, her voice strangely conversational. 'Another corvette, I learned later, two oil tankers and a ship carrying grain. All destroyed by the same U-boat pack.'

'The 23rd of November 1941?'

'Yes.'

When Max spoke again, it did nothing to kill the suspense. 'I fire on British ships, many times. You know this.'

The resigned tone, as if killing was a regretful necessity, brought Gwenna to her feet. She took a half-pail of warm milk to the churn and tipped it in. 'Don't you ever dwell on what happens when your torpedoes slam into the side of a ship? When the fuel tanks go up, and the water pours in?'

Max came to empty his pail. 'Yes, I think,' he said earnestly. 'Do you ever think what it is for the crew of a U-boat to be surrounded by enemy ships dropping *Wasserbomben*? Water bombs, they explode beneath the surface. They wish to break your hull and flood you. Drown you. It becomes a game, to drop these bombs around us, to hit us.'

'It's only the reverse of what you're doing to them.'

'Their sonar locates us, and they drop their charges. We are trapped. It is killing the animal in the pit.'

'Like bear-baiting.' She hadn't thought of it like that. 'Is that worse than stalking convoys, picking them off, ship by ship?'

Memories broke surface in Max's eyes. Trauma, death escaped, death served up. She was seeing the man he must have been in his last hours aboard his U-boat. He said, 'It is not only your people, your sailors, who suffer. A U-boat ripped open at depth fills with water, but that is a quick dying. If we must stay under too long, and cannot surface to take on fresh air, we fill with poison gases. Men wait then to die slowly. If we break surface, we are bombed or fired on, or we surrender.'

'As you did.' The pragmatic option. 'Were you forced to the surface?'

He inclined his head. 'In the end. The *Kriegswolf* was boarded and we were captured. This is my decision.'

'Well, as you say, better than dying slowly in a steel coffin.'

'I lose respect of many of my crew but I ask them if they like better being alive to hate me, or dead with me as their hero.'

'What is their answer?'

'All are glad to be alive, some hate me, some plan my trial when we are home again in Germany. Captains who fail are hanged.'

Nothing more was said. Gwenna still did not know if Max Reiner had given the order to fire on the *Bee Orchid*. She checked her watch. They needed to work a bit faster, or she and Lotti would miss their bus. When Max called her over, she went reluctantly.

He was milking an older cow who was hugely pregnant. 'This bag... you call it...?'

'It's her udder. Udd-er.'

'Ah. This udd-er is big now, very full. She is sick?'

Gwenna placed her hands where his had been. The cow's udder was swollen but she felt no unusual heat in the tissue. Nor redness, suggesting mastitis. 'She'll be calving in two months so it's possible everything's swelling in preparation. She could be birthing earlier than we think. Well spotted.' Realising her hip was resting against Max's shoulder, Gwenna stepped away. 'I'll tell Ezra; he'll want her dried off.'

'Dried?'

'It means that after today, we stop milking her.'

Sitting back on her stool, Gwenna reflected that an eavesdropper would have heard their conversation swerve from U-boats to udders. It felt slightly crackpot that she was milking cows in the company of a U-boat captain who had just confessed to killing her compatriots. Max lived alongside former crewmen who'd like to see a noose round his neck. He had found peace here at Colvennon, while dropping a bomb into her world.

When the milking was done, churns wheeled to the cooling sheds, they walked behind the cows to the meadow. Lotti, looking neat in a cotton skirt and blouse, had joined them, but when she spied the postman, she ran back to take the letters from him. Gwenna watched her go, and was momentarily deaf to what Max was saying.

'You tell me there were five ships sunk in one night, and I think once you have told me it was near the Ireland coast, yes?'

They were back there again, were they? 'As I understand it. My sister-in-law is secretary to a member of parliament who sits on some naval committee or other, and he extracted information that wouldn't normally be shared.'

'My U-boat is in the seas off Ireland on the night of November 23rd. But I think that three ships were sunk. One is an oil tanker. My memory is clear on such things. An oil tanker, a merchant ship and one smaller defence vessel you call a corvette.'

'Edward's *Bee Orchid* was a corvette.' She rested her hand on the undulating tailbone of the cow closest to her, to keep herself moving forward. 'If you knew what you'd hit, couldn't you or other ships have gone to their aid?'

'It is possible.'

'Can a U-boat pick up survivors from the water?'

'*Ja*, if it surfaces. If the captain chooses.'

Bile flooded her tongue. 'If you were there at the kill, then tell me if he did or not.'

Max clicked his tongue to urge a slow-moving cow onwards. 'We followed the convoy many days. Oil tankers, merchant ships, destroyers and smaller escort ships, they are sailing together across many miles of sea. Kills were made that night in November. This, I do not enjoy to tell you. I gave order for *Kriegswolf* to fire on a tanker and the sky lights up with red fire. There is no chance for survivors, and the night is not clear to see. A small ship I see all at once, a shadow in glowing flames. This is also destroyed.'

'You fired on that small ship? November 1941, in the Atlantic, off the south coast of Ireland?'

His mouth tightened. He drew in a breath. '*Ja*.'

Whoever said ignorance was bliss had not lived through this. There was only one person in a position to tell her if Max had fired on Edward's ship. One man who might furnish her with precise information about the whereabouts of HMS *Bee Orchid* that fateful night.

Contacting that person might be illegal. It would certainly offend her dignity.

But she had to know.

That night, when Lotti was in bed, Gwenna took up pen and paper. She sat staring into the pulsing halo of the oil lamp and wrote:

Dear Mr Avril-Whiting,

I am asking for information surrounding the loss of my husband Edward Devoran's corvette. I have thought long and hard about how much I wish to know of the last hours of his life, and my answer to myself is now clear. I want to know everything. From your position in Naval Intelligence, and as Edward's friend, you are my best hope of learning the circumstances of the *Bee Orchid*'s sinking. I hope you will be generous and share what you know. Most particularly, if Edward's corvette was sunk by a German U-boat, shortly after the destruction of an oil tanker, as I have heard through other channels.

She signed the letter 'G. Devoran' and addressed it to Old Admiralty Building, Whitehall, London, telling herself that she didn't have to post it.

36

And she might not have posted it, except that the following morning, Lotti saw it on top of the bookcase and said, 'We can take this with our reply to Aunt Freda.'

Freda's most recent letter had contained a response to Gwenna's suggestion that Miryam Gittelman should be laid to rest in the Quaker meeting house of Come-to-Good. Freda had written that she'd hoped Miryam's body could have been brought to London, 'for interment in a Jewish cemetery close to me, but bureaucracy has frustrated this. They cite the difficulties of transporting a body under wartime restrictions. One cannot argue, so it seems your idea must prevail.'

Freda was agreeing to Gwenna's suggestion, though ever Freda, she went on to say, 'I am contacting Quaker Friends in Falmouth who will organise Miryam's final journey from Truro. They will keep you informed, Gwenna dearest, and take the organisational burden from your shoulders.'

At the post office, Mrs Andrews gave Lotti a quick up and down. 'Now then, little maid. I do believe you're growing.'

'I have grown two whole sugar cubes.' Lotti opened finger

and thumb to demonstrate two thirds of an inch. She dropped Mrs Andrews her little curtsey.

'Well I never. What a rare creature you are.' The post-mistress gave her a rather sweet smile, then unashamedly read the address on the front of the letter which Gwenna passed over. 'Now what do you want with the Admiralty, Mrs Devoran?'

'A long-range weather forecast.'

Mrs Andrews looked sceptical. 'I don't know what they'd know in London that we don't know down here. My niece, whose husband has a boat at Port Isaac, says we've a bad storm coming.'

'A storm in May?'

'That's right, when they do come at this season, they're wicked fierce.' The postmistress turned to nod at someone who had just come in. 'Good morning, Mrs Hoskens.'

'You too, Mrs Andrews.' Hilda gave Gwenna a bristling side glance and said, 'I heard you won't have your Germans much longer. There's trouble in Tregallon, and they're likely to be downgraded.'

'To what?' Gwenna asked.

'To "unsafe". Unsafe to be around decent folk, because they're Nazis.'

Gwenna paid for her stamps and took her change. 'While we're on the subject of "decent", Hilda, would you kindly tell your youngest sons not to come thieving in my sheds?'

'What d'you mean by that?' Hilda's cheeks inflated, rosy colour suffusing her forehead.

Gwenna sketched the attempted snatching of seed potatoes.

'They would never do that. They're well brought-up lads.'

'There were witnesses, Hilda. I haven't yet reported them to John Wormley, but I will if there are any more transgressions.'

'Oh, you will, will you? Perhaps I shall start speaking what I know about your doings, Gwenna Devoran.'

Gwenna recalled Auntie Nancy repeating Hilda's insinuations, something about her undoing too many buttons on her blouse to emphasise her bosom. As if she had the energy. She spelled out to Hilda, 'Tell your boys not to set foot on my farm.'

As they left the post office, Gwenna fended off Lotti's anxious questions. Was Max being sent away? What did Hilda mean, about him being unsafe?

'I honestly don't know,' Gwenna said. 'Being in a prison camp is not easy, and sometimes the men fight. I think that's all she was saying.'

'No, Aunt Gwenna. She said they were being downgraded because they were Nazis.'

'That's just her sounding off.'

'I don't know what downgraded means.'

'Neither do I, in this particular case.'

'But I do know what Nazis are. Max isn't one.'

'Well, he says he's not. He says he never joined the Party. I don't really know if that proves anything much.'

'It proves a lot.' Lotti sounded absolutely certain. But of course, in her eyes, Max could do no wrong.

Hilda's words gained the weight of a prediction when, next morning, Wiggy sounded her horn twice as she drove into the yard. Only Jürgen got down from the truck, and he had new bruises all over his face and was limping badly.

'Can't stop,' Wiggy called to Gwenna. Because her cab was doorless and Mrs Andrews' predicted storm was arriving in a sweep of rain, she was bundled in oilskins. 'It's all gone bonkers at Tregallon, so we're on high alert today.'

'Bonkers how?' Gwenna asked but Wiggy didn't hear over the roar of her truck.

MAX

On his back on a hard plank bed, Max stared sightlessly up at the tin roof. At some time during the night, the rain had come and it was like being under a torrent of dried peas. These huts were built so badly, drips found their way through. All night, all day so far, he had been listening to the stamping of feet outside and the coming and going of trucks. He'd woken a short while ago with sweat on his brow and an unbearable pressure on his chest. To breathe was hard. Fuhrman had kicked him full in the ribs.

He had not let Fuhrman claim victory in front of his men.

In a move that made him gasp in pain, Max tucked his arms under his head. Jürgen had warned him not to provoke Fuhrman.

'Say nothing of why you no longer wear your iron cross, Kapitänleutnant. Do not say you threw it into the sea. The men will not understand.'

'I know. Until they carry the burden of all they have done, and question the orders that made them do it, they will not understand, Jürgen.'

So why, as they ate dinner in the mess hut, had Max himself called for silence and revealed that he no longer wore the medal placed there by the commander-in-chief of the German navy?

Some men had looked away, others down to their food. Fuhrman's eyes had turned cruel as he'd slammed his knife into the table. Only a tin knife, it folded like a flower stalk. Moving fast in his rage, he'd got around the table and pulled Max to the floor. A boot to the throat, then so hard in the ribs Max had felt bone break. Last time Fuhrman had done this, Max had been hand-bound to a chair. Now he was better able to fight back.

You do not plough behind horses, striding deep in soil, to end up a weakling. Fuhrman was in a hospital bed and he, Max, was locked up for fighting. He had refused to go to the sanatorium.

He went back in his head to the moment he had given the order for his U-boat to surface and surrender. They had been pummelled by depth charges rolled off the ships that had surrounded the *Kriegswolf*. One, exploding close, had knocked out some of their electrics. More would come and the U-boat would start to sink and be trapped in the blind depths, and he would die listening to lads crying for their mothers. He had felt an unbearable desire to survive and his boys too and gave the order to surface and raise the white flag. Some, like Fuhrman, blamed him for a choice they would not have dared make. Most were glad.

They would never understand why he had hurled his iron cross into the sea. They did not see as he saw now, that in war men close ranks and call atrocity 'valour'. He could no longer bear the hypocrisy and had thrown the cross away for those he had killed, and for Lotti too. And for Gwenna, who he feared could never forgive him.

He reached into his pocket. Because he was an officer, the guards had not searched him or taken his possessions. A broken bit of pencil was there, and the small diary that had gone to sea with him, and which, like him, had survived his surrender and capture.

They were all he had to make his case to the one he cared for most.

37

'Where is Max?' Gwenna followed Jürgen towards the stables in the wake of an 'I don't know' shrug. Rain dripped off his waterproof hat. He was hobbling still, but trying to conceal it.

Gwenna leaned over Lady's stable door as he took down the net that had held the mare's night hay. The horses had been stabled overnight, when it had become clear that the rain wasn't going to ease. 'If you won't say what's happened to Max, then what happened to you? *Was ist los, Jürgen?*'

'I slide over.'

'And Max?'

Jürgen gave a shake of the head. 'Bad.'

'You mean, hurt?'

'*Ja.*'

'Hospital-bad?'

He said he didn't know. A stubborn back told her she'd get no more. If, as she suspected, camp politics had again spilled into violence, Jürgen probably hadn't the vocabulary to explain.

A farming day never stopped for anyone's feelings and Gwenna ate her breakfast toast while checking the last of the heifers who would likely calve before the weekend. 'See the pointy bones each side of this one's tail?' She showed Lotti. 'They've sunk, which means she's getting ready for labour. For birthing a calf.'

'Can I watch this time?' Lotti asked.

'If Ezra says yes. It's his province.'

With unerring stockman's instinct, Ezra arrived as they were closing the field gate behind them.

'I'll get a mothering pen ready,' he said. 'You heard about the trouble at Tregallon?'

'Only that Max hasn't come to work and is hurt.'

'Fighting. The commandant had to bring in reinforcements. They say morale is rock bottom among the POWs.' Ezra spoke as though he was quoting an official report, though most likely his information had flowed across the bar at the Mermaid. 'Did the Ministry of Agriculture turn up yet, missus?'

Gwenna hadn't yet seen John Wormley, if that's what Ezra meant. Her thoughts were elsewhere. Max, fighting? Or defending himself.

'I think you'll see Mr Wormley very soon.' Ezra cocked a hand to his ear. 'Hm, now I say it, I hear an engine.'

Gwenna couldn't hear anything.

'Heading from Truro way and sounds like it has John Wormley at the wheel.'

'You can't possibly know that – unless you already know. Do you?'

'I might have seen a car with him driving on my way here.'

'Then why not say so? Stop pretending to be a wizard.'

Ezra laughed. 'Once upon a time, you believed I was one.'

'I'm no longer eight years old.'

As they brought the milking herd into the yard, a car splashed through puddles on the other side of the gate. Out got John Wormley.

Who visited a dairy farm at milking time? Gwenna thought crossly. It was the sort of thing Angela would do, sailing in on a ship named *Ignorance*. Wormley tied the belt of his raincoat as he strode towards her in worn leather cavalry boots. 'Too wet to 'oss it today,' he said. Meaning, too rainy to come on a horse.

In spite of his genial approach, Lotti stiffened. Gwenna sensed a primal panic, and realisation dawned. It wasn't men that Lotti was afraid of, nor even Germans per se; it was authority. To Lotti, authority wore a particular kind of clothing. Authority walked with a certain intent.

Gwenna took the small hand and squeezed it. 'Mr Wormley, please make your own way to Colvennon Glaze. Milking trumps all, as I'm sure you appreciate. Pop in to see me when you're done and I'll bring you up to date.'

Half an hour later, John Wormley returned, saying that he was satisfied she had done everything required of her. 'That field is being harrowed to perfection, though obviously not today. Far too wet. By the way, I took a quick look at your pigs and met their keeper.'

'That'll be Jürgen. If it were dry, he'd be harrowing the Glaze. Did you get a word out of him?'

'No, and what he lacks in chit-chat, he makes up for in dogged contempt for my kind. Still, this isn't charm school. Where are the other chaps? We sent you three, didn't we?'

'Oh, er, one got his nose broken and was invalided out of service. That was Walther, who was shaping up to be a good pig man.' *And an even better Nazi*, she added silently.

'Ah, bad luck. And the other fellow, the officer chappie?'

'He didn't turn up today.'

John Wormley nodded. 'All is not calm, all is not bright at Tregallon. I called in on my way somewhere else last night and you could have eaten the air with a spoon. Were your potatoes delivered?'

Gwenna was momentarily thrown by the conversational swerve. 'Oh, yes, mountains of the wretched things.'

'May I see?'

Gwenna led him to the barn. 'Rain permitting, we'll plant end of next week. So long as my other workman comes back.' *Max, where are you? How are you?*

'I could send you a couple of replacements,' Wormley said thoughtfully.

'No! I mean, Max Reiner is pretty much trained. To be honest, he and Jürgen together are all I need.'

Wormley gave her a waggish look. 'What about your hankering for land girls? Are you now convinced that you got the better bargain?'

'Not at all,' she said, sticking up for her sex. 'But I like routine, Mr Wormley. I don't care for change.'

'Home Guard variety?' Wormley asked, picking up a sprouting tuber. 'One of the better new types, in my opinion. Mind you, you'd go a long way to beat Duke of York, in my opinion.'

After some minutes' conversation on potato varieties, which Gwenna could not have recalled five minutes later, she ushered Mr Wormley outside. 'Now you've seen Colvennon Glaze, am I back in the ministry's good books?'

'Yes, for now.'

'What does that mean?' She'd heard of farms being commandeered, the tenants or owners evicted because the land was needed for aircraft runways or weapons silos, or even for secret tunnels to be dug. She couldn't believe Colvennon would fit any of those requirements. Its name meant 'back against the hill' and the sheer cliff that curtailed its fields made it impractical for anything apart from what it was – a mixed farm. 'You've said it yourself, Mr Wormley, I've done all you asked. Ploughed up a meadow that was my father's pride to plant potatoes. Blood, toil, tears and sweat and we'll have them harvested by Lammastide.' No need to explain Lammastide to a countryman; it began on August 1st. 'Put my mind at ease. Tell me I have nothing to fear.'

He laughed. 'I see no looming problems, Mrs Devoran, other than those of frail flesh.'

'My frail flesh?' Had he been speaking to Hilda Hoskens? 'I take that rather amiss, Mr Wormley.'

'Dear me, I wasn't referring to you, Mrs Devoran, but to your missing worker. Men caged together will fight, I suppose, but it won't do for them to carry on pulverising each other as they seem to be doing at the moment.'

She snatched the opportunity to ask him what he thought 'downgraded' meant. 'Someone mentioned the POWs might be downgraded. To what, though?'

'Oh, it refers to their category. Safe or dangerous. If they're deemed to be a risk, they'd downgraded and moved to high-security accommodation. If the inmates of Tregallon wish to remain in a relatively open camp, they need to adjust their behaviour. If you'd rather not have that officer fellow back, I'll understand. I don't like to think of a lady coping alone with a renegade.'

'Max Reiner isn't violent. Not in the way you mean and...' *he makes Lotti happy, and my stomach go into knots.* 'He knows how to use the machinery, and the horses trust him.'

'In that case...' Wormley raised his palm to the air. 'Here we go, the rain's coming back.'

The clouds split. Gwenna ran for the shelter of the milking parlour, Wormley for his car.

A stillborn bull calf arrived at five, ending the day on a sad note. It was not an unusual event with a first-time birth, but still it felt like a failure to Gwenna. The exhausted mother's distress as she tried to nudge the lifeless body pulled hard at her heart. Lotti, who had sat in on the birth, wept copiously.

'Comes of putting them to graze in Fairy Tump,' was Ezra's comment. 'I knew it would go bad soon enough.'

'Oh, don't. It doesn't help, Ezra. I don't want Lotti's head filled with nonsense.' Imagine if, when they made their visit to Freda's, Lotti piped up about the fairies' curses at Colvennon.

While Jürgen and Ezra were removing the calf to bury it in the orchard, Gwenna washed down the mother and Lotti hand-fed her a warm bran mash. 'I'm afraid this is farming life, Lotti.'

'No,' Lotti answered, her eyes on the pink tongue scooping mash from her cupped palms, 'it is all of life, Aunt Gwenna. May I go inside now, and finish what I was writing?'

'Of course.'

Gwenna was washing her hands under the yard pump when Wiggy drove in. Gwenna had taken off her watch, but it felt early for the transport to arrive.

'We're still all to pot, queen. Can I grab Mr Chatterbox and go?'

'Jürgen's doing a job... Wiggy, can you tell me what's happened at Tregallon? Everyone knows either nothing, or nothing very useful. I want to know if Max is—'

'Fit and well?' Wiggy's tone held a teasing note.

'Fit enough to come back to work.'

'Oh, right. There was a brawl over dinner, fists and fury, boots in the ribs,' Wiggy answered. 'I heard enough from the chaps in my truck to know Max started it. Basically, he renounced Nazism over the soup. It didn't go down well with some of his audience.'

'Kurt Fuhrman for one.'

'Those men know our air force is bombing their cities, and they're like rats in a sack, imagining high explosives raining down on the folks at home.'

'Same for folk in London.'

'And Liverpool. Tell me about it, queen. I'm not pitying them, but they're as human as we are. Some are resigned to the fact that their war is over, and they'll go home to a different world. A few still want to be fighting and believe the Thousand

Year Reich actually is that. Max blew a fuse. I don't know why. Perhaps you do.'

'I don't.' Gwenna shook her head. She couldn't stop herself asking, 'How bad is he?'

'Two cracked ribs and he's in the cooler.'

'The cooler?' Gwenna pictured Max sitting among milk churns.

'The lock-up. He's an officer, so they won't keep him in too long. Any road, you were right about Fuhrman. He used to spy for the Gestapo, and the guards know that.'

Jürgen hadn't shown himself yet, so they walked together to the orchard and found him and Ezra still digging a pit.

'Oh, poor little mite,' Wiggy said of the calf lying on a tarpaulin.

Gwenna said, 'As with human babies, they don't always present in the best way. This one was bottom first.'

'It happens when you don't pay heed to the small people,' Ezra threw over his shoulder.

'He means the fairies,' Gwenna explained to Wiggy. 'I put the heifers in the fairy field without offering the small folk their tribute last midsummer, and now I'm paying.'

Wiggy nodded. 'Same where I come from. We have to pay up too, only our small folk are lads armed with wooden clubs with nails in.'

'And you want to go back there?' Gwenna asked.

Wiggy threw a glance towards Jürgen. 'Maybe. I mean, what's to keep me here?' She looked around. 'Where's the nipper?'

'Doing her English homework.'

'Poor kid.'

'Not at all. My problem is stopping Lotti doing it all in one sitting. She particularly loves maths.'

Wiggy blew out her cheeks. 'I suppose it takes all sorts. Jürgen, pet, put your spade down. We have to go.'

As Jürgen stomped past, Wiggy took a tightly folded piece of paper from her pocket and handed it to Gwenna. Max had smuggled it out to her, she said, a friendly guard acting as a go-between.

Gwenna's initials were on the front, in pencil. The note must have been composed against a rough, damp wall and as she read what Max had written, pressure built in her head. Aware of Wiggy's scrutiny, she kept a poker face.

'So, what's he saying?'

'He's apologising for missing a day's work.'

'That all?'

Gwenna nodded.

'Oh, well, I'll go back to my romance novels. You'll have to go back to being a cow's midwife. Not much of a life, is it?'

'I suppose not.' Much as she liked Wiggy, Gwenna wished she'd go. Max had written: 'It should not have been so, what I have become and done. Mrs Devoran, dear Gwenna, if I can cut out my heart for you, I will do it. Write your feelings for me, the truth good or bad.'

'I'm supposed to take a reply,' Wiggy said. 'Though if I get caught smuggling notes, I'll probably be court-martialled.'

Gwenna took a pen from her bag and wrote three words in reply.

She folded the paper and handed it back to Wiggy, saying, 'Don't peep, and don't get caught.'

Lotti's homework, to be given in the following day, had been to write a story involving a colour and an animal. 'A little bit of fun,' Miss Linley had said, 'because next week, we start on the examination syllabus.' Gwenna was so delighted with Lotti's story, she asked her to copy it out. 'We'll send it to Aunt Freda. She'll see how excellently you write, and it'll make her chuckle too.'

Three short words in reply. Morning came and Max did not. Broken ribs took time to mend, but he would have her message by now. Another morning came and went, then another week and still he did not come back. In the meantime, Freda's Quaker contacts in Falmouth wrote to Gwenna with detailed arrangements. Miryam Gittelman's funeral would take place the following week.

38

In the Quaker tradition, the service was simple, with time for silent reflection. A psalm was read as the coffin was lowered. Trees cast dappled shadows on the plain walls and thatched roof of the meeting house of Come-to-Good.

Gwenna was asked if she wished to speak. Her mind went briefly blank and she sputtered out a few halting words. 'I am sorry you did not get to live at Colvennon Farm, Miryam, and that your life was cut short. I will guard and love your daughter as my own. I am sorry you endured so much and had to travel so far.' She cast into the grave a bunch of pink thrift, gathered early that morning above Colvennon Cove, and their gentle landing felt like a premature full stop. She whispered to Lotti, 'Would you like to speak? You don't have to.'

Lotti shook her head but reached inside her coat and, for a heart-stopping moment, Gwenna thought Rumtopf was going into the grave. Instead, there came a flash of colour. A mustard-yellow beret landed beside the flowers. Lotti had discovered the hat in the drawer where Gwenna had hidden it and together, they'd brushed it clean. There had been tears.

'Your nicest hat, Mutti,' Lotti said into the grave, then with a confidence that made every face around them lift in surprise, she told the assembled company, 'The label says "MiGi of Paris". Mutti was MiGi of Paris because it is the first letters of Miryam Gittelman, which is her name. She wanted to be a Parisian milliner, but the Germans came and took my papa, and we had to leave.'

A gentle murmur passed around. Lotti spoke into the grave again. 'I am sorry, Mutti, for leaving Rumtopf on the train. I was scared of the man through the window with Berlin in his eyes.'

Fuhrman the Nazi, she meant, who had outstared Miryam and Lotti as they sat in the dining car at Truro station. Lotti was taking them back to the critical moments before they left the train.

She said, 'I thought he was a policeman because he did not blink. Policemen can look at you until you forget you have a name. We didn't realise we'd arrived and Mutti was shaking from hearing the Germans singing, and because of the man staring. She put her hand on the window to stop him seeing. He put his hand on the window too, like a bad game, and Mutti pulled me off the train. I left Rumtopf behind.'

Birds warbled and a leisurely breeze shook the leaves on the trees. Talented, frightened Miryam Gittelman was laid to rest in a place she'd never dreamed existed, and shortly afterwards, Lotti and Gwenna left. There seemed little point going back to Colvennon as Lotti had a lesson with Miss Linley later, so, getting off the bus in Truro, they went to the tearoom by the cathedral. They could have taken refuge at Fendynick House, but Gwenna felt instinctively that Mill needed more time alone with her emotions.

There had been no reply to the letter Gwenna had written to Charles Avril-Whiting, and until she knew more about Edward's death and Max's role in it – or was told there was no more to know – she would keep a respectful distance.

As they ate fish paste sandwiches, Gwenna let Lotti choose

the subject of conversation. She chose to speak of the man she was meant to call Oncle Gael, whom Mutti had liked and Lotti had not.

———

When he smiled, he showed teeth full of invisible cigarettes. He had bundled her into the dark back of a van, very early in the morning, and told her to be quiet. They'd held on tight because the van had tilted and bumped, sometimes going fast then going slow. At one point, it had stopped, and there had been shouting outside. Oncle Gael had hissed: 'Lie down, don't move.'

He had thrown tree trunks of cloth on top of them. The van had suddenly roared away again and Lotti had felt it bump and bump. At some point, the rear doors flew open. She could feel daylight on her legs. Oncle Gael had fired a gun – it must have been in the truck, though Lotti hadn't seen it. There was shooting, shooting and Lotti could smell hot metal. Hard things smacked against the parts of her not covered by the rolls of cloth.

Later, Mutti had told her they were cartridge cases from the gun.

When they got to the sea, and had to jump into the boat, the van's back doors were half hanging off and Oncle Gael lay on the floor of the van, his head all on one side, and blood on his clothes.

When Lotti had finished speaking, Gwenna took her hands and held them above the salt and pepper set on the table. 'You poor child, to think what you have been through, the things you have seen.'

'Mutti cried and cried, "No, no, Gael, Gael!" Am I bad, Aunt Gwenna, that I did not like him as she did?'

'There is nothing bad in you, Lotti. You are careful whom you trust, and that is entirely right. But let's not forget, this man

Gael helped you escape. He gave everything to get you out of France.'

Doomed Gael must have been a member of the local resistance, Gwenna thought. An ordinary man, helping fugitives from safe houses onto fishing boats which then made the clandestine trip to southern Cornwall. Had love sprung up between Miryam and a rough-speaking Breton?

Why not? Love was a seed that planted itself in any viable ground, gap or crevice. Driven only to live, it didn't care about social class, nationality, or gender. Nor for the havoc it wreaked in its host.

The three words she had written to Max, which Wiggy had, hopefully, smuggled to him, were a simple reflection of this truth.

I need you.

She could not now imagine a life at Colvennon without Max. She wished passionately that Charles Avril-Whiting would reply and inform her that a U-boat called the *Kriegswolf* had been nowhere near Edward's ship on the night of November 23rd 1941. But she didn't suppose he would. If he'd even received her letter, he'd most likely have torn it up in contempt.

May gave way to June and Max returned to Colvennon in time to help bring in the hay. He'd shed a little weight, to Gwenna's eye, and complained of losing fitness.

'Eight hours a day with a scythe will soon fill you out, my lad,' Ezra promised. Gwenna and Lotti drove the horses and the hay cart and the days were filled with the drowsy, malty scents of new-mown grass, the fields full of butterflies and darting hares. When she wasn't driving the laden cart off the field, Gwenna was baking for ravenous men. Or sitting with Lotti, who was studying hard for her exam.

Like a ticking alarm clock, the moment loomed when they'd go to London for Freda's verdict on Lotti's progress, and her future. On June 24th, examination day arrived. Dressed in a yellow blouse and cotton skirt that had belonged to one of Lady Copping's daughters, and worryingly quiet, Lotti was signed in by the school secretary.

'You may come back later, Mrs Devoran. I will show Charlotte to her seat.'

'May she...? I mean, you don't mind if the bear goes in with her?' Rumtopf was wedged under Lotti's left arm. In her right hand, she clutched a bag with pencils and a geometry set Miss Linley had given her. 'You see, the bear is—'

'It's fine,' the school secretary said. 'Lots of the girls bring mascots in with them. It helps calm the nerves, though we draw the line at live mice and rabbits. Back in three hours, yes?'

Gwenna waited until Lotti, with a final nervous smile, disappeared around the corner of a corridor. Gwenna spent most of the time in the cathedral grounds, trying to read a novel. She was twenty minutes early to pick Lotti up, and when the girls filed out, Gwenna searched for a fair head, and waved vigorously. 'Lotti, over here. How was it? How did you do?'

Lotti did not answer until they were well away from the crowd. 'There were a lot of questions, Aunt Gwenna.'

'Could you answer them?'

'I think so. Rumtopf fell off the desk, though.'

And that was as much as Gwenna got.

39

While the hay cutting was in full swing, three new German POWs arrived to swell the manpower. The newcomers were set to hoeing between the rows of potatoes to get rid of weeds and keep the air flowing around the plants. When the hay was cut and turned, the five Germans, under Ezra's instruction, learned how to build hayricks.

This year, 1943, could be written down as 'Good so far'. Gwenna had adopted her father's habit of keeping a diary. Hers this summer would have bewildered him. 'What's this about barley?' he'd have demanded. Colvennon had never grown the crop.

'Barley is improving, growing stronger,' wrote Gwenna. And, 'Barley is keeping me awake at night.' 'Barley' had thrown himself into the work on the farm each day, helped by a tight band of loyal men, who loved him.

Gwenna needed Barley, but it was dangerous to write his name, except in code. For his part, Barley would catch her eye across the shorn grass and speak from his soul.

'You need me but it is not enough. It is nowhere near enough.'

On midsummer morning, Gwenna rose at dawn and walked to Fairy Tump field where she dug a small hole. In it, she laid Charles Avril-Whiting's letter to Edward. After a moment's painful twisting and pulling, she got her wedding ring off and threw it in too. Her final offering to the fairies was the remainder of her whisky. 'I hope that's tribute enough,' she said. 'Be kind to us, you small folk. Let this war end soon. Bless Colvennon and all who work and live here.'

On the last day of June, the farm made the transition from early summer sunshine to searing heat. A standing army of green-yellow hayricks marched alongside her sunken lane, bringing the comfort of fodder the coming winter. In two days, Gwenna and Lotti would board the Cornish Riviera Express, to go to London for Freda's birthday. It would be the moment of truth for Gwenna and Lotti. Under Miss Linley's tutelage, Lotti had flourished, but would it be enough for Freda?

Not on current evidence. Lotti's story, which had so delighted Gwenna, had been received by Freda but the gesture had backfired. Miss Linley had asked for a piece 'involving a colour and an animal' and Lotti had conjured up a purple cow which produced 'the yellowest milk'. A purple cow would produce the most golden milk, because the cow and the milk stood at the furthest ends of the colour spectrum. A red cow would produce green milk, which was why there were no red cows. Gwenna had enclosed Lotti's illustration of a violet cow and a milkmaid with yellow plaits.

'Most imaginative,' Freda had written back, 'but Gwenna dearest, you do Lotti no favours doing her schoolwork for her. Education specialists advise that children should be allowed to explore their own abilities and to fail, if need be.'

Gwenna had felt all the blinding fury of injustice. After what Miss Linley had told her, it was clear that Freda was capable of underhand tactics if her primacy was threatened.

Gwenna resolved that in London, she would not allow herself to be browbeaten.

Today, they would pack, so there'd be no last-minute rush. Tomorrow, St Morgan's entrance examination results would arrive in the post. Never had the postman been so feared or so wished-for. Gwenna felt as though her stomach was being pushed through a sieve.

Needing to be busy, she was weeding a corner of the bean field. Straightening her back, leaning on her hoe for a moment, she watched two Cornish choughs hopping across her path. She gave them a greeting. In her grandmother's youth the cliff tops had glittered with them. She remembered her grandma recalling that sometimes you could hardly hear the waves over their cries. They'd sunk to a few pairs after her grandfather stopped grazing sheep along the cliffs and the gorse had taken over.

'Is it tea break?' Max shouted as he walked towards her, teasing her for standing idle. He lobbed a stone, which landed a few feet away. She averted her eyes.

They had no privacy in which to explore the dangerous complexity of their lives. She wished Charles Avril-Whiting would write.

'Aunt Gwenna, Aunt Gwenna!'

Lotti was jumping the rows of potatoes, her skirt gathered in one hand so she could run. She held a letter. Oh, Lord. Had the results come a day early?

Lotti thrust the envelope at Gwenna. 'It has the school badge on the front.'

Gwenna's mouth was suddenly dry. If Lotti had failed, if Miss Linley's confidence had been misplaced, she wouldn't forgive herself. She'd have to confess to Freda, 'I made her sit the exam with too little preparation.' She kicked a clod of dirt, which had a thistle embedded in it, then rustled up a bright smile. 'Shall we see what it says?'

'Wait for Max. I want him to see too.' Lotti urgently called Max to hurry.

Gwenna smoothed out her expression and thought how well Max looked as he walked across the field towards them. Upright as a lusty oak, his arms swinging. A Cornish summer was driving away any remnants of submariner's pallor. His hair had grown out of its prison crop and gleamed dark gold. He rarely wore a hat. He was in debt to the sun, as he put it.

He looked concerned when he was close enough to see what Gwenna held in her hand. 'All is well?'

'It's Lotti's entrance exam results for her new school. Hopefully, her new one.'

'She is got in?'

'I daren't open it. I feel more nervous than when it was my results. Well, here goes.' Fingers like wooden clothes pegs, she prised open the envelope and removed a crisp sheet of paper. Her eye dived into the typed letter, searching for 'sorry' or 'regret', any clue that would prepare them for disappointment.

'Have I passed, Aunt Gwenna?'

'Oh, Lotti. No. No, you haven't passed.'

'Freda, Lotti sat her exam for St Morgan's.'

They were in London, in Freda's kitchen. Freda had brought them in here, saying she and Norbert always ate huddled around the fold-out table because the dining room was overflowing with paperwork. They were drinking tea, eating a cake Gwenna had bought on the way here from the station. It was a chocolate cake, eye-wateringly expensive, and sweet enough to feel like a crime.

'Did she pass?' Freda asked, with a voice that expected the answer 'No'.

'Um... not exactly.' Gwenna took out the letter with the St Morgan's crest on it and passed it to Freda. 'I didn't want to disclose her results in a telephone call. I wanted to show you face to face since it affects us all.'

Freda took the letter and read it. She frowned. 'You said she hadn't passed.'

'She hasn't "passed".' Lotti had been awarded a distinction. 'Don't you see, she's done remarkably. She's got the Mabel Perdew scholarship.'

'The Perdew...?' Freda frowned. 'But that's for the girl who—'

'Scores the highest result in the entrance exam. Exactly.'

'How?' Freda shot a glance towards her husband, who was wedged up against a kitchen trolley, eating cake hungrily. Norbert Fincham had always seemed to Gwenna to be too tall for his own body, and with his shoulders hunched to wolf down his cake, he made Gwenna think of a prematurely aged street child. Keeping him fuelled under food rationing must be a challenge for Freda.

'Norbert, what do you say?' Freda flashed the results letter towards him.

'I say, jolly good cake.' Norbert kept his tone light.

'Don't be obtuse. I want your opinion on this exam result. Should we take it seriously?'

Gwenna's tense smile turned ferocious. Keeping her voice steady with an effort, she answered before Norbert could empty his mouth. 'Lotti did it, Freda, that's the point. You cannot argue with a scholarship. Miss Linley deserves praise, but the true victor is Lotti's own incredible brain. Lotti, tell Aunt Freda what your result was.'

Gwenna beamed with pride as Lotti replied, 'Ninety-four per cent but only because I forgot how to spell some words. I would have remembered, except Rumtopf fell off the desk and I had to put my hand up to ask the in-in—'

'Invigilator.'

'—that lady to pick him up.'

Norbert Fincham had sputtered on hearing 'ninety-four per cent'. Now he laughed. 'Brava!'

Freda stared down at her plate. 'Have St Morgan's formalised their offer?'

'There hasn't been time, but Miss Linley, Lotti's tutor, telephoned. Lotti can start this September and because of the scholarship, I can afford to let her be a weekly boarder. We need your permission, of course, but Freda, it's a wonderful chance for Lotti.'

'This is a bit sudden.' Freda looked the closest she ever did to being flustered. 'We haven't discussed Lotti's future.'

'We're discussing it now. We have done all you asked of us.' The spectre of John Wormley rose up in front of Gwenna. She'd done all he'd asked too, and he'd had the grace to admit it. 'She's speaking English fluently, she laughs and smiles. Don't you, Lotti? And she's grown out of all the clothes she arrived in, and into the ones my sister-in-law found for her. She passes exams with flying colours. And by the way' – Freda had begun a counter argument, which Gwenna ruthlessly overrode – 'the story about the purple cow was all her own work. I may not be the perfect guardian, but one thing I have never done is underestimate Lotti's intelligence.'

'You misunderstand me,' Freda said stiffly.

'No, she doesn't,' Norbert said robustly. 'You told me bold-faced you thought Gwenna had written that little essay. "Just like her to blither on about cows," you said.'

'Norbert!'

'Dear heart, you are usually so full of grace, and now is the moment to back down.'

A truce was declared as nobody wanted the visit to descend into ill feeling. There was a birthday card and gifts to hand over to Freda, and lunch to be thought of, and later, Holland Park to be walked in, where a shadow from the past caught up with them. Before they went out for their walk, however, a mystery was solved. Norbert showed Gwenna a battered suitcase, a vanity case and a child's satchel.

'These arrived a few days ago, from Paddington Station's lost property office. Apparently they've been sitting in the chief clerk's office, gathering dust while he was off sick. They're full of Miryam and Lotti's things.'

'Hide them,' Gwenna said. 'The clothes won't fit Lotti anyway. When she's a bit older, we'll let her decide what she wants to keep. It's too soon now.'

That afternoon, Gwenna, Freda and Lotti strolled along a gravel path in Holland Park. The truce still held, and their conversation dwelled on the weather, the wildlife and landscape. They were approaching a circular garden planted with cabbages and runner beans when Gwenna realised that Lotti was lagging behind.

She turned. Lotti had stopped dead a few yards back. She hadn't seen the child's body stiffen like that in weeks and she hurried back. 'Darling, what is it?'

'Here. It... here.' Lotti's breathing was ragged. 'Mutti and I.'

Gwenna looked to Freda, who, having realised she was walking alone, had also turned back. 'Something happened here,' Gwenna said.

Freda glanced about, and recognition dawned. 'Oh dear. This is where she and her mother were surrounded. Remember, I described it in court? Miryam spoke German inadvertently, and they were encircled. It's changed so much, I didn't realise. Lotti?' Lotti's eyes were fixed on the circular garden. 'This isn't necessary. The past is gone, dearest. Yes? The past is not the present. Now, calm down and breathe properly.'

Lotti stared blankly. Gwenna put her arm around her and linked her other through Freda's. 'Come on, best foot forward.'

. . .

Later that night, when Lotti was in bed, she said to Freda, 'We don't always get it right, however hard we try.'

'Clearly not. I should have realised, Holland Park was bound to be traumatic.'

'It doesn't mean we're unfit guardians. It means we're human.'

Freda allowed a smile. 'By that you mean, you are more human than I. I've become a Mrs Pardiggle, neglecting the children for the sake of the charity.'

'That's beyond me, Freda, but I will say this. We have to allow ourselves to get things wrong. Just occasionally, to act with passion rather than with mechanical precision.'

'Easy for you to say. Lives depend on me, Gwenna. My work literally brings people to safety from the brink of disaster.'

'What you and Norbert do is remarkable,' Gwenna agreed. 'If it comes to an argument as to which of us is the better person, it's you by a long way. But I'm tired of being judged. All I want is to love and be loved, and...' She'd practised saying this but it still required a leap of faith. 'I'm taking Lotti home with me.'

Contradiction flared in Freda's eyes. 'No. I feel she needs time in London, to help her make up her own mind where she wants her future to be.'

That small, invisible axe swung and found its target, Gwenna's lacerated heart. 'I have proved myself a fit carer for Lotti, more than fit, and I'm taking her home to Colvennon, Freda. You won't dare stop me.'

'No?'

'No. Because you owe me.'

Like Mr Beecroft, Freda was able to raise a single eyebrow. 'What do I owe you?'

'An apology for failing to tell me in time why Edward Devoran could never love me. Not the way I wanted him to, because he had no sexual feelings for women.'

Freda gaped momentarily. 'You're saying I should have brought up such a subject?'

'Yes! You broke off your engagement with him, then watched me blunder into the same situation. I got no love and no children. Why did you send me that one half-baked hint months and months too late?'

'What could one say, Gwenna? One doesn't talk of such things.'

'I'm your oldest friend!'

'And I am a Quaker. We seal our lips against gossip.'

Gwenna would never know if Norbert had been eavesdropping, but he thrust the door open at that moment, bringing a tray loaded with their evening drinks. He had a telegram clutched between his front teeth. Like a bumbling retriever barging into a difficult conversation, he dropped the buff-coloured sheet in Freda's lap.

'Family of five, homeless, mother with four children, father sent by ship for internment in Canada. I've said we can take them in. Can we?'

Freda swung into action with an energy Gwenna suspected came not only from a passion to heal the brutalities of the world, but to evade a most awkward allegation. No more was said of Edward, or of Lotti staying in London. At the end of their stay, Freda was too busy to accompany them to Paddington for the journey home. Norbert went instead.

Lifting their luggage onto the rack in their compartment, he whispered to Gwenna, 'Freda's deeply anxious that she may, in some way, have failed you.'

Gwenna decided Norbert could cope with a candid reply. 'Freda didn't tell me why she called off her engagement to Edward but I am pretty sure it's because she discovered he was in love with Charles Avril-Whiting.'

Colour in Norbert's cheeks told Gwenna that he had

discussed this already with his wife. 'A tricky thing to say at any time.'

'But Freda specialises in difficult things. She was my dearest friend, who let me go to the altar regardless. Still, there were others with a stronger duty to tell me. Edward, for one.'

'I understand why you're angry,' Norbert said gravely. 'Freda should have warned you. And if it's any comfort, I think you're doing a splendid job with Lotti. I shall tell Freda so.'

They shook hands, Norbert lingering long enough to say to Lotti, 'Ninety-four per cent. Well done you.'

Later, as the train carved through the city's western suburbs, Lotti looked up from the atlas she was studying. Norbert had presented it to her, and it was much more up to date than Gwenna's old school atlas.

'What are you thinking, Aunt Gwenna?'

'What a lot of roofs there are in London.' And under one of them, Charles Avril-Whiting lodged, feeling perhaps as empty as she did. He'd have replied to her letter by now, if he meant to.

'Canada is really big,' Lotti said, turning a page.

'I believe so.' Gwenna moved seats, to sit next to Lotti. This atlas was very detailed. The state lines of Canada were ruler straight, she noticed, not like the wiggly boundaries of British counties. 'What intrigues you about Canada?'

'It's where Papa wanted us to go. This book opens out into a great big square and you can see the whole world. Can we open it now?'

'I think we'd better wait till we're home, in the dining room. If we move the table, we can spread it on the floor.' This was the first Gwenna had heard of Lotti's father wanting to take his family to Canada. Other family members had gone to Norway, so Freda had told her.

Lotti asked an unconnected question. 'Will I like my school?'

'I hope so. I did.'

'Will I like being a weekly boarder? That means I come home on Friday and go back on Monday.'

'Exactly right.'

'You'll be there when I come home?'

'Always. Always and forever.'

'I don't ever want to leave you, Aunt Gwenna.'

'And you don't have to. It's been agreed, you will stay at Colvennon. Now, close the atlas. We can't have the Mabel Perdew scholar growing short-sighted. There is such thing as too much study. Let's play I-spy. You have time, Lotti, all the time in the world to grow up and teach me the things I never learned. Yes?'

Lotti filled her heart by saying, 'Just like you taught me to milk the cows and that a calico cat is three colours.'

'Just like that.'

40

July brought blowing meadows and a final cut of hay by the middle of the month. The potato harvest was dug and carted off to the wholesaler. Gwenna hoped that king, country and John Wormley were now satisfied.

The weather turned sultry, storms grumbling as the heat thickened. Soon, everyone was praying for a cleansing burst.

Lammastide, the 1st of August, brought a dry spell and it was all hands to the broad beans, which were in danger of darkening in the pod. Village women came to help, and for two weeks the fields were colourful with hats, head scarves and baskets. Their children lent a hand though the locals kept their distance from the Germans, Gwenna noticed. Two tribes.

Max commented on it. 'We can never be accepted.'

'Do you need to be? One day you will go home.'

He pushed his hair off a forehead where trouble sat. 'They take our labour but not our handshake.'

'Those women have loved ones in North Africa, fighting a desert war. They have sons who are bomber crew and get shot down. What do you expect?'

The end of July had brought news of the toppling of the

Italian Fascist dictator, Mussolini. Tension had soared among the Germans at Tregallon, Wiggy reported. 'Mussolini was Hitler's best chum. Now Hitler's beginning to look like a man who starts a fight in a bar, looks round and discovers all his mates have legged it.'

The war would turn, but in which direction? Defeat for Germany, or the victory fanatics like Fuhrman still believed in? Colvennon carried on bringing in the beans. The cows still came in twice a day to be milked, the churns went to the road and the empties came back. The air grew hotter and muggier. Gwenna made sure a water bowser was always on hand for the workers and took cold beer to Max and the other men to keep their energy up. They were all sick of slapping midges on their necks.

The storm broke on the 18th of August, which was her wedding anniversary and, more importantly, four days before Lotti's eleventh birthday. The storm coincided with the arrival of Solomon, the bull from a neighbouring farm who would run with Gwenna's cows and create next year's calves. Rain teemed down on his butter-coloured magnificence as he pawed the ground and bellowed. After seeing him led into his paddock, Gwenna went into the house. She snatched a long glass of water and turned on the wireless that was tuned permanently to the BBC. Important news floated out. After five weeks of sustained and successful Allied attack, Sicily had finally been liberated from German occupation. Max ought to hear it from her, she decided.

She was on her way to tell him when she saw Roddy and two of his sons parading along the lane than ran parallel with her fields. They were the boys she'd caught stealing her seed potatoes. Union Jack bunting fluttered between them. The boys were beating biscuit-tin drums, while their dad hollered over the hedge towards Gwenna's POWs, 'Who's winning the war? We're winning the war!'

Gwenna went to intervene. 'Scare my cows,' she warned Roddy, 'and I'll shrink your head and hang it on my belt.'

Ezra, coming up alongside, voiced his opinion too. 'You lummocks might as well bash your heads as those tins. They'd make just as much noise.'

'What d'you know, old man?' one of the boys jeered.

'Cheeky little wazzock.' Ezra told Roddy to teach his lads some manners.

But Roddy was drunk on the BBC news. He waved his bunting. 'Tell those Germans you love so much that they're beaten, Mrs Devoran.'

'Don't be ridiculous.' Gwenna was listening more attentively to the news lately, tracking the advance of the war on Lotti's atlas. 'They're far from beaten.'

'On their side now?' Roddy sneered.

'I'm on the side of good sense. The war isn't over, by a long mile.'

Roddy's answer was a long, spittle-filled raspberry, which had his sons cheering. 'Come on, boys, let's share our good tidings with they Nazis.'

Gwenna watched them go. Lotti had come out to find her, taking a break from her studies. Miss Linley had imposed a strict schedule during the holidays, so Lotti might join her new school without gaps in her education. She was currently reading up on the Malayan rubber industry and its role in the prosperity of Victorian Britain.

Gwenna urged her to go back inside. She wasn't going to give Roddy or his unpleasant offspring any excuse to tease or mock the child.

'What's the banging?' Lotti asked.

'I'll explain later, darling.'

'All right, Aunt Gwenna.' Lotti obeyed happily, saying, 'I'll make a salad for us.'

Gwenna ran towards the bean fields. She got ahead of the

Hoskenses, who had tangled their bunting round a gatepost, saying as she passed, 'If you bring your racket anywhere near my cows or set that bull off, I will complain formally to John Wormley. I won't spare you, Roddy.'

Another raspberry pursued her as she cut along a path between fields. Reaching the pasture where Solomon was pacing, Gwenna climbed the gate. Head lowered, she walked calmly across his turf.

There were five Germans at work today, including Max and Jürgen, and with the beans now harvested, they were grubbing up the stalks, which would be stored for pig fodder and cow bedding. They'd worked out a system, pulling up the roots and raking them onto tarpaulin mats, which they then rolled like giant pasties, and passed up to a man standing on the back of a high-sided cart. Lady and Prince were harnessed to the cart, munching on fibrous stalks when they weren't tossing their heads against the flies.

Max set down his rake and came over. 'What is worrying you, why are you running?' he asked.

She told him the news. The Hoskenses' chanting and their drumbeats could be heard quite clearly. Her threat to report them had not deterred them. 'It seems your troops have retreated from Sicily, and landed on mainland Italy. I suppose that's where the fighting will be now. Do you think—'

She broke off as Max's face tightened.

'Go on, please,' he said quietly.

'Will your side see the value of surrendering, now you've lost your footing in the Mediterranean, and Mussolini is in prison?'

'No.' Said without inflection. 'We will fight on.' Roddy and his sons were now visible with their flapping red, white and blue bunting. Max swore. 'Are the pagans returning?'

Roddy had acquired a headdress, made from stems of hogweed rammed into a neckerchief he'd tied around his head.

He looked like a straggler from a May Day pageant. His sons beat their improvised drums and they'd lashed themselves together with the bunting, which meant they had to move with careful synchronicity. The Germans all stopped work to watch. Jürgen left the horses, harnessed to their cart, and came to stand close to Max.

'We're winning the war. We're winning the war,' the Hoskens boys chanted over their drumbeat while their father beat his chest and roared, 'We've kicked your German arses out of Italy. Out of *Italee*.'

'Only from Sicily,' Max said, his voice pitched to carry over the racket. 'A small island and we hold Italy. We will fight to hold Italy.'

'You won't,' Roddy countered. 'You'll scuttle away back to your burrow, like the vermin you are.'

'Like vermin,' echoed the eldest boy with a flourish of drumsticks, which Gwenna realised were his mother's wooden kitchen spoons. Hilda wouldn't thank him for that. He was loud, though, and the horses shied, backing against the cart's shafts. Gwenna touched Jürgen's shoulder, and he returned to stand by Lady's head.

Max addressed Roddy. 'You damn fool. Your wireless tells the happy news but Germany will fight for Italy and her mountains will run red. Our blood, your blood.'

'That's what you hope!' Roddy hollered back.

'It is not. I want the damn war to end, so all may go home and men can stop killing each other.' Max's voice cracked. 'What I am saying is, my country will not give up after one retreat. They will fight.'

'That's what we want too, a good fight. Get rid of you lot once and for all.'

'Don't you see? Italy is a narrow country of mountains, and when war rages in the mountains, there are many dead. Yours and ours.'

. 'Then you should be fighting, boy, if that's what you think.' With a yell, Roddy charged at the watching Germans. Only, he forgot that he and his sons were connected by yards of bunting and within a couple of strides, he was on his face in a pile of bean stems, the boys tumbling on top of him. It would have ended in farce, had one of the boys not hurled his biscuit tin as he fell. It struck the side of the cart, and Lady shied and plunged. Prince, spooked by his mother, bucked. Jürgen was dragged as they bolted. The man on the back of the cart fell to the ground.

Max and Gwenna ran after the cart that was jerking as the horses bucked, reared and plunged. Gwenna gave a silent scream at the splintering thump of wheels on hard earth. Jürgen was hanging on to Lady's harness, half running, half dragged.

Max shouted, '*Jürgen, mein Bruder*—' Telling Jürgen to hold firm, he sprinted to get in front of Prince's head, and pulled him up by brute strength. Between them, Max and Jürgen brought the horses to a stop.

Gwenna ran to Jürgen's side and began to unhitch Lady. She could feel the mare's terror, smell it in the sweat streaming off her white back. Lady's rolling eyes and the solid set of her neck warned of imminent panic. In rare moments like this, the weight and power of these animals was terrifying. The cart they'd been hitched to many, many times had become a predator. Gwenna saw a dash of bright scarlet on Prince's back leg, which lay on the wrong side of the shaft. Now she understood why the horses had not outrun the men. 'Max, Prince is caught up. Keep him still.'

They had to free both horses, quickly. 'There now, easy, good Lady,' Gwenna crooned. The harness leather had swelled in the humid air. It needed stronger fingers than hers to unbuckle the loin strap, the first stage of releasing the shafts.

'Gwenna-maid, you let me do that.' Ezra Jago's oak-aged

voice came into her ear. 'You go to her head; that's where you're best use.'

She let Ezra take her place and stroked Lady's solid neck as he, without any apparent haste, unhitched first the loin strap, then the girth. Lady was freed, but they kept her where she was. She nuzzled her son's withers.

Ezra plodded round to Prince's side and repeated the process. The shaft was gently lowered, releasing his injured leg.

Max and Jürgen led the horses away from the cart. Gwenna breathed.

Ezra checked Prince's back leg. 'I'd say that hurts like blazes. The skin's been rubbed raw,' he said. 'Back to their stables, please, lads. I'll be along in a moment.'

Gwenna nodded to Max. 'Take them.'

'Of course,' said Max. 'But keep those thickheads away from us.' The man who had fallen off the cart was being helped to walk. He was clearly badly winded.

'We'll take him to the house,' Gwenna told Max, 'and I'll give him first aid.' The man looked dizzy. It was a long way down from a cart, and he'd come off backwards.

Roddy and his boys, meanwhile, were unravelling their bunting. Covered in soil and plant shreds, they looked surly, as if the ignominious end to their prank was someone else's fault. Ezra went to stand in front of them.

'Show your face here again, Roddy Hoskens, or go near they horses, you'll have me to answer to.'

'Give over, Ezra. 'Twas only a bit of fun.'

'Fun? A horse that might have broke his leg, who never did you no harm? We were that far from the creature being put down here in front of us.' Ezra measured a half-inch between thumb and finger. 'That far. I saw enough of that in the last war, horses a-dying. You're a no-good, miserable bastard.'

Gwenna stared. She'd known Ezra all her life, and never heard him use a profanity. He was crying, she realised, some buried grief welling out of him. Or perhaps it was shock. She knew better than to comfort him and turned away.

The other Germans murmured among themselves. Gwenna went to them to instruct them to take their fellow to the farmhouse. 'Then I'm afraid it's back to work without horses.' Lady wouldn't work without Prince, and they'd have to be reintroduced to the cart before they could go back in harness.

Only a bit of fun. She'd give Roddy Hoskens fun. What she did was tell him, in front of his boys, that one German was worth ten of him.

Out to sea, lightning flashed. Thunder came twenty heartbeats later. The air darkened.

41

The storm hit the coast at five in the evening and Gwenna thought she could hear the booming flares of stricken ships. She hoped it was the crash of oversized waves on the rocks. The man who had fallen off the cart was on the couch in her sitting room. His comrades were sheltering in the barn.

She was in Prince's stable watching while Ezra and Max cleaned the horse's leg. A bucket of rags in bloody water stood to one side, and Max was applying diluted gentian violet to the wound while Ezra held the head collar. Gwenna looked at the leg and flinched. Skin had been scraped off over quite a patch. As Ezra had said, it must hurt like blazes.

'I'll call the vet in the morning,' she said. 'I won't catch him now; he'll be on his rounds, probably taking shelter somewhere. I'd say Prince is on box rest for the foreseeable. Who's doing the pigs?'

'Jürgen, Martin and Heinz will go, if you tell them,' Max said.

'I'll bring the cows in for milking, then. There's nothing else we can do in this weather apart from carry on regardless.' Rain was sluicing off the stable roof. Gwenna was soaked. They all were.

Ezra was reluctant to let her get the cows in alone in these conditions. 'And we should bring them under cover tonight. That old Solomon must go in a shed too. Any volunteers to lead a bull? Max?'

'All right.' A thread of humour had returned to Max's voice, but Gwenna knew it would take more than Ezra's coaxing to melt the anger, the despair, she'd heard in his voice when he had tried to explain mountain warfare to a dense trio of Hoskenses.

Max led Solomon into the shed prepared for him with a rope clipped to a brass ring through the animal's nose. The cows, their coats darkened to teak by rain, filed into the milking parlour. Gwenna's feet were squelching in her boots. She reckoned the only ones comfortable on the farm right now were the pigs, wallowing in liquorice-coloured mud, the Old Spots distinguishable from the black Cornish hogs only by the lesser size of their ears.

Heinz slipped and fell trying to persuade the black boar, Pendragon, to quit his glorious hollow. He limped back to the yard, clutching his knee.

'*Lieber Gott*, such a day,' Max said heavily. 'May he go also to the house?'

'Yes, though it will resemble a field hospital. Don't you fall over, Max,' Gwenna pleaded.

'I know. You need me.'

Rain streaming off her face and her hair plastered flat, she couldn't summon a clever riposte or even manage a blush. 'I do,' she said. 'Now more than ever. Tread carefully, Max Reiner.'

Thundery weather and humidity could send milk sour, so they worked fast, in silence, at opposite ends of the parlour.

Getting the churns down the sunken lane would be double the usual chore, and Gwenna suggested waiting for Wiggy. 'I'm sure she'll let us put them in the back of her truck and the other POWs can help lift them off.' Gwenna asked herself: *Do people have any idea when they splash milk into their tea what goes into getting it to their table?*

There came the moment when there were just two cows between her and Max. 'Nearly done,' she said, and was surprised to get no answer. 'Max?'

Concerned, she got up and found him on his feet, leaning against the cow he was supposed to be stripping, his elbow on the animal's withers. 'Max.'

He looked at her and seemed not to recognise her. She'd seen this pallor on him before, when he'd asked her the name of Edward's ship. 'Are you sick? It's been a heck of a hard day.'

No answer. Had he been hurt, and she hadn't noticed? Struck his head? 'What is it?'

'Rudi.'

She knew the names of the new Germans on the farm. Martin, Heinz and the winded Andreas. Rudi was new to her. 'Who's that?'

'My younger brother. I saw him just now.'

'Impossible.' Nobody could have come into the parlour without her being aware of it.

'No, I saw him *here*.' Max tapped his forehead. 'In my mind, so clear. This is how I know.'

'What do you know?' The desolation in his eyes answered her. 'You think he's dead?'

'*Ja*. He is in a Panzer division. Tanks, North Africa. I know he is now dead. When we left to fight, we said we would come to the other, if we died.'

Max wasn't given to fanciful ideas, but she suggested he was overwrought. Arguing with Roddy earlier, trying to get through the thick walls of his skull, had brought this on.

Max denied it. He was shivering. 'Rudi brought the touch of his soul.'

She did the only thing she could, offered the only solace she had, and put her arms around him. Their cold cheeks collided and she willed warmth from her body to flow into his. She could feel him crying inside and she thought of her own pity for Edward, which had been not one bit lessened by her reading Charles Avril-Whiting's words to him.

'You didn't ever tell me you had a brother.'

'I feared to remember; it is easier sometimes to keep things silent. He was younger than me.'

'I'm so sorry.'

They kissed. Not a kiss of scorching passion but tentatively, after weeks of restraint. The cow beside them lifted a hoof and slammed it down but still they kissed. Eventually, they broke apart.

'I love you, Gwenna.'

'I – I think I love you too, Max. I think so.' She spoke in a rush, in case she lost courage. Putting a finger against his lips, she said, 'I'm freezing; I'm covered in muck.'

He smiled sorrowfully against her cheek. 'I too. I wish so much I did not have to go away tonight.'

'I know. Could you escape?'

He gave a wild chuckle. 'Yes, easily maybe, but they will catch me and send me to a rocky island.'

'Then we need to think of another way.'

The scrape of a footstep made them both spring apart. Hilda Hoskens stood just inside the parlour, and from her expression, she had watched it all.

'You're a disgrace, Gwenna Devoran, a German-loving disgrace. I came out in all this weather to see if that horse was mending. My Roddy was concerned but I should have saved my trouble.'

Gwenna had stepped away from Max. Now she wrapped

her arms around herself. She might as well have been naked and pinned to the wall, every flaw of her character on display. 'I don't believe you,' she shot back at Hilda. 'You came to see if I mean to inform the camp commander about your husband's behaviour to the men today.'

'And I shall say what I've seen here.' Hilda jutted her lower jaw. 'You'll not dare show your face in the village after I've finished.'

It was more than a threat, as Gwenna discovered early next morning on going out to telephone the vet. She took Lotti with her. At the post office, Mrs Andrews stood guard as Gwenna made the call, and afterwards marched behind her to the door, saying, 'And don't come back. I don't want Germans here, nor a German's fancy piece.'

In case there was any misunderstanding, Mrs Andrews spat in Gwenna's face.

42

It was the 23rd of August and Lotti's birthday. Eleven years old. This morning, it was birthday cake in the field. Lotti didn't know that Max had a gift to give.

Since Mrs Andrews' attack, Gwenna had kept her distance from the village. The sensation of spittle on her skin had stayed long after she'd washed her face. Gwenna checked her watch. It was five to eleven. 'Come along, birthday girl.'

When Lotti continued frowning down at the pages of her geography textbook, Gwenna leaned across and closed it. 'I know the cocoa crop of Ghana encroaches on natural forest, darling, but imagine a day without our favourite drink. Maybe not now so much' – the August weather was still and humid – 'but I couldn't survive winter without it. Get your shoes on.' Most parents fought to keep a child at her studies. Gosh. Had she just thought 'parent'? She wasn't that. Lotti was still Freda's ward, a stateless person.

'You know they cut down the trees to plant the bushes, Aunt Gwenna.'

'Does the book say that?'

'No, the books say, "Acres of virgin forest are being cleared to grow the valuable crop." They make it sound like a good thing but where do the animals go?'

'I don't know. Oh dear, I don't want you worrying today of all days and I need your help.'

'All right.' Lotti obligingly got to her feet. Since the incident in the post office, she'd done all she could to cheer Gwenna up; walking home that day, she'd said, 'It happened to Mutti and Papa too. In Berlin, and even in Paris where people ought to have known better. Papa used to say, "It doesn't matter in a world where we have soap."'

Gwenna picked up the cake tin. She'd been up in the night, baking a cake flavoured with rhubarb and apple jam. After a frantic search, she'd found eleven part-used birthday candles.

They pulled on outdoor shoes. Both of them were wearing cotton dungarees and straw sunhats, and it took Gwenna back to distant summers, when casual workers would come to help with the harvest. She remembered running down to the cove with the workers' children when the day's labour was done. They didn't always understand each other's accents, but they'd built sandcastles together. That could teach Mrs Andrews something and Hilda, too.

Ezra had been upset by the attack on Gwenna. The village was split, he'd told her, between those who thought she was bringing shame on herself, consorting with a German, and those who thought, *Good luck to the maid.*

'Which side do you stand on, Ezra?' she'd asked.

'I always favour my right foot, missus,' had been Ezra's deadpan reply.

Lotti and Gwenna made their way to Colvennon Glaze, stopping off at the paddock where Lady and Prince were grazing to feed them each a carrot. The vet had advised two weeks' rest for Prince's abrasions and strained tendons to heal, and as Lady would not be separated from him, Gwenna had hired a horse from another farm to take on their work. A stolid black mare named Emily was out in the field. Lady was in mischievous mood, reaching out and plucking Rumtopf from the bib of Lotti's dungarees, and dropping him on the ground.

'Poor bear,' Lotti cried. 'He doesn't understand.'

Gwenna wouldn't mention it for the world, but since Lotti's soaraway success in the entrance exam for St Morgan's, Rumtopf had spent more time than usual on the kitchen table. Lotti was growing up. The school had sent its formal offer of a heavily subsidised place. The new Perdew scholar would become a weekly boarder on the 8th of September.

Passing the field where Solomon filled the eye with his stature and the gleam of his nose ring, Gwenna checked the gate was fastened and the chain that secured it. The day before, she'd found a roadside gate open and suspected the Hoskens boys.

At the Glaze, the men were preparing the soil for the next crop, picking stones and hurling them into a cart. Emily dozed between its shafts. Someone had fastened a straw hat to her head, her ears poking through holes in the brim. Flies were a menace on these late August days and they'd be worse by the end of the week, when the muck spreading began. Gwenna waved to Max, though not before checking to see if they were being observed. She hated being the butt of gossip, the despised object. She hadn't been to chapel for three weeks now, staying cocooned at Colvennon. Even here, she twitched and imagined eyes implanted in the hills.

Max came towards them, giving a whistle that made the others straighten up. As he picked his way across, she thought how she'd revolted against having Germans on her land, yet she could not have got through the last weeks without them.

Max looked at his watch. His own watch, guarded fero-ciously during the early weeks of his capture and now the protector of a pale band of skin on a tanned wrist. 'You make good timing,' he said, glancing at the cake tin. 'Everything stops for tea.'

Coffee, in his case. The men got the billycan boiling, Ezra wandered up from some corner and took his preferred seat, an elm stump that somebody had provided for his comfort. Everyone else slumped on the grass. Gwenna put the cake on the tin lid.

Lotti's face split in a grin. 'You told me it was a turnip cake!'

'Every birthday deserves a surprise.' Gwenna had forgotten to bring a knife, so Ezra offered the one that hung from his belt. Gwenna gave Lotti her present, a clutch of coloured art pencils tied with ribbon. Max gave her a necklace of wooden beads. Another of the POWs had made it, he said. The medic who had been in his crew. 'We all find ways to make our living.'

Lotti was congratulated, in German, in English and in Cornish by Ezra. Though she thanked everyone in turn, she did so quietly. Her first birthday without her mother was bound to bring sadness. Gwenna cut the cake and acknowledged that she'd excelled herself. Moist and tangy. She watched the faces around her and felt a twinge of defiance. Her mother had been known as a fine baker, so maybe she was growing to be a worthy mistress of Colvennon and the old cats in the village could hate her but they'd never destroy her. On the back of that came a sudden resolve. 'We'll go to chapel this Sunday, Lotti.' Let them see her with her head high.

The flies kept away, discouraged by the campfire. Emily the mare ambled to the edge of the field, pulling her cart and looking like something from a child's picture book. Lotti got up to feed her the last crumbs of her cake. The horse's broad mouth could do nothing with it and the bits dropped onto the grass.

Max fished a carrot from his pocket and tossed it to Lotti. He and Gwenna locked eyes, words passing between them in a silent flash. *We're allowed to be happy.*

. . .

Sunday morning, and as Gwenna rolled out of bed, she remembered her vow of going to chapel. 'Must I?' she asked herself, bleary-eyed in the mirror.

Yes. A promise to the self is a promise to God. She wasn't sure who'd said that, but she wished they hadn't. She hurried through her morning work and by nine, she and Lotti were dressed in Sunday clothes. The air was sticky again and they walked towards the village at an equally heavy pace. Gwenna had said to Lotti, 'You don't have to come.' Lotti's answer had been a shake of the head, as if to say, 'You think I'd let you go on your own?'

She must be suspecting trouble, though. She hadn't brought Rumtopf.

The chapel's interior was blessedly cool, its white-plastered walls and elm-wood pews holding a memory of chillier days. The service had started – they'd walked too slowly and they entered to hear the congregation singing 'Rock of Ages' a tone flatter than the miniature organ that accompanied them. Though she closed the big door as gently as she could, heads turned. She recognised Hilda Hoskens, in a hat like a small bucket, Roddy and their children alongside. Mrs Andrews glared at her from under the brim of an ancient felt cloche. Gwenna stared sightlessly ahead and squeezed Lotti's hand too hard.

They took an empty pew at the back. The hymn ended. Ezra, near the front with his extended family, turned to look at them. He gave her a little nod. *Head high, maidie.* She saw Auntie Nancy Jago wearing a straw boater, porcupined with coloured hat pins.

The sermon was delivered straight at them, on the virtues of patriotism and female chastity. Gwenna wondered if this was the sermon the minister had written, or if he was improvising. There were probably few women in this chapel more chaste than Gwenna, she and Edward having never achieved what was laughably called 'the pleasures of the bedroom'.

'We'll leave after the last hymn,' Gwenna whispered after the sermon ended. The organist played the opening chords of 'Abide with Me' and unusually, the minister walked down to stand in front of the door. Lotti and Gwenna pressed hands. When the final prayer and 'amen' rumbled around the chapel there was a surge of movement. Chapelgoers spilled from the pews, blocking Gwenna and Lotti's way out.

'There she is, bold as brass,' Hilda Hoskens shrilled.

'Shame on her,' boomed Roddy.

'Nazi lover,' crowed one of their boys.

Feeling Lotti cringe, Gwenna searched for the minister. He'd known her parents; he preached love and equality twice on Sunday and once on a Wednesday. She silently entreated him to come to her aid but he made no move.

Something struck her cheek. It was a hymn book, which Gwenna picked up and pressed to her stomach for comfort. 'Shame!' someone cried. 'Shame!' And the word grew into a chant, swelling from twenty or more throats. Gwenna felt something more than physical fear. It came from a primitive part of her, the despair of the beaten animal, the outcast, the doomed prisoner. Beside her, Lotti gave two harsh sobs.

'You're a whore, Gwenna Devoran.' Roddy's face loomed close and, pushed to the edge, Gwenna slammed the hymn book against his teeth. He yelped in pain.

'Judge me if you will, Roddy Hoskens, and I judge you right back. Your boys thieve with your blessing!'

Roddy gurgled in fury and reached for her. Gwenna expected to be lifted and hurled. But before he could take hold of her, Roddy gave a bellow worthy of Solomon the bull and backed away, clutching his backside. Gwenna saw Auntie Nancy wielding a hatpin. The old lady brandished it at the congregation. 'Go you on your way, friends. What are you about?'

'We don't like Nazi lovers,' Hilda Hoskins thrust back.

'And I say, he or she who is without sin may cast the first stone. Will you cast a stone, Hilda?'

'I'll cast stones all right,' agreed Hilda. 'And more.'

'Then I shall remind the company that in your day you came to me with a child in your belly and a man who wanted to scarper back to Devon.' In the sudden hush, Nancy flashed her hatpin at Roddy. 'Aye, there he is, who planted his seed but wouldn't stand to his duty.'

'That's a lie,' Hilda spluttered.

''Tis no lie.' Ezra's voice carried across the chapel nave. 'It was your father's shotgun got Roddy to the altar with you, Hilda. There's sin aplenty in this gathering and if this maidie dares love a German' – Ezra moved towards Gwenna and held out his hand – 'then she's no worse than many another. I've worked alongside Max Reiner these last months and I'll tell you, he's a good man.'

Gwenna gratefully took Ezra's proffered hand. Her other hand sought Lotti's. The congregation dispersed, Hilda and Roddy making the fastest exit.

'We'll see you home,' said Ezra.

As she passed the minister, who looked suddenly six inches shorter, Gwenna said, 'From now on, I shall pray in a corner of my field.'

It took hours for Lotti's shaking to subside, and that night her slumber burst open in shrill cries.

Gwenna took her into her bed, and Rumtopf too, and sang every verse of 'The Sweet Nightingale' twice through. As she lay there, attuned to Lotti's breathing, she knew something had changed in her. In the chapel, she had glimpsed the bloodlust of the mob and though it had scared her almost witless, she knew she'd experienced the worst her neighbours could throw at her. She wouldn't be ruled by them, and in time they wouldn't frighten her at all.

All she need do if Hilda railed in her direction was say 'hat-pin'. The thought liberated her. It emboldened her.

It emboldened her to the point that, a few days later, she stopped Max on his way to the fields. 'When Prince is better, shall we take them for a walk in hand around the fields? He'll need to start moving again.'

'*Ja*, sure,' Max said. 'But I prefer to be on his back.'

'You can ride?'

'I can. Can you?'

'I used to. They'll be full of beans; they'll throw you on the ground.' She leaned earnestly towards him, adding, 'Unless you'd rather I did that?'

A smile cut across Max's face. She thought he was going to say something tender, but he spoke gravely. 'When Prince is well, I wish nothing but to ride away with you, to where the sunset ends.'

43

A week before Lotti was due to start school, the vet declared Prince to be fit. Ezra grumbled when he saw Max and Gwenna bridling the horses, but she reminded him that her father had often ridden with her down to the sea when the day's work was done.

'That was when Duke was around. Him and Lady, they were quiet as lambs.'

Not when they got into the sea, Gwenna recalled. In the waves, they played and bucked. 'Lady and Prince have sea-swum in their time. It's just that since Dad died, I haven't had anyone to ride with.'

Ezra swung his disapproval to Max. 'I want to see sound horses come home, and the missus too. Are you allowed to go off on a jaunt?'

'No,' Max answered. 'Are you going to report?'

'Huh. You forget sometimes you're a prisoner, at His Majesty's pleasure.'

Max looked bemused at the mention of the king. Gwenna assured Ezra and Jürgen, who had come over to see what was going on, that Colvennon Cove was her land as far as the tide reached, and that Max would not be absconding if they stayed in the bay. She didn't mention her plan to ride around the headland. 'It's good for the horses to get sea water on their legs. Vet's orders.'

They had no saddles so Jürgen gave them a leg up. With Gwenna leading the way on Lady, they rode to the highest point of the farm, then descended a winding path which had been the smugglers' route to the cove in the days of contraband and customs men. The horses snorted as they scented the sea, and the breeze caught their manes. Gwenna hadn't felt so alive in months.

They tried to keep the horses to a walk, but it was hopeless and they jogged to the sea's edge. They had to go quite a distance as the tide was right out. Lady broached the water first, stirring it with powerful forelegs. Prince skittered as the surf broke around his feet until, with a huge lunge, he joined his mother. Gwenna and Max laughed as it had almost unseated him. Once the horses were confident with the swell of the water, Gwenna led the way around the headland where the sand shone with freshly washed pebbles and razor clams.

'I have never seen this,' Max said as they entered a bay whose wide mouth stretched a quarter of a mile.

'This is Black Jem Cove. Jem was a lady smuggler, two hundred years ago.'

'This is also your land?'

'No, my neighbours' but they won't mind us riding across it.'

'But your king will mind. I am not allowed off your property.'

She shot Max a grin. 'Then we'd better do it fast, before he catches us.' She squeezed the mare's sides and dug her hand into the thick mane. Lady gave a slight rear and took off at a canter. Prince raced his mother and for next few minutes, the slam of hooves on wet sand, the rush of wind, was all her ears could hold. She didn't care if she came off. She was Ezra's

Gwenna-maid, outrunning shame and her worries for an uncertain future. At the furthest end of the bay, they wheeled around and plunged again into the waves to slow the horses down. They headed back towards Colvennon Cove, soaked to the elbows, the horses wet to the withers and their tails raised behind them like banners.

In Colvennon Cove they pulled up and stared out into the misty distance, until an unspoken pull turned them towards each other. Gwenna leaned until her lips touched Max's. They kissed, slowly then hungrily. His hands strayed into her hair, then took root as the horses, used to working side by side, responded to the shift in their weight and came closer. Gwenna dropped her reins and linked her hands around Max's head. Her need for him was clawing its way out. Years of misplaced love for Edward had murdered the sensual part of her, so she'd thought. She now knew it was far from the case.

Max drew his head back. 'I want you, Gwenna, but I do not think it fair.'

'I want you too, Max, but—' And she looked towards the cliff top and gave an unsteady laugh. He followed her look.

'Who is there?'

'Nobody, but I wouldn't put it past Ezra to check up on us. Why can't life be normal? Why I can't I love you and be with you?'

Max's eyes were arrestingly light in his summer-tanned face. 'You can, if you will do it,' he said. 'Will you?'

'Be with you – officially courting, you mean?' How many neighbours would spit at her?

'Courting is to have an understanding, yes?' he asked.

'And intention, if it's done right.'

'Until I am free, we can have intention but I think it is not permitted to be official. War does not last forever, Gwenna.'

'No...' A past conversation with Freda trickled back. The Thirty Years War. The Hundred Years War. She had a vague idea there'd been a seventy-year one too. 'It might go on for a decade.'

'No.' Max looked solemn. 'I am hearing of defeats in North Africa and it goes not good for us in Italy. In Russia, once again, we are made to turn back with terrible loss.'

'Who tells you all this – the guards?'

'One of them. Before the war, he is a teacher of language and he tells me what he thinks I should know. For Germany now, the end is beginning and our people suffer. I will one day be a free man, Gwenna.'

'You'll want to go back home.'

Will I? said his shrug. 'My mother is dead. I have there a stepfather who has no care of me, and stepbrothers I hardly know. The one I loved, Rudi, is dead.'

'You have older sisters, you told me.'

'And I hope they are well, but they turn away when I do not join the Nazi Party.'

Was he saying that Colvennon was where he wanted to put down roots? She dared not believe it. 'Family and home exert a strong pull. I came back to Colvennon, so I know how it works.' Something Max had said pulled her thoughts to his past. 'Was it hard, refusing to join the Nazis?'

'Yes, and after I join the navy, much harder. Refusing to carry the National Socialist Card is to play with the hangman's rope. I was a good submariner but always being watched.'

'By Fuhrman and Walther Franz.'

He smiled coldly. 'I was a good captain, I would have died for my men and my country but I would not join the Party. I do not like the belief that makes a man into a god, and obeys his every order when it is cruel, or foolish, and throws away lives. They put Fuhrman and Walther Franz into my crew to spy and report me. See this scar?' He stroked the pale line beneath his eye which she'd often wondered about. It was too perfect in shape to be an accident.

'Fuhrman attacked you?' she ventured.

'Many times. Walther too, but not with his hands because he is afraid of me.'

'And yet you brought him here, to my farm.'

'Walther volunteered himself, so he can watch me. It did not matter, until I met Lotti, and then it matters.'

And you dealt with him, she thought. Broke his nose and fingers, ensuring that Walther could never again do farm work. *Ruthless*, she thought. 'Did Fuhrman and Walther get you into trouble, in Germany?'

'Most certainly. When we are called back to base in west France, they report on me.' He told her how, in the autumn of 1942, a few days short of his thirty-seventh birthday, he'd been given a 'surprise gift' as he docked his submarine. 'I am arrested.'

'Actually arrested, a captain and decorated hero.'

Max's smile turned ironic. 'The Gestapo do not trust heroes. They are waiting for me.'

'Lotti has nightmares about the Gestapo.'

'Poor child. The Gestapo are barbarous to Jews. I am a different matter. I have a use to them. It was middle of October 1942; I bring the *Kriegswolf* back to base at Saint-Nazaire. That is my home port since almost the beginning of war. Many German troops are stationed there and where there are German troops is also the Gestapo.' Max described an ordeal that had echoes of Lotti's father's fate: thrown into the back of a car, taken to a place unknown. 'Underground somewhere. I do not know where, as I am blindfold. They tie me to a chair – arms, wrists, ankles – and they beat me. They use rubber hose filled with sand. It is bad, when you do not know where comes the next blow. Very bad.'

She stroked his face. 'You don't have to tell me.'

'I like to tell you. When they take off the blindfold, Fuhrman is there, accusing that I remove a picture of Hitler from the crew mess room. All U-boats must have a painting of the Führer to eat with.'

'Did you take it down?'

'For sure. Walther Franz writes it in his little book and also reports this to Fuhrman. The Gestapo want a confession that I am making my crew believe Germany will lose the war, that I plan to go across to the enemy. Nothing is more untrue, but Fuhrman wants my command from me. And the Gestapo need a man to... how to say it?' Max stared between Prince's twitching ears. Mother and son had been nibbling each other affectionately all this time, but Prince had got a bite in and his mother punished him with one to the shoulder. 'The Gestapo need a man to carry the sin. You understand?'

'Oh... a scapegoat. They wanted to make a scapegoat of you.'

'Ah, in German, "*Sündenbock*".' Max explained that the German navy had, by and large, a looser affiliation to Nazism than the other services, something the Gestapo was determined to stamp on. 'We are free men, in our minds. The Gestapo want to take me to trial and find me guilty to scare others into obedience. That I do not join the Party makes me the perfect... what was the word?'

'Scapegoat. Did they wring a confession from you?' Gwenna ran her finger along the scimitar curve of his scar.

'No, what can I confess? All my sin is in Walther's little book already. I am beaten, tied to a table, my head wrapped in a sack so I fight to breathe and then a – a pipe, a piece of hose, is pushed into my throat. They pour water into my mouth. So much, I will drown.' Max paused, and Gwenna knew he was reliving the horror of drowning on a hard table, lights flashing in his skull, unable to move. 'Fuhrman beats my belly with his fist, so I throw up the water. When I do not confess to being a traitor, he will take out my eyes and then they will beat me again, blind and on my knees.'

'This man was your crew member, your colleague.'

'To Fuhrman, I am less than human. I stand against all he worships. All who are not like Fuhrman are worms, even you, my dearest Gwenna.'

She remembered Fuhrman's expression as she'd encountered him jumping down from Wiggy's truck. Wiggy had said of him, 'It's all show.' But Wiggy had changed her mind about Fuhrman, the more she knew. 'You survived him,' Gwenna said shakily.

'Because I have a friend in Admiral Dönitz. He is supreme commander of the U-boat fleet.'

'Good. I mean, good that he is your friend.'

'You will not like him, Gwenna.' Max took the hand that had stroked his face and kissed her palm. 'He develops the wolf-pack tactic for the U-boats which kills your husband, but he has a good memory. It is Dönitz who gives me the Iron Cross for valour, six months into the war.' It was Jürgen, Max went on to say, who got a message to Dönitz's HQ, and secured Max's release.

'Jürgen's a true friend to you.'

'I know,' Max said. 'I trust few men but one is Jürgen. He takes punches for me now, in the camp and in the train when we arrive. He and Fuhrman are fighting then because Fuhrman insults me always. That is enough of the past, Gwenna.' He laid his hand on her leg, heavy with intent. His eyes grew lazy with desire, and an invitation she couldn't pretend not to see.

Why should she pretend? She wanted Max, not in some nebulous future but now. Gwenna knotted Lady's reins and slid off the horse's back.

'You are leaving?'

'Join me.' She took off her boots and shoved her socks inside them. Her dungarees were easy to get off; all it needed was to push the straps off her shoulders.

'You are taking a swim?'

'Yes. The sea's had all summer to warm up.' She dropped her watch into a boot, then unbuttoned her blouse, and looking down was confronted by her body in weekday underwear. Even so, no point getting it wet. She pulled off her brassiere and pants, did a delicate curtsey to place them on top of her boots, and walked sedately into the water.

Max had dismounted and the horses were now free to roam, though the furthest they could go was back up the path to the farm. Turning as a wave broke against her stomach, Gwenna saw giant, churned footprints on the sand, and Max throwing off his boiler suit as if he hoped the tide would take it. The horses were ambling towards rocks to browse on seaweed. Gwenna waded deeper. She had never seen a naked man in her life. Edward had insisted on turning off the lights, and eventually, he had taken to sleeping on a divan in their bedroom, joining her in their bed as morning broke to keep up appearances. She'd believed her body repelled him.

It wasn't repelling Max – a glance was enough to tell her that. Just as she had never looked on a naked man, she had never been looked at like this. *You'll be thirty-three on Christmas Eve,* she reminded herself. *It's high time you got used to it. No blushing.*

His arms encircled her and she leaned back against him.

'Your king will not approve,' he said gruffly into her ear.

She faced him, sighing as the sea swelled like warm silk around her and raised her lips to his. Nothing short of an amphibious landing craft coming into shore would stop her giving herself to this man but... having only ever slept with a husband whose mind was with his lover in London, Gwenna had not considered the practicalities of making love standing up in the sea. She fell over and pulled Max down with her. He stood up, choking and laughing, and fished her out.

'We cannot, this is not respectable for you.'

'I don't care.'

'But what if there is a child from this?' He was erect against her, his breathing taking its tempo from the waves, holding her as if he feared the tide might drag her from him. 'This will not work. We will fall over again.'

'Then let's get covered in sand.' She caught his hand and led him into the shallows.

Yes? his expression asked. 'I will be careful.'

'I'm infertile, you'd better know that.' She and Edward had tried to begin with, because he had wanted children. Something to show the world, she supposed. He must have been clever at distancing his mind during the act. They'd given up when Gwenna had failed to conceive. Sad and humiliating, but she let it go, like a rude sketch in the sand erased by a wave. Max led her to the shelter of the rocks she'd looked down on so many times in her life. They lay down in a warm hollow, violating the rules laid down for the good conduct of prisoners of war.

44

Later, she lay in his arms, the wind whipping over her sand-streaked flesh. Her body had felt sated at first and was now waking up to new, sharp sensations of hunger. *Perhaps I'm insatiable*, she thought. *A demon female who can't get enough of her man.* She'd have to be on her guard once they were back among the others. Would Ezra guess what they'd been doing? Or Jürgen?

The moment of doubt allowed in the hornet that had buzzed around her ever since she'd learned that Max was a submariner. 'Will you get my clothes, please?'

'Of course.' He got up, unabashed by his nakedness. Wide-shouldered, narrow-waisted, he'd regained all his previous strength and more from a summer of harvesting. Gwenna lapsed for a moment into admiration. She had cried out under him, gouging shapes in the sand. What evil fate had decreed she should love and desire a man who had all but confessed to sending her husband's ship to the bottom? For the first time, she wondered how Charles Avril-Whiting would see her were he eavesdropping now. Not as a little country mouse, for sure.

The horses were returning, seaweed stains around their

mouths. Gwenna saw Max stop, clothes in his arms, and stare up at the cliff. He stood for several seconds, focusing on something above his eyeline, and out of her vision, then came to her, laying her clothes in front of her.

He said, 'Someone is watching.'

She stared at him, desperate to believe he was teasing. 'Ezra?'

'Not unless Ezra wears now a brown suit like mine.'

Jürgen, then. Why would he... *Oh, God*. Gwenna retrieved her watch and stared at it. Four o'clock. Where had the time gone? 'We have to get the cows in. Jürgen won't say anything?' She waited for his assurance, which he didn't give. 'Max?'

'I think it was not Jürgen.' He knocked his boots together, releasing sand, then pulled her to him and kissed her mouth. 'Come, I help you on your horse.'

Back at the farm, Gwenna stabled and brushed down the horses so Max could bring in the cows. He was anxious, shouting in vain for Jürgen. It had to have been Jürgen watching them, because the other Germans, Heinz, Andreas and Martin, no longer came. Who else could it have been?

Gwenna put up hay for the horses, then hurried to the house.

Lotti was spreading butter on bread that Gwenna had cut earlier and smiled over her shoulder. 'I am making sandwiches with boiled egg and sauerkraut.' She'd expressed a longing for foods of her childhood and, having watched her mother make the fermented cabbage dish, had shown Gwenna and they'd experimented until they got it right.

'Sounds—' Gwenna didn't get as far as 'delicious'. She turned to the window, saying, 'What's that odd noise?'

Lotti joined her. 'It's like the air raid sirens we had in London.' A hooning wail. Gwenna's thoughts flew to the cows, the possibility of a repeat of the German bomber attack of last summer. Telling Lotti to stay inside, she went out, peering upwards. Max called to her as he crossed the yard. Jürgen was a few yards behind him.

'You haven't brought in the cows,' said Gwenna, over the noise.

'I leave them in the field. It is the camp siren,' Max said. 'Means trouble.'

Gwenna searched his face. 'Trouble of what kind?'

'An escape, maybe. Jürgen and I will be recalled, for roll call.'

She let that sink in, then asked, 'Max, who did you see staring down at us? It wasn't Jürgen, was it?'

'No. I am thinking it was Kurt Fuhrman.'

The siren ceased, its absence making Gwenna's next question sound too loud. 'You think Fuhrman's on the loose?'

Max nodded. 'It is possible. Sometimes, the guards don't check all the fence. Gwenna, go into the house and lock doors and windows. Jürgen and I stay outside and keep watch.'

Gwenna didn't argue. She strode inside and found the kitchen empty. The egg sandwiches were abandoned on the cutting board. The table Lotti had set for their tea was messed up, the cloth runkled, cutlery heaped about.

She ran to the stairs, calling, 'Lotti, are you there?' Getting no response, she checked Lotti's bedroom. A search of the other upstairs rooms brought nothing, nor, when Gwenna went back down, did a search of the dining and sitting rooms. She went to the front door, which was always heavy with hanging coats. Lotti's red coat was there. Dread pushed through Gwenna's veins as the front door whined open at her push.

'You don't lock it?' Max seemed incredulous when, in a frantic state, she fetched him in.

'Usually, but I unlocked it after the rain, because it swells in the wet. I must have forgotten...' Not bothering to finish her sentence, Gwenna tore back to the kitchen, hoping that Lotti would have come in. The room was empty and coldness stole over her as she noticed the most telling clue that something was dreadfully wrong.

Rumtopf lay on the floor, by a table leg. She screamed for Max and when he saw her holding the bear, whose eye patch had fallen off and whose waistcoat was half open, something changed in his face too.

Wiggy's arrival a couple of minutes later answered Gwenna's deepest fear. 'That siren was for an escapee from Tregallon. Kurt Fuhrman. He smuggled a trowel from his workplace and dug under the wire.'

Fuhrman, who hated Jews and believed he was still fighting a war. Gwenna burst out, 'Wiggy, you can't take Max and Jürgen away. You have to help. Lotti's gone and I'm terrified she's been taken.'

45

Wiggy was appalled but she was under strict orders. 'If I don't take the lads back, they'll think they've run off too.'

'And they will send guards,' Max agreed. 'So, let them.'

Wiggy shook her head. 'Come on, Max, play fair.'

'Tell them we refused. Say we offered you violence.'

'And get you both sent to a high-security camp? I don't want that. Where's Jürgen?'

'Staying too,' Max told her. 'I saw Fuhrman here, looking out at the sea.'

Wiggy's eyebrows shot up. 'Bloody hell. You sure?'

Gwenna, gnawed to a frenzy by the delay in searching for Lotti, intervened. 'If he has her, she'll be scared half to death.' An awful thought struck her. 'What if Fuhrman persuaded the bus to pick them up... they could be anywhere by now.'

'The bus will have pulled up as soon as the siren sounded,' Wiggy assured her. 'The driver will have followed emergency procedure, which is: lock the doors, put no one down and pick no one up.'

That was something.

'If you are refusing to get in the truck,' Wiggy said to Max,

'I'll have to drive back to the camp and report the sighting. I'll say I couldn't find you.' She poked Rumtopf, who was tucked into Max's overalls. With his eye patch missing, the bear's one good eye shone all the brighter as he peered from the gap between Max's buttons. 'Find her, all right?' She gave Gwenna a quick hug and walked to where she'd parked her truck.

Ezra passed her on his way in. He must have popped home for an hour or so, as he often did, to tend to his chickens and the pig he shared with his neighbours. 'Sounds like a rumpus Tregallon way.' When told the news, he nodded as though he had expected as much, some day or other. 'Why are you gathered like a prayer meeting? That maidie needs to be found, and from the noise in the meadow, they cows are waiting to be milked.'

Gwenna pleaded with Ezra to do the cows. 'I know it's a lot, on your own.' She caught back a sob.

'There, now.' Ezra patted her shoulder. 'You leave the beasts to me and if I see the little maid, I'll come and tell 'ee.'

Jürgen, who had been missing for a while, came and spoke to Max, something about searching the house. Gwenna said she'd already done that, top to bottom.

'Jürgen goes up into the attic,' Max said. 'Nobody is there but he says that in the pantry is a dish on the floor that had meat.'

'There was cold beef in there. I didn't think to look in the pantry.'

'Now is only the plate, no beef.'

Had Fuhrman broken in to find food, then? 'He'd have come in through the front door and found Lotti on her own. Oh, God.'

Max's gaze dug into hers. 'She will be all right.'

'With Fuhrman?'

'He is not a fool. He knows the penalty for hurting a child.'

But men on the run did not think rationally. And men like Fuhrman did not think Jewish children really counted.

'Where have you looked for this runaway?' Ezra wanted to know. 'The hay store, the barn?'

All of those – Max and Jürgen had searched all the buildings around the yard before they came to the house.

A scream cut the conversation short.

'That sounds like Wiggy,' Gwenna said, and they all ran, at their different speeds, towards the sunken lane.

46

There they found a grievous scene. On the other side of the gate, Wiggy was bent double, looking so stricken Gwenna thought at first her friend was having a heart attack. Mud over her breeches and jersey told a story of violence.

'Threw – me – out.' Wiggy could hardly speak.

There was someone in the truck... no, there were two figures behind the windscreen. Gwenna was first to clamber over the gate and reach the open cab. Kurt Fuhrman sat in the driver's seat, holding Lotti by her braids. So tightly, the little girl's head was drawn right back.

Max and Jürgen joined Gwenna, and stood tense but help-less because Fuhrman had a knife that shone against Lotti's exposed throat. Gwenna recognised her own kitchen knife. Long-bladed with a horn handle and very, very sharp. She kept it that way.

'Let her go, Herr Fuhrman. You can take the truck.' Gwenna's voice was squeezed thin. Lotti's frantic eyes met hers and Gwenna tried to convey love, reassurance, optimism in a single smile. She shifted her gaze back to Fuhrman. Had he under-stood? He looked overwrought, but there was still room in his eyes for a certain glee. As though he knew he could make them dance to any tune he chose.

He spoke German to Max and Jürgen, telling them to stay out of his way.

'He will not go far,' Max said quietly for Gwenna to hear. 'Soldiers will have blocked all the roads.'

'They might kill Lotti, trying to take him.'

'I do not think so.' But Max didn't sound wholly sure. War tore up the rules. He patted Rumtopf's belly through his overalls. 'Nobody will risk a child's life.'

But what if somebody told the camp guards that Lotti was a foreigner? A German. They might not be so careful then. Gwenna reached her decision so fast, she wasn't aware of it until her boot was on the footboard, and she was inside the truck. She grabbed Fuhrman's arm. 'Take me. Take me instead. Let her go!'

Fuhrman uttered some obscenity and lunged with the knife. Gwenna jerked to avoid it. She could hear Lotti's wild breathing and, risking another slash of the blade, threw her arms around Lotti and hauled, dragging the child like a large fish she was determined to land. The truck's engine roared to life. Gwenna felt its vibration in her bones. The vehicle lurched and she fell out, striking her head on the ground. She was aware of violent pain, of the truck's great wheels inches away, spinning to get a grip on the surface of the lane. Fuhrman thrust the truck into reverse and she heard Lotti screaming.

47

MAX

As Gwenna made her foiled attempt to save Lotti, Max slipped around to the driver's side. He jumped onto the footboard of the truck as Fuhrman reversed and he now had no choice but to hang on.

Gwenna had fallen out, but Lotti was still on board and Fuhrman was accelerating like a man escaping a fire. With his left foot on the running board, his right planted on the wheel arch, the only thing stopping Max from falling too was the handgrip welded to the outside of the cab. He held on to it like an infant to his mother. His free right hand was clamped over Fuhrman's on the steering wheel and they were wrestling for control as the truck slewed side to side. Lotti had crawled into the passenger footwell.

About the safest place for her. Fuhrman held Gwenna's carving knife against the steering wheel, and whenever the wheel moved, the knife jerked, kissing Max's throat. Fuhrman liked knives; he was skilled with a blade. In Berlin, in civilian life, he'd been a furrier and knew how to skin and fillet. When he'd had Max in his power, he'd whispered about flaying the skin from his face.

He might have knife skills, but Fuhrman was no driver, and if he got to the open road, he'd cause carnage. Maybe kill one of the camp sentries, hurtling down the lane on a motorbike in search of him. What Max cared for most right now was the little girl huddled in the footwell, her arms hiding her face.

Ach! The knife caught his throat.

Fuhrman pulled it back, visibly excited by the blood on its tip. Removing one hand from the steering wheel, he punched Max hard above the eyebrow, shouting over the roar of the engine, 'I'll kill you, Reiner, and they will give me the Iron Cross when I go home.'

'Home? They are already bombing Berlin, Fuhrman.'

That earned Max a blow to the bridge of his nose, but he absorbed the pain. If he fell, he'd tumble between the stone bank of Gwenna's lane and the wheels. Fuhrman was re-angling the knife for a plunge at Max's throat. To Fuhrman's thinking, there was everything to gain from killing a man he viewed as a traitor. The fact that he might hang for it in a British jail would not have penetrated his fanatical brain. His left hand steadying the wheel, Fuhrman pulled the knife back for a final thrust.

The rear wheels smacked into a rut and the steering wheel spun, forcing Fuhrman to seize it with both hands. As he fought to control the truck, the knife flashed like a needle on a gigantic dial.

Max had pushed the milk churns to the end of this lane often enough to know that the gate at the end was always open. If Fuhrman failed to brake in time, he'd hammer into the bank on the other side of the road, and Max would be done for. And Lotti too, probably.

He had to make the lorry turn as it came through the gate. *Now.*

He grabbed the steering wheel and leaned back, hanging all

his weight off it. He and Fuhrman battled in a test of strength. Fuhrman had the advantage of two hands, but Max had a passionate desire to live. Those he cared about most in this world were variously crumpled at the top of the lane and hunkered in the footwell and he was going to see them happy and upright again, even if it pulled his arm off.

The truck slewed violently as it hurtled backwards through the gate, its wheels locked in a tight turn. It winged the standing stone before striking the concrete stand where, on a normal afternoon, the milk churns would have been proudly sitting by now. The impact was ear-splitting. Fuhrman was thrown backwards, then forwards, his nose exploding against the steering wheel. With Max still hanging on for dear life, the truck ploughed on, screeching like a demon with the milk stand wedged under its tailgate. It ground against the turf-and-stone bank that bounded the road, sending out sparks, until, with a crunching sound and the stink of over-heated tyres, it finally stopped. Max stared with his heart pounding towards the footwell.

He saw Lotti peering up. There was blood on her face, her eyes were wide and unblinking, but she was conscious.

Drenched with sweat, shaking in every muscle, Max said in the deafening silence, 'It was always coming to this, Fuhrman. You would not accept my command. You believed you had a higher authority to obey.'

'*Heil Hitler*,' Fuhrman slurred. His face was against the steering wheel. 'There is only one leader for a true German.'

'Not on a U-boat. Not with the lives of eighty men resting on your decisions. There is no place for rats on a submarine.'

Fuhrman slowly turned his head sideways. His nose was a palette of blood and crushed bone. His eyes were swelling fast, their blueness shining in the slits. He spoke through broken teeth. 'You surfaced the *Kriegswolf*, gave the order for surrender. We were captained by a coward.'

'You will die believing that, Fuhrman. But you will die breathing fresh air, because of my decision that day. You call me a coward – you who took a little girl hostage to make an escape you knew would fail.'

'A Jew. Who cares?'

Max spoke into Fuhrman's ear. 'I do.' He'd thought Fuhrman had dropped the knife. Wrong. Fuhrman reared back and rammed it at Max's torso and the blade lodged deep.

'Die a traitor, Max Reiner.'

Max smiled. 'Not today, Fuhrman.'

He read bewilderment in the man's stream of profanities.

'Kapitänleutnant?' It was Jürgen, his voice ragged as if he didn't know what he was about to discover. 'Is Fuhrman dead?'

'No. Help me down, then go to the child.' Max let Jürgen take his weight and sank into a squat at the edge of the road. 'Gwenna, is she—?'

Jürgen muttered, 'Hurt.'

'Say more. Three words at least.'

'I think, alive.'

His patience broken, Max let fly at his friend. '*Verdammt noch mal*, go and help the child.'

He heard someone panting up to him on unwilling legs. It was the girl with the red mouth and bold eyes, though he couldn't at that moment recall her name. Jürgen was in love with her, though not even his own mother would guess. 'Is Gwenna good?' he asked her.

'She got knocked out, but Ezra's with her.' The girl dropped down beside him and he smelled her perfume. Surprising and sweet, like violets.

'God love you,' she gasped. 'What's that sticking out of your chest?'

Max looked down. 'Kitchen knife.'

She grasped his wrist. 'Don't touch it; I grew up on a street with a rough pub on each corner so I know you never pull a blade out— What are you doing? Don't! Leave it!'

The knife came with dry rasp. Wiggy. That was her name, except he could never pronounce it properly. 'It does not enter my body.' He tilted the blade. 'See, no blood.'

'What was it sticking into, then? Because it was stuck in something.'

'It is a friend who again saves me.' Max extracted Rumtopf. 'He is here to bring me luck, and now has a new hole to be mended. Lotti?' He recognised the small face bending close to his. Lotti had been lifted down from the truck. He asked her if she was in pain, and when she nodded, added gently, 'Fuhrman put a knife into your bear but he will be—' He didn't get as far as 'all right'. He felt suddenly, violently sick. His ears had picked up the mass growl of motorbikes and a distant jangle of bells. Police cars? Max groaned, hoping he would not be put back in the cooler.

48

There was a feel of autumn in the air, and the first leaves blew across the yard. In three days, Lotti would go to St Morgan's and be allocated her bed in the junior dormitory. Unless she healed in the interim, she'd be taking some bruises with her.

They were doing the evening milking, seated in stalls side by side, when Lotti broke her silence over her terrifying ordeal at Fuhrman's hands. 'I was so scared. Were you, Aunt Gwenna?'

'I'll say, from the moment I found you missing.' Gwenna leaned around the side of her stall. She'd feared Lotti might have regressed, back into mute trauma, after being lifted out of the cab by Jürgen. But over the last few days her self-possession had returned. 'When I realised that horrible man had you in his power, I didn't think, I simply grabbed you. I'm worried I only scared you more.'

Gwenna had underestimated Lotti's near-adult grasp of situations. 'No, it's like me, holding on to Rumtopf when the lady who isn't your sister tried to snatch him. Are we going to tell Aunt Freda?'

'About your experience...? We ought to.' Gwenna's conscience was clear on that.

'Only,' Lotti continued, 'she'll feel she has to come and make sure I'm all right, and she will probably think it was your fault.'

Undoubtedly, Gwenna reflected.

'Aunt Freda has so many other people to look after, it would be inconvenient for her.'

'You think we shouldn't, then?'

'No, and anyway, it would be breaking the law if we did.'

Sergeant Couch had said as much. After Kurt Fuhrman had been transferred to a police van, the sergeant had patiently interviewed a shaken Lotti, Gwenna and Wiggy in the farm-house kitchen, then driven them to a doctor's in Truro for their injuries to be checked. He'd said, 'You must keep today's shenanigans quiet, ladies. It'll be subject to a D-notice.' A D-notice was a government order sent to newspaper editors and the BBC to suppress news likely to undermine national secu-rity. 'Mum's the word. I hope you understand?'

None of them had any desire to dwell on the horrible event, and they solemnly assured Sergeant Couch that he could rely on them to be silent. For a while, the only sound in the parlour was of hissing milk and the steady chomp of cows at their hay. Then Lotti said something unexpected.

'Did you know, Jürgen doesn't want to learn English, Aunt Gwenna?'

'I thought as much.'

'Because when he goes home, if he learns English, he will have too much to remember.'

'How do you know that?'

'Oh, he speaks to me sometimes in German. He asked me if Wiggy was stepping out with anyone.'

'And what did you say?'

'That she probably had lots of admirers as she is the prettiest woman in the district. Apart from you, of course, Aunt Gwenna. I think poor Jürgen was upset.' In the evening half-light, Lotti's face, arms and hands glowed luminously, marred here and there by plum-coloured grazes. Worried this might make Lotti an object of curiosity at school, Gwenna had offered to write to Miss Saddler, St Morgan's headmistress, to say she'd been injured by a cow.

Lotti had seemed quite put out by the suggestion. 'Not a cow. Say I was dragged by a bull.'

'No! They'd come and arrest me for neglect. Can we say you fell off a haystack?'

'Do you think Jürgen really likes Wiggy, then?' Gwenna asked now.

Lotti was sure of it. 'But he doesn't think he has a hope. Papa used to say that despair steals the tiles from a man's roof, but hope mends the holes in his ceiling.'

'Your papa had quite a turn of phrase.'

Lotti considered this. 'He did and I'm going to write a book one day of all the clever things he told me. I shall write it when I go to Canada.'

'When... you go to Canada?' Gwenna tried to keep the 'when' casual.

Lotti's answer was matter-of-fact. 'When the war is done, we will meet in Canada.'

'Who? Who is we?'

'My Grandmama Sonia, my Oncle Otto and Tante Helen. That's where they are. They travelled there after they escaped Norway.'

'Aunt Freda never told me that!'

'She doesn't know. Rumtopf says so.'

Ah. The child was drifting into a dream world. 'You write that book about your father, Lotti, but don't forget, it's important to enjoy today.'

'I know. But I will take the path across the sea, when the war is over.'

She sounded so completely certain, a cold rock settled in Gwenna's belly.

When Lotti had gone to bed that night, Gwenna sat alone, wishing that she hadn't poured her half-drunk bottle of whisky into a hole to appease the small folk. Solitude pressed on her. Max and Jürgen had been absent since being escorted off in the wake of Kurt Fuhrman, and with them presumably confined to barracks, Wiggy hadn't come either. Gwenna had no idea if the men had been put under some kind of house arrest. Fuhrman had hit Max hard, and he'd torn ligaments hanging on to the side of the truck. So Wiggy had told her after the drama was over. He'd have died of a stab wound but for Rumtopf.

She didn't know if Sergeant Couch had passed on her urgent message to the camp commandant, that Max was a hero. She feared he'd be implicated in Fuhrman's escape, transferred to a more secure camp, never to be heard of again.

The idea that Max might one day simply disappear was unbearable. What if she lost Lotti *and* Max? Needing to be busy, she picked Rumtopf out of the mending basket and set to with a needle. Lotti had repaired the fissure where the kitchen knife had gone in, and Gwenna began sewing buttons back onto his waistcoat. He had his eye patch back and his good eye watched her inscrutably.

At four o'clock on Tuesday, the 7th of September, Gwenna delivered Lotti – with suitcase, books and a brand new hockey stick – to the boarders' entrance of St Morgan's. Lotti would sleep her first night in the dormitory, and meet her form mistress and classmates in the morning. They hugged, and

Gwenna said, 'I'll see you right here, same time Friday,' then left before her emotions leaked.

At that same hour, the POW camp at Tregallon was stood down from its state of high alert, and eligible prisoners were told they might resume their outside duties from the following morning.

Gwenna had her face pressed against a golden flank of cow number twelve when Max tapped his knuckles against the milking parlour doorway.

'It brings me suffering that I am late.'

She looked up and saw him smiling. From the exaggerated German accent, she knew he was sending himself up. 'I don't want you to suffer, and you aren't late.'

'But you are suffering too, Mrs Devoran. You are thinner. Where is Lotti?'

'Having breakfast, I hope, in the company of other girls. Today's her first full day at school.'

'Ah, I am sorry I am not here to say "good luck".'

'She'll be back for the weekend. It's good to see you. I thought they'd locked you up or sent you to that rocky island.'

'No.' He picked up a stool, put it down near her and sat on it. 'I and Jürgen are interrogated for a long time, but it is seen we are not in bond with Fuhrman.'

'In cahoots, you mean? I spoke up for you.' She needed him to know that.

I do know, his nod implied. 'I would write, but Wiggy is not around to take secret letters and my friendly guard is not so friendly now.' Max patted his shoulder blade, made a face. 'My muscles are with fire but it is good to move them. We must finish picking the stones today, Jürgen and me, and the stand by the lane is still broken. I mean, the table for the churns.' He still struggled with the word 'churn'. 'We must make new.'

'Is Jürgen here too?'

'With the pigs, feeding. Can you not hear?'

She could indeed hear the happy symphony of snouts, now he mentioned it. 'Help me with the milking, then I'll join you for stone picking.'

Mid-morning, she and Max were in the kitchen having their elevenses – tea for her, coffee for him – when the postman called. One letter only, and Gwenna immediately recognised the handwriting on the front. Her heart lurched.

'I go, if you wish privacy,' Max offered.

'No, it's all right.' The letter was from Freda. Gwenna had written to her, wanting to understand Lotti's fascination with Canada.

Orme Mansions,
    Bayswater,
    September 4th 1943

My dearest Gwenna,

How odd that your letter should arrive when it did, as at last I have news of Lotti's father. Through French contacts we have learned that Leopold Gittelman was taken as part of the systematic round-up of Jews in Paris in July 1942. He went to Drancy internment camp, north-east of the capital, from where he was transferred to hospital suffering internal injuries. He died in hospital. My dear friend, yours is the task of telling Lotti that all hope is lost. Comfort her with the knowledge that her papa was cared for at the end and did not endure deportation. As for potential relations in Canada, I cannot add anything. I simply don't know.

All my love,

Freda

Gwenna read the letter out loud. 'How will I tell her, Max? She's said a few times that she knows her papa is dead, but it's different having it confirmed in black and white.'

He put down his coffee. 'Telephone her school, ask if you can visit her today.'

'Her first day? No, no, I can't.' Nor could Gwenna face going to the post office and asking Mrs Andrews' permission to use the telephone. Ezra had posted her last letter to Freda on her behalf. 'I'll tell her on Friday, here, when I've brought her home.'

'Take her to the sea edge, tell her there.' Max put his hand, warm from his cup, over hers. 'She will weep but Lotti is young, and the young know how to adapt.'

That evening, the BBC broadcast news that Italy had surrendered. The following day came an announcement that Allied troops had landed in the south of the country. Italy's surrender robbed Germany of its principal ally and brought Max's prediction of a German defeat a stride closer. Wiggy brought news of a fight among the prisoners at Tregallon, men of different ideologies turning on each other. Kurt Fuhrman, only just out of hospital, had stabbed a crewmate with a sharpened toothbrush, filched from the sanitorium, and was later shot dead trying to escape a second time. The sentry who killed him made use of the yellow target sewn onto the back of Fuhrman's prison-issue boiler suit.

Max arrived for work on Thursday morning silent and pale. Wiggy's eyes were red. The prisoner who had been knifed was Jürgen. Gwenna made up a basket for him, including eggs and fresh milk, for Wiggy to take.

Max said later, 'This will make him happy because he is in love with her.'

'Lotti suggested as much. I didn't notice a thing.'

'Because your mind is on me.' Though he joked, Max's mood had darkened. He was worried not only for Jürgen but because news had seeped into the camp of Mannheim in south-west Germany being bombed earlier in the month by the RAF. A huge part of the city was destroyed, so he understood. One of his sisters lived there.

On Friday, Gwenna got to St Morgan's too early, and decided to pay a quick call on Mill. Getting no answer to her knock at Fendynick House, she wrote her mother-in-law a note explaining that she had got rid of "the compromising letter". It was gone and she, Gwenna, felt lighter for it. She added that she would love to bring Lotti to visit, as soon as Mill wished it. Folding the note, she wrote Mill's name on the front and printed "Strictly Private" before pushing it through the letter box. Janet would find it and would certainly not open it. Whatever Janet's shortcomings, she was a stickler for good conduct. At the end of Lemon Street, however, Gwenna saw Angela driving past in her car and her heart plunged. There was little she could do, with only five minutes to get to the school to greet Lotti as she came out. She had to hope that her sister-in-law would step over the note on the doormat, or if she saw it, would respect the embargo on the front.

Loaded with prep, and ebullient at having made her first best friend, Lotti chattered without pause the whole way home. Gwenna hadn't the heart to immediately pass on Freda's news. She waited until Sunday morning, when, taking Max's advice, she suggested a walk in Colvennon Cove. Sitting beside Lotti on a weed-strewn rock, she told her. 'Your father passed away in hospital in France. So he was spared any journey.'

'But I know, Aunt Gwenna. I've felt it since before we reached England.'

'But Lotti, there is feeling and there is knowing. The heart always hopes for a miracle.'

Lotti picked up a razor clam shell, cleaned out by a seagull's beak, and turned it so its enamel surface caught the light. Then she looked at Gwenna. 'Please, I don't want to be sad. I like being happy.'

'Then be happy, my darling. I needed to tell you, but your papa would not want grief to go on, so let's throw it into the sea.'

'Can you throw sadness away?'

'We can try.'

As they skimmed stones into the breaking surf, Gwenna's mind returned to the moment she'd seen Max hurl his iron cross, the silver flash as it hit the water. Had Max been casting off a prize he no longer valued, or hurling away the grief and shame it caused him?

A golden Indian summer mocked the gloom that hung over Colvennon while Jürgen fought fever from an infected wound. There had been ill luck, on and off, all year. Those damnable, ungrateful fairies. Gwenna directed her distress and anger at them until a new target presented itself.

Angela.

49

She and Max were taking their mid-morning break, as had become their habit. Rumtopf was on the table, and Gwenna was sewing him a bow tie from a scrap of red fabric.

'My mother was good with the needle,' Max said, his eyes on her work.

'You're saying I'm not?'

'Your stitches are too big. For a tie, they must be soon invisible.'

'*Near* invisible, you mean. I don't claim to be a seamstress.'

'Because you are too much in hurry. Suppose it is a cow, then you will go slow and make small stitches.'

She laughed, then peered out of the window. A car was drawing up. Moments later, Angela stepped in without knocking, bringing with her a preview of autumn in town, from the tawny colours of her ensemble to the shiny surface of her leather handbag. She scowled at Max.

'Get him out.'

Max looked to Gwenna. 'You want?'

'Max is staying.' Gwenna tucked her needle and thread into the cloth.

'Don't be ridiculous. You could be arrested for aiding the enemy.'

Angela sounded as though she knew what she was talking about, and as secretary to an MP, perhaps she did, though Gwenna doubted there was any actual law banning the sharing of elevenses between an Englishwomen and a POW. She suggested to Angela that it would be awfully difficult to enforce.

Angela was unimpressed. 'You discuss the progress of the war, you and this man?'

'Er, generally, we talk about soil. Cows. Udders. Muck-spreading.'

'Pigs,' Max added.

Angela recoiled, as if the words themselves carried an odour. 'Then I will say what I have come to say.'

'Please do.'

'You are to stay away from Fendynick House and never again make contact with my mother.'

She found that note and blasted well read it. Gwenna asked, 'Is this what she wants?'

'Mummy does not wish to see or speak with you again.'

'Then why hasn't she told me so?'

'I'm here, saying it. What you did, telling those lies about Edward, you've destroyed her.'

Gwenna shook her head. 'Angela, she knows what Edward was like.' She glanced at Max, who looked soberly back. She hadn't confided to him why her marriage had been a failure. 'The last time Mill and I talked, in the rose arbour at Fendynick, she passed on a letter. She knows Edward's secret.'

'I don't know what you mean by "secret".'

'Charles Avril-Whiting.' Gwenna watched Angela's face.

A flicker in the cheek, a dart of the eye. Angela's voice remained steady, however. 'They played in the same orchestra, didn't they? Until Charles left to join the Admiralty or some such.'

'Naval Intelligence. They kept in contact, Angela, particularly after Edward joined the Navy himself. Close contact. They used to meet, whenever Edward had leave.'

'I know what you're suggesting. You're impugning two decent men, one of whom cannot defend himself. Worse, you flung your dirty-minded insinuations at my mother.' As if the words had unleashed a desire to strike out at Gwenna, Angela drew back her arm.

Max stepped between them. '*Gnädige Frau*, leave now or I put you out of the door.'

Angela hit him instead. Her handbag smacked him on the shoulder, the one he'd badly strained gripping the side of Wiggy's truck, but Max didn't flinch. 'You must leave,' he said calmly.

'Yes, I will. But know that I intend to sue *your woman* for defamation against my brother.'

'You can't defame the dead,' Gwenna said wearily. 'And you'll drag Charles Avril-Whiting into it. He won't like that.'

Angela lifted her chin, reminding Gwenna of Mill's assertion that her daughter always had to have the last word, or the last action. 'And I will report you for consorting with a German prisoner.'

'I'm a widow and he's unmarried. Who cares?'

Triumph changed Angela's face. *Gotcha.* 'As a prisoner, he is under government protection. You are taking advantage of his dependent status. I wonder if you'll be considered a fit guardian for Lotti when I make this public.'

'You wouldn't do that.'

'No?' Angela had scented victory. 'My mother is in shreds, turning over every day of her son's life, thanks to you. Trying to piece together what and who he was.'

'He was Charles Avril-Whiting's lover. I wasn't ever going to tell Mill. She found one of Charles's letters to Edward under your mattress, Angela. Why in God's name did you keep it?'

'I don't know what you're talking about.' True to her character, Angela would not give in. She denied the very existence of any letter. 'I shall report you to social services and recommend that the child, Lotti, is removed from your care.'

Gwenna's gaze went to the kitchen table where her tea was growing cold. Rumtopf lay next to the cow's head butter dish. 'Fine. I might find myself mentioning that you received illegal butter from my dairy.'

Angela looked affronted. 'I have no recollection of that.'

'Really? Mill says you passed it on to Sir Henry Copping, for his lady wife who detests margarine. It will add a piquancy to my defence to social services when I mention that your member of parliament abused the rationing system. Ignorance is no defence in law, Angela.'

Angela searched visibly for a counterattack and landed on the picture of her brother which stood in its usual place. Fearing she was going for it, Gwenna blocked her. Instead, Angela snatched Rumtopf, calling him a repugnant, one-eyed gawper, and flung him across the room.

Max opened the door and said, 'Out.'

After she'd left, Max said, 'I think you have just told me why you have no children with your husband.'

'I suppose you despise Edward now.' She fetched the picture from the bookcase and laid it in front of Max, who gazed at the image for some time before saying:

'This word, "despise"...?'

'It means to think little of someone, and I don't want that. In many ways, Edward was remarkable.'

'In Germany, are men like him but for them there is no compassion.'

'There isn't all that much here.'

'But in Germany, they are beaten to death.'

'Oh.' She looked hard at him, delving for his own feelings,

but he hid them so well. 'Would you have allowed Edward on your submarine?'

'If I knew?' He shook his head. 'It is bad for discipline, but I would not leave him to those like Fuhrman or Walther Franz. I would report him as too much suffering the *Klaustrophobie* or seasickness.'

'You're kind, then. You were born in the wrong country, Max.'

He refuted that. 'No, but in the wrong time.' He kissed her until she had to push him away, because she wanted to drag him upstairs and make love to him on her bed.

'I can't take any more name-calling, Max. Immoral. Fancy piece. Traitor. Any of it.'

'If we love, we can withstand, *ja*?'

'I don't know, Max. Loving you... I don't feel I have permission. It keeps swinging back at me. What if it was you who fired on Edward's ship?'

'I have already confessed to the possibility. I can never know the truth.'

'I can't bear the thought of losing you, Max, but until I know for sure, I can't be at peace.' Her words had the ring of a nail being knocked into a coffin.

On the first day of October, she was taking the dairy cows back to their grazing when she heard a vehicle. Her first thought was, *Angela, come back for more.* Then she realised it wasn't a car but a motorbike. And then she identified the distinctive throb of a Norton, such as her vet used. By the time she'd got back to the yard, the rider had parked and was dismounting. He wasn't wearing the vet's usual rust-red helmet, but a military green one. And unlike her Cornish vet, this man was very tall. She went to greet him. 'Hello, are you lost?'

'I don't know. Depends who you are.' The cut-glass accent

brought Gwenna's insecurities racing in like Alsatians. Had Angela reported her to the moral authorities, risking a dirty battle after all? Or was it to do with the farm? Her milk yield was slightly down this month. And she had sold an Old Spot weaner to a pig club in nearby Trenwithy before their full-grown one was slaughtered. Only a few days' overlap, but illegal. Her voice shook. 'I am Gwenna Devoran. This is my farm.'

'In that case' – the man took off his helmet and thrust his arm over the gate to shake her hand – 'I'm in the right place. You're a devil to find, Mrs Devoran.' Grey hair that was once fair, a side parting. An impassive face, long nose. Middle forties... she was catapulted back to a dockside street in Plymouth and her vigil outside Edward's rented house.

'Oh, God. It's—'

'Avril-Whiting. Charles Avril-Whiting. We met numerous times, of course, and we've always had Edward in common.'

50

Making tea, serving it, shooing Josephine off Avril-Whiting's lap, used up the first ten minutes of their re-acquaintance. Gwenna was astonished she could be so outwardly calm while inside her emotions spun like a turbine. Edward's lover, who thought her some kind of rustic rodent, had come down from London to find her in a pleated skirt, thick stockings and clumpy boots. Thinking it was the vet making an unexpected call, she hadn't even wrenched off her headscarf.

'You got my letter, then,' she said. 'I wrote ages ago.'

'I didn't want to reply,' Avril-Whiting said. 'Too risky. Ah, thank you.' He took a teacup from her. 'It played on my mind all summer, and I was due a few days' leave so I rode down yesterday. I've been staying in town near the cathedral. Last night, I walked around, imagining I was stepping in Edward's footsteps. I even stood outside Fendynick House.'

Taking her seat, sipping her tea, she waited for him to say more.

'As I say, I didn't want to write,' he said finally. 'Working where I do, my correspondence is highly sensitive – and probably opened – which is why I received your letter with something less than joy, Mrs Devoran. In requesting information about the loss of the *Bee Orchid*, you asked me to break the Official Secrets Act.'

'But here you are,' she said flatly.

'Here I am, proving that nobody is proof against blackmail.'

That wasn't what she'd expected. 'That's unfair. I haven't sunk to that!'

'Now you disappoint me. Was it not a very "generous" letter you sent me? And equally "generous" of me to respond?'

She went red. *A shack and one generous hammock would suit us well enough.* Had she unknowingly echoed that word in her letter to this man? Meanwhile, Avril-Whiting had noticed Edward's photograph. He went to examine it, as poker-faced as Max had been. 'I work in intelligence, Mrs Devoran, and men like me are highly vulnerable to blackmail. It makes us thin-skinned.' He replaced the picture. 'I haven't one of Edward, you know, not a recent one.' He cut her off as she began to speak. 'Let's avoid personal detail. Suffice to say I am here and will answer your questions, if I can. You want to know how Edward died.'

She was finally able to agree with something. 'I got the barest information at the time.'

'It's what everyone gets.'

'Then a bit more through my sister-in-law, who is a secretary to Sir Henry Copping. He's the MP for—'

'Oh, I know Copping. He won't have got anywhere near the nub of the matter; they'll have fobbed him off.'

'Who will?'

'The Admiralty. You want to know more. You want to scrape the barnacles off the hull, so to speak, and get to the smooth metal.'

'I suppose so.' He was looming over her. It was what Edward had always done. Very boys' public school, she thought, using height to express status.

'Why?' Avril-Whiting slid back onto his chair.

'I need to know how he died, and whether it was quick or not. And mostly, who fired on his corvette.'

'It was a German submarine. A torpedo, hitting the ship broadside. As for whether it was quick or not, do you really want to know?' Avril-Whiting steepled his hands, his long, narrow fingers threading together. He'd been a talented violinist, Edward had said. Now he looked almost thin enough to be considered ill. Abruptly, he got to his feet again.

'Shall we walk out? They say walls have ears, don't they?'

She took him through the orchard whose trees blushed with fruit almost ripe for picking. The late roses topping and tailing each line of trees drooped, their petals blown. She judged her guest would prefer dry grass and blackberry-studded hedgerows to a view of the pigs, so her feet turned towards Colvennon Glaze. As they neared it, the thump of sledgehammers reminded her that Max and Heinz, who was standing in for Jürgen, were repairing fences. Some heifers had got out of their field recently and enjoyed an afternoon's freedom before being rounded up. She could have turned away, but something pushed her on.

Charles Avril-Whiting glanced at the two men in their conspicuous brown suits, particularly at Max, who was ramming in a round post. 'They look young and fit. Conscientious objectors?'

'Germans, and rather warlike.'

'Well I never.' Avril-Whiting watched, until his unblinking gaze fetched Max's in return.

Gwenna discerned a change in Max's posture. Curious, suspicious? Jealous? In all the months they'd known each other, he'd had no rivals. She would reassure him, she decided. It would be cruel to tease a man who had to leave each day to sleep behind barbed wire.

Avril-Whiting walked on and she followed him into Fairy Tump field, where he seemed fascinated by its succession of tumuli and hollows.

'We think they're burial mounds,' Gwenna said. Max had moved on to a second post and the rhythmic thud of his hammer echoed down the slope. 'Iron Age, probably.'

'Certainly Iron Age,' Avril-Whiting agreed, crouching to look into one of the dips. He had on a tweed jacket and cavalry twill trousers, and she saw he was losing his hair on top. This man had carved a thick slice off her life without knowing it. Or if he did know it, had done so without caring. And now, he was making her wait for information. 'They're not burial mounds,' he said, straightening up. 'Almost certainly you've got an ancient iron or tin mine on your property.'

'You're a historian?'

'Archaeology, Oxford. I might have spent my life fumbling around with a trowel in the dirt, only I also wanted to be a professional violinist. A choice was required. In the end, the intelligence services tapped me on the shoulder. A lot of mining went on two thousand years ago,' he said, indicating the hollows. 'It was often open cast, tunnels being dastardly hard to dig. The mounds are spoil heaps; the little pits are where they dug out the ore. Sorry. Have I spoiled the magic?'

'Thoroughly. The fairies will be offended, so drive carefully on the lanes back to Truro.'

'Thanks for the warning. Edward said you had a touch of otherworldliness about you.'

'Whereas you thought me a mere mouse.' Gwenna hated the idea that they'd discussed her. How to offload her so they could get to that island paradise they dreamed of. 'Are you going to tell me what I want to know?'

'I suppose so.'

This was it. Within a minute, she might discover for certain that Max had killed Edward.

Avril-Whiting stretched his mouth like an actor warming up to perform and said, 'You were told that the corvette HMS *Bee Orchid* was torpedoed off the coast of Ireland, along with four other vessels in a convoy that had left South Africa en route to Plymouth. Right?'

'Um...yes.'

'On November 23rd 1941. Yes?'

She nodded. That accorded with what she knew.

'The truth is, the convoy was badly mauled by a German wolf pack that night, resulting in the loss of three ships: a merchant vessel, an oil tanker and a corvette, the *Gilly Flower*.'

'No, it was the *Bee*—'

He raised his hand. 'Let me speak. *Three* of our ships were sunk by German U-boats that night. The convoy got strung out in bad fog, and Edward's corvette and another destroyer got separated from the rest. While the main convoy continued its allotted course, they entered a heavily mined area off the south-western coast of Ireland.'

'No – they were off the south coast.' Nobody had said anything about "south-western". She had to have accurate details or there was no point in this. 'They were among five ships to be sunk that night, not three.'

'Mrs Devoran, am I speaking to an agent of Naval Intelligence?'

'No.'

'No. You are a keeper of pigs and cows.'

'I'm a lot more than that but I apologise. Go on.'

'Only if you commit to listening.' His disdain for those who failed to latch on quickly was evident. Edward had possessed a lightning-fast mind too.

'Please continue,' she said humbly.

'Understand that on that vast ocean, in the dark and the fog, even with modern instruments, ships go off course. When they're being trailed by German U-boats, they make decisions they would not make on a Sunday afternoon in the park. Are you clear?'

'Yes.'

'The destroyer Edward's ship was escorting left the convoy and veered towards the south-western corner of Ireland, into waters that had been heavily mined—'

'What do you mean, "mined"?' With their conversation about Iron Age tin extraction fresh in her head, Gwenna was grappling with images.

'Laid with naval mines. Steel-cased explosives hidden under water. Think of enormous party balloons tethered to the seabed, only far less fun. They explode when a ship blunders into them. The Germans have laid hundreds off the Irish shore.'

'What made them head into those waters?'

'An error of navigation. The destroyer's captain chose the course, possibly to avoid a German submarine that was stalking his ship and Edward's corvette had no choice but to stay with it. I'm afraid awful things happen at sea.'

She stared into Avril-Whiting's eyes. They were dull in a way that indicated fading health. Desperation made her say, 'No. You're lying.'

He arched an eyebrow. 'Mrs Devoran, really.'

'What's the point in coming all this way, making me feel stupid and then lying to me?' *Don't let that stalking submarine have been the Kriegswolf.*

They stared at each other, until finally Avril-Whiting smiled. 'Edward said you were fierce. Rather soppy about animals, but he felt they ought to name a corvette after you because you were compact, sturdy and a challenge to handle.'

'I thought we weren't going into personal detail.'

'No, indeed. Well, you've caught me, Mrs Devoran. There's a razor-sharp brain under your headscarf after all. You were right. The destroyer and Edward's corvette sailed clear of the German-mined area, taking a course directly west of the Emerald Isle where, unbeknownst to us in Naval Intelligence, one of our allies had laid mines in what should have been a safe sea lane. Classic cock-up: they dropped them in the wrong place, fudged their report when they realised their error and two of our ships went to the bottom because of it.'

'You're saying Edward's ship hit mines laid by an ally?'

'Yes. Meanwhile, the remaining convoy was attacked by U-boats in the South West Approaches, off the Cork coast. South of Ireland as you were told at the time, with the loss of three ships.'

'An oil tanker, a merchant vessel and a corvette.' She echoed what Max had told her.

'Details were changed on official reports to imply that all five ships were lost in the same area—' Avril-Whiting stopped. 'Hello, friend or foe?'

Max was coming towards them, though still half a field away. Gwenna asked quickly, 'Which ally laid those mines?'

'Do you need to know...? I suppose you do. The Free French navy.'

'The French?'

'*Free* French, those who have come over to us. Or should I say, whom we allow to use our ports, though I often think we're fighting a different war. They're touchy when it comes to taking orders from the Royal Navy, hence the hush-hush, because rapping their knuckles might cause a diplomatic rift.'

Gwenna cared for none of this. 'They sabotaged the sea lanes.'

'That's a little extreme, Mrs Devoran, but under the circumstances, I will agree.'

'And it was covered up?'

'Absolutely. It happens all the time, and it makes no difference to Edward that his death was caused by error rather than a

German U-boat having a lucky night. Death by mine, death by torpedo, the end is ghastly. I like to think it was quick for Edward, or that he had time to get off his ship and die in the water, staring up at the stars.'

'It was too foggy. Or so someone told me.'

'I see.' Charles Avril-Whiting took a deep breath. When he spoke again, his voice was ten years older. 'Edward only wanted to play his cello and write symphonies. I made him join the navy. My doing. He shouldn't have been pitched into a war.' Pain scored grooves in Charles Avril-Whiting's face. He then asked, 'Have I answered your question to satisfaction?'

She nodded, too full of emotion to speak. It made a world of difference to know that blundering allies had doomed Edward's ship. It did nothing to lessen the tragedy of her husband's death, but it lifted that ice-cold rock from her heart.

Max had reached them. He and Avril-Whiting stared at each other.

'Good God,' said Avril-Whiting. 'I know you.'

'And I you,' Max said tonelessly.

'I interrogated you in Scotland after you were brought ashore from your submarine. Reiner, aren't you? I'll never forget your face or your Iron Cross.'

Max dipped his head, in ironic greeting. 'I too remember that you struck me across the face and said, "That is for the *Bee Orchid*. That is for Edward."'

'You struck Max?' Gwenna demanded. 'Isn't that against the Geneva Convention?'

'Thoroughly, but I didn't care then,' Avril-Whiting said in a tone that held no shame, 'and I still don't. I knew this man's U-boat hadn't fired on Edward, he wasn't anywhere near, but thumping him was an opportunity to offload some rage.' He told Gwenna to forget everything he'd told her. 'I think we're now even, so could I ask you – generously – to destroy any letters you might find?'

She said she already had, aware that the only letter of his she'd ever seen was buried close by, almost under his feet, along with her wedding ring. She wasn't aware of Avril-Whiting walking away, only of arms embracing her, of hair tickling the tip of her nose.

'This man makes you cry; what does he say to you that I did not hear?'

'I'm not allowed to tell you.' She buried her face against Max's shoulder as he stroked her hair. 'One day perhaps. Only, now I can love you, Max. It's all right. I can love you.'

'This is permission?'

They walked around the field, hand in hand, noticing that the oak crowns were touched with copper and field mushrooms had appeared by magic. They planned their future. When, eventually, the war ended, nobody would stop them marrying.

'What of Lotti?' Max asked. 'You want to adopt her, but with me as your husband it will not be so easy. You may have to choose between us.'

'I think,' Gwenna said, 'it's more about Lotti, and what she will choose. She still speaks of going to Canada.'

51

Mill's birthday came in October and Gwenna sent a card, 'with love'. Meanwhile, to help Gwenna with her relentless workload, Miss Linley offered to pick Lotti up from school on Fridays, and give her tea along with whichever friend was coming home with her that weekend. The arrangement allowed Gwenna to finish the milking and get the bus without having to go at double speed. Verity Linley became by degrees a trusted friend.

On the farm, there was ploughing to do. Jürgen returned to work, but Heinz stayed on. The days shortened. She and Max rode the horses on the beach whenever the tide and weather allowed and made careful love in their private spot. Careful, because Max refused to rely on Gwenna's certainty that she was infertile.

Lotti adored her school. Gwenna's fears that she would be seen as too clever, 'the scholarship swot', receded as it became obvious that Lotti possessed a talent for coming top at almost everything without stirring up resentment.

October half-term was two days away and Lotti was bringing a girl called Sheila back with her, to stay a couple of days. 'She's nearly a year older than me,' Lotti had warned

Gwenna, 'but she says I'm quite grown up for an eleven-year-old.'

With this in mind, Gwenna decided that Rumtopf should be temporarily removed from Lotti's bed. Lotti still treasured her bear, but Sheila might pass comment.

Something struck Gwenna for the first time as she took Rumtopf into her own room and sat him against her pillow. He had leather patches under his feet, like little bear's pads. One of them was coming unstitched, probably from Angela picking him up on her last visit, and flinging him as she left the house in her rage. Gwenna decided to remove it and restitch it so it didn't get lost.

She discovered that the egg-shaped patch had writing on the underside. Taking it to the window and holding it to the light, she expected to see a maker's mark. What she read changed her world in the time it takes to swat a fly.

'Otto Gittelman, Victoria Street, Amherst, Nova Scotia.'

Wasn't that in...?

Gwenna found Lotti's atlas and looked it up. Nova Scotia was part of Canada. She sat down, feeling faint.

That weekend, while Sheila was petting Josephine in the sitting room, Gwenna showed the leather patch to Lotti.

'It's Papa's writing,' Lotti said.

'Did you know it was there?'

Lotti nodded, her eyes searching Gwenna's for signs of displeasure. 'He showed me before he stitched it on, saying nobody would ever think to look on a bear's foot. I was never to say it to anyone, not even Mutti, because when Mutti got scared, she would tell things she shouldn't.'

'I understand. This place, it's where your aunt and uncle went, from Norway?'

Lotti was vague. She thought so. 'Papa only said that they were safe in Canada now, and my Grandmama Sonia too, and we would go over the sea to find them. Aunt Gwenna, don't look so sad.'

Mastering her emotions, Gwenna wrote to Freda with what she had discovered. Freda contacted the Canadian High Commission and asked if they could confirm if an Otto and Helen Gittelman resided in Amherst, Nova Scotia.

Weeks went past and no information came back. Weeks turned to months. Autumn became winter.

On Christmas Eve, Gwenna's thirty-third birthday, they brought the cows in for milking through drifts of snow. Lotti baked her a cake with caraway seeds, which had been her grandmother Sonia's favourite. Max gave Gwenna a wooden brooch, a pagan-looking horse's head, that he had carved himself. New Year arrived, and the war ground on.

On February 1st 1944, Candlemas Day, the cows left their sheds to go out to permanent pasture. Some early piglets were born, seed was planted. On midsummer day, Gwenna and Max slipped away to Fairy Tump field and gave the small folk a bottle of beer and a jug of coffee.

In September 1944, Lotti moved up a year at St Morgan's, and that Christmas, she played the innkeeper's daughter in the nativity play, revealing a talent for comedy. She won the science prize that term, the youngest ever recipient.

Mill came to the nativity, and afterwards, Gwenna and Lotti were guests at Fendynick House for supper. Angela was attending an event at the town hall, to Gwenna's relief, and the evening rang with laughter. Charles Avril-Whiting's letter was not mentioned. Gwenna still kept her nightly diary, but these days she wrote Max's name in it, clearly and proudly. They were engaged, though only Jürgen, Wiggy and Ezra knew.

. . .

The winter of 1944–45 was the most severe of an unusually cold series of years. Snow began falling on Gwenna's thirty-fourth birthday. By New Year, the snow was so deep in the sunken lane, the milk churns had to be driven down in Wiggy's truck. The milk then froze solid overnight. One churn burst open, and they discovered milky icicles clinging to its side in the morning and a frozen white lava coating the new concrete stand. Lotti became a temporary full-time boarder, as the buses could not get through. POWs at Tregallon suffered badly, some going down with pneumonia. Outraged that no provision had been made for extra fuel or blankets, Gwenna broke her prohibition on speaking to Angela.

'Ask your member of parliament how he'd have liked to spend last night in a single-skin hut with a tin roof, gaps under the floorboards and no coal on the stove.'

Extra coal was delivered within days and Angela's picture appeared in the *Cornishman*, shaking hands with a dusty-faced coal heaver. She began collecting unwanted blankets and men's clothing, and within a month, the POWs were more warmly dressed than most men in the town. Gwenna thawed slightly towards her sister-in-law and her comment, 'You know, you really ought to stand for parliament yourself,' brought a reaction she'd never before experienced.

Angela smiled. 'I don't believe Cornwall is ready for that yet but thank you, Gwenna. I take that very kindly.'

Hardly had the snow melted at the close of February 1945 when Gwenna felt a change in Max that frightened her. He got out of Wiggy's truck one day, only his nose and forehead visible above a muffler, and a woolly hat pulled down over his ears. Without speaking, he veered towards the pig sties. Gwenna went after him, stewing in dread. She found him breaking ice on a water trough.

'Don't you dare,' she said furiously.

He finished what he was doing, then faced her. 'Gwenna,

please, not now.' His voice seemed to come from the bottom of a pit.

'Yes, now! Don't you dare walk away from me as if I'm nobody.' Edward's bored expression when she'd tried to provoke some gesture of affection from him was scored on her memory. 'Have you stopped caring?' The pigs grunted, upset by her wild hand gestures. 'Are you ill or have you suddenly remembered you're German, and have another home waiting?'

People were daring to believe the war in Europe would be over soon and while Gwenna longed for it, she was hearing the sonorous ticking of a timer. When – if – Germany surrendered, Max, Jürgen and the others would be repatriated. 'Please tell me, Max.'

'Your air force bombed Dresden, Gwenna. My home.'

She went to him, took his hands. 'I see. Was it heavy bombing?'

'Heavy?' Max echoed. 'What is "light bombing"?'

She thought of blitzed London, and Liverpool and Coventry. Back in 1941, the burning docks of Plymouth had painted the sky orange, visible from the south of Cornwall. Heavy bombing was when planes flew over in waves and the falling ordnance darkened the air.

'My city is destroyed. It no longer has its centre, only burning. Two of my sisters...' He gave up and crouched, his forearms over his face. Gwenna crouched beside him and held him. The destruction of historic Dresden was, she found out later, part of the pulverisation of Germany that took place that winter and spring of 1945. It was the finishing off of a wounded animal.

Winter gave way to spring. As May blossom frothed in the hedgerows and bees flew jagged courses between corncockles and buttercups, bells chimed across the fields. On May 8th 1945, Winston Churchill came on the wireless to announce that the war in Europe was over. When Wiggy arrived to pick up Max and Jürgen, she and Gwenna danced around the farmyard. As the men appeared, Wiggy said, 'This is it, then, queen, the moment of truth. Is it the rest of our lives together or good-night, Vienna?'

'You and Jürgen...?'

'Yes, but I'm not looking forward to telling me mam and da. Are you and Max making it official?'

'Yes, and I can't wait to place the announcement in the *Cornishman* and see everyone's face.' Gwenna was lying. The thought of it terrified her but not as much as the prospect of him being forced home. Her other constant fear was that, as the fog of war rolled back across Europe, somebody would claim Lotti.

Eight weeks later, in July, Freda wrote thanking Gwenna for remembering her birthday and saying that she had at last heard from the Canadian High Commission. An immigrant family named Gittelman had been located living precisely where Gwenna had suggested, in Amherst, Nova Scotia.

52

AUGUST 1946

They stood together at the rail of a passenger ship which had left Southampton the previous day. It was the first time Max had been at sea since his capture, a day he remembered as grey as only defeat could be. On this very different afternoon, the breeze played infinite arpeggios on the sea's surface and rippled their lightweight clothes. To starboard, Ireland's west coast shimmered halfway between reality and mirage. A sailor had told them that they were sighting the Dingle Peninsula. The same sailor came over, saying, 'According to your coordinates, madam, we'll pass the spot in five minutes.'

Gwenna lifted a wreath of dried roses and peonies, resting it on the rail. The flowers had been picked and dried from Mill's garden. Tags attached to the wreath carried messages from Mill, Angela and Gwenna.

The sailor gave Gwenna a friendly smile, and Max a wary nod. 'Any time you're ready.'

Max thanked him, not attempting to disguise his accent. He never hid his identity as a former U-boat commander and he'd been received on board ship with guarded courtesy. He ignored outright hostility and as Gwenna now bore his name, she was learning to ignore it too. Their wedding had taken place in London. 'Just in bloody time,' Wiggy, her adult bridesmaid, had commented. 'You'll show any day now.' Gwenna was four months pregnant. Freda had been matron of honour and Freda's husband, Norbert, had given Gwenna away. Lotti had stolen the show in her bridesmaid's dress, her fair hair cut to shoulder length.

'One bit of sea is much the same as any other.' Max scanned the horizon. 'Are those the islands you spoke of?'

'That's right,' the sailor confirmed. 'The Blasket Islands are the last specks of inhabited land before Newfoundland, Canada.'

Gwenna stared at the smudges of grey to starboard. The *Bee Orchid*'s crew probably wouldn't have spotted them in their last, doomed hours as night and fog closed in.

'Go on, it is time,' Max said.

'I was hoping Lotti would join us. Where is she?' Panic hit Gwenna, as when Lotti had escaped the house in their first days together. 'I shouldn't have taken my eyes off her.'

Max stopped her running from the rail. 'She is talking with that old lady she befriended, and she is not a little girl any more. This is your own moment, Gwenna.'

'I feel every moment we're travelling that I'm losing her.'

'Throw your wreath, darling.'

Gwenna hurled it as far as she could. It rocked on the choppy surface, pirouetting in a pink and green blur before sinking. 'Goodbye, Edward,' Gwenna whispered. Here, or somewhere near, his ship had struck a rogue mine, exploded and sunk. Charles Avril-Whiting, who was dying in a hospice and no longer cared much for the Official Secrets Act, had revealed to Gwenna the coordinates of the *Bee Orchid* in its last minutes. He'd also said, 'Tell Edward I'm on my way, would you?'

She placed her hand on top of Max's, on the rail. Next stop

Nova Scotia. The ship was sailing into the immense unknown and at the end of the journey was a separation that felt like a kind of death.

LOTTI

The old lady was an excellent listener, and in the course of their conversation, Lotti had arrived at two important decisions. She would be fourteen by the time the ship arrived in Halifax, Nova Scotia, so it was right that she should have reconsidered her choice of career.

Instead of opening her own museum when she left school, she now intended to become an eye surgeon. That's what the old lady had done before retiring. It was a good job for a woman, she'd told Lotti, 'Because we have delicate hands, and can give people back the thing they take most for granted but can least afford to lose. That being sight.' She had let Lotti try on her lovely gold watch, saying, 'It's a well paid profession too, which is rather useful.'

This new ambition fitted with Lotti and Sheila's plan to have a flat together in Kensington or Mayfair when they left school. London was the best place to train in ophthalmology, apparently.

Lotti's second very important decision involved the adults at the ship's rail, holding hands. They believed she intended to stay forever in Nova Scotia with her real aunt and uncle. But much as Lotti looked forward to seeing those dear ones from Berlin, the fact was, a person could not live in two places. Her aunt and uncle did not really know her now and her Grand-mama Sonia had died before the war ended. At Colvennon were Aunt Gwenna, Uncle Max, Ezra, Josephine and the horses. There was Sheila and her other school friends and Mutti in her grave at Come-to-Good.

Papa had told her that Canada was safe, and they would go

there, but as the old lady had said, parents do their best for their children at the time. 'But times change.' It was hard to remember exactly what Papa had said about Canada, and trying to rehear his voice was like sketching a cloud after it had drifted off and become something else. She didn't know how she was going to explain to Uncle Otto and Aunt Helen that she wanted to grow up in Cornwall, and keep going to her school, and visit Mutti's grave every other Sunday.

She'd said this to the old lady, who replied, 'It sounds like a difficult conversation.' The lady then mentioned that it was a good idea to write down thoughts, so that one didn't get flustered. Lotti saw Aunt Gwenna coming over to her with her hand on her tummy, wearing her worry-face. Poor Aunt Gwenna was trying to smile her way to Nova Scotia but Lotti knew she cried with every nautical mile.

Why were there nautical miles, different from ordinary ones? She would ask the sailor who made a click with the side of his mouth and said, 'Morning, miss' when they passed on deck. There was something Papa had said when she was very little. Thinking of it, she almost caught a corner of his voice.

'If ever you don't know what to say, *bubbeleh*, say nothing.'

Good advice for a child but not for someone of almost fourteen who had just decided to become the country's leading eye surgeon. Aunt Gwenna believed she was doing the right thing, taking her to Nova Scotia and handing her over to Otto and Helen. But it was time to tell Aunt Gwenna and Uncle Max that the absolute fact was, she *would* return on this ship and begin the new school term at St Morgan's in autumn. Albeit a bit late. *Of course* she would.

Why would she have left Rumtopf behind at Colvennon if she did not mean to go back?

· · ·

In the kitchen of an old farmhouse that stood with its back to the hills, a well-loved bear sat on top of a cupboard, reviewing the emptiness with his one good eye. Under his bright suit of clothes, his belly was darned, his innards a muddle of lumpy stuffing and a tattered yellow star. Lotti had hidden it inside Rumtopf because she didn't want to see it but dared not throw it away. She wasn't afraid of German policemen any longer, but it was important not to forget. Nobody should ever forget.

A LETTER FROM NATALIE

Dear reader,

I want to say a huge thank you for choosing to read *The Girl with the Yellow Star*. If you enjoyed it and want to keep up to date with all my latest releases, just sign up at the following link. Your email address will never be shared and you can unsubscribe at any time.

www.bookouture.com/natalie-meg-evans

It has long been my wish to write a book set in beautiful north Cornwall, a location I fell in love with from my first visit thirty years ago. We all have our 'happy place', where we retreat in times of stress. For me, it is a wild Cornish cliff, yellow with gorse blossom, staring out across a sparkling, copper-green sea. Whether you are familiar with Cornwall or visit through the medium of words and images, its unspoiled nature speaks to us all. As a backdrop to intense and passionate human relationships, I can think of no better place.

So, I hope you loved *The Girl with the Yellow Star* and if you did I would be very grateful if you could write a review. I'd love to hear what you think, and it makes such a difference, helping new readers to discover one of my books for the first time.

I love hearing from my readers – you can get in touch on my Facebook page, through Twitter or my website.

Thanks,

Natalie Meg Evans

www.nataliemegevans.uk

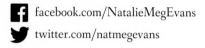 facebook.com/NatalieMegEvans
twitter.com/natmegevans

Made in United States
North Haven, CT
29 May 2023